HINTERAEVUM

Brian Lancaster

ACKNOWLEDGMENTS

The author would like to thank Steve and Andrea for proof-reading during the making of this novel. The support and encouragement was invaluable.

Thanks also to Kevin and Kim for proof-reading the first draft and taking the time to give informative feedback.

And thank you to Lynne, Jayne and Joe for providing such constructive critique of the second draft.

0

Wednesday December 24th, 2014 (H)

Monty angled the bottle and listened to the familiar glug as he poured two equal glasses of wine. The kitchen, Karen's kitchen, was dimly lit and a Christmas tree glowed in the far corner of the open plan dining area. An artistic mix of red baubles dangled amongst the crystals from the modern light fitting that hung above the island. He put the bottle back down and paused for a moment to admire the twinkling reflections bouncing back off the shiny surfaces around him. It was his favourite time of the year. It was a perfect time to reminisce.

To say that this had been a difficult period in their relationship would be an understatement in anyone's books. One hears of couples going through trial separations but this separation had been totally different. They had been worlds apart. He loved her deeply, he'd never given up hoping and waiting. She hadn't stopped loving him but, as far as she knew at the time, she'd never see him again. Yet now they were back together. It wasn't quite the way he'd have wanted things to work out. His mind was a confusing cocktail during their time apart. Desperate to be reunited with her. Desperately not wishing that transition journey on her so soon in her Realworld life.

He picked up the two glasses of red wine and carried them through to the lounge where she was sitting on the sofa with her legs tucked up. He walked across and handed her one of the glasses, kissed her cheek, then sat down beside her. Karen shuffled her legs around so that she could lean in to his side. He raised his right arm and wrapped it around her as she drew in close. They chinked their glasses together, implicitly declaring a mutual love, before each taking a sip.

They began to chat. A second Christmas tree decked with memorabilia from all their time together as a family filled the opposite corner of the room. Mind you, they both recognised that it would be a long time before they might share another festive season as a complete family with their children, Sam and Gemma. In the background a CD was playing a selection of the "best ever" Yuletide songs at low volume. Monty loved Karen more with every day that went by. It had been such a heart aching time waiting for her since his fall on the building site.

1

It had materialised quickly. Sienna had called into his office on Monday to have a private chat. She was running through the payroll procedures and had spotted something odd. This was normally Pat's domain but there had been a gaffe in February when she had taken ill and the salaries weren't paid on time. It wasn't quite mutiny, but there were some stern questions asked about why something so critical to all the team was so dependent upon a single individual in the admin office. Pat had been distraught. She was still apologising to everybody by the time the next salary run was set to go which put everyone on heightened awareness. It hadn't gone unnoticed that any delay at the end of March would extend money pain across the Easter weekend.

They all knew that it wasn't Pat's fault but they couldn't resist teasing her in the form of some exaggerated pampering during the last week of the month. Clare had been out shopping with two of her colleagues over the weekend and when Pat had arrived at work on Monday the 28th she found her desk littered with an assortment of cushions, scarves and woolly hats. Not to mention a selection of herbal remedies and medicinal rubs.

Monty had reassured the team by asking Pat to show Sienna the ins and outs of the banking operations so that there would at least be a plan B in the event of any future hiccups. Sienna had sat alongside Pat taking copious, detailed notes as the March pay details were loaded up on the PC. She was going through a dummy run in the middle of April using her procedure so that she would feel comfortable to fly solo in two weeks time. However, she found that she just couldn't reconcile some of the numbers and didn't like to mention this to Pat because it might seem that she was trying to rub salt in her team-mate's recent wounds.

There were 19 salary payments showing up on the system, but Hanson Scott only had 18 named employees. Pat was so used to processing it by rote every month that she hadn't even noticed the discrepancy. Sienna brought a fresh pair of eyes to the task and was checking everything meticulously as she went. She didn't want to make any errors on her first go at the payroll.

Monty told Sienna not to say anything to anybody until he had had time to get to the bottom of it. He certainly didn't want to generate any more fear, uncertainty and doubt, especially with the recent pay trauma being so fresh in everyone's minds. He'd asked her to send him the list of monthly amounts and a salary listing off the HR system so that he could check all of the figures. It was probably a minor oversight going back to January when Richard Fletcher had resigned. They might have to try recovering the overpaid amount from Fletch, though it was more likely they'd have to write it off. It would be a few thousand pounds damage. Not exactly a matter of life or death, but it would come straight off the practice's bottom line.

He stayed later on Tuesday, doing a bit of analysis after he'd finished his meetings and other commitments for the day. Multiplying the numbers by twelve he was able to match eighteen of the salaries without breaking sweat. The nineteenth, for £3500, was not so obvious. After a bit of head scratching he went through the paper payroll reports that Pat prepared for Nick every month. Monty didn't get involved in the money side of the business, he left all the financials to Nick. He assumed that the payroll reports were always given a thorough review to make sure that the overall totals were correct and that there was nothing untoward with the overtime or alarming with the expenses.

As he looked through them he found something strange. The value seemed to remain the same going back for three years, then it dropped by a few percent in March 2007. £3350, times twelve, £40200. That was his salary at that time. And Nick's. He looked up the bank account details on the personnel system and compared them with Pat's payroll listings.

It was Nick's. But he had a vague memory that Nick had moved banks around that time. Something to do with him investing in an apartment in Turkey with a group of friends. Sure enough, a change of account number and sort code had clearly been entered into the personnel database in April 2007. Monty was able to trace Nick's salary payments going into that new bank account for the last three years, including the increases they jointly agreed for each other, right up to the numbers showing in Sienna's spreadsheet for April 2010. So, it appeared that the slip had happened much longer ago than Monty had first thought. Nick's previous salary payment instruction had not been cancelled out of the system when the new instruction had been added and nobody had picked up on the oversight. Probably because it coincided with the annual salary increases taking effect, possibly because a busy period had triggered lots of overtime claims.

But if Nick had closed that old account, why on earth hadn't those other payments bounced back in error? Had the bank messed up and not shut down the account correctly? If that were the case, it ought to be easy for Nick to call his old bank and get the money returned into Hanson Scott's coffers. After all, it amounted to a tidy sum over a three year period. A hundred and twenty grand couldn't be written off as small change.

There was another possibility. That for the last thirty six months Nick knew he was getting two salaries and had deliberately kept quiet about it. But Monty couldn't entertain that thought for more than a few seconds. No, that wasn't the way they worked together.

Monty finished off making notes alongside his calculations in the spreadsheet and saved it to his private share of the disk space on the main computer. He didn't want anyone else catching sight of that information.

He had found Nick in his office late on Wednesday afternoon and explained the results of his research into Sienna's find from two days earlier. Nick had listened with growing unease.

'So, I think this should be easy to fix. It will require a call from you to your old bank to find out what's gone on and to get the money credited back to Hanson Scott.'

When he looked at Nick he was disturbed by what he saw. His friend was squirming noticeably, avoiding direct eye contact, and seemed lost for something to say.

'Nick ... did you get the confirmation from the bank that this account was closed off?'

'Err, I can't really remember. I've had a few nights sleep since then, Monty' he replied, his voice faltering. He had swung his chair through ninety degrees and angled his head away from his inquisitor to stare out of the bay window.

'Nick. Look me in the eye and tell me you really didn't know that account was still live.'

If there was one thing in the world that Monty detested it was people not telling the truth. And he was now picking up strong vibes that the person he'd invested the last ten years of his life building up this company with just might be falling into that bracket. It was inconceivable. He didn't know what to say next. He had dismissed this possibility without any hesitation. But now ... now he was erring towards that conclusion. He felt a sickening sensation deep inside. Nick duplicitous. It struck at his core value. A rage welled up. How could Nick have done that to him? Where was the loyalty between them? Why would his co-director have cheated him? And so flagrantly?

Uncharacteristically, Monty jumped up from the chair and snapped.

'You bloody bastard! You sneaky, cheating bastard! What the bloody hell do you think you're playing at?'

'Hold on Monty. Keep the noise down, people will hear.'

'Keep the noise down? You cheeky sod. You're lucky I haven't put you through that flaming window.'

Monty thought of the others still working. And himself. He needed to bring himself back under control. He never worked well when he let himself get too hot under the collar. He paced across the room, gradually calming and containing himself.

'You knew this was happening, didn't you?'

But Nick could only huff and puff some politician answer that skirted the direct question, leaving Monty in no doubt that his trusted partner wasn't so trustworthy after all. Did Nick still have the money? Another politician answer suggested it had been spent, but it was unclear on what. Quite possibly that place in Turkey!

Having heard enough, and having got his emotions under wraps, Monty stopped pacing the room. With a stony expression he looked down at Nick in the swivel chair behind his heavy, antique, dark mahogany desk. Speaking in a low and very direct voice, Monty made his position clear.

'That money should have been additional profit, split between the two of us, but you've had the whole lot as additional salary. You greedy bastard. You knew that I took out a loan so that Karen and I could afford that extension at home. I could have had it paid off already if you hadn't ripped me off. I can't believe you've done this to me after all the time we've spent making Hanson Scott successful. Hanson Scott. That's two of us. Equal shares. Or at least I thought that's what it was.'

Nick was about to make a weak argument about it still being a partnership but Monty spoke again.

'What are you going to do to sort this mess out?'

'Look, I'll sort it out, Monty. Just can't do it straight away. I'll have to talk to the Bank. Work something out.'

'You had better talk to them pretty soon. Or I'll be talking to my solicitor. I may even be talking to the police.'

'Hang on, Monty, there's no need for that.'

'Really? You've stolen fifty grand off me.'

'I haven't stolen it.'

'Well, what have you done? If that's not stealing, then what the hell is it?'

'Stealing's a bit of a harsh description, Monty. I didn't realise that …'

But Monty cut him off short.

'No more, Nick. I'm bloody livid about what you've done. Just get to work on fixing this problem. Go talk to your bank manager. Or your bank managers. I want to hear your proposal next Monday morning. And it had better be good. I don't know what this means for the future of Hanson Scott. I can't see how I can continue with you as a business partner. Not after this episode.'

With that Monty turned and made his way out of Nick's office.

But it was far from over and the timing was far from perfect. Tomorrow afternoon was the team building event, followed by an evening out together.

2

'Thsssssssst.'

Nick Hanson sucked the air in through the slight gap between his two front teeth, his tongue pressed up against the back of them. He didn't know he was doing it, but he knew he did it. It was part of his zoning in, his routine for concentrating on the job in hand. And the job in hand right now was a rifle. Weighing in at just over 8 pounds it was cushioned in snugly to his left shoulder. His eyes were fixed on the target. His head was raging with the memory of that confrontation with Monty yesterday afternoon and he couldn't help feeling that his left hand was squeezing too tightly on the trigger. He knew better than that. Ease off a little, stay calm. Composed.

He and Monty Scott were partners, they had been running the architecture practice for nine years and it was flourishing. Nick felt as though he had had the upper hand when it all started. After all, it was he who had instigated the whole thing and prompted their departure from a larger and less imaginative design group. But as Hanson Scott had grown, the tables had gradually turned. Monty was a much calmer and easier person to deal with. He had the architectural flair that brought in the business. No matter what Nick did as the prime salesman, wheeling and dealing the financial numbers, it was Monty who usually persuaded the clients by assuredly walking them through the strengths of the design features.

Monty was a good deal smarter than Nick, and Nick knew it. Deep down, Nick was envious.

Monty was unwaveringly respected by the team at Hanson Scott. He had a gorgeous wife and two children that anyone would be proud of. His house was mock Tudor, five bedrooms, period features, with a modern extension to the rear that would surely appear in one of those design magazines one day soon. Bought cheaply and renovated, it was now worth a tidy sum. Monty enjoyed a perfectly stable family lifestyle.

They were all the things that Nick didn't have, nor seem capable of grasping for himself. Single and finding himself in his mid-forties, he was clunky and awkward around women, particularly those that he took a fancy to. He was a perennial rented apartment dweller. He'd never established himself firmly on the property ladder, there'd always been other things higher on his priority list. No need for a garden as there was nobody to share it with. No warm family to come home to after a day at work. No children to take to the park.

Monty was a daily reminder of all Nick's weaknesses and self regrets.

When he'd got the business rolling, Nick had joined the local Chamber of Commerce and quickly developed lofty ambitions of being as wealthy as some of the people he was now mixing with. He developed an unhealthy taste for expensive luxuries, he even went in with some of them to take a share in a yacht in the Mediterranean. But he found it tough keeping up with the demands of this persona. After seeking some advice from a friend who knew enough about book-keeping to outwit the tax man, Nick had taken to diverting money from the Hanson Scott coffers. Monty didn't display a great interest in the accounts so Nick, rather naively, thought his partner wouldn't spot the odd dubious transaction here or there.

And then it all blew up yesterday afternoon. Monty had come into his office and questioned him about the salary bill and Nick was caught off guard. He'd not got a well rehearsed answer and was instantly incriminated by his bumbling replies. He'd never seen his partner act like that, he was completely thrown by Monty's display of aggression. Nick found himself in a tight corner with Monty demanding recompense.

He tried hard to put on a casual veneer, making out that all was okay, it was a genuine mistake and everything would get sorted out soon enough. But underneath he was panicking. The money wasn't going to be that easy to find. He weighed up his options. His growing resentment for Monty was now blurring his judgment. It was time to show Monty who was boss. Send a bit of a warning shot across the bows.

He realized his finger was pressing far too hard on the trigger again. Calm. Regain composure.

'Thsssssssst.'

Was this the best way to do it? Surely not. Too messy. Too obvious. Stay focused. Too easy to unravel, too easy to find the perpetrator. His eyes locked on to his target. There must be a better way.

'Thsssssssst.'

'You're doing it again' the voice behind him whispered.

The left arm relaxed, the rifle lowered, the shoulders dropped.

'Thanks very much!' Nick's voice was slow and slightly sarcastic. He crooked his head round to face Liz. She'd been a good friend of Nick's for a long time and had eventually cajoled him into reacquainting himself with the rifle club after far too long an absence.

'Sorry Nick,' she said. 'I lost myself there. I'll keep quiet.'

Nick began to compose himself again, nuzzling the rifle butt back into position and making fine adjustments to the balance of weight through his right arm.

This was his first visit since he was given his marching orders nearly ten years ago. His trip to the 2000 Olympics had been nothing short of a disaster. His self-fuelled confidence had convinced him that he'd won the gold medal before the plane had even touched down in Australia. Trouble was that the same message hadn't reached three of the other competitors. Licking his wounds, he had gone absent without leave for three days, venturing off limits to drown his disappointment in drink and drugs with two old university friends who were working in Sydney at the time. So he returned home with no medal and a formal warning from the team management.

Back at the local rifle club he was subjected to some persistent and petulant jibes from a fellow member. Ken was a prominent person at the club and had designs on becoming president. Jealous of Nick's abilities, Ken looked upon him as a threat to that ambition. This actually made precious little sense as Nick had no interest at all in taking on that mantle. Still, Ken seized this opportunity to goad. And goad. And goad. He just didn't let it drop.

Then, one Friday evening, it came to a crescendo. Nick had been drinking to excess. Ken had been goading to excess. Nick snapped when he heard yet another snide remark behind his back. He turned, threw a large whisky in Ken's face then thumped him so hard that the president-to-be was out cold for several minutes. An ironic twist, considering the motto for Sydney 2000 had been 'Share the Spirit'. By the time Ken came around Nick had already been transported off home. He was banned from the club. Word spread to the country authorities and Nick soon found out that he wouldn't need to pack his bags for any future Olympic venues.

A lot of water had flowed under that bridge. Nick was now back at the rifle range, having had a number of discussions with Liz about the whole situation. There was a big gap there, she'd told him. A lot of younger members would benefit greatly from his coaching and experience. And it really was time for mutual apologies and a mature shake of hands with Ken. It was Liz who had ferried him home that unfortunate evening. She was now brokering reconciliation back at the club.

'Thsssssst.'

Calm, controlled, concentrating carefully, Nick sent 20 rounds down the range with an accuracy that belied how long it had been since he'd picked up a gun. He relaxed, exhaled and turned to face Liz.

'You know, that's pretty good' she said, deliberately understating what had just played out in front of her. 'You've not lost it at all, Nick. You've got such a good eye for this.'

'Yeah' he sighed, disappointed that he'd left it so long. 'It's as though I've been persecuting myself.' The look in his eyes informed her that he'd enjoyed the last few minutes.

'You've cut your nose off to spite your face. Come on over on Tuesday evening and see Ken. I know he'd be happy to see you. Come on,' she continued her gentle pleading. 'Time is a great healer. Hold out the olive branch? Bury the hatchet? …'

'All right,' Nick relented. 'OK, just ease off with the clichés.'

'I've run out' she smiled back at him.

They carried on their conversation as they ambled across to the main club house. Strangely he was more comfortable in Liz's company than he would normally be with women. Probably because his interactions with her were very functional and transactional. He wasn't sexually attracted to her and that was always a significant factor in determining his demeanour.

'If you're free a week on Sunday we're having a bit of a social event to promote the club. We've invited some of the local big wigs along, a shameless attempt to see if we can get some new members.'

'I get it now. You just want me there so that you can brag about the club having an ex Olympian in its midst!'

'Oh dear, you've spotted my cunning plan. Who knows, you might pick up some leads. Who's that man that your team has recently designed a large house for?'

'We've designed quite a few houses. You'd better give me a bit more of a clue than that.'

'Oh, crikey,' she shook her head slowly. 'I can't remember his name. He bought that old farmhouse on Boothby Hill and is having a big extension built onto it. I think he runs a factory that makes tablets?'

'Ah, Connor,' Nick answered. 'Dan Connor'

'That's him. Dan, Dan, the Medicine Man. He's going to be

there.' Liz went on, 'I heard that he's planning some sort of office-come-factory over on that light industrial estate beyond the railway station. He'll be looking for someone to design it for him.'

'Yes. He mentioned it to us a few months ago, although he was a bit guarded about what he could tell us at the time. Mind you, I think that's understandable. As soon as something like that gets out, the price of the land starts nudging up. Anyway, I'd like to think he'd give us a go at winning the business.'

'Well, if you come along to the event you'll be able to ask him how it's going. Can't do any harm, can it?'

'No, I guess not. It would be useful to find out what he's intending doing. I hear he's pleased with how the house is coming on.' Nick glanced at his watch. 'Look, I'm sorry Liz, I need to be getting off. Got to be back at the office before half past ten. Thanks for talking me round to this, I've really enjoyed this morning.'

He handed the rifle over to Liz. He looked admiringly at the rifle. 'See you soon.'

'See you here around seven on Tuesday evening?'

Nick smiled in agreement, then set off across the car park. He got into his BMW and left for the office. He normally looked forward to this event, the outdoor challenge played to his strengths and reminded him of his military training exercises, albeit on a much smaller scale. But he didn't have the usual buzz about today's proceedings. It was marred by that argument about money. Why did Monty have to go digging around in all of that? Where on earth would he get that sort of cash from at such short notice? The money had been sunk into an apartment in Turkey and a few other nice-to-haves which Nick certainly wasn't ready to part with just yet.

As he travelled he wondered whether he had been wrong to pay himself the extra amounts. Those sums were effectively his sales bonuses for going out and getting the business for the firm. He was always the one at the coal face when it came to the hard negotiations about the price. He was the one who had to know exactly what the margins would be. Where he could give a little, if he had to trim the bid. Monty was hardly ever involved in pawing through the contracts. He was always back in Cartmel House doing the easy bit at the drawing board. Then he'd show up at the end and claim the glory.

If it wasn't for Nick, the whole Hanson Scott thing wouldn't have got off the ground in the first place. He was the one that had taken the biggest risk.

Yes. Those were his commission payments and he deserved every penny. He would tough it out with his partner. Argue the sales incentive angle. He'd need a bit of a backup plan. Some items to negotiate on. Some leverage. And that could be Clare.

Nick liked Clare and he was convinced that she liked him. But Monty had always taken her under his wing and was very protective of her. On two occasions in the last few months Nick had had to listen to 'advice' from Monty about some of his interactions with Clare. According to Monty, Clare felt uncomfortable when Nick had asked her out recently. She liked Nick as a work colleague, but nothing more. Whilst they might be well meaning, they were creating unnecessary tension for her in the office.

Nick didn't get that impression though. He had become more and more convinced that there was something illicit going on between Monty and Clare. Monty, a married man with two children. Clare, single. Nick, single, a free agent. It just wasn't right. Nick had tried talking to Clare in the pub last Friday after work, but she had been evasive again, which only served to fuel his suspicions. It was curious that Monty should then bring up the money business a few days later. Was that too much of a coincidence? No, he was certain that this was Monty's attempt to put him off the scent. Put him on the back foot because he was getting too close to the truth about those two.

Nick was very business-like about the whole thing. Monty was beginning to be his number one problem and it was time for him to put any emotional considerations he had for his partner to the very bottom of his priorities. Nick was more used to a dog-eat-dog philosophy.

And maybe he'd just landed upon his way out of his current predicament. Perhaps Monty ought to just put this whole money thing to bed, or Karen might find out who her husband's been putting into bed.

3

It was Thursday morning and Monty Scott was travelling across to the Barker's Court site. As he drove along his thoughts kept returning to yesterday afternoon's conversation with Nick. What the devil had got into his partner's head? How long did Nick think he could get away with it? Monty had been cross. Angry, in fact. He'd almost lost it at one point, which was so unlike him. He had to use all of his will power to return to his usual calm and unflappable self. He wasn't going to give his colleague the upper hand simply by losing his temper. Besides, the last thing he wanted was to alarm all the team at work. What would they think if they overheard a heated argument between the figureheads of the practice? Monty had also decided to keep it under his hat at home. There was little point in Karen worrying about it unnecessarily. Hopefully all would soon be resolved.

However, it was still gnawing away at him. What else had Nick been up to? Would he be able to trust his business partner again? And what troubled Monty most was that he knew Nick could be highly irrational when hemmed into a corner. He could be volatile, aggressive, bordering on violent.

Monty fixed his attention on the road again, not knowing quite how much danger he was in. Fortunately his rural route kept him away from busy traffic, otherwise his drifting mind might have brought about a few close calls along the way.

He arrived at the site, pulled in and parked up, and stepped down from his new 4x4. It had that fresh-off-the-assembly-line smell and he was still counting its age in days, not weeks. It was twelve days old to be precise. He'd researched it thoroughly before making the purchase and he could safely say there wasn't a feature that he was in the least bit disappointed with. He'd chosen a gentle platinum metallic paint which he felt sure would soften the car's appearance, disguising the considerable mass under the skin. Unsurprisingly he was right. After all, he was an architect and had a sixth sense for these things.

The driver's door closed with a reassuring clunk which spoke of the manufacturing quality. Monty pressed the remote key fob and the car responded with a chorus of quieter clunks synchronised with a mild beep, signalling that the car was now locked. He paused, admiring for a few seconds. He watched the wing mirrors smoothly fold inwards to the accompaniment of three flashes of the indicator lights.

Yes, he was smitten. He loved it.

Monty had just turned forty two. Standing a little over five foot ten, with black hair and youthful features, he was considered a very handsome man. A passion for cycling helped keep him fit and trim. He was a calm and moderated person, both at work and at home. He had a knack of being able to connect with the younger members of the team and help them develop, being paternal without being patronising. All in all, he was a very likeable guy.

Thankfully the new car had pushed the unsavoury business with Nick from the forefront of his mind. He took one last longing look at it before turning away and heading towards a two storey terrace of prefabs. The engineers' office was one of the less than des-res maisonettes on the upper tier. This was where he'd arranged to meet Ged, one of the younger Hanson Scott architects. He clambered up the metal grating steps to the gantry that serviced the top row. A short distance along the walkway he pushed open a door and stepped in.

Ged looked up from the desk where he was reviewing an A1 sized drawing and greeted him with an enthusiastic 'Hiya Monty!'

'Morning Ged' he replied. 'Is Maria here?'

'Yes, she picked me up this morning. We got here about ten minutes ago. She's just popped to the loo, she'll not be long.'

'Great.' He scanned the room. 'I see you've not had Freeman's Fabrics in to decorate yet.' The prefab was very basic, housing three desks and a draughtsman's drawing board. There were several cupboards and half a dozen shelves, all crammed to overflowing with drawings and lever arch files. Several soiled coffee mugs randomly littered the surfaces. His mind wandered a little.

'They have been on site this week, actually.'

Monty turned his head back towards Ged, a slightly vacant look on his face.

'Freeman's Fabrics,' he said, bringing him back in to the room. 'They were checking out where their store is going to be. Maria couldn't manage to persuade them to give us a few off-cuts of curtain fabric for these windows though.'

As Monty smiled back at Ged the Portacabin door opened and

they turned to see Bob Hart enter. He was the senior engineer on site. He was rough around the edges and gave the impression of being very much from the old school, but his experience was invaluable and he always took time to pass on his knowledge to those willing to learn. This trait was probably why he and Monty had struck up such a good rapport.

Barker's Court was a moderately sized shopping centre, one of those out-of-town retail outlets. It was by far the largest commission that Monty had designed and this was the first time he'd worked with such a large engineering outfit. Monty had got to know Bob well during the two years in which the structure had mushroomed up from the brown field.

As they all greeted each other Bob shuffled over to his desk, placed his bag on top of the filing cabinet, put his coat on a peg, then sat down in his chair. He arched back and clasped his hands together behind his head.

'Aahh, another day, another dilemma, eh? What are you here for Monty? Checking up on us again are you? I've put a few big buildings up in my time, you know.'

'Couple of things to look at with Maria,' Monty explained.

'Aye, that girl's definitely got a couple of things worth looking at.'

Bob would often throw in the odd bit of building site humour, usually to bait Maria into giving as good as she got. He enjoyed the sparring. In the far corner Ged shook his head as if to acknowledge that he and Maria would never alter Bob's behavior in the office.

'That must be a record. Your backside had hardly touched the seat when you uttered your first derogatory remark.'

'Can't understand why these lasses want to be in a game like this, Monty. It's all heavy lifting, getting your designer outfits dirty and breaking fingernails.'

He belched and let off wind, almost simultaneously.

'Sorry folks. Curry last night, I'm afraid.'

'Should we go see where Maria's got to?' Ged interrupted. 'I think it's time for some fresh air' he added, wagging his thumb in the direction of Bob's seat.

'Yes, come on.' Monty opened the door and they both stepped outside where they bumped into Maria.

'Hiya Monty! Are you ready for action? Have I got time to pop in and get my note book?'

'You have, but I'd recommend you don't inhale when you're in there' Monty cautioned. Maria looked at both of them

'Have we been Bobbed out by Hart the Fart?'

'Yup' said Ged, nodding knowingly. Clearly it wasn't the first air pollution incident they'd experienced in the cabin. Maria took a deep breath and, pinching her nose theatrically, plunged herself into the site office. Monty held the door open, waiting for her. She noticed Bob had a lewd grin on his face.

'What have you been up to now?' she asked him.

'Monty was just saying that you were going to show him a couple of interesting things.'

'Yes, that's right. Two boobs on the west wing, upper floor. Will you be joining us?'

She had grown accustomed to working with Bob and knew that matching him with double entendres would unlock the door to his thirty-five years of construction wisdom.

'I think I can trust you to do the right thing, lass.'

'Okay, thanks. Won't be long. Why don't you make a brew while I'm sorting this out?'

She exited, leaving him to put the kettle on. Maria guided Monty and Ged into the construction site to take a look at two locations where suspended cable trays were interfering with the routes for some water pipes. As a site engineer Maria knew exactly what needed doing, she just needed the architects to agree that there were no aesthetic issues. They were soon back at the cabin where they found Bob Hart enjoying his first pot of tea of the day. As Ged gathered his things together Bob had a quiet chat with Monty.

'You don't seem yourself today. What's up?'

'Just got something unsavoury on my mind.'

'Oh. Anything I can help you with?'

'No, but thanks for offering. Had a bit of an argument with my partner.'

'Her indoors?'

'No, not that partner. Everything's fine there. No. My business partner.'

'That Nick fella?'

Monty nodded.

'I'd watch him, Monty. I've heard a few bad reports on the grapevine and I've not been impressed by any dealings I've had with him. Just watch your back.'

Monty nodded again. He respected Bob Hart's opinions and that last comment un-nerved him. He looked round to see that Ged had picked up his belongings and was ready to go, so they both left Bob and Maria to their work and went off to the car. He'd offered to squeeze in the site visit so that he could give Ged a lift into work for the team event. They were due at base in forty minutes. There was ample time, especially if he took some of the country roads again to cut a few corners.

'Thanks for the lift, Monty.'

'That's okay.'

'So, this is the new motor.' Ged was eyeing up the onboard equipment. He was a keen gadget man. As well as being a very promising designer, Ged looked after all of the computers for Hanson Scott. He quickly found himself tinkering with the integrated sat nav and computer screen.

'This is really neat.'

'Yes, it is,' Monty replied. The tone of his response was just subtle enough to inform his passenger to stop as it was distracting him from the job of driving the vehicle.

'Oh, I'm sorry. Can't help it, I'm afraid. I love all these gizmos.' He changed the subject. After a little pause he continued.

'I've got a question for you, Monty.'

'Go ahead. Seems only fair considering how many I ask you when we are on site.'

'Your certificates on the wall at work, all the references I've seen, they all say David M Scott. So, I was wondering, what made you decide you were going to be Monty, not David?'

'Oh, it was just one of those daft things that came about when I was a teenager. We'd been playing cricket and I was berating my best friend for getting a duck. He came up with this lame excuse about being left handed and having to play with a right handed cricket bat. So I told him my dad's got a left handed wheelbarrow, my mum's got a left handed sweeping brush, and I'm going into town to buy some left handed ink.'

'And … coming on to the Monty bit …?' Ged reigned him back to the question in hand.

'Ah, well, he rattled on about me having a stupid middle name.'

'I wouldn't say that Montgomery is particularly odd.'

'Nor would I. But he knew that the M didn't stand for Montgomery.'

'Ah. Montague?'

'Nope. Look, I don't think you'll guess, so I'd better put you out of your misery. It's Montpellier.'

'That's a place, isn't it?' Ged was a promising, if not well travelled, young architect.

'Yes. It's in the south of France. Very nice too. My parents were on holiday there when I was conceived.'

Ged snorted a laugh. 'Sorry,' he said, 'it's just a bit weird calling your son after the place where you've procreated.'

Monty turned his head away from the road momentarily and gave him a raised eyebrow.

'What's the matter? Made love. Is that better?'

'Mmmm. Anyway, my sister got a much better deal.'

'Did she? Let me guess. Kitchen-Table isn't a common Christian name.'

'Do you mind? That's my parents you're talking about.' Monty imitated a reprimanding tone. 'She was conceived in Florence, if you must know.'

Ged went quiet for a minute before sheepishly offering up a confession.

'My middle name is Henley.'

'Ha – hoisted by your own petard, eh!'

'Hoisted by your own petard … I wish I knew what that meant.'

Monty managed to educate Ged with a brief explanation of the saying just before reaching the entrance to the office car park. It was nowhere near as full as usual. Most of the team had left their cars at home so that they could have a drink that evening. Instead the area was busy with people gathering in groups near the two minibuses, which had been borrowed for the day from the local scout troop. Monty and Ged could see that a few of their colleagues had already taken seats onboard and were either chatting patiently or fiddling with their mobile phones. The 4x4 purred into Monty's reserved space and a few moments later they both pulled their gear out of the back of the vehicle. Ged began to sort out his walking boots whilst Monty ambled across to the nearest congregation.

'Hassawa Misser Monty!' Three of the group greeted him with hammy Japanese accents and a flourish of oriental bowing and deference.

'Nineteen' he replied.

'Seventy four!' they roused, punching the sky twice with their fists. It was a regular little ritual they offered up to recognise his fastidious preaching about the importance of the 1974 Health And Safety At Work Act. He'd seen a pretty unpleasant accident in one of his early sojourns on a building site and he never wanted to see another. At least he'd succeeded in getting that snippet of history cemented in their heads.

'Everyone here?' he asked, trying to do a quick survey of faces.

'Just about,' replied one of them. 'Nick's not here yet.'

'Oh. That's not like him, what with his military background.'

'And there's still a couple up in the office.'

'I suppose that's to be expected' acknowledged Monty. 'I'll just put my kit on the bus then I'll go in and prize them away from their CAD machines.'

'Just leave your bags here Monty. We'll load them up' offered another. Monty handed his rucksack and walking boots over and nodded his appreciation. He walked up towards Cartmel House, the large Victorian property that served as their base. It was incongruous, considering their highly modern architectural output. The double entrance door opened into a high-ceilinged, spacious hallway. He took the first door on the right which led into the reception room where the secretarial team carried out all the necessary admin. Pat was tapping away at the keyboard, she said hello to Monty without even looking up to see who it was. She just knew it was him.

'Hello Pat. How's it going?'

'Can't complain' she replied. 'You've got a nice afternoon for the charity walk, if we're to believe the weather forecast.' Pat was quite a bit older than the other admin staff and always volunteered to man the fort and the phones for these events. She considered it her contribution to the team effort. She wasn't one for all this walking nonsense and, besides, she'd still be able to meet them later for a couple of drinks and the meal.

'Do you know where Nick is?' he asked.

'He said something about going to the shooting range.'

'Blimey. They've lifted his ban' he laughed. 'There again, it's been a long time since it happened.'

Monty paused for a moment to reflect. He hoped that Nick hadn't done something stupid. At the same time he couldn't help feeling a little apprehensive about seeing him today.

'Mind if I leave these car keys here? Karen's going to drop by later on and pick up the car.'

'Of course you can. It'll be nice to see her again. How is she?'

'She's fine, thank you. Sounds like there's something going on with her sister, so Karen's hoping to go find out what it's all about.'

'Oh dear. There's always something sent to try us'.

'Yes. It's not clear whether it's home or work. Might be my brother-in-law, he tends to be away quite a lot with his job.' Monty

19

shrugged his shoulders. 'Karen's going to take her out this evening when they've both finished work. She said she'd be here before five to pick it up.'

'Oooh, that means I get time to take it out for a spin this afternoon' smiled Pat.

'Just as long as I don't find out about it. And you don't miss any calls from some rich tycoon wanting us to do a multi-million pound design for him.'

'Or her' said Pat, dropping in the vote for women's equality.

'That's a fair cop.'

He went out into the entrance hall and, thinking back to the earlier conversation with Ged, had to accept that his last comment to Pat counted as being hoisted by his own petard. He went upstairs to round up the stragglers. It was time to set off.

4

The hike passed off uneventfully. Nick kept his own company for the most part of the eight miles, but he couldn't help noticing a couple of occasions when Monty and Clare were walking alongside each other chatting secretively. What Nick was less observant about was Monty spending equal amounts of time with all of the team members, encouraging the slower ones up the hills and showing interest in everyone's topics of conversation.

Later on Pat picked up a text informing her that the gang had arrived back at The Half Moon. It was two hundred yards along the road from Cartmel House, they'd stopped there to let an advance party off to set up a tab in the pub. She tidied around, locking filing cabinets and her desk drawer. A couple of minutes later she saw both minibuses arrive in the car park and knew that the peacefulness of the office was about to be broken. It didn't take long for all the equipment to be unloaded and carried into the building. There was an ample stationery cupboard on the ground floor that served as a temporary store. Mind you, Pat wasn't too happy about the prospects of being greeted by the stale aroma of sweaty socks and boots the next morning.

Very shortly the last few left the building and Nick prepared to run through the procedure to close up and secure the office. He suggested to Pat that she made her way over to the Half Moon with the others as he had just remembered that he needed to get some things from his desk. He wanted to make sure he was alone for that task.

Nick pulled out his mobile phone and despatched a message to Ged who was one of those who'd been dropped at The Half Moon about twenty minutes earlier. Ged picked it up and continued calling out the instructions to Arthur and Stella behind the bar. They were a popular old couple and very few locals could remember The Half Moon ever being under different stewardship. Arthur was very short of hearing in his left ear and always jerked the right side of his head forwards to pick up what was being said. The lads in the team would deliberately ask for 'arfer Stellar' just to confuse him.

Everyone had arrived and there was a happy hum of conversation

21

in the lounge room. It always proved to be a fantastic way of getting all the firm's employees together and fuelling morale. Timing was excellent in one sense because Nick had announced on Tuesday that a substantial contract had just been won.

Ged was telling Clare all about Barker's Court when Monty came over. Clare was his chief protégé. She'd joined them soon after he and Nick had got the new partnership on its feet. Whilst attractive and lively, she was thirty and unattached. She was hesitant when it came to long term relationships having seen her parents make a complete mess of their marriage. She'd suffered from being caught in the middle of their infernal bickering, it was as though they were fighting over her for possession rights. The best thing she ever did was leave home and secure a place at university to study Architecture. After qualifying she gained experience in some small practices and first came to Monty's attention when she joined Parker Priest.

'Hey Monty, when are you going to show me the mall again? Ged's just been telling me all about it.'

'Whenever you want. It's certainly moving on at a good pace. When were you last there?'

'Three months ago. It was bloody cold.'

'Ah, you'll see a lot of difference now. I was planning on a slow day at the office tomorrow, get some paperwork cleared up. I could find some time to pop over there instead. What have you got planned?'

'Nothing much. Nothing that desperately needs doing before the weekend.'

'Okay. Let's do that.'

During the exchange, Pat and Nick had walked across from the bar to stand with them. Spotting a gap in the conversation, Pat offered Monty an update

'Karen picked up the keys just before five o'clock, Monty.'

'Excellent, thank you very much Pat.'

Pat turned towards Nick

'Oh, and I forgot to tell you, there was a message from a Mister Connor.'

'Dan Connor?' asked Clare.

'Yes, I expect it will be' said Nick.

'He wants you to call him about a new project' Pat added.

'So, Clare, I hope you're making a first rate job of that new house for him' said Monty. 'I think it's time I took a look. How about we add it to our itinerary for tomorrow? We'll do a grand tour.'

They were at it again, thought Nick, his demons instantly added up two and two to make five. This was another opportunity for Monty and Clare to slope off somewhere private at lunch time for a little bit of steamy passion. He listened attentively as they developed their schedule.

Aside from the turmoil inside Nick's head, the evening buzzed along nicely. They had a couple of hours in The Half Moon and then walked a little further down the road to The Kashmir Room, one of the town's two Indian restaurants. They'd booked for eighteen a few weeks ago and had reduced this to sixteen because two people weren't able to stay on after the early evening drinks. The party entered noisily and made their way to a part of the room where the tables had been arranged to form two parallel rectangles, each seating eight people. Clare sat down and within seconds found Nick occupying the seat to her left. Monty had automatically gone to the other table so that each eight-some enjoyed management team representation.

During popadoms Clare had to endure the management representation, rather than enjoy it, as Nick made numerous attempts to manoeuvre his right leg so that it was pressing against her left. This was usually done in tandem with him leaning his upper body into her personal space on the pretence that he could listen more closely to what she was saying. Clare could handle the lime pickle, but Nick brushing up close beside her was not so palatable. She spotted her moment when the last scraps of popadom were being picked at. She jumped up.

'Hey everybody, your attention please! Listen for a moment. We're going to have a shuffle around so that we all get time to talk to each other. I'm going to number you all one or two, then the number ones from this table can switch with the number ones at this table,' pointing right and left as she explained the instructions.

It was a smart move. The plan was for each table to get the same food - popadoms and pickle tray, the same selection of starters, and an equal mix of main courses, rices, and breads. So it really didn't matter where everyone sat and this introduced a social merry-go-round to make the meal more fun.

She started by declaring herself a 'one' and quickly worked her way around both tables before giving everyone the go ahead to move. There was a mixed reaction and a lot of bustle, with people climbing out of their places and making sure that they took their drinks with them to their new seating positions. The majority were able to do the drill with ease. Pat got a little bit confused by it, but was soon helped to a new seat. Nick found himself sat between two of the men, neither of whom he wanted to rub his thigh against. Nor was he revelling in the prospect of a discussion about their pet subject, cricket. He looked over his shoulder to see that Clare was now sat next to Monty.

'Typical,' he thought. He wasn't at all happy, but nobody noticed him slowly fuming away. Everyone else was having a great time. There was an excitement in the air about the message from Dan Connor, it could mean another big job in the offing. It was highly likely that the brief would call for a very high tech design.

During the starter course Clare didn't hog Monty's company, but she did complain in his ear about Nick's attentions whilst she'd been sat at the other table. When the starters had been cleared there were some calls for Clare to get everyone organised for the next table swap. She had her wits about her and was able to remind everyone whether they were a one or a two. Then she instructed all the number ones now sat at Nick's table to swap with the number twos from Monty's table.

Pat stood up to move and was jovially mocked and told to sit down again by at least half of the company. She was staying put this time. Monty stepped across to the other table and took the seat where Clare had sat for the first course. If nothing else, he would be preventing any of the other females from suffering what Clare had put up with half an hour earlier. He set his drink down very close to Nick's and decided that this was as good a time as any to detour out to the gents before the main course arrived.

In the general hubbub that accompanied the musical chairs Nick felt inside his jacket and extracted a small packet. He picked up Monty's glass of Cobra beer and pretended to take a sip before lowering it just below the table. He was able to sprinkle a tiny amount of Rohypnol powder into it without anyone seeing, before raising it near his mouth a second time then returning it to the table. Each action involved a subtle shake to help the powder dissolve its way through the thin frothy head, losing itself in the amber liquid underneath.

His intention was to give Monty a bit of discomfort, not to do any serious harm. He'd considered spiking Clare's drink, and maybe he would have done so had she remained in the seat next to him. He had, however, reached the right conclusion that his name would be the last on the list when it came to figuring out who was the most appropriate person to take a very tipsy Clare home.

Monty returned to the table and remained civil and pleasant throughout the remainder of the meal, despite having to sit next to a very sullen Nick. As the group began to disperse he held his partner back so that they could attend to the final bill. This also gave Monty a bit of time to talk to Nick alone when they stepped out into the night. The fresh air hit Monty and he immediately felt a degree more drunk than he thought he ought to. Nonetheless, as they stood waiting for taxis to arrive, he broached Nick about what had gone on at the table earlier in the evening.

'Will you bloody well back off Monty? You're worse than my flaming parents ever were. Don't do this, don't do that. What gives you this divine right, eh?'

'Nick, calm down, for Heaven's sake. I've a right when it involves the overall well being of the staff that work for us.'

'You only seem to want to practice that right when it comes to one particular member of staff. What else are you practicing with her Monty? All seems a bit close and cosy if you ask me.'

'What the heck are you insinuating?'

'I'm absolutely sure that you won't want Karen to know that you're playing around with someone from the office.'

'Don't be so bloody ridiculous. That's a very wild accusation, Nick. Are you.... Are you trying to threaten me?'

This ludicrous conversation was giving him a strange feeling of nausea and he was becoming weary, desperate to be settled down in bed.

'I don't know what has got into you, but I'm not going to stand around and listen to any more of this crazy nonsense. Look, perhaps I've been a bit too hasty demanding that you resolve that money position so quickly. You can have some more time to sort it out.'

'You're changing your tune. You're backing off. You've got something to hide, haven't you? I thought so.'

'Absolutely not. Now, why don't you just go home. Stay off work tomorrow and try to calm down, get your head straightened out. Come back on Monday in a far better frame of mind and we can talk this money thing through properly.'

'Press me any more on the money front, Monty, and I'll have no reservations about making sure that Karen knows about you and Clare.'

'I'm not listening to any more of this rubbish. There's nothing at all to know about me and Clare. Just your crazy theory. I'm going.'

With impeccable timing a taxi pulled up in front of them. Monty slalomed his way across the pavement towards it and clambered in, relieved that he was about to be transported home. He was feeling light headed and his insides were beginning to grumble.

Nick watched Monty depart. The second cab that the Indian restaurant had ordered for them appeared within a couple of minutes. He was pretty mad about Monty being so patronising, but he took some sadistic satisfaction from seeing that the dose of Rohypnol was kicking in. He settled himself into the back seat and told the driver to take him to the Black Jack Casino. It was only half past eleven and that meant plenty more drinking time. Besides, Monty had already told him to stay away from the office for a few days.

During the taxi ride he pulled a different packet out of his jacket, wet his finger, dabbed it in the powder, then sucked it clean. 'Purely medicinal' he thought to himself. The driver pretended not to notice the deed, just like the football manager who didn't see his prima-donna goal scorer dive in the penalty area.

Fifteen minutes later Nick was showing his black membership card at the reception desk. He went to the gents and washed his hands, then furnished himself with a drink and shuffled into position at a busy roulette table. Whilst he played the table his imagination wandered off into a swamp, spinning out of control as the roulette wheel sucked the money out of his wallet. There was no telling what lengths he might go to in order to protect his ill gotten gains.

5

Friday April 16th, 2010 (R)

Monty woke, again. He'd been up three times during the night with a really bad stomach and a terrible headache. One of those headaches that pierced deeply, as though someone had forced a sharp knitting needle up through his left eyeball to exit his skull three quarters of the way along the top of his head. The only way he could dull the sensation was by shutting that eye as tightly as possible. When he did so, he could see dull coloured blotches in the midst of the blackness. The temporary relief afforded to his head only served to remind him that his stomach was still churned up. He felt pretty lousy all round.

He looked at the clock on the bedside cabinet. 07:42 shone back at him. He simply could not have heard the alarm. He turned to check the right hand side of the bed to find that Karen wasn't there. Through the fuzziness that shrouded his head he could hear movement about the house and he knew it was high time he got out of bed. Slowly he rolled and raised his heavy body so that he was sitting over the edge of the mattress. Instinctively his elbows found his knees and his forehead found his hands. He puffed out a long breath as he slumped. He'd been here once or twice before, but not very often. He was a healthy living individual. This wasn't a regular sensation by any stretch of the imagination. And, besides, he'd only had four pints throughout the whole evening.

He gave his sockets a hard rub with the heels of his hands, then lifted his face to the point where he could continue the massage with his fingertips. He pressed them into the bridge of his nose and brought his hands together so that his fingers ran down the flanks of his nostrils and his palms met, cupping round his mouth. His thumbs pointed in towards his neck, providing a cantilever under his chin to support the dead weight of his head. In this praying position he decided it was time to force open his eyes. A squint. A faint gap that let in a hazy grey light. He closed and opened a few times, broadening the fissure ever so slightly with each cycle. Finally he mustered the energy and confidence to hoist himself up. He felt a dull pain that started in the back of his neck and carried on downwards to his shoulder blades, marking out the tip of a triangle at the top of his back. He steadied for a few seconds, then dragged himself over to the en-suite and into the shower.

Downstairs in the kitchen Karen had made a pot of tea and was half way through her bowl of cereal whilst reading the newspaper. Describing herself as medium height at five feet three inches, she had a slight physique which was maintained at the expense of a gym membership and at least three visits per week. Her blonde hair was parted on the right, but the parting dissolved into a fringe as the light strands came down together over her forehead. Her hair was styled in such a way that it cleverly softened her quite linear features.

Karen was an interior designer at a small furnishing and decorating shop in the town. It was a business with a strong reputation that brought her an interesting breadth of commissions. It was important to her that she always dressed smartly for work and today was no different, even though she was only going in for a half day. A navy blue dress with bold grey and white flowers helped present her attractive figure perfectly, whilst also striking a strong contrast with her blonde hair. A pair of light grey shoes elevated her up another three inches.

Every room in this 1930's detached house had her artistic stamp on it. The kitchen had been their most recent upgrade. A steel and glass extension to the back of the mock-Tudor property gave Karen a large canvas to work on. She'd had great fun considering the various styles and finishes for the cupboards; annotating a long list of appliances; and deciding how to get the right blending of materials for the floor and the work surfaces. Monty had more say in the layout, he was adept at thinking through how the family would use the space. Together they'd arrived at a gem which gave them a fantastic focal point, both for relaxing as a family and for entertaining.

Sam sat at the breakfast bar with her, engrossed in his magazine while two slices of white bread warmed up in the toaster. He wasn't particularly comfortable. His knee had taken a blow during a football match at sixth form on Wednesday afternoon and had stiffened up worse last night than it had the night before. Karen sensed he was suffering.

'How is it this morning, Sam?'

'It's not too bad. I'll be alright.'

'Let's take a look. Is it swollen?'

'Yeah, a bit.'

Sam slid off the barstool and tried to roll the bottoms of his jeans up. The left leg wasn't playing. He rolled them down again, but wasn't going to be defeated that easily. He undid his belt and button, pulled down his flies and dropped his trousers to his ankles. He presented his legs in clear view for his mother to carry out a comparison inspection. But Karen was distracted by his bright pink pants.

'Where on earth did you get those?'

Gemma breezed into the kitchen just as the toaster ejected its finished products.

'Haaa! Are those the ones that Sophie bought you for your birthday?'

She continued straight across to the other side of the kitchen, picked out the two pieces of toast and soon had them dressed in butter and Marmite. Caught with his pants down, Sam was unable to launch any form of defence. The mention of Sophie had aroused a blush on his face.

'Hey! They're mine! You know I hate Marmite.'

'Oh, I'm sorry' said Gemma, taking her next bite right under his nose. 'You're tough enough to wear pink today, are you? Will Sophie get a private showing in the sixth form common room?'

'Gemma, there's no need for that, thank you' said Karen, calming the situation. 'That knee does look swollen. Let me see.' She felt around Sam's knees and took a close look from several angles. 'It's badly bruised but you'll be alright. Just avoid knocking it against anything. Now pull your trousers back on. Gemma, put two more slices in for Sam, please.'

Gemma did as she was asked then took Sam's place at the breakfast bar, despite there being another two unoccupied. The Easter break was behind them and they both had some serious exams to build up to. Sam's were more overtly important as, being seventeen, he would be relying on these results to help him in the race for university offers after the summer. Gemma was two years younger and had another twelve months before facing exams that would have an influence on her future.

Karen's phone began beeping.

'Is that your alarm, mum?' asked Gemma.

'Oh, it might be. I thought I'd turned it off ten minutes ago.'

'It looks like you put it on snooze' said Gemma after inspecting it.

'Can you switch it off for me?'

'Mum. You really should learn how to do this yourself. What would you do if we weren't here to help you?'

Gemma looked around the kitchen and looked back at the phone to double-check the time.

'Where's dad? He's normally up and about by now.'

Karen explained that their father hadn't been very well during the night. She went on to tell Gemma the latest trials and tribulations about their Auntie Debbie, with whom she had been out for dinner the previous evening. Two inches taller and of slightly heavier build, Debbie was Karen's younger sister. She resembled their mother, whereas Karen took her looks from their father. Whilst she could occasionally be a bit of a drama queen, it was nice to have her living within easy reach. Debbie didn't have children and had always taken a close interest in Sam and Gemma. She had been a regular babysitter when they were younger. The need for that service had now passed, or at least that's what Sam and Gemma maintained.

The second round of toast had been ejected and Sam took another seat alongside his mother and sister, eating his breakfast at last.

'Where's dad?' he asked. 'Isn't he normally up by now?'

Karen looked at Gemma and raised her eyebrows. Gemma turned to Sam, snatched his guitarist magazine, part folded it, then playfully clipped him over the head with it.

'What?' Sam looked at both of them in mild puzzlement, turning his outstretched hands upwards. At which point they all heard a noise on the stairs.

Monty entered the kitchen and made for the television controls. The breakfast news programme was on and it was a little too loud for his sensitive head this morning. Nobody was really listening to it, anyway. The shower, shave and brushing of teeth had left him feeling considerably better, though he was still a long way from being back to normal. He sluggishly filled a glass with water and searched out some headache tablets, breathing heavily throughout. He was wearing a pair of red chino trousers, a bright purple and white striped shirt, and a matching purple tie.

Sam looked up.

'God, you look rough, dad. And is there an option to turn down the volume on that shirt and tie?'

'What did you get up to last night?' asked Karen. 'It was nearly midnight when you got home and you were very drunk.'

'I know. We just had a few rounds at the Moon and then went along to the Kashmir at eight o'clock for a curry. I really didn't drink much at all.' Monty had been trying to recall what it was that could have affected him so much.

'Are you going to be able to drive?'

'Yes, I'll be fine. I wasn't planning on going in as early as usual. Going to take a run out to Barker's Court again with Clare, so that she can see how it's looking. Then she's going to show me the farm extension she designed for that pharmaceutical chap.' His speech was slow and his voice hoarse.

'Well, be careful. Make sure you're not over the limit.'

'I'm not, love. I just feel really rough. I wonder if I'm coming down with something. Sorry if I disturbed you during the night.'

'You did, but I'll forgive you.'

'So, how was your evening? How's Debbie going to cope for the next month while Chris is in Qatar?'

'Has Uncle Chris got a guitar?' Sam was suddenly sparked into life again, speaking with a half mouthful of toast and marmalade. Gemma gave him another slap with the magazine.

'Ow! Stop that!'

'No, he hasn't got a guitar' said Karen in a slow and pronounced fashion. 'He's going to Qatar for a month. It's in the Middle East.'

'Yes, I know. I am doing Geography A-level. I thought you said…'

'No.' Karen closed her newspaper. 'Come on! Chop chop!' She clapped her hands twice, gently, to chivvy the two teenagers along. 'It's time you were both thinking about school. Go and get ready, now.'

Sam and Gemma wove their way around the kitchen, and each other, putting rubbish in the bin and their cutlery and crockery in the dishwasher. Monty grimaced slightly as the intermittent shock waves hit his ears.

'Oh, Sam? Would you set the sat nav up for me before you disappear please?'

'Sure. Where is it? And where do you need to go this time?'

'It's on the hall table. And this is the post code.' Karen handed him a scrap of paper with the destination address. He went off to program the device. Gemma gave her mother a knowing look on her way out of the kitchen.

Karen began to tell Monty about the previous evening. She had taken her sister to Brindley's Bistro, over by the canal. Debbie had been tearful at times as she told Karen about her unsuccessful attempts to persuade Chris about having children. They didn't see eye to eye on the subject and now Chris was spending more and more time away from home. Karen would have to keep an eye on Debbie over the next few weeks.

'And what are your plans for today?' asked Monty.

'I'm going in to work this morning, I have a client visit at eleven. Then I'll come home and start packing everything. Have you got all of your clothes sorted out yet?'

'No, not yet. I'll do it before I head over to the office.'

'Well, you'll need to be in better form than this for your niece's wedding tomorrow. Otherwise your big brother will be very disappointed with you.'

'I know. I'll rally. I'll be as right as rain by the time we have to drive up there this afternoon.'

'If you leave your clothes on the bed, I'll deal with them when I get back home. I want us to be leaving as soon as Sam and Gemma get back. So, can you be home for 4:00pm?'

'Yes, no problem.'

'And where's your suit carrier?'

'In the wardrobe.'

'Okay.' Karen stood up and began tidying around. 'Right, I'm going to go and finish putting my make-up on. You get yourself sorted out and, whatever you do, don't do anything stupid with that lovely new car today. I'm looking forward to our first long distance run in it to the Lake District. The weather's supposed to clear up nicely tomorrow.'

She picked up the newspaper from the breakfast bar and was about to take it through to the magazine rack in the lounge.

'Leave the newspaper. I'm going to have five minutes looking at it with a cup of tea. I don't think I can face any breakfast just yet.'

Karen looked at him. He was in a sorry state.

'That shirt doesn't really go with those trousers' she said. She smiled, turned away and went upstairs. Monty slowly sipped at his tea and continued to pull himself around. Karen reappeared some ten minutes later.

'I'm off now. I'll see you later. Hopefully you'll be looking a bit brighter than you are now.'

'Hopefully' he echoed. 'You look fantastic. I always like to see you wearing that leather jacket. Very smart indeed Mrs Scott.'

Karen came over to him. He swivelled on the barstool, and wrapped his arms around her. She looked down on him. They kissed once, lightly, then held for a few more seconds.

'Got to go. See you later' she said as she eased away, slowly. Her heels clicked as she walked across the kitchen to the doorway, before turning to muffled footsteps on the carpet in the hallway. Monty heard the front door open and close. The house fell silent.

By 8:45 he felt stabilised to the point where he could negotiate the stairs and the remainder of his preparations for a day at the office. The last fifteen minutes had been peaceful for him once the rest of the household had departed. Eventually he emerged from the front door and crunched over the gravel drive to his Land Rover. It was a duller day than yesterday and he reflected how fortunate they'd been with the weather for the charity walk. Today was forecast to be a good deal more cloudy with a strong probability of heavy rain around lunchtime.

He reversed the car down the drive and out through the gateway. A loud horn sounded, startling him to brake just before the rear of the car traversed the boundary of pavement and tarmac. It was the man from two doors along. Fortunately he hadn't picked up much speed and was able to pull up short of any potential collision. Monty signalled an apologetic hand wave to his neighbour.

'Come on, get a grip Monty!' he said to himself.

6

Monty arrived safely, though he was not confident about his handling of the car this morning. He steered into his bay in the car park. He checked in to the admin office, saying his good mornings to Pat and Sienna. They both remarked how pale he looked.

'Would you like a nice hot cup of tea Monty?'

'I'd prefer a coffee please, Pat, if you don't mind.'

'I don't mind at all. I'll bring it up to you in a few minutes.'

He trudged upstairs to his office, settled into his seat and made himself comfortable. He started to flick through his notebook. He plugged his laptop in and lethargically shuffled around his tasks, making minimal headway. It was a welcome interruption when Pat came in with the cup of coffee. She asked about Barker's Court, remembering the conversation from the Half Moon the previous evening. She knew that Monty and Clare had come up with a plan to visit the site today. They chatted for five minutes, with Pat expressing some concern about his state of health and advising him to seek out some paracetamol. Monty persevered at his desk for an hour, which took him up towards the time he'd arranged to meet Clare.

During that hour, the office gradually filled with noise as people drifted in and generated conversations about the night out. The ground floor kitchenette proved the most popular place as groups came together to brew tea and make coffees in attempts to bring themselves round. There was a loud outburst up on the second floor, a good humoured bout of mickey-taking between three of the younger architects. The noise abated almost as quickly as it had flared up, but it had broken Monty's limited concentration. He stood up from his desk and went off to find Clare, picking up his green jacket on his way out of the room. They both set off downstairs and Monty poked his head round the admin door and checked out with Pat.

'We're heading out now. We should be back at around three this afternoon' he said, withdrawing again to the hallway.

'Monty,' she called after him.

'Yes,' he poked his head back around the door.

'That shirt doesn't really go with that jacket.'

Monty smiled, acknowledging his sartorial deficiency. He exited the front door of Cartmel House with Clare. Setting off was not smooth. The car lurched forwards and Monty was slow to bring it under control. Clare looked across at him and asked if he was alright. He confessed to being very dull. It was highly irregular for Monty to be so badly hungover.

'Are you sure nobody spiked your drink last night? You're in no fit state to drive. Come on, jump out, I'll take over.'

She had three motives for offering to swap seats. One being that she really fancied driving his new car. Another was to prevent Monty losing his licence. The third was pure self preservation.

Barker's Court had three similar wings branching from a square courtyard. Monty and Clare didn't need to cover the entire building, it would suffice to see one wing and the central square today. It was a slow amble as neither of them felt like going at a sprint. Monty explained all the design points as they walked and talked. They were returning to the central court when they bumped into Bob Hart.

'Good grief, Monty, another bleeding woman. Who's this one?'

'This is Clare. Clare, this is Bob.'

'Hi Bob.'

'Haven't you got any fellas over at that place of yours? You'll be getting hauled up for racial discrimination against us men, Monty.'

Clare had heard all about Bob Hart and was able to detect he wasn't being serious.

'I think you'll find it's sexual discrimination, Bob. We do have a couple of lads in the admin office who make the tea, but the rest of the practice is wall to wall females. You'd love it.'

'Nice one,' said Bob, 'I like your fighting spirit.'

Clare had an ability to muck in with the men at work and was hardened to dealing with the alpha male behaviours of the building trade. A lot of that resilience had been developed during the period when her parents were constantly squabbling around her. She'd quickly gained a lot of respect on the sites by standing up to some of the macho foremen and pointing out, very firmly, that they wouldn't get far by trying to pull the wool over her eyes.

'I know that's not right,' she would often say to them. 'You know that's not right. And I know that you know it's not right,' she would continue. 'So, now that you know that I know that you know it's not right, don't come trying to pull that kind of trick again. Do we understand each other?'

At this point they'd usually be baffled to the point of not understanding at all, but they'd give a submissive nod of acceptance.

They talked for a few minutes then Bob said that he was going to check how the pipe fitters were getting on in the north wing and he set off in search of them.

7

Clare and Monty had made their way back across to where the 4x4 was parked. Monty went to get into the driver's side but was directed back to the passenger door. He climbed in and turned to Clare as she pulled on her seatbelt.

'I actually feel a bit peckish now. Shall we stop off somewhere to have lunch?'

'Sounds good to me. I'm hungry too.'

Clare drove off. Monty knew of a good roadside café which was only a few miles out of their way. It wasn't long before they were sat at a table scrolling down the menu. Mushroom soup and a bread roll would satisfy Monty. Something middle of the road, and the roll would help soak up whatever was left inside. Clare had a healthier appetite and went for a toasted sandwich with chips and salad. Another coffee helped the gradual recovery process for Monty.

They talked about Clare's impending holiday. Three weeks ago she had booked flights to go to Chicago where one of her old friends was now living on a two year work secondment.

'Wow, the windy city. Birthplace of the skyscraper. I'm very envious, Clare. I've always wanted to go there.'

'My pal loves it. She's got a downtown apartment and commutes out to work. She gets all the benefits of having the city lifestyle at the weekends. Plenty of restaurants to enjoy in the evenings, too.'

'I'd just luxuriate in the architecture. The Hancock Tower is one of my all time favourites, I'd love to see it for real. And Mies van der Rohe, Frank Lloyd Wright ... it would be fantastic to look around some of their work.'

This developed into a conversation about what their respective world architecture tour itineraries would look like, if money and time were no object. Several American cities were offered up. Both agreed that New York's Empire State Building simply could not be missed, it was such a historic icon. Their deliberations quickly moved East, through Dubai to Kuala Lumpur, Hong Kong and Shanghai. Clare doodled a route map on her serviette. It exposed that cartography wasn't her strong point, but it was sufficiently accurate that they could re-trace the steps of the discussion. Monty's final throw was to nominate Sydney Opera House.

Monty looked at his watch. The time had flown by. They had spent almost two hours chatting. He paid the bill and left a small tip in the cup by the cash register. Clare pocketed the napkin for posterity and they walked out of the café into a huge downpour. They ran across to the car and hurried inside. Clare turned the key in the ignition and the wiper blades began swishing the rain off the windscreen. She really was enjoying the loftier driving position in the 4x4. They turned away from the café and back out onto the main road.

It only took fifteen minutes for Monty and Clare to get to the Dan Connor house, by which time the rain had eased off to a light shower. Clare parked up near three other vehicles, including two white vans, then led Monty across to the entrance.

A little earlier another vehicle had pulled off a country road to park up in a clearing at the far side of Boothby Hill woods. The driver stepped out and set off through the trees. The area was popular with dog owners, but they tended to be out early morning and late afternoon. So, it being lunchtime, the event went unnoticed.

Dan Connor had bought the old stone farmhouse and engaged Hanson Scott to design a scheme for considerably extending the property. Clare had produced a proposal that added a wing at ninety degrees to the existing house. Taking advantage of the slope, the plan introduced a lower ground floor level, resulting in an imposing three story gable end that faced down the hill towards the town and beyond. The whole house would have a structural frame of exposed oak timbers, giving it an aged styling that blended into the older farm building.

The timber frame was erected and most of the walls were now in place, though the external scaffolding still cloaked the whole house and masked the full dramatic effect of the gable. The roofing was complete and some of the windows had been fitted, so most of the inside was protected against the weather. Monty and Clare stepped in through the front gable, the one section that was yet to be made watertight.

It would be a high glass façade and the first six feet of the roof would also be glazed, forming a tall atrium. They paused and looked up. It was a superb open space. There was a staircase to go in here, but there would still be plenty of light. It hadn't been constructed yet, so there were long ladders reaching up through the void. Some of the scaffolding poles protruded in from outside. They interfered with the view, but it was easy enough to block these out of one's mind and imagine the final effect.

'Watch the toilets,' warned Clare. Monty was so busy looking up that he hadn't noticed the array of porcelain features that lay on the concrete slab just behind him. 'The plumbers are starting work on all of the bathrooms' she explained.

They came across two electricians who were busy setting all the cable runs for this new wing.

'Hiya guys. It's quiet today.'

'That's Friday afternoon for you, Clare' the taller one replied. 'Now, if you'd been around an hour ago... Loads of folks. Most of them have taken a flyer. I think the tiler's still working somewhere in the old wing. And there was a chap from the glass balustrade place measuring that top balcony when we got back from our lunch break.' He gestured upwards to above where they were standing.

'Again? I'm positive they measured it just a few weeks ago.'

'Expensive stuff. Probably don't want to make any mistakes.'

'Did you speak to him? Was it a guy called Alex?'

'Don't know. Sorry, Clare. Didn't really get a good look at him. We've been down here all day.'

'Didn't see him turn up, or go' the other electrician added.

Clare left the electricians to get on with their cabling and took Monty through to investigate the remainder of the lower ground floor. It contained an extensive kitchen and entertainment rooms, all opening out onto what would be a south facing patio. Returning to the atrium, they took the shorter set of ladders to the ground floor. They had to clamber off the top of the ladder under a wooden bar that acted as a safety barrier, preventing anyone inadvertently walking straight off the edge. It was quite awkward, even at this low level. Clare commented that she wasn't confident to take the other ladder to the upper floor, she felt much safer using the existing stairs at the far end of the old wing.

They continued exploring the first floor and it was evident that Clare was extremely proud of how she had laid it all out. The proportions were excellent and there was a natural flow through the whole house. Their circular route took them back into the old part of the house, which had been subtly remodelled such that it functioned as a wing of the whole. They were able to access the top floor via the safe staircase rather than having to confront the challenge of the longer ladder in the atrium. When they got there Monty was impressed by how the bedrooms were arranged. Each had an ample en-suite, though they didn't delve into all of them because the tiler was at work in one of them and had his gear littered about in the others.

Clare was eager for Monty to see the end of the upper corridor. Beyond the final bedroom the gable came into view again. He found himself in a terrific open landing looking straight across the atrium and out through what would be a huge curtain of windows opposite.

'Ahhhh, now that will be some view once all the scaffolding is out of the way.'

'That was the idea.' Clare was glowing inside at the sound of her mentor's compliments.

They stood for a moment, taking in the surrounding air. Then Clare got a shout from down below. The electricians wanted to discuss the kitchen layout. It was the room with the most sockets and appliances, some of which would take very high current loading. Careful planning was a necessity and they wanted to double check which appliances were going where. Clare left Monty on the gallery and caught a glimpse of someone in one of the bedrooms as she returned along the top corridor towards the staircase. She checked her stride and took a couple of steps back to look into the bedroom but saw nothing. It was probably the lad that was helping the tiler, disappearing off into the en-suite to pick up a specialist tool. She made her way down to catch up with the electricians again.

Back on the gallery landing, Monty stepped over towards the edge and placed his hands on the temporary wooden bar that ran across at waist height between the vertical oak timbers. He leaned forward and relaxed, taking in the fantastic view. Seeing his pride and joy outside in the temporary car park, he pulled the keys out of his pocket and began to subconsciously fumble with them in his right hand. Usually a stickler for safety, on a normal day he would have noticed that the temporary bar retaining him had been nailed into the oak frame on the atrium side, rather than the landing side. Unfortunately today wasn't a normal day, he was still feeling light headed and this point didn't register with him at all.

He felt a sudden surge forwards. His weight on the bar simply teased the nails out on the far side and there was nothing to counterbalance him. It gave way and Monty fell forward. He scrambled with his feet but his centre of gravity was already carrying him over. He flapped to grab hold of the ladder with his outstretched left hand. He couldn't get any great purchase. The rungs were greasy where the tradesmen had clambered up them earlier with wet muddy boots. Monty spun in the air and as he tumbled he managed to clumsily connect his right leg with the ladder. His boot slipped on two rungs and he lurched to his left. His face met directly with the end of a scaffolding pole which ran under and supported the ladder. His left eye and cheek felt the full force of the impact, his hard hat offering no protection. His body rotated to the right and he dropped through the air.

There was a set of crash bags on the ground down below, a safety measure in case of such an accident. But the flight of his fall, particularly after the interaction with the ladder, meant that he was always going to miss the benefit of them being there. He landed awkwardly on the toilet pans that he'd nearly tripped over earlier, the car keys coming to rest inside one of the U-bends. He lay motionless. It was highly likely that he was dead before he hit the sanitary-ware.

Clare and the electricians heard the disturbance and raced out into the atrium from different directions. They found Monty's broken body and Clare let out a scream. Within seconds the tiler and his sidekick appeared at the top landing, looking down from the point where Monty had dropped to his death.

8

Friday April 16th, 2010 (R)

It was devastating for Clare. The only saving grace was that she hadn't seen the full acrobatics of Monty's gruesome fall. The police and ambulance service arrived within twenty minutes, though the paramedics were only able to confirm what everyone there already knew. The site would be closed for a couple of weeks to allow the necessary safety inspections and any remediation activities to take place. Dan Connor would also be notified by the police. He'd be upset, as he had grown to like and respect Monty. However, the delay wouldn't concern him too much, just as long as it didn't drag beyond the fortnight. There would be some repercussions with the site insurance policy, and that did concern him.

The police took on the grim task of informing Karen. It was just after 3:30pm when they arrived at Monty's house and rang the bell. Karen was busily arranging the weekend outfits into special carriers and placing all of the other clothes into the suitcase. She glanced at her watch and assumed that Sam had forgotten his front door key again. She and Monty slept in the back bedroom, otherwise her natural reaction may have been to take a look out of the window to see who it was. She placed the blouse that she had been about to pack over the back of a chair and went downstairs.

Karen could make out the forms of two dark figures through the glass panel of the door. It wasn't Sam. Or Gemma. And neither would bring a friend home today because they knew that the plan was to make an early departure. She opened the door to see two uniformed police officers, one male and one female. She knew by the look on their faces that something was horribly wrong. Had there been an accident at school? Or had one of their children been knocked down on the way home? Was it drugs? Had Sam got himself involved with the wrong crowd in sixth form?

'Mrs Scott?' said the policeman.

'Yes.'

'I'm PC Taylor and this is WPC Walker. May we come in please?'

She invited the officers in and led them off the hall into the lounge.

'This must be serious,' she said as she offered them a seat. Her pulse was beginning to race. 'Whatever is the matter?'

'Please, Mrs Scott, please take a seat. I'm afraid we have some bad news for you.'

The WPC gestured to Karen to sit on the sofa and she sat close by. PC Taylor went to the single armchair and eased himself down.

It was hard for her to compose herself. Her mind had stalled into an emotional tailspin. Possible reasons for their visit were randomly rebounding around her head like a game of pinball. They all involved her two offspring until she suddenly remembered the state her husband had been in that morning. He's crashed that new car! He's in a ditch somewhere. Is he in hospital? Which one? How bad? Where is he? Is he alright … oh, pray he's alright …

PC Taylor slowly and considerately explained the facts of the accident at the Connor farmhouse. Karen listened, hanging on his every word. Fighting to keep the mulch of grey brain noise out of the way so that she could digest what he was saying. She sat for a moment in sheer disbelief. Then she collapsed, distraught, in a heap of tears. The policewoman comforted her and said that she would remain until friends or relatives arrived. Her colleague made calls to Karen's sister Debbie, and their mother, Pauline. Debbie dropped everything and rushed across in no time at all. It was a reversal of roles, Debbie looking after her older sister for a change.

Fortunately Debbie had managed to hear the full story before Sam and Gemma arrived from school, full of excitement about the weekend ahead. The sight of a police car outside the house had sparked their curiosity and they sensed the worst as soon as they came into the house. Debbie stepped in to take the unenviable duty of telling them the harrowing news. She and Karen were glad to see their mother arrive shortly afterwards to give much needed support.

'Has anyone called Ritchie to tell him?' Pauline asked Debbie.

'Yes. I managed to catch him before he went off to work. He was really cut up about it.' Karen and Debbie's older brother lived in Seattle where he'd been working for Boeing for over ten years. He'd be sure to make the trip over for the funeral.

Karen tried her level best to hold herself together through the evening, a sign of strength to comfort Sam and Gemma. But all three of them found it far too difficult. They went to bed very early with the help of some prescribed sleeping tablets.

Clare had composed herself and phoned Nick's mobile. She felt duty bound to relay the news to her boss. He was in the car. There was a lot of background noise and at least one of them must have been in a poor reception area, so the conversation was rather jilted. Clare didn't register Nick's reaction, she was in such a state of shock. Had she been more compos mentis she might have thought that he didn't appear to be so upset at the news of his now former partner and friend.

He was lucky that he'd received that call when he was on the road. Clare informed him that the police would be coming over to the office very soon, so he immediately decided to re-route there instead of returning home. It could generate some unnecessary questions if they turned up and nobody had seen him all day.

He arrived at Cartmel House shortly before the police, and having had some time in the car to think. Time to compose himself. Time to get his story straight. But he was very jittery. Had anyone spotted any friction between him and Monty developing over recent weeks? Had any of the team been lurking around and seen the altercation outside the Indian last night? Would the circumstances prompt an autopsy? And if so, what would be found in Monty's system? He'd have to rummage through his drawers in that old antique desk and make sure everything was clean. He thought back over the tensions of the last few days. They weren't the most positive memories to cherish. But they were his last interactions with Monty and nothing could change that now. He wondered whether he ought to have been a little less confrontational with him?

A constable arrived and Sienna showed him up to Nick's office. The PC talked through the details of the accident. Nick had to disguise his relief when he heard that term. Accident. There were no suspicious circumstances. The retaining bar had simply worked loose. Had it been nailed into the other side of the oak beams it would have held Monty in situ. The same mistake had been made on the lower floor. The electricians and the tilers had given statements to the police. There were some routine enquiries to do with the person who'd been seen measuring the balcony, though it was quite possible that this was some local lowlife checking out the place to see if there was anything worth stealing. Monty's hangover was curious, but not so alarming to spur anything more than a recount of how many beers he'd had the previous evening. There was no mention of a vehicle parked over by Boothby Hill woods. Mind you, that could have been the lowlife on his scouting mission.

When the policeman had left, Nick gathered everyone together in the hallway. There was an inquisitive babble as people swapped theories about what was going on. It was very rare that they were brought together at a moment's notice like this. Nor was it normal for the local constabulary to have been on the premises either. Nick rose up to the fifth step on the staircase to make the announcement. A hush descended, not least because they all noticed that he looked as white as a sheet. Was that grief or anxiety? There was stunned silence, a far cry from the lively spirits that had been on display twenty-four hours earlier. Nick informed them of Monty's accident with a heavy heart and a wavering voice.

A state of utter shock descended and there was an immediate outbreak of sorrow from Pat, her last words to Monty that morning resonating in her ears. She broke down and was helped back into the admin office where she crumpled into one of the two easy chairs that were used for waiting visitors. She was inconsolable. Ged hung his head to avoid the others seeing his tears and he slowly made his way up the stairs past Nick. He was going to sit by himself at his desk for a little while. Others stepped up and offered to go over to the Dan Connor house to collect Clare. Three of the youngest members of the group hugged together, sobbing.

Five minutes later everyone had gradually dispersed to various corners of the building. They mingled around desks saying how they couldn't believe it and eulogising about the departed Monty. Four of the more senior men found themselves together in the kitchen brewing tea and ferrying drinks throughout the building, checking up on everyone. Nick had already told all of them that work was over for the day but he steadied himself and went on a tour round all of the rooms to make sure that they everybody knew to pack their things away. Nothing else would get done in the office that afternoon. They would all go to The Half Moon, the least they could do was raise a glass to their great friend and ex-colleague. Once Pat's husband had been to collect her, almost everyone else managed to pull themselves together and walk to the pub. Arthur and Stella were surprised to see them turn up a good half hour earlier than usual. It was normally after 5pm on a Friday when the Hanson Scott gang descended to kick off the weekend. Nick had to tell Arthur three times before the news sank in. Stella retreated to the back room of the pub and wept.

Monty's brother was all for cancelling the wedding but Karen insisted that it should still go ahead. Whilst she was in no fit state to be there she knew that Monty wouldn't have wanted it to be cancelled on his account. It was dreadfully difficult for anyone to carry on through such a joyful event against such a sombre backdrop. There was a toast to absent friends.

Monty's new car was returned to the driveway on Conway Road. Karen couldn't quite make her mind up whether she was pleased to see the vehicle or not. The next week was extremely trying for everyone.

9

For Monty everything was black. Jet black. Hardly surprising, really, now that he was dead. There was an occasion when he and Karen had taken Sam and Gemma for a short Easter holiday break in Wales. Nearby, a disused mine had been reborn as a tourist attraction and they had decided to pay it a visit. At one point, deep below ground, the guide had asked everyone in the group to switch off their head torches. There was complete absence of light. No stars, no light pollution from nearby street lighting, nothing. It was just black. And that was what Monty was experiencing now. Pitch black.

The strange thing was that he felt sure he could see the black. It wasn't the same as being asleep. When he went to sleep he completely shut down, didn't register anything. Didn't even see the black. This was odd. It was just still and quiet and black. It stayed that way for a while, though there was no time reference to monitor exactly how long.

Then it started to change. A dappled pattern formed. Though it was very faint to begin with, tiny flowery shapes began to crystallise. Each one the size of a pin head, with dull blue centres and dark green outers. They were barely distinguishable against the black backcloth. A small cluster grew quickly and in no time there must have been a hundred, gathering centrally and coalescing. The flowers ebbed away and the background took on an orange hue. A band of greyness fused across the bottom half of this optical screen. It swirled through a vague yellow to a light green, the colour of lime cordial. Despite being dull in tone, all of the light seemed to have a certain blotchy glare. It pulsed backwards and forwards through the prismatic spectrum, gradually brightening. The cycles increasing in frequency. It all moved and morphed. A variety of shapes began to show more vividly. Brighter straight bars appeared, like pink neon strip lights, before ceding behind fuzzy golden ellipses. A rectangle of blood-orange red with equally spaced black horizontal lines took shape. It resembled looking at a terrific sunset through Venetian blinds.

Then the first one appeared.

It was his older brother James walking to school. It didn't last long. He saw his old school hall, heard himself in the nativity play, saw his early classrooms, the first goal he scored for the school football team. They were all short flashes, but they were gathering speed. Helping his father in the garden, spending time at his best friend's house, birthday parties, snowballs in the playground. The views were vivid and had texture and depth to them. They were becoming more and more clear as they followed the time line of his younger life. Monty could only watch. He couldn't really think. He couldn't interact, his body was motionless. All he could do was observe. The images were appearing just as photographs would when viewed in slide show mode on his computer. But they were richer in substance, having three dimensional reality and elements of motion about them.

The process continued at a quickening pace. He saw his teenage years zip by. There he was, sitting with Mark and Steve, taking the micky out of Jacko about his left handed cricket bat. Fond memories of sixth form, going to pubs, his first girlfriends. Then the journey to Nottingham University to read Architecture. His room in hall, nights out, the student union bar, making life-long friends, particularly Ritchie. Especially Ritchie. Meeting Ritchie's sister, Karen, for the first time. And so it sped on, unveiling the substantial weight of his life story. His wedding to Karen. Their first Christmas together. Sam and Gemma. Occasionally there were items that didn't sit in the correct chronological order. Items that had a flatness of image, no depth of being there in the moment, just the still image. Then it was back to holidays, decorating bedrooms, family, funerals. Everything was there. Even a glimpse of Jacko's funeral. It was the first funeral he'd ever been to and it was so sad that it had to be that of his best friend. They were only eighteen years old. There hadn't been any comments about a left-handed coffin that day.

He saw Karen. Plenty of Karen. So close. So beautiful. So many wonderful memories. So precious. Exciting times. Mundane and routine, doing the weekly supermarket shopping. So together.

Then there she was in her leather jacket, turning away from him at the breakfast bar and walking across the kitchen, her heals clicking on the tile floor. She went through the door into the hallway. His last recollection of his soul mate. Finally there was a napkin with a half recognisable map of the continents.

And everything stopped right there. It went blank. A fuzzy blank. Not quite the same as the jet black he'd first been aware of. It remained that way for a brief interlude.

The alphabet coursed through his head. A through to Z. The

number system, his times tables, and some binary. His form teacher had taught the base two number system when he was ten years old and he'd been so proud that he could count all the way up to thirty-one on one hand. 1066, Hastings, Senlac Hill, Harold, William, Stamford Bridge. 1215, Runnymede, Magna Carta. The dates streamed through. There were facts that he would have found impossible to dredge up when he had been alive, now they were sweeping through in front of him with incredible ease. Such accelerated recall would have been an amazing boost at the Half Moon pub quiz.

The contents of his school learning came next. A year by year syllabus, all accounted for, subject by subject. Interspersed were all the other things that he had picked up from magazines, books, television. Facts followed facts. Theories, methods, maths, art, sport, winners, semi-finalists, goal scorers, famous cricketers. Comedy sketches, all the words, parrot fashion, the order of songs on his favourite albums, lyrics. Shakespeare, Macbeth. Catcher in the Rye. Some of this knowledge must have been buried so deep in the dusty furrows of his brain. Yet it all emerged. Still he could only observe. No feeling in his limbs, no way of making anything move. Just watch it all flow past.

And everything stopped again. He got a wall of deep purple. It remained that way for less than a minute. The colour began to evaporate and the blackness gradually closed in. Then it was just pitch black and Monty was out cold.

10

It was almost 3:25pm. Everybody rose to their feet. Some stood with their heads bowed, saying a final prayer for him. Others concentrated their stare on the coffin in front of them, as if transmitting their final farewell thoughts across the ether and into the wooden casket. The harmonies of Simon and Garfunkel began warming the room. Karen and Monty had never discussed this moment, but she had selected 'So Long Frank Lloyd Wright' as her soothing and personal goodbye. The curtains drew slowly, reverently, around the plinth and the final mechanics of Monty's body rolling through the hatch were masked from view.

The service at the church had been lovely, a fitting remembrance of a much loved man. Despite the best efforts of the minister the crematorium had been an almost entirely functional experience. Colder and utilitarian. The music faded and they all filed out in somber silence. Once outside people milled around awkwardly, looking at the floral tributes, gathering in random groupings to chat, then breaking apart and merging in new formations.

The entire Hanson Scott troupe was in attendance. It hadn't been a very productive five days at Cartmel House, this event had been on their minds all week. It was one they just had to pull through together. They would be able to get on with things once they had all paid their respects and given Monty an official send off. Pat took a moment to walk over and hug Karen, though it was probably more for her own benefit than Karen's. Her emotions were spilling over and she was grateful to receive some comfort from the strength and stoicism of the grieving widow. Nick looked on as Clare intervened to release Karen from Pat's well meaning and close attention.

They're very similar, thought Nick. Roughly the same height, medium length blond hair, both very pretty, Karen slightly slimmer than Claire. It wasn't the first time he'd seen them together, but it was the first time that he was struck by the likeness. Perhaps he noticed because of his recent theory about Monty and Clare. He'd made a very determined effort to step back from any close interactions with her in the office this week. Recent events had given him a little bit of a shock, sufficient for him to realise that he should be very careful about his actions for the time being.

Refreshments had been arranged at the Village Hall where Monty and the family had some happy memories of Scout and Guide gang shows, local amateur dramatic productions, and friends' birthday parties. Everyone socialised whilst sipping tea and coffee and picking away at the cold buffet. Gradually people relaxed into less reserved moods, relatives and friends catching up on stories having not seen each other for many months, or even years. Funerals tend to have their lighter moments. It's a paradoxical feature that comes about from bringing many people together to mourn one person's departure.

Nick felt a vibration in his jacket pocket. He pulled out his mobile phone and saw that he had a new text message. It was from Liz, his friend at the rifle club. 'How was funeral? Am free for few hours, fancy meeting up for drink?' He remembered her saying something to that effect earlier in the week, something about a sympathetic ear when the proceedings were over. He looked at his watch and concluded that it was a suitable time for him to go. He replied to Liz then went over to say a final word to Monty's wife before making his exit. He received another text from Liz which simply said 'The Jolly Ploughman'.

She arrived ahead of Nick and, seeing that his car wasn't there, sat waiting in her convertible in the car park. She had never been far away from money. Liz had grown up in Gloucestershire, the daughter of a wealthy MP. She attended Cheltenham Ladies' College and went on to read Philosophy, Politics, and Economics at Oxford, following in her father's footsteps. After graduating she found a job in the media, writing about parliament and the vagaries of Westminster. She thrived on the wine bar lifestyle with the social set and eventually found Peter, the man who she would marry in haste when she was thirty. Despite the fact that she was a very attractive woman and extremely good company, deep down inside Liz had had a growing concern about being left on the shelf.

Her husband was also from a well heeled background. His parents owned a large pile in Surrey and had set him up through top class education and monetary support. He was an MP for a North Yorkshire constituency and Liz was very attracted to the idea of moving out to the countryside. Whilst she would always look back fondly on her time in the City and London's party life, she was keen to get back to what she felt would be cleaner air and the chance to go riding again. It would also be an ideal place to start a family of her own.

True, the rural life was all that she hoped it would be. It soon became evident that the marriage, on the other hand, was falling sadly below expectations. He would be in London most weeks and would stay at his parents' home every other weekend. Liz got used to seeing him for a few days every fortnight and relied heavily on her own abilities to make plenty of friends in the neighbourhood.

On their first wedding anniversary, her husband came clean. He was homosexual. His old school upbringing lead him to believe that marrying Liz was a perfect front to deflect any adverse publicity. He made it very clear that he was very fond of her, he did love her in his own particular way. However, he couldn't help himself finding other affections elsewhere with the male gender. They agreed to a deal. They would remain together as a couple and each would be free to develop relationships as they desired, just as long as they were kept under the radar. Everything must be kept low key, away from any prying members of the press.

Liz found she had all that she wanted – money, fine house, car, and a freedom to do what she wanted and to party when the mood took her. Her nominal husband was able to continue visiting mummy and daddy in Surrey, which had the advantage of being within very easy reach of Marcus, his special advisor and personal assistant. During those weekends the assistance offered up by Marcus would often get very personal.

Liz had several flings, choosing her relationships carefully. She had known Nick from shortly after the move north, mainly through the rifle club which she had been introduced to via the local hunt and some of the nearby land owners who ran shooting parties on their estates. There was something about Nick that she was drawn to. The military background, well spoken, a bit clumsy, that little bit of an edge. She couldn't put her finger on it, but she had warmed to him over the last 4 months as she had spent more time in his company persuading him to rejoin the club.

After five minutes she saw his car turn in off the road. She got out of her car and waited for him to park up and join her, then they went into the lounge bar together. Nick ordered the drinks and carried them across to the table that Liz had occupied. She was immaculately dressed, as always. He talked about the funeral. There really wasn't that much to say, but he did remark how elegant and dignified Karen was. Liz tried to gauge how upset Nick was about the whole episode, drawing on some of her earlier journalism skills. She couldn't draw any clear conclusions and decided to lead the conversation in a different direction.

'Now that that's over, what are you planning to do this weekend?'

'Back to the mundane tomorrow. I've got to go to the supermarket and buy my usual round of ready meals to get me through the week. Then I am due a visit to my parents on Sunday. At least I'll get some proper food there. I can look forward to a home cooked roast dinner for a change. A meal that doesn't need a ping from the microwave to tell me it's ready.'

Liz smiled. 'And what about this evening? Are you going to drown your sorrows in your local?'

'I expect so, though I really don't feel like it. The only other option I've got is to have a couple of whiskeys at home and watch some inane rubbish on the TV. I don't have any better offer.'

'Well, Peter is staying at mummy and daddy's this weekend. So I shall have nothing on at all this evening. I'll just be draping myself across my leather sofa and watching a romantic film in front of a nice log fire.'

'Oh dear, it sounds as though we're competing to see who wins the award for loneliest Friday night.'

Liz's thinly veiled invitation fell on stony ground.

'Never mind,' she thought, 'probably not the best time to offer him company.'

Next time she'd consider being a little more obvious to reduce the likelihood of her suggestions going straight over Nick's head.

11

Monty felt a convulsion, an upward surge that started low in his intestines and rose through his stomach and lungs. He awoke with a light shudder. He was sitting down and the back of his neck felt stiff. Perhaps he had nodded off whilst watching the television. No. The seat was hard, it definitely wasn't an armchair or a sofa. Monty yawned and forced open his heavy eyelids. He looked around. No television. In fact the room was very spartan. The surprise of it all catalysed him like a sniff of smelling salts and he very quickly came to. He properly surveyed his surroundings and it dawned on him that he was in the foyer at the Village Hall. He went to stand up, but was taken aback by how heavy his body felt.

'Hello Monty. I'm Angela. I'm going to be your hostess this afternoon. How are you feeling?'

He turned his head to the left and saw a young woman, in her mid twenties. She had just entered the foyer through a door which connected with the main hall. She had a very soft voice, one you could listen to all day. But he had absolutely no recollection of ever seeing her before. How did she know him?

'Err, hello. Erm, okay. Cold, actually. A little bit cold.' His state of great confusion was evident in his stammered response. 'What's happened? What's going on? What am I doing in the Village Hall?'

'It's alright. There's nothing to be alarmed about. When you're ready, if you'd like to come through. All in your own good time.'

Monty wondered what on earth he had got himself in to. There certainly didn't seem to be anything sinister or threatening about the situation. It was calm and peaceful, there was very little background noise. She was gentle and welcoming. It was just completely baffling to him. His head was clear and there were no signs of sickness at all. That stiffness in his neck had already soothed away too. He had another go at standing up and this time found that he was able to rise to his feet without any hindrance. He looked around once more, as if to confirm that he was where he was. He took a deep breath and exhaled, long and slow. He shook his head a few times, then turned to the left. She stood waiting patiently.

'Okay? Please, this way.'

Monty followed the girl through the doorway into the main hall. Dividers were set out down each flank of the large open room, marking out four meeting areas on either side of a wide central aisle. At first it reminded him of an Election Day when the hall would be transformed into a polling station. Monty observed that each bay had an armchair and a small two seater sofa set around a coffee table. Two bays were currently in use. A young hostess was chatting to an older man, probably in his late seventies. A second hostess sat talking in another bay to a lady who Monty guessed was about ninety. He followed his hostess to the third bay on the left where she gestured for him to sit down on the settee. He noticed that there was a glass of water on the table in front of him and a set of leaflets to one side. She sat down opposite him.

'Welcome. Are you comfortable? Can I get you anything before I begin?'

'No, I'm fine, thank you. I think I'll feel a lot more comfortable when I understand what's happening and why I'm here. How did I come to be round here in the Village Hall?'

Angela wasn't so sure about that. In her experience, accumulated through a great many years of distinguished service, she knew that this first conversation wasn't easy for any new arrival.

He had warmed up. Leaning forward, he took his jacket off. She scanned him and smiled, cast her eyes down at her lap, then angled her head up to engage directly with him again. She was still smiling. Monty returned an inquisitive look.

'What's the matter? What's so amusing?'

'That shirt really doesn't go with that jacket.'

'You're the third person that's told me that today.'

'Hmmm. Well, that's not a bad place for us to start' she said. Monty remained upright and forward on the settee, a bemused expression fixed to his face. 'Tell me, Monty, what was the last thing that you can remember?'

'Everything, my whole life, flashing in front of my eyes.'

'And before that?'

'Being in the café with Clare. She was drawing a map of the world on her serviette.' Monty was a little surprised at how quickly that came back to him.

'Good, that seems to have worked.'

'What? What seems to have worked?'

'Let's go back to the comment about your shirt and jacket. I'm actually the first person to tell you that today. The other two occasions took place a fortnight ago.'

Monty took another deep breath, as though he had begun to figure it all out.

'Are you saying that I've been in some sort of coma for two weeks? I must have suffered some short term memory loss. Where have I been? Have I been in hospital?'

'It's a little bit like that, Monty,' she said, tilting her head to her left in a slightly apologetic fashion. 'But there are some, erm, some subtle differences.' She looked to make sure he was in a suitably prepared frame of mind for what was about to be unveiled. His face inquisitive, he waited for her next piece of information with baited breath. 'Here we go' she thought.

'Exactly two weeks ago you were involved in an accident. Rather a serious accident, in fact. Now, I'm afraid there is no easy way of saying this, Monty. That accident actually resulted in your death.'

'My death?' he echoed softly and froze. That couldn't be right. If he was dead, why was he still feeling so alive? And why was he sitting in the Village Hall? What was this all about? And, more importantly, what was going to happen next? How long was he going to be here? Was he going to be taken somewhere else? Was this it now, forever, or was there some other end ahead of him? He felt sick in the pit of his stomach, his mind was jumping erratically in reaction to this body blow news. Then he suddenly stopped himself.

'This is some sort of a joke. A prank set up by the lads in the office?'

'It isn't any form of fun and games from the office. It would have to be a very elaborate plot, Monty. What do you think has happened?'

'Well, perhaps they put something in my drink at lunchtime then transported me over here. And you're one of their friends who I've never met, which would explain why you know my name. And ...'

Monty dried up as he recognised how outlandish this was sounding.

'And your friends in the office, do you really think that they would go to the lengths of knocking you out to play a trick on you?'

'No, not really' he said sheepishly.

'And why would they bring you to the Village Hall, of all places, and go to such great lengths to set it up like this?' She paused a moment to let Monty look around and weigh up the odds. 'And who did you say you had lunch with?'

'Clare.'

'And Clare would have been happy to go along with all of this?'

'No. Not Clare. No.'

'I realise this is very difficult, Monty, but you do have to believe me.'

If it was true, how had he died? Car crash? He was distracted momentarily by an irrational worry that his new car could be a write off. He'd only had it a couple of weeks. He drew himself back from the materialistic. Actually, the state of the car is of no importance now if he really is dead. But he was healthy, so it couldn't have been natural causes. Must have been something pretty horrible. Something sudden. He quickly inspected himself. No signs of any accident. No broken bones, cuts or bruises. No damaged clothes. He felt no pain. He looked back at his hostess.

'I still don't get it. If I've had some devastating accident, surely there would be some aches and pains. A few cuts and bruises for my troubles.'

'True. You were in need of some repair work.'

'Repair work … what do you mean … Repair work?'

'We clean you up and make sure you're in pristine condition' Angela said. 'There is a transition process that we undertake with every new person who comes through.'

'I'm sorry, this is just too daft to believe. Transition process. Come through. Just a little bit too sci-fi for me. The lads in the office have put you up to this, haven't they? I don't know how. I've got to hand it to all of you, you've done an awful lot of planning and preparation. Goodness knows why you've gone to all this trouble. And why me?'

Angela looked a little forlornly at him and tried a slightly different angle.

'Do you have any distinguishing marks?'

'Ah, very good. OK.' He looked around to see if he could work out where the gang were hiding. He honestly thought they would have called an end to the mischief by now and come out laughing. He decided to play along. 'I've got a small scar on my right wrist. Got it when I was doing some washing up and a jar smashed, cutting me in the act.'

As he spoke, he began undoing his shirt sleeve button with his left hand and folding back the cuff. He went to offer over his right arm but stalled. Monty brought his arm back towards himself so that he could give it a closer inspection. He was puzzled. He'd had that scar for at least fifteen years and now it was gone.

Angela moved some of the paperwork aside on the table and

picked up a buff wallet. She opened it and took out a photograph which she offered up for Monty to see.

'Was it like this?'

He took hold of it and looked at a picture of his right wrist, complete with that scar. It wasn't a big scar, but it was there, clear as day, exactly how he knew it to be. Meanwhile his hostess held up a second. It could almost have been a photocopy, but the scar was no longer evident on this one.

'That's before and after' she said. 'Can Clare do that? Or any of the lads in the office? Or anyone else you know, for that matter?'

He'd been trying to convince himself that this was all just a clever game. He wasn't succeeding, he really had to accept that this was far beyond tomfoolery. But he still didn't understand where he was and what was happening. Monty was increasingly perplexed. He knew it wasn't a dream, it was too real for it to be a dream. Yet, strangely, he didn't feel at all stressed about the situation he found himself in. There were plenty of questions buzzing around in his mind, but he felt calmly inquisitive. It was then that he remembered having seen his life pass before him, a phenomenon he'd heard of many times before. Perhaps there may be some truth in what she had just been trying to tell him.

'It is now Friday the 30th of April' said Angela. 'You died two weeks ago and your funeral took place last Friday.'

Funeral. That was a grim word to hear. It provoked a multitude of emotions and thoughts about what he must have left behind.

Who would look after Karen, and Sam, and Gemma? What about the garden? The shed needed a coat of creosote. And who would take the meter readings for the solar panels? What if something needed repairing in the house? Sam couldn't do that. And he'd be going off to university soon, anyway. And when Sam went, how would Karen cope with just her and Gemma at home? What about money? Karen should get the money from the life policies, but when would she get it? Did she even know where to find them? Would she be able to manage until that money came through?

There was an important site meeting on Monday, who would cover that for him? No, he remembered, he'd just lost two weeks in hibernation, so that meeting had already happened. Who went, did they handle things correctly? Who would oversee the Barker's Court development for him? Clare?

He returned to the question of 'where was he'. Surely Heaven doesn't look like the local Village Hall. If he stepped outside would he find that the Village Hall had been transported off onto some cloud somewhere? Were the Pearly Gates just outside? He'd broken into a cold sweat and his stomach was churned up.

'My funeral' he uttered, from a very dry mouth. He reached forward, picked up the glass from the table and took a gulp of water.

'Yes. I'm afraid so. You have been in a holding pattern for two weeks whilst we worked through the transition processes.'

'Holding pattern? Transition processes? Transition to what?'

'You've come through to Hinteraevum. It's a second phase in your life, sitting between Realworld and Afterworld. I'm here to welcome you and to give you an introduction to this new world.'

'There's a hundred and one things I want to know. The first of which is why am I still so relaxed? Surely I really ought to feel differently about being dead. More agitated, cross even?'

Angela paused for a moment. No need to hurry. Everything was tranquil. She looked down at the table and rearranged the booklets, turning one of them towards Monty and sliding it over in front of him.

'I think this is a perfect time for a short break. I will get some refreshments and the best thing for you to do right now is to read through this pamphlet here. It explains the transition process and introduces you to Hinteraevum. I can answer any questions once you have read through the material. You will also see that there are some lifestyle options available. Don't worry too much about those, I will go into more detail after our break.'

'Will you be long?' Monty felt a tiny bit vulnerable.

'It's OK, I'm not actually leaving you. I will sit with you whilst you read.'

He picked up the pamphlet and looked at the cover. It stated

'Hinteraevum – A Satisfying And Wonderful Afterlife'

He looked at it for a few seconds. There was something curiously familiar about it. Then he spotted the connection … H.A.S.A.W.A.

If only he knew. Ironically, his final moments had been the result of a breach of his favourite six letter directive.

12

Sienna stepped into the doorway of Nick's office and knocked lightly on the open door. Nick looked up and summoned her in with a little wave of his hand. He was just finishing off a letter on the computer, a quote for another potential commission for Hanson Scott. It had crossed his mind that in the long term he ought to rename the company Hanson Associates, or something similar, but he knew that he needed to keep Monty's surname there for the time being. Half ownership would now rest with Karen Scott. Monty had said right from the beginning that if anything happened to him his share would go to his wife.

During the week, Nick had held meetings with three prospective clients. Each occasion had been a reminder of just how important Monty had been in the entire process of convincing people of Hanson Scott's abilities. His architectural flair helped to win business. This week he had been accompanied in sales meetings by Clare and one of the other senior architects. They both did a very professional job, but neither was as good as Monty. Clare was close. What she lacked in terms of experience, she compensated for in enthusiasm and inventiveness.

Nick looked up again. Sienna was half way across the room. He asked if she would mind closing the door. She retraced her steps, attended to the door, then walked over and sat opposite him. He continued typing for a further minute, exercising his two index fingers, then eased back from the keyboard and spun on his chair so that he was facing her across his expansive desk.

'Now Sienna, before Monty had his accident he had a quiet word with me about the payroll. Said that you thought there was another person on the books.'

'Yes, I found it out when I was having a dummy run at this month's salary payments.'

'And did you talk to anyone else about it, other than Monty?'

'No. Monty said that I should keep it quiet until it had been investigated. He thought everyone would go into meltdown if they heard any whisper of further problems with the pay.'

'Quite right. Well. Monty asked me about it and I happen to

know what that extra item is for. Unfortunately we've all been a little bit at sixes and sevens for the last two weeks so this is the first time I've been able to catch some time with you to explain.'

Nick told Sienna that it was to pay a quantity surveyor who did a lot of work on all of the projects for Nick. Rather than be self-employed, this particular person preferred to be treated as a part time employee of the two companies he did all of his assignments for. It made it a lot easier for him to handle his affairs – tax, accounts, and all of those administration headaches. It wasn't common. But then it wasn't uncommon either. Nick threw ample jargon in to minimize Sienna's latitude to ask any more questions.

'Can you keep that to yourself? It's just that I'd rather not have all the staff here know that I have such an arrangement in place.'

'Yes, of course. And at least I know that I don't have to worry about it in future months. I suppose Pat knows about it already?'

'No,' Nick shook his head, 'and she doesn't have to.'

'Ah, okay,' Sienna nodded in return and stood up from the chair. She was ready to make her way back downstairs to the admin office when she remembered another point.

'Did Monty give you his analysis spreadsheet? I sent him all the pay figures and he was using a spreadsheet to compare them with the annual salary data.'

Nick was caught off guard for a split second, but covered up by pretending his mind was back on the quote he'd been preparing.

'Err, spreadsheet. Oh, err, yes. He sent me something, I'm sure it will be the one that you're talking about.'

Sienna left the room and Nick pushed himself back from the desk. He clearly needed some help and he knew who to go and ask. Ged did all that nerdy stuff around the office. Nick went to find him.

'What do you intend doing with the computer in Monty's office, now that he's gone?'

'Nothing special, not until someone new joins. Then I will reconfigure it, put all the latest fix packs on, alter the drive mappings and change the directory settings …'

Nick was already glazing over. He interrupted Ged's technical spiel.

'I'd like you to clear it down straight away. Delete all the files on it. Spreadsheets and things like that.'

'Erm, I can do that, but don't you think someone should have a good look at it first?'

'No, there's no need to do that. We shouldn't go prying into

Monty's personal files on his computer.'

'But, what if…'

'No. Ged, just go and delete it all straight away. I'd like it doing before you leave this afternoon.'

'Okay. I'll get onto it now.'

'Thank you. And let me know when you've done it.'

Ged went across the first floor to Monty's office, sat himself down at the desk and began booting up the PC. Clare noticed him sitting there as she walked past the doorway.

'Crikey, you gave me a fright,' she said as she entered the room. 'I thought you were Monty's ghost for a moment.'

'I don't look a bit like him.'

'Yes, I know, but I just caught sight of someone sitting at his desk and it gave me a bit of a start. What are you doing?'

'Clearing his old computer down.'

'Why? I thought you usually left them until they were needed by a new member of staff.'

'Nick wanted it doing asap. Got to get it sorted before I go home today.'

She couldn't understand why Nick was in such a hurry to have Monty's computer wiped. All of their design drawings and other project information were kept on a central machine, but Clare felt sure that there must be a wealth of useful material on Monty's machine. There might be something important that they would need in months to come.

'Ged, I recommend you take a copy so that we don't lose anything important. Can you put it somewhere safe on the main computer?'

'Yes, sure. I was already planning on doing that.'

Clare was suspicious. Was there something on it that Nick was particularly concerned about? She cast her mind back to the last few days before Monty's fall. She felt sure that there was something secretive between him and Monty, something that had been niggling away at their working relationship. And what had made Nick back away from her since the accident? She was pleased that he hadn't made any other advances in the last two weeks. Far from it, he'd been fine. Friendly, yes, but nowhere near over-stepping the mark.

Something wasn't quite right.

13

Monty began reading, but he wasn't at his most fluent. His mind was in a distracted state and he just wasn't taking the text on board. He read the first three paragraphs seven times and nothing was going in. He stopped and looked across at Angela. On the table between them sat a tray with a cafetiere of coffee, two cups, milk, sugar, and a small selection of Danish pastries. He'd not noticed them arrive. Angela leaned across and poured the coffees, Monty reached for a Danish. He took a few sips and munched through the pastry, pleased that they had coincidentally brought one of his favourites. His hostess knew that it wasn't in the least bit coincidental.

He picked up the pamphlet and returned to paragraph one. It began with an introduction to Hinteraevum. Whilst he couldn't say that it all made perfect sense, at least he was now able to absorb what it was telling him.

Hinteraevum is a second life, entered upon death from Realworld, a preparation for the third life in the Afterworld. The name has changed a number of times over the years. This most recent and more modern moniker was fashioned a little over two thousand years ago. Bearing a Latin influence, the name refers to being between worlds.

Monty looked up for a moment. 'It says it's a modern name. I don't call two thousand years modern.'

'But that is relatively modern, considering how long we have been in existence. I recommend that you continue through the pamphlet. We have plenty of time. Once you've read this we can cover anything that you would like to explore in more detail.'

He took another drink and returned his attention to the documents. He read.

Hinteraevum is a step in the evolution towards the Afterworld. You may remain here for any length of time up to a maximum of one hundred years. During your stay you will not age, your appearance and state of health will not change. As part of transition we address any damage caused in death and remove all existing ailments so that every individual can enjoy their time here without fear of interference from illness. It is an extremely peaceful way of preparing for what lies beyond.

Because the Afterworld is a very different place altogether, the purpose of Hinteraevum is to prepare you for that in more familiar surroundings. An environment where everyone and everything is calm, there is time to enjoy life, reflect, make one's peace with whoever or whatever may have upset you in the past. With rare exceptions, everyone gets longer here than in Realworld. You have a hundred years ahead of you and the pace of life is much slower. Think about it. The prospect of eternal life may seem very attractive on the surface. However, coming to terms with the concept and reality of eternal life is considerably harder than one might imagine. That is what Hinteraevum helps you to get ready for.

He looked up again.

'So, Two thousand years ago. Welcomed by Angela the Angel. Am I right in saying that Hinteraevum is actually Heaven? Where's Saint Peter? Surely he should be part of the greeting party as well.'

'Pete is in the back room, he's catching up on some work on the computer system. We usually assign our welcoming staff to match the individual's faith and, you being Christian, that's why Pete and I are here for you today. It doesn't really matter to some people, but a lot of new entrants find it comforting.'

'So ... it is Heaven.'

'No. It is a stage in the process of moving to Afterworld. And everybody comes here. It is as multi-cultural as Realworld. We have people from all backgrounds and not every religion would recognise the term Heaven. It is fair to say that the construct has many similarities to Afterworld, but so do constructs from other beliefs. Suffice to say that we try not to emphasise the subject because it helps to enter Afterworld with as few preconceived ideas as possible.'

Monty settled back in his chair. Bemusement was giving way to intrigue. Angela could sense that Monty had another question on the tip of his tongue.

'What's the point of it all?'

'You're not the first person to ask that, and I am sure that you'll not be the last. You've heard the expression 'life's too short'?'

'Of course. And I should know, because mine certainly was.'

'Precisely. Life is too short and people don't get enough time to really enjoy it. Too many worries. Too much pressure. Work life balance. Or imbalance would be closer to the truth. All of the things that you would have liked to have done with friends and loved ones, but didn't seem to get the time.'

Monty found that he was nodding in agreement.

'Hinteraevum gives you the chance to do that.'

'But... doesn't that same opportunity arise in whatever this Afterworld is that you say we eventually go to?'

'It does, but the change from Realworld to Afterworld is so considerable it was decided a long time ago that it was best done in two stages.'

Monty was quiet for a moment, processing Angela's comments. He read some more.

It is important to know that acts of aggression and violent behaviour meet with instant removal from Hinteraevum. Whilst we do have a very high success rate in cleaning up brain logic, some of the darker instincts can remain deep down in the mind. Not enough to justify rejection, but enough to rise to the surface during tenure. Thankfully we are able to catch the act before any damage can be done. In such circumstances the perpetrator is summarily deliquesced.

'Deliquesced?'

He hadn't intended saying it out loud.

'Yes. It means that they dissolve with immediate effect, fade away to nothing. Deliquesce also has Latin origins. Please, keep reading. The more that you read, the sooner it will all fall into place.'

He realised that she was repeating her recommendation for the third time, so he decided to hold back any more questions and just plough through the remaining eight pages. There was a little more about Hinteraevum itself, then a section on the transition procedures.

When you passed away your instincts triggered off certain processes that prepare you for the transition into Hinteraevum. One of the most important procedures involves the removal of any aggressive emotions or antisocial tendencies. It is one of our fundamental values that this whole world is an extremely safe place for all its inhabitants. It is intended that everybody enjoys their time here, so we simply cannot tolerate people getting cross, using threatening behaviour, committing burglary, or any form of violence.

It all starts with a reset and reorganisation procedure. After a short time lapse, when we know that you are not going to return to your Realworld life, we step in to take control and run those functional routines through to completion. It is a cleaning up process. We take a copy of all of your memories, starting with the photographic image bank in your head, then running through all of the facts and knowledge that you have accumulated over time. As you have grown older it is only natural that you have forgotten things. Those forgotten memory store areas have been freed up and reused to accommodate newer memories. So we shuffle it all into an orderly sequence and place it back in your mind. It makes it much easier and faster for you to recall.

During this activity, any particularly bad memories are removed and discarded. A topical example at this juncture is that we eradicate anything relating to how you died. Most people don't want to know anyway. We ask that you kindly observe another of the key principles here - that you must not tell someone else how they passed away. The only exception being, of course, when they specifically ask to know.

Monty nodded sagely. It crossed his mind that maybe he ought to have been curious, but he found that he didn't want to know how he had met his end.

Once we have secured a full copy of every piece of your memory we clean up the inner workings of your brain. We have to reorganise and clean up the memories first before we can start working on the inner circuitry. Any negative aspects are removed. This takes away the majority of aggression and violence. In most cases it is completely successful. Sometimes, however, remnants of those feelings and instincts linger. In some extreme situations we find that it isn't possible to re-establish the brain's logic to a point where we feel comfortable to continue. Occasionally we have to acknowledge that the level of resident evil is too high, too deeply written into the person's DNA. Such people will never be able to meet our core values and standards of behaviour. We cannot allow them entry to Hinteraevum.

He paused again and looked up at his hostess. He couldn't help it. He was just an inquisitive type. She smiled, as if in acceptance that the customer was always right.

'This transition process. It's the whole life flashing before your eyes experience?'

'Yes, I'm sure you've heard of it before.'

'I've heard about people having near-death experiences where they claim that has happened to them. Why is that?'

'It depends upon the individual and the specific circumstances. It usually occurs because a person's instinctive trigger is so strong that the process is initiated extremely quickly. It only gets a little way through before he or she springs back to life. In those split seconds they get to see a very small subset of their image history.'

'I noticed that some images seemed a little artificial. I felt a real part of other memories, as though they were lasting. They had motion. I had a much stronger sense of being there in the moment.'

'Yes. Those that didn't feel quite as real would be photographs that you have seen. You may not remember the actual occasion, perhaps because you were so young. But you remember seeing a photograph of yourself.'

Monty jumped to another line of question.

'Let me get this right. This is saying that everybody who has died in the last one hundred years is here?'

'The majority are here. Some are rejected at transition stage. And then there are some who pass through to a specialist care unit. The ones who do not have the ability to cope here.'

'The ability to cope? What do you mean?'

'Young children, babies, for example. There is a recommended minimum age. One has to be capable of looking after oneself. We make an exception with younger entrants. We place them in an incubation facility and they are allowed to grow to the minimum age of twelve under our supervision.' Angela paused again. 'Shall I go on?'

'Yes please.'

'Some people find it hard to adjust to being here. That's particularly true for those in the twelve to twenty-one age group. Too old for the special treatment, too young to be fully mature. As I'm sure you can imagine, most of our population are of a much older generation nowadays and that isn't always fun for the younger minority.'

'Of course.'

'Some teenagers find it a very lonely existence amongst so many elderly people. Some, on the other hand, acclimatise and thrive. You see, once you are here you can keep on learning – knowledge, skills, everything. You don't physically age, but you still have an active mind.'

'What happens if you don't want to stay for a hundred years?'

'You have a Life Expectancy setting that can be adjusted. Nobody else can do that for you. You are the only person who has access to your own personal parameters.'

'And where would I find those parameters?'

'In the very next section on pages nine through to twelve.' Now her smile was broad and her eyes twinkled at him.

'Advantage, Angela' he conceded. He turned the page to see that the next section was indeed all about lifestyle options and parameters.

'Hmmm. Set point, Angela.'

This time Monty read without stopping.

Life Expectancy
You may remain in Hinteraevum for up to one hundred years. We have found that this gives ample time for acclimatisation and preparation. Your Life Expectancy parameter (LE) has been set to the default 99 Y, representing the maximum stay of a century. You will receive a notification message when you have 6 months remaining in Hinteraevum. A second message will be posted three months before your LE date, and a final message one month before the LE date.

If for any reason you decide to leave before this time arrives, then you have the ability to alter your LE via the Soul Destroyer application interface on your Hinteraevum computer. LE can be set to any number between zero and ninety nine, and the Y may be replaced by M for months. The system will check your current Hinteraevum age to make sure that the new value does not take you beyond the maximum permissible stay. Extreme care must be taken with this parameter and nobody else can access your LE. You are strongly advised not to change your LE without seeking counselling and consultation. Your local support team offer a range of education sessions to help you learn how to use all elements of the Hinteraevum systems.

Your View of the World
The Global Reality Action Synchronisation Parameter (GRASP) controls how many of the changes happening in Realworld are seen by the individual. If set to zero, your view of the world would stay the same as it was on the day that you died. If set to the maximum, it would allow sight of every moving inanimate object from Realworld. This is not recommended as it can cause sensory overload for our inhabitants, making it far too difficult for them to lead a normal lifestyle. The GRASP default is 0.3, which allows one to accommodate changes in the Realworld on a week by week basis – new houses, buildings, roads, bridges, fixed objects. This level of volatility doesn't conflict with the normal movements of our inhabitants.

Privacy and Sharing
There is a strong possibility that inhabitants may need to share particular facilities. The most common example occurs when multiple unconnected people wish to live in the same dwelling because they have each occupied that facility in Realworld at different points in time. This is overcome by a virtualisation technique which eliminates any knowledge or visibility of those who are sharing the facility with you, making it appear that you have dedicated use.

Control of this virtualisation is achieved through the Visible Unit (VU) parameter. VU enables us to keep inhabitants' existences private within suitable boundaries of the shared facility. Usually this means a distance of a hundred metres, though it does depend on the exact nature of the facility and the location.

Within that zone you remain totally oblivious of anyone else who is sharing the facility with you, and they remain totally oblivious of you.

Transport

The Transport Recognition and Instantiation Parameter (TRIP) governs what modes of transport one could see from Realworld. The default of 0.6 is a level that blocks out Realworld road traffic from view but gives access to less numerous items such as ships, trains, and aeroplanes. Removing visibility of Realworld traffic makes it easy and safe for people in Hinteraevum to have their own vehicles. You have complete flexibility over which type of car you use. All vehicles are automatically monitored and controlled to avoid excessive speed.

Booking travel on public transport is simple through the Virtual Seat Information and Ticketing System (ViSITs). Flights are always available for reservation because, through the use of the VU parameter, multiple Hinteraevum inhabitants can occupy the same seat without ever knowing they are sharing.

Accessing Your Data

Everything is at your fingertips by logging on to the Hinteraevum Personal Profile Information System on any computer. This service is available to all inhabitants, every hour of the day, every day of the year. A selection menu will lead you to your personal lifestyle options and a wealth of information about people, places, travel, hobbies, shopping, eating and drinking. Everything you could possibly want is featured.

Finding friends and family couldn't be easier. The SoulSearch application helps you find contacts quickly. Details will be visible alongside an image of the person you are looking for. SoulSearch has a set of menu buttons to help you locate family, close friends, and other personal connections. When retrieving information the system will display all of the current residents in Hinteraevum that match your criteria, sorted by closeness.

You will receive a message to inform you when anybody with whom you may have a connection is about to come through from Realworld. You may choose to keep or ignore these connections.

Further Information

Detailed descriptions of all the Lifestyle parameters and how to access them can be found in the full Hinteraevum Manual, which you will find in your induction pack.

Monty finished reading and placed the booklet on the table in front of him, open at the start of the Lifestyle section on page nine. He'd stored up his questions and was working out where to start.

'Tell me, what's outside? When I walk out of here, what's through that door?'

'It will all be familiar to you. It is the same as the physical world that you were living in. The same roads, same buildings, everything. The big difference is that it is inhabited by people who are in the same condition as you.'

'Dead people?'

'People who have died and come through from Realworld, yes.'

'It sounds to me as though I'm going to walk out and find myself in the midst of a whole load of Zombies.'

'No. Absolutely not. There's no witchcraft and wizardry here. Everybody has a lucid mind, everyone is conscious and self-aware. It takes a few weeks to get used to Hinteraevum, but once people know how everything works they generally tend to have a wonderful time. People really do enjoy it.'

'Are my parents here?'

'Yes they are.'

'And Karen, Sam and Gemma. I didn't notice anything in the material that explained how I get to see them. I assume that you've devised some clever way of making that possible?'

'Ah,' she gave herself a few seconds. 'No, I'm afraid not. You can only see inanimate things from Realworld. You have no means of seeing people there, and they have no means of seeing you. Your parents haven't been looking down on you from above, contrary to popular belief. Similarly you won't be watching over your wife and children. All of that is a myth.'

This hit him hard. He wouldn't see his loved ones until they passed away and entered Hinteraevum. He suddenly felt very emotional. It was a hammer blow.

Angela saw his reaction and leant forwards. He'd finished his coffee, so she poured a glass of water and offered it to him.

'Here, take a drink Monty. We'll have another short break, you can have a little time to absorb everything. When you're ready I will take you through to one of the other rooms and demonstrate the computer information systems to you. Would you like another coffee now?'

'I think a tea would be nice, thank you.'

Angela stood up and walked away from the bay. Monty took the pamphlet again and began trying to look back at the sections he had just read. He kept returning to one line of thought - not seeing Karen until she died. That would be another thirty years, maybe even forty. And when he next sees her she could be eighty years old, and he would still look forty-two. How would that feel? After such a long separation, how would their relationship feel? How would he be able to deal with that unorthodox age difference? And how long would it be until he got to see Sam and Gemma again. He would miss all of their growing up. Who would they marry? What about their children, his grandchildren? Would Sam and Gemma arrive, sixty years from now, looking much older than Monty?.

14

The realisation of his death began to sink in. The implications were incredibly painful to get to grips with. He was very upset. Tears were welling in his eyes when Angela arrived with a strong cup of tea. Setting it down in front of him, she said 'Would you like some more time alone?'

'No, I'd rather you were here. That's if you don't mind watching a grown man cry.'

'I don't mind at all. I do this a lot. I'm used to the reaction. All of your friends and family in Realworld have been through that rollercoaster ride during the last two weeks. So have all of your family and friends in Hinteraevum.'

Monty looked up at her.

'Yes, they were made aware that you were transitioning. It's one of the reasons that we hold you for two weeks. The processing only takes a few days, but we like to give a little time for folk in Hinteraevum to come to terms with your death too.'

Monty sipped at his tea. He took another look at his booklet then he turned to Angela and told her that he was ready for further instruction. She took him to another room, a small office behind the stage. They each took a seat at the desk and Angela switched on the computer. The display phased itself in within a few seconds and the welcome logon screen soon appeared, bearing the branding 'Hinteraevum – A Satisfying And Wonderful Afterlife'. Angela pointed at a section of his welcome leaflet which contained his personal details. She invited Monty to log on. He did so and the screen refreshed to show a menu of options under the heading of 'Hinteraevum Personal Profile Information System'. All of the wording was set against a pale blue background, everything was designed around a sensitively placid colour palette.

'Okay, this is the system that you will use for all of your needs. HPPI Sys. You'll hear everyone referring to it as HappySys. It allows you to set up all of your personal preferences and it gives you access to travel booking, news, data archives, knowledge information databases, and, perhaps most importantly, all of your people links here in Hinteraevum.'

Angela began by walking him through the guiding parameters that were used for orchestrating his life in Hinteraevum. They became much more understandable when he saw them on the screen and his hostess spent time explaining them.

'This technology ... have you had this for thousands of years? Are we just beginning to catch up in real life?'

'We have always had the transition process. The rest has developed over the years. We are always ahead of Realworld but we can't appear to be giant leaps ahead because it would be too unsettling for people as they come through. And some of the technology would look out of place. Remember that you will still see the world as you knew it when you left Realworld. The buildings, houses, the infrastructure. We know that there are new, weather resistant road surfaces coming in the next ten years, but we can't show you that until it happens in Realworld.'

'Thinking about houses,' said Monty, 'what do I do about a home? Where do I go to live? What is the protocol?'

'Most people go to the house they were living in prior to dying.'

'And everything is there? Books, cutlery, crockery, clothes?'

'Yes. You can elect to see or block particular items. It's just as you left it two weeks ago. I must advise you, though, people find it difficult stepping over the threshold for the first time. It is a peculiar sensation and it can take a few weeks to grow accustomed to being in the house when you know that your loved ones are probably also there at the same time in Realworld.'

'What's to stop me living somewhere else?'

'Nothing at all. You could choose to go and live in Buckingham Palace if you want to. The great majority of our guests want some stability and that is more likely to be achieved by living in their own home. Some decide to move at a later date, when they find that their house has been redeveloped, or their partner arrives and they want to settle abroad. Some opt for a house in the sun.'

'My house dates back to the 1930's.'

'Yes, I'm aware of that.'

'So, there must have been other occupants who have died during that time and decided to live there already. The idea of sharing the house with my wife and children, who I can't see, is bad enough. Sharing it with some complete strangers who I can see ... that really does bother me.'

Angela reminded him of the VU parameter in his pamphlet and gave him some example scenarios of how the virtualisation boundary zone worked.

'That sounds bizarre. As I am walking along the road I'll see people vanishing in front of me as they enter the hundred meter exclusion zone. Or I'll suddenly bump into someone who has just magically appeared, coming out through the boundary? Sounds like I'll have to watch my step when I draw close to the perimeter.'

'We manage it with much more subtlety than that. They may turn a corner, and they're no longer in view when you reach the same corner. They may step across the road and you lose sight of them behind a car. You really shouldn't let it bother you.'

'If you say so. You really seem to have everything figured out.'

'You forget that we have had a great many years perfecting this.'

Monty nodded.

'And how old are you, Angela?'

'I'm twenty-five. Though I have been around for some time.' She smiled and said nothing more on the subject.

'You said something earlier about my connections being informed of my death. They know I'm here?'

'Yes they do. A posting goes to all of your relatives and friends, and to others who have known you in the past. People who were in your year group at school, though they may not have been your close friends. Neighbours. People you may have known at work. You may be surprised by what the system has identified for you. It gives you the opportunity to make contact with old friends.'

'Jacko,' Monty uttered.

'Yes, he's here. Let's briefly look at the other two categories, you'll probably see him in there. Then I will leave you alone to spend some time searching through the system.'

When Monty had understood how to switch between the various options, Angela rose up and left the room. She gave Monty some space to find his way around the computer system.

His time in the Village Hall had brought out such a mix of feelings. Deep sadness that he would not see Karen, Sam and Gemma. A warm expectancy about seeing his parents again. Curiosity about a reunion with Jacko after a gap of more than twenty years. Then there was the question of how he would feel walking back into his house. Being there alone. But knowing that his wife and children were there in some other living existence.

He explored the system for a good thirty minutes. Certainly enough time to polish off that cup of tea. There was a tap on the door and an older man entered. Monty guessed at late fifties. The man had brown hair and a neatly maintained beard and moustache. He was wearing a thick cotton shirt which was off-white with a soft red and green checked pattern. Below he was sporting a pair of brown moleskin trousers.

'Good afternoon Monty and welcome to Hinteraevum. I'm Pete. I work here with Angela and the rest of the team.'

'Good afternoon.'

'It's very sad that you have left Realworld. However, their loss is our gain. We are really pleased to welcome you here. I sincerely hope you settle in and have an enjoyable time with us. Has Angela explained everything for you?'

'Yes, she has been very helpful.'

Pete came closer and sat himself down on the seat next to Monty.

'Good. It is drawing to that point in the afternoon where you will be wanting to step outside and begin your new life here. I know that it can be quite daunting. There's always an element of fear and uncertainty. Please try not to be frightened in any way. We have arranged a series of return appointments for you. They are marked in your induction pack.'

He picked up the brochure from the table and flicked to the page which contained Monty's itinerary.

'Here they are' he said, pointing to the particulars. 'It is our normal practice. We encourage new guests to take advantage of our counselling services. Everybody has questions in the first few months. However, please don't feel that you have to wait for a specific appointment to come round in the calendar. If you want to come back to see us at any time, then do so. We're open all of the time, twenty-four seven, as they say nowadays.'

'I do have a couple of questions' Monty ventured.

'Go ahead.'

'What about food and drink? Buying things, shopping?'

'Hinteraevum is something of a slave to your imagination. The shops are there, just like you have been used to. You simply go and obtain what you want. Stocks are always replenished. Nobody goes without. And everybody settles into a moderated behaviour. Some people grab far too much in their first few months, but they soon come to understand that that greed is rather pointless. It serves no purpose.'

'And eating? What about cooking, restaurants?'

'You can cook at home. You can go out to restaurants. You identify what you want from the menu and it appears for you. You'll get used to it. You enjoyed your cup of coffee and Danish earlier?'

'Yes, very much, thank you.'

'And we got there without you even having to tell us on that occasion. Give it a try. You might want to visit someone you know, they'll show you the ropes, help you get started.'

'I was thinking of going to see my parents first.'

'An excellent idea. And how will you get there?'

'I hadn't really figured it out yet.'

'Well, you could go by train. Or by road? What car would you most like to drive whilst you're here?'

That was easy for Monty. He knew the specification for that 4x4 and was able to recite it like a well-worn nursery rhyme.

Pete helped him gather his things together. Jacket, induction brochure, leaflets.

'That shirt …' began Pete.

'Yes, I know' interrupted Monty. 'Doesn't go with this jacket.'

Pete nodded. They stepped out of the little office and followed the corridor round the side of the stage to come back into the main hall. Monty's eyes caught sight of a large mural on the wall advertising what was now becoming a familiar strap line:

'Hinteraevum – A Satisfying And Wonderful Afterlife'

He was ready to step out of the Village Hall and see just how satisfying and wonderful Hinteraevum was.

15

If anything, it was an anticlimax. Friday, April 30th. The High Street looked every bit the same as it had done on Sunday 11th when he had walked along to the newsagents to pick up the paper. There were less than a dozen shops, but they all seemed a little busier than he'd normally expect them to be at this time on a Friday afternoon. He resisted the minor temptation to step into the The Blue Lion, one of four pubs in the village, and made his way along the upper side past the bread shop, the butcher's, and the florist's. The latter had branched out to specialise in selling a range of aromatic candles over recent years which lead all the locals to refer to the row as the butcher, the baker and the candlestick maker.

It was known as the upper side of the High Street because the pavement was almost a metre higher than the road level. Between them was a cobbled incline where people could park their cars. And today there wasn't an empty space to be found. The cars all appeared to be relatively new and each had a personalised number plate. The people, on the other hand, were of a more advanced age demographic. He didn't recognise anyone, which he found irregular. The village wasn't particularly large. It was a very friendly place and he thought he knew a fair proportion of the inhabitants, but the majority of these people pre-dated his and Karen's move there.

He crossed over the road and made his way out of the centre of the village, turning left into Sandringham Road. After a hundred yards he turned right into Conway Road. His road. At last, someone he recognised. Mrs Sowerby was walking towards him. She used to be his next-door neighbour until three years ago, when she died at the age of seventy-five.

'Hello Mrs Sowerby.'

'Hello Monty. I saw the notification that you were joining us shortly. Have you just come through?'

'I arrived this afternoon. It hasn't really sunk in yet.'

'No, I wouldn't expect it to have. It usually takes a few weeks.'

'And how are you, Mrs Sowerby?'

Monty and Karen had always referred to her with a formality that respected her age. They never knew Mr Sowerby as he had passed away shortly before their arrival on Conway Road. So it had always just been Mrs Sowerby.

'I'm very well, thank you. Very well indeed. And I've got Mr Sowerby to keep me company now. You'll have to come and meet him.'

'Yes. I'd like to meet him. Once I get myself accustomed to the place.'

'You won't know the Franklins, will you? George and Betty.'

'No, I can't say those names ring a bell with me.'

'They're in your house too. They used to live there before the Johnsons.'

'I remember that we bought the house off the Johnsons.'

'Yes, that's right. It's nice to know that they're sharing the house with you. Although I expect you won't actually see George and Betty, because of your privacy view settings.'

Monty wasn't so sure he agreed. In fact he found it slightly off-putting to know that an elderly couple were going to be around the house. He would rather have remained ignorant of that fact.

'How old are your boys now?'

'It's a boy and a girl, Mrs Sowerby. Sam is seventeen and Gemma is fifteen.'

'Of course it is. One soon forgets. And what about Carole?'

'Karen is fine.'

'Good. It's such a shame they haven't got you at home anymore.'

Monty winced under the surface as the remark scraped across his heart. He didn't want to be rude to Mrs Sowerby, but he just felt the need to escape this particular line of conversation. He felt the need to wallow in the comfort of his own home, although even that idea was now tarnished with the knowledge that he was doubling up with the Franklins. He politely brought their chat to a close and committed to catch up with Mrs and Mr Sowerby in the coming days.

He resumed his route along Conway Road. There were six more houses to go before he would arrive at his own. The level of anticipation gradually increased with each one he passed, not knowing quite how it would feel to arrive back home after the ordeal. He reached the neighbouring house. The high hedge at the front of their garden masked the view of his own house until he arrived at his gatepost and turned into the driveway. He was immediately confronted by the sight of his 4x4 parked just in front of the garage. It was the same colour, same model, same specification. The number plate read M, zero, N, T, Y. As he got closer he realised it wasn't a zero, it was simple straightforward MONTY in capital letters. There was no real need to follow restrictive number plate protocols here.

He ran his hand down the rear side of the car, before turning towards the front door of the house. His right hand instinctively reached into his pocket and there were his keys. There, as if nothing had happened. He brought out the cluster, selected the one to open the front door and crossed the threshold into the hall. Monty stood for a few seconds, looking along the hallway towards the kitchen door. He turned round and closed the front door, locking it from the inside. He turned back through a hundred and eighty degrees and surveyed the hallway again. The door through to the lounge. The staircase. The light fittings. The peacefulness. It was so quiet. Quieter than at any time he could remember. Quieter than when he'd been home alone in the house.

He took off his jacket and hung it over the end of the banister at the foot of the stairs then began a slow circuit of the ground floor. He'd start from the front and work his way to the back of the house. That meant the lounge first. He'd do the open plan kitchen and dining room later. That was the social hub of the house. Every room oozed Karen's personality, but the kitchen was her finest hour. He knew that was the one that would be the most difficult for him to experience today.

Monty gently tossed the wad of papers onto the coffee table in the centre of the living room and walked across to the window that looked out over the front garden. He stood for a few minutes, just staring aimlessly, mulling everything over. He ambled across the room and sat in one of the armchairs. Fireplace, television, pictures on the wall, mirror over the mantelpiece, two sofas, armchair. Everything looked to be in order. Leaning forward, Monty picked up the material from the village hall and flicked through it casually. He eased back in the armchair and started to read it in earnest.

He awoke with a bit of a start. He must have been snoozing for a couple of hours. The daylight was beginning to fade outside and the Hinteraevum booklet had slipped down to nestle between his left thigh and the inside of the chair arm. He felt fuzzy headed, as if he'd been through some sort of hospital procedure under anaesthetic. Pulling himself round, he sat the booklet on the table with the rest of the information pack and rose to his feet. He made his way through to the kitchen, switched on the coffee machine, collected a mug from the cupboard and went across to the fridge.

By the time he had poured a centimetre of milk into the bottom of the mug the machine was well into its start-up procedure. For whatever reason, he had an instinctive urge for pizza. Perhaps he'd subconsciously noticed one sat in the fridge? He re-opened the door and, yes, there was a ham and mushroom pizza on the shelf waiting to be unwrapped and loaded into the oven. He removed it and placed it on the island temporarily because the coffee machine was now ready to brew. He positioned the mug, made his selection, then turned to sort out the pizza.

He sat at the island with his cup of coffee, the oven cooking his meal with a gentle background hum. Then, with relaxation came realisation. He remembered his circumstances and took a deep breath, followed by a long sigh. He was sat in the kitchen, alone. Karen's kitchen. He cast his eyes round. For someone who knew every inch of this house, he felt very lost.

'Right. Stop,' he said to himself. He said it out loud, but there was nobody there to hear it for him. 'Can't change this, so I've just got to get on and make the best of it. Let's have this pizza, then we can go and take a look at the computer. Let's see what it's all about. Let's see who is on my contacts list.'

He had no idea why he had used the plural form, but he did make a mental note of caution that he should avoid talking to himself at all costs. That would be a very bad habit to lapse into.

After taking a reminiscent look around all of the rooms upstairs, he sat down at the desk in the study and turned on the computer. The boot up process looked unfamiliar, but was far quicker than usual. The Hinteraevum logo appeared and he responded with his logon details and password which took him straight into the welcome menu. He had to go back downstairs to collect the information pack so that he could guide himself through his debut session on the screen.

He began by exploring SoulSearch. He took a long look at his parents' pages, reacquainting himself with their appearance and making sure that they were still living at the same address. He continued through his family ties, then on to his close friends. Jacko was the entry he was most keen to read. There were plenty of others, ranging from those that he could remember well, to those who he had no recollection of. SoulSearch allowed him to tag those that he wanted to connect with, so he soon compiled a target group.

Second point of interest was his message box. He opened it up and began to work through the list. After the standard set of welcome messages from Hinteraevum he found that he had about a dozen from family and friends, all of which had a similar look and feel. He read the one from his mother and father. It was very simple and actually didn't say very much at all. It didn't need to. They were looking forward to seeing him. He read it several times. This was the first communication he had had from them in years and he found it incredibly moving. He was eager to see them and this message served to reinforce that conviction. He typed a reply saying that he would drive up tomorrow.

He worked his way down the messages and decided that he would leave any further investigation of the system until later. After all, he had a hundred years ahead of him to get used to it. He logged off and turned out the light as he left the study.

Going to bed. That was going to be the next hurdle. But he'd resolved to be positive about this new lifestyle, if lifestyle was indeed the correct word for it. He retired to the master bedroom at the rear of the house. It had been enhanced when they did the extension work, gaining a walk-in wardrobe and dressing area, plus a sumptuous en-suite bathroom. He peeled off his clothes and settled into bed for his first night's sleep.

After two and a half hours of tossing and turning in bed, Monty still couldn't get comfortable. His mind kept returning to the idea of sharing a bed with the Franklins. He couldn't see them, he'd had neither sight nor sound of them since entering the house, but he knew they were there. And that was unnerving, to say the very least. He tried to displace the Franklins by thinking of Karen. She would be here, in this bed, in the Realworld. That was a nice thought. An odd concept to come to terms with, but picturing his ideal bed partner did offer him some semblance of comfort. But it was no use. George and Betty Franklin kept bouncing back in there.

He couldn't bear it any longer. He got up and shuffled out to the landing, where he switched on the lamp. He took a look in at Gemma's room. She would be lying there asleep. He pushed open the door to Sam's bedroom and stepped inside. Monty put the light on for a moment and looked around at the items on the desk and the posters on the wall. He turned the light off and popped into the bathroom to use the toilet before deciding he'd try the guest bedroom at the front of the house. Monty slipped in between the smooth Egyptian cotton sheets and was soon in a deep sleep.

16

Karen felt something, or someone, next to her. Partially awake, but still in a drowsy slumber, she turned over and cuddled the form beside her. As she gathered her senses she found that it didn't feel like Monty at all. And there was a smell, a perfumed smell. That wasn't like him. Was she still dreaming? Confused, she slowly opened her eyes to find Gemma lying at her side.

'Morning mum' she said, cuddling in closer.

'Good morning. What are you doing in here?'

'I couldn't sleep, and I thought someone had put a light on in the middle of the night. And why are you sleeping in here, mum?'

'I couldn't sleep either. I kept thinking about your dad, so I decided to come in here to see if it made any difference.' She too had relocated to the guest bedroom in the middle of the night. 'I put the landing lamp on and took a little peep in at you and Sam. Sorry if that disturbed your sleep.'

It was quarter past eight. The sun was up and it looked as though it was going to be a warm day, not that they could tell that in the front bedroom as it was north facing and shaded. The door pushed open and Sam entered.

'What are you both doing in here?'

'We couldn't sleep,' they replied together. Gemma followed up with 'how come you're up so early?'

'I had a bit of a strange night. I thought someone was snooping around in my room.'

'That was me,' confessed Karen. 'Just checking up on both of you.'

'Oh.'

Sam trudged across the room and sat on the bottom of the bed.

'You do know that it's the first Saturday of the month, don't you?'

Traditionally that meant doing something fun as a family. Bowling, or the cinema, or a meal out somewhere. It went back many years to when Sam and Gemma were young and Monty was working hard with Nick to get their architects practice established. At the end of the month Monty and Karen would check their bank balance and evaluate whether there was sufficient funds left over for a family treat. The number of tight months gradually diminished over those early years and going out 'en famille' on the first Saturday of the month had become normal custom and practice.

'I think your dad would have wanted us to keep that alive.' Karen immediately recognised the irony in what she had just said and quickly continued. 'Why don't you have a look at what's on at the pictures Sam?'

Sam took to the task straightaway and was soon in his bedroom searching out the options on his laptop. Karen decided it was time for her and Gemma to vacate the bed and make a start to the day.

17

Saturday May 1st, 2010 (H)

Monty stirred. He felt better than when he'd woken up in the armchair the previous evening, it had been a fitful night's sleep once he'd managed to settle down in the spare room. He opened his eyes and took a few minutes to wake up properly.

'OK, time to get motoring and see what this place has to offer' he said out loud. 'Doing it again,' he thought. He swung himself out of bed and went through to the back bedroom where the sunlight was already raising the temperature in the room, despite the curtains being drawn. After a refreshing shower he set about getting dressed. It was usual to catch up with current affairs at breakfast and Monty wondered if newspapers would feature in this new existence. As he made his way downstairs he caught sight of the paper poking from the letter box like an irreverent tongue, as if to say 'Oh ye of little faith'. He checked the banner on the top of the front page to reassure himself what day it was. It also reminded him that this was the first Saturday of May.

As he lay the paper down on the surface of the island in the kitchen his mind turned to whether Karen, Sam and Gemma would uphold the first Saturday of the month tradition. Were they sat at the island right now debating what film to go and see? It certainly was going to be hard getting used to the idea of being with them at the same time as being without them.

A cup of coffee and a bowl of porridge consumed, he cleared up and went back upstairs. Monty packed a small case and after ticking off the items on his mental checklist he left the house and walked over to the car. He was putting his things in the boot when Mrs Sowerby said hello from the mouth of his driveway. She was on her way into the village.

'How was your first night?'

'I think it was as good as I could have expected. It took me a while to settle down to sleep.'

Instinct made him look up at the window of the spare bedroom and he realised he hadn't been back in there to open the curtains. Mrs Sowerby followed his line of sight.

'At least you wouldn't have been woken by the sun this morning' she said, with a nod of her head to the same point on the facade. 'George and Betty have always liked having their main bedroom at the front because they don't get woken up too early by the light streaming in.'

Monty kicked himself. Why had he assumed that the Franklins would be in that same rear bedroom last night? Why had he tortured himself? It was crystal clear to him now. The Franklins would have known the house before the extension was added, at which time the largest bedroom had been that one at the front. He smiled, acknowledging the perverse outcome of his nocturnal migration.

'And, besides, they've gone away to France in their caravan for three weeks.'

He smiled again, then told Mrs Sowerby that he was going to stay with his parents for a few days and asked if she would watch the house for him while he was away.

'Why?' she replied. 'Nothing's going to go wrong. You've no need to worry about anything untoward happening. You go and enjoy seeing your parents again.'

He said goodbye, climbed in and started up the engine. Once he got underway Monty felt a sense of security and normality from being behind the wheel concentrating on his driving. He switched on the CD player and it picked up in the middle of the album he'd last been listening to in Realworld - Simon and Garfunkel singing 'So Long Frank Lloyd Wright'.

He soon arrived in Darlington, his parents' home town. It had been a while since his last visit. After his mother and father had died there was no real reason for him to go back here. It hadn't changed much, he thought, as he turned into Durham Road. The glow of expectation had developed throughout the journey and now that he was so close his head was full of thoughts of how they would react when they saw him again. He slowed down and pulled to a gentle stop by the kerb outside number 23. Monty jumped out and pulled his belongings from the back of the vehicle, took a long look at the familiar facade in front of him, then walked up the path.

Marianne opened the front door before he had a chance to ring the bell.

'David!'

A torrent of emotions gushed through them both as they embraced. In her first few years in Hinteraevum his mother had acclimatised to the knowledge that she would see Monty again at some point in the future. However, despite her maternal instincts, she had geared herself up for that interval being a lot longer than seven years. She would have much preferred for Monty to live to a ripe old age in Realworld.

She had just come through a fortnight of diametrically opposed feelings starting with a deep, deep sadness at learning of her son's death. What had happened to him, what had caused him to die so young? Was it something sinister? She hoped that it hadn't been a painful death. Was anyone else involved, was David to blame? Had he enjoyed the last seven years, had he been happy? Was it natural causes, had it been a long illness? She and Roger had both died in their early sixties through cancer. They both remembered the pain of dealing with cancer in their final years and Roger's older sister had accidentally confirmed their cause of death shortly after her arrival in Hinteraevum two years after Marianne. It was all too easy to leap to conclusions about Monty's passing.

And how was Karen? Marianne was confident that Monty and Karen were still together. There were signs to watch out for - in the home, for example - that make for reliable pointers. Marianne had warmed to Karen very quickly and they had always got on really well, so it was very upsetting to think of the distress that her daughter-in-law must be going through. And what about Sam and Gemma? Goodness knows how they must be feeling without their father around. Marianne had done the sums. She knew their birthdays, she knew exactly how old they were. She still loved her grandchildren, even though she had no true sense of who they were now. They would have done so much growing up since she had come through.

All of this grief had gradually morphed into eager expectancy. Day after day the excitement of being reunited displaced the sadness. Her mind had switched from thinking about how he'd left Realworld to being preoccupied with his pending arrival in Hinteraevum. What would he look like? How much would he have altered in those seven years? When would she and Roger get to see him? Hopefully very soon. How long would he stay? What could she do to make his visit special? She would arrange a fish pie. Did he still like fish pie? It was comforting to have that two week transition period to prepare for this moment.

It had been quite the opposite for her son during those gap years. Monty had had no idea that he'd ever get to see his mother and father again. Yesterday he had learnt differently. All the way up in the car he had been picturing the pair of them, remembering from his induction talk that neither would have aged from their respective times of death. Sure enough, his mother hadn't changed from when he last saw her in 2003. The absence of any signs of ageing seemed peculiar at first, something that might take a little getting used to. The age perspective hadn't really occurred to him when seeing Mrs Sowerby because she was a lot older anyway, and her passing was more recent.

All in all, it seemed strange to be hugging his mother again. Strange, perhaps, but truly wonderful.

'Come along Marianne, dear, put the boy down.'

'Hello dad.'

Monty released his mother and stepped via a handshake into a man hug with his father. It was a strong hug, and a silent one. Roger broke it by saying 'Let's go inside. We've got a huge amount to catch up on.' There were some dignified tears to wipe aside for all three parties as they stepped through the doorway.

It was a full afternoon of information exchange. Monty talked about Karen and the children while Roger and Marianne listened intently, interjecting with lots of questions and recounting their memories. They also wanted to know what Monty had been doing at work. They were proud to hear about the formation of Hanson Scott and impressed at its level of success. They also enjoyed hearing about how Monty and Karen had purchased a large detached property and made some modern developments to it. Roger's sister had brought news of Monty and Karen's house move at the same time as her protocol breaking comments about cancer, so Marianne and Roger had actually been to see it and were able to relate to his descriptions.

In return, Monty was very interested to hear that they had found it so easy to enjoy living in Hinteraevum. He was brought up to date with all of the recent history of relatives who were here in this new world. Life seemed to be so full and yet so care free. Between them, Roger and Marianne reeled off a gazetteer of foreign trips.

'I know you always liked a holiday abroad, but you've become professional globetrotters' Monty observed. 'How do you manage it?'

'Everything is so simple to book' replied Marianne. 'I can do it, so it must be simple.'

'Your mother's being modest again. She's very adept at searching out where to go and how to get there.'

'If you're going to stay here with us for a few days I'll show you how to find your way around the travel system. I'm sure you'll be better at it than me, you're more used to how these computers work.'

'That would be really helpful, mum. I was planning on staying for maybe three or four days, if that would be okay with you?'

'Absolutely, son' said his father.

'Stay longer if you'd like to,' Marianne added. 'Most people tend to use a family support network to get themselves through the first few weeks'.

She knew he would stay longer once he got the first couple of days over with, so there was no need for any persuasive talk today.

'Yes, your mother can show you the ropes.'

Marianne decided it was time for more tea and went through to the kitchen to sort out drinks and some light bites.

'I see you've got sorted with a car. I like the colour.'

'Yes, I love it. Bought it two weeks before I … well, erm, before I came here. Actually, that reminds me, something I was thinking about on the way here.'

'What's that?'

'How do I pay for it? How do I earn money to pay for the diesel?'

'You don't need to. There's no currency, you don't need to buy anything at all.'

Monty's bemused look prompted his father to explain.

'You understand that you can see material items that exist in Realworld, don't you?'

'Yes. It's dependent upon my parameter settings' replied Monty, though in a tone that sought confirmation more than it oozed affirmation.

'That's right. When you go into a department store you'll see all the clothes on display.'

'Yes…'

'If there's something that you like, you just pick it up and take it away.'

'That sounds like shoplifting to me, dad'.

'No, it's not. At that point it's all down to your imagination, your natural subconscious resolves it all for you. The real shirt is still in the store, you have a virtual one. No need for transporting goods all over the place. No lorries on the roads.'

'Hmmm, now you mention it … I don't remember seeing any lorries. But the Realworld lorries … they're material … so I should be able to see them?'

'That's down to your settings again. Your settings block out the Realworld traffic because it would be just too insane to have to deal with that and the Hinteraevum movements.'

'Who flys the planes in Hinteraevum?'

'Airport travel is very ordered, less chaotic. It's so different to the roads. The vast majority of us can happily drive a car, but we can't drive a plane. So it makes a lot of sense to exploit Realworld aeroplanes. Where it makes sense, use it. Where it doesn't make sense, block it out. We get the best of both worlds, literally.'

'I see.' He paused to absorb before asking another question.

'Back to my car. Is that virtual too?'

'Of course. Did it feel any different to the real one you were driving a few weeks ago?'

'Well, I didn't really notice. No.'

'There you are, you see. Have faith. You'll get the hang of it. It will soon feel very natural.'

'And the food is virtual?'

Marianne returned with tea and scones.

'Yes, it's all figments of your imagination' she said. 'You'll get used to it. It will soon feel very natural' she said, blissfully unaware that she was repeating her husband's comment.

Roger decided that they should go out for dinner that evening. It would serve both as a celebration and an education. Marianne agreed that it was an excellent idea. 'I was going to arrange a fish pie, but there will be plenty of time for that during your visit.'

Monty didn't quite catch the nuance of 'arrange' rather than 'cook'. He'd latched on to using the term 'Realworld', but he wasn't fully tuned in to the place yet.

Marianne switched the topic of conversation. 'Jacko was asking after you earlier in the week. He's a lovely boy, David.'

'Don't forget, Marianne, Jacko's a lot older than he looks' Roger corrected. 'Underneath the surface he's the same age as David.'

'I know, Roger. It was such a shame he died so young. He'd already been here fifteen years when I arrived. He had some difficulties at first, but he's really made something of this place.'

'I had a message from him on SoulSearch' said Monty. 'I sent him a reply saying that I would be here for a few days and it would be great to meet up. I'm going to see him tomorrow.'

'The joys of Hinter-mail' said Roger. 'It will be an interesting encounter for you because he will appear just as he was when you two were back at sixth form. Just remember, though, he's actually the same age as you and he's lived a very different lifestyle for the last twenty-odd years. I think you'll be quite surprised when you talk to him.'

Monty took all of this on board.

Later that evening he drove out into the countryside with his parents to The Wise Fox, an old coaching inn that had always been a favourite with the whole family. Monty had fond memories of the food and the atmosphere. As they walked through the restaurant he knew he'd not be disappointed. The warm aromas were sublime and he was catching sight of elegant dishes on the tables. There was a busy mixture of conversation, chinking of glasses, and clinking of cutlery on crockery which gave the room a light and welcoming feel. They found a table and within no time at all their conversation was bouncing around the room with everyone else's.

Monty saw that there was a menu just to his left. He hadn't noticed it as they sat down. He picked it up and read intently. There wasn't a dish on the menu that he didn't like. They each arrived at their choices quickly and the pace of their chatter regained its meter. At the back of his mind he was conscious that they'd not had their orders taken, but equally he hadn't spotted any staff circulating. He put that down to the distractions of the company. Feeling an urge for the toilet, he excused himself. When he got back to the table he saw that their starters had arrived.

'That was quick service. They've hardly had time to relay the order to the kitchen staff.'

Roger made a point of scanning the room as they began to eat. 'Who are you referring to?'

Marianne smiled at Monty. Monty studied his mother, then his father, before running a concentrated survey of the restaurant for himself. No sign of any waiters or waitresses, though he was sure he'd seen some people behind the bar as they had come through.

'Alright, I'm beat. What's the trick?'

'There's no trick,' replied Marianne. 'It's all subconscious. We were ready for our starters so they just materialised when we weren't paying attention.'

'Okay. I'll make sure I pay attention in future.'

Marianne and Roger exchanged knowing looks, provoking a 'What?' from Monty.

'Nothing' said his mother, 'just relax, dear, and enjoy your meal.'

Monty was going to be on heightened alert for the rest of the evening. He was going to see this in action. As he tucked into his starter he looked at what his father was eating.

'I don't remember seeing a ravioli starter on the menu,' he said.

'I don't remember you liking ravioli.'

'I don't, but…'

'So why would it be on your menu if there was absolutely no

chance of you wanting it?'

They finished their first course amid continued chatter and Monty found himself absorbing a wide variety of informative tips that would ease him in to his new environment. He was particularly engrossed by the travel. Marianne explained ViSITs, the online booking system which took advantage of Realworld transport combined with Hinteraevum virtualisation. No check-in required at the airports, no need to arrive hours ahead of your scheduled flight, no searching baggage or emptying out contents. Fly in style - business class or first class luxury. No cost.

'What if the flight is full? I suppose it's relatively easy to reserve a seat on an alternative route?'

'You're still having trouble with this concept, aren't you?' his father said. 'Use your imagination. You have a seat. There could be any number of other people booked onto that seat, but as far as you are concerned you've got that seat. You don't have any awareness that others may be sitting there because your VU parameters take care of blanking out all of that for you.'

Monty was doing his best to sit back and take it all in. He looked down to see that his main course was sitting on the table in front of him. The look on his face was registered by both Marianne and Roger.

'Have you been paying attention?' his father asked. Monty had to smile in acceptance of defeat. Perhaps he just had to go with the flow after all.

18

The forecast was for a dry day with occasional showers. Jacko had suggested meeting at 10.30am at the cricket pavilion on the edge of town, not far from their old school. Monty walked across from his parents' home, actually passing Jacko's old home on the way. It was a trip down memory lane, the route they'd always taken to get to school. Fifteen minutes and his Alma Mater appeared ahead of him. He crossed the road and turned right, following the boundary fence to the corner of the cricket field. The club house had been there since the 1950's, a single storey building made from brownish red bricks with a high rosemary tiled roof. He needed to be around the other side, the side facing the pitch, where three steps led up to a recessed entrance area under the overhang of the roof. Up above was the dormer opening from which the scorers had an uninterrupted view of every ball bowled.

As he drew close to the steps a familiar scene came into view. A wooden bench seat to the left, underneath a panelled window. A pair of panelled entrance doors. A second wooden bench seat to the right. And there was a youthful Jacko, sitting casually. When Jacko saw his old friend he got to his feet and greeted him with a warm handshake.

'Hello matey' Jacko began. 'You look well, all things considered.'

'So do you, all things considered.'

Jacko sat down again on the bench and Monty sat beside him. They both looked out onto the green expanse with its pale rectangular wicket running from left to right, parallel with the pavilion. The first few minutes were quiet and peaceful, as if they didn't need to say anything to each other. They had been best friends. Monty absorbed everything around him. He was struck with a strong feeling of melancholy. He thought of the many times he'd gone into bat on that field, often with Jacko, representing their school first eleven.

'Played a few times on there, eh?' Jacko broke the silence with a soft voice.

'Mmm. A few times more than you, I'd say.'

'A few less times than me, I'd say.'

Monty turned his head slightly towards Jacko, as if to ask 'what do you mean?'

'You might have carried on playing here for a few years after I passed on, but I've been playing here for twenty years since we last partnered each other out there.'

'I'm sorry, I didn't think. This is all still very weird for me.'

'It will be for a while. Don't worry though, you'll get used to it. It will all seem so natural before too long.'

'It's really good to see you, Jacko.'

'I'm really pleased to see you too, Monty. Pleased, but sad at the same time. It always happens this way. Conflicting feelings when someone you like comes through.'

'Mum said that you had a tough time when you first arrived.' Monty hadn't got used to all the colloquialisms yet, so it was 'arrived' not 'came through'.

'Yes.' Jacko looked down at the wooden floor for a moment. 'It was tough, matey. Really hard. Hardest time of my life.'

They continued to look out over the cricket field as Jacko went on to describe his first few years in Hinteraevum. Monty listening sympathetically, whilst trying not to be distracted by the bizarre circumstances – sitting next to an eighteen year old who was the same age as him, but he'd not seen for over twenty years.

'I was very bitter about being here before my time. Only eighteen. Eighteen. I didn't know how to cope, how to look after myself. And there aren't many young people here. The average age on entry is way above fifty. It wasn't easy finding friends and company, I can tell you. My granddad took me in and looked after me, thank goodness. Mind you, I was a real pain to him for months. He had the patience of a saint.'

'When did he …'

'When I was thirteen. And he only lived a few miles away, so I knew him well enough. You know, it wasn't as though he'd passed on before I was out of nappies. Anyway, I certainly couldn't have gone to live at home in my parents' place on Chester Drive.'

'I went past there on the way here' said Monty.

'Yes I know. I'm living there now. Couldn't have done it twenty years ago.'

'What? You've made me walk all the way over here?'

'Yes. Of course. This was the right place for us to meet, Monty.'

'I'm just joking. I think you've picked the best place imaginable. Go on, how did it all work out?'

'Granddad gradually managed to calm me down over time. He

took me along to play bowls with all of his friends, which was not my idea of fun to begin with. But, you know me, I got competitive and I've a good eye for most sports. Soon became good at it and as I got to know them I recognised that all of those people had a story to tell. I started to learn a lot from them. Firstly about playing bowls. Then they got to me, psychologically. Made me realise I wasn't going to achieve anything by strutting around in a foul mood all of the time. It must have looked odd – a young lad like me knocking about with a bunch of old wrinklies. But it did me good. They brought me back from being on the verge of throwing in the towel and setting myself to deliquesce into the next existence.'

'So you're now top at bowls as well as being very handy at cricket and football?'

'Yes, I'm very handy with a nice pair of woods.'

He smiled, knowing full well that Monty would pick up on the double entendre they'd employed so often at sixth form together.

Jacko explained how he had managed to stabilise himself and learned to thrive on what Hinteraevum had to offer him. He had studied his favourite subject, physics, and his grandparents had taught him a wide range of practical skills which had helped him to feel very independent at home. Eventually he had moved back to Chester Drive, though he maintained very close ties with his grandparents.

He told Monty how he had also followed his love of sport.

'One of the bowling wrinklies told me there's a network of football clubs all across the country playing at Realworld stadiums. Given that we're all here for a hundred years, you soon find that there are enough people aged between 17 and 35 who can play a bit. It may not be right up there with the professionals, but it's a very high standard. In fact most clubs have an ex professional or two in the side. And there's no shortage of people who have been coaches and managers in their former lives. I've really improved as a player, I've learnt so much over the years. And being in an eighteen year old body is a massive advantage because I'm as fit as a fiddle.'

'And the same happens for cricket?'

'Yes. So I play all the year round. Football through the winter, cricket in the summer. That reminds me,' he paused. He turned to his left, away from Monty, to pick up a package that was leaning against the wall beside him. He handed it over. 'I got this especially for you. I picked it up a long time ago. I've been waiting to give it to you, and now the time has come'.

Monty took it with a quizzical look in his eye. It was a cardboard box measuring approximately a metre in length, 20 centimetres wide and 10 centimetres deep. He opened it up to find the item inside was wrapped in cloth. As he unraveled it the gift became clear. A cricket bat. Not just any cricket bat. It was a left hander. Monty snorted a laugh.

'Is this one of yours?' he said

'No' replied Jacko. 'It's special. It belonged to Sir Colin Andrews.'

Monty's head jerked ninety degrees to look at Jacko. Colin Andrews had been an opening batsman for both county and country.

'I knew he was one of your boyhood heroes.'

'But he gave up playing around the time of ...' Monty had to pause. What are the right words for your friend's death?

'My death?' Jacko finished off Monty's sentence. 'Yes, you're right. However, I found out that he was playing in a charity match nearby and I went along.'

'And he gave you this bat?'

'Well, he didn't exactly give me it. I took it.'

'Stole it, you mean?'

'No. Took it. Took my virtual copy of it. Do you like?'

'Yes I do.' Monty relaxed. 'It was very thoughtful of you, and it means a lot to me. Thanks Jacko.'

'It's a pleasure, matey. Now, I've done my history lesson, it must be your turn. Advantage is that I know a little bit already because your mum and dad have told me about you.'

'So you probably know that I got to do that architecture degree, found myself a wonderful wife, Karen, and have got two fantastic children. You'd really like Karen.'

'Yes, I'm sure I would. She's very attractive and you look happy together.'

The comment threw Monty completely. Seeing the reaction, Jacko explained.

'Your parents told me where you were living, so I took a trip there one weekend and had a nose around.'

'Spying on me. Is nothing sacred?'

'Nice house. Very nice house. I saw the photographs on display – you and Karen, your children. How old are they?'

'Gemma is fifteen and Sam is seventeen. He's almost as old as you are.'

'No he's not, Monty. Don't forget, I'm the same age as you. Only difference is that you're forty-two, zero. And I'm eighteen, twenty-four. Some people say 18r/24h.'

It only took a few seconds for Monty to register the number scheme which, after all, wasn't rocket science. Jacko looked at his watch.

'Come on! Let's take a walk along to the Beehive, they do a cracking Sunday roast. You can tell me all this over a beer.'

As the day went by Monty got to see that Jacko was a middle aged man in a young body. His appearance had stood still, but he had grown up in all other respects and conversed on a maturity level with his 42r/0h friend.

Monty also found out that his mother was indebted to Jacko. She had experimented with some of her personal settings, as one does when one first comes through. However, she had misunderstood advice from one of her friends and made some big mistakes along the way. Jacko had tidied it up for her and spotted that she had set her LE parameter to the bare minimum. Had he not helped her correct it, she would have deliquesced back in 2003.

'Surely that's what friends are for' was his parting comment as they left the pub later that afternoon.

19

'What have you managed to find?'

Clare pulled a chair up next to Ged's desk. It was lunchtime and the office was quiet. Most importantly, Nick was out meeting clients and doing site visits all day. Ged explained that he had managed to take a copy of what was on Monty's old desktop computer but there was hardly anything there of any significance. Most of the folders were projects that Monty had been working on and they were all backed up to the main office server already. He showed Clare the only curious thing that he had found, a folder called 'xfer2laptop' that contained one spreadsheet file.

'I can't actually open the spreadsheet,' he said. 'It's password protected.'

'I thought you could get into all of the computers.'

'I have admin rights and I know what Monty's normal logon password was, but it doesn't work with this file. He's given it a separate passcode altogether.'

Clare leaned across at the keyboard and Ged rolled his chair to the side to make room for her. She went to open the file and attempted a password when the prompt appeared.

'Access denied'.

She repeated this cycle five times without success. Ged wondered how long she would be prepared to keep up the guesswork, she could be there all day. Clare tapped her fingernails lightly on the surface of the desk, thinking intensely, trying to work out what would have been in Monty's head.

'What was his normal password?'

Ged pointed at a post-it note that was stuck to the display screen and read out the characters, just in case Clare couldn't decipher his scrawl.

'5-4-m-6-e-m-m-4'.

Clare scrutinised the password and asked him to repeat it. As he did so, she wrote it down herself in capitals. '5-4-M-6-E-M-M-4'

'Sam, Gemma,' she said proudly.

'Who?'

'It's Monty's children, Sam and Gemma. Monty's used four, five,

97

and six to replace A, S, and G. Just like you might do on a personalised number plate.'

It was time for another go. She typed 'k4ren' and confidently depressed the enter key. Denied yet again. Not to be defeated she typed 'k4ren5cott' and slowly squeezed the enter key down until the PC reacted. The grid opened up in front of them and within a few seconds they were sat looking at a table of data. Two columns of numbers, a column of four letter names, and a fourth column containing a fourteen digit number. It wasn't a large array, almost all of the rows were visible on the screen. Their eyes danced around the contents and Ged spoke first.

'Well done with the password. I think you're going to have to do some more detective work though. I'm not getting any clues. Nothing is leaping out at me. The only thing I can think of is that right hand column … could it be a membership number of some sort?'

'It might be. These names don't ring any bells, so it could be something to do with the cricket club. Phil, Alan, Mark, Jill ...'

'Can't remember him saying anything about women playing at his club,' said Ged. 'Nope, I don't think I can crack this one Clare. Do you mind if I leave you on your own, Miss Marple? I'm ready for some lunch.'

Clare nodded, her eyes still sweeping across the data in front of her. She began moving the cursor around the cells and noticed that all of the second column entries were calculated by multiplying their first column neighbours by twelve. And they were five digits, with the odd exception. Instinct told her that these must be salaries but she still couldn't work out who the people were in the third column. She selected all of the data and sorted it based on ascending order of that second column.

She still couldn't figure out who they were. Thom, Lola, Adam. And several that made no sense at all, including Ctsu. How could she test her hypothesis? The fourteen digits were no help at all, so she went back to the second column once again and ran her finger down the screen. 32400. Her finger stopped. She looked across the row. The name was Cjen. The fourteen digit number was instantly recognisable. It was her sort code and account number. £32,400 was her salary. Clare Jenkins, Cjen.

With that key the rest fell into place. It was all of the team at Hanson Scott. Pat Hillbrook was Phil; Arnie Dambury was Adam; John Illingworth coded as Jill; Anna Langford became Alan. And of course it made sense of the non-names like Ctsu and Itho, which represented Cheung Kit Tsui and Ian Thompson respectively.

She resisted the urge to compare her earnings with those of her colleagues, she might find time for that later. Her immediate priority was to search for anything odd that could have given rise to the task that Nick had set Ged the previous Friday. She scrolled down to the bottom rows, where the salaries were highest. Sure enough, the names at that end of the data included Msco for Monty and Nhan for Nick.

But there were two rows with Nhan. She checked the other cells. The salaries were not the same. The fourteen digit banking reference was also different. Why would Nick Hanson get two rows on the spreadsheet? She was convinced this was out of the ordinary and her thoughts turned to whether there had been an argument behind closed doors before Monty's fall.

She heard some people coming up the stairway, so she closed the spreadsheet and made a mental note to ask Ged for help in getting a copy on to her PC later. She thought back to the folder name, 'xfer2laptop', and wondered if there was anything more substantial on Monty's laptop. Moreover, where was that laptop? Could it be sitting somewhere inside Cartmel House? If so, she had better find it first.

It was time for her to go and get some lunch. And some fresh air.

20

'Thssst'

His mind was on the top of Lose Hill again. Nick focused his eye on the bull. The target was only 30 metres away, but he was still getting used to handling the bow. It was very different to a rifle and he had to concentrate hard on the release to make sure that he didn't pull to one side and send the arrow astray. He was ready. Don't rush it, make sure it's accurate. OK, now....

Thwang!

The arrow accelerated up to speed in an instant, converting the bow's potential energy into its own kinetic energy. Nick heard the whoosh close to his left ear as the thin sliver of wood set off on its trajectory. He relaxed out of the hold with perfect timing and his right arm drew the weapon down through a ninety degree arc, coming to rest by his side.

The arrow hit the red centre circle with a thud. In the space of a couple of centimetres it lost its kinetic energy, as quickly as it had gained it, the target absorbing it with a mild judder. The arrow stood firm, perpendicular to the roundel, alongside the other four that he'd dispatched during the last ten minutes. He was pleased with the result, especially as this was still a beginner's lesson.

'I think my work here is done, as it were,' said Ken. 'That's very good indeed, as good as anyone I've seen, that's for sure. Your technique is excellent, your posture's great. And as for your aim, well, the results speak for themselves, as it were.'

In the period since Monty's accident Nick had made a particular effort to renew friendly terms with Ken. Perhaps the loss of his business partner had had a sanguine effect on him. Whatever, Ken had responded by meeting Nick half way and they were now able to spend time together without any brickbats. They'd started talking again at the archery event which had taken place the day before Monty's funeral. Since then, Ken had been giving Nick instruction on how to use a bow.

'Okay? Done?'

'Yes. Thanks Ken. I've really enjoyed these lessons.'

'Fancy rounding it off with a pint, as it were?'

'I'm afraid I can't today. I have some things that I've got to drop off at a friend's house and I really shouldn't call too late in the evening. Next time, eh?'

'Indeed. Now, let's get this murder weapon locked away in the club house.'

There was a stock room where all the equipment and munitions were kept. When the bow had been placed in its cupboard, they each secured the locker door with separate keys. Part of the club's safety procedure. Nick went to exit.

'Not that way, that takes you out into the car park. It's just the fire exit. In case of emergencies, as it were.'

Nick turned and followed Ken through to the main hallway of the clubhouse and then said goodbye as his archery coach took himself off into the bar.

He didn't have to go far from the rifle club. It only took a little over ten minutes to drive. He stepped up and rang the bell. The door opened and there stood Karen.

'Hello Nick.'

'Hello Karen. We've been having a bit of a tidy out in the office and a lot of Monty's things have surfaced. I thought you might want them, rather than us throw them out.'

'Oh, thank you. Err, come in.'

Nick entered, bearing a cardboard box, one that had previously contained packs of A4 paper. He followed Karen through to the kitchen and placed the box on the island.

'Would you like a coffee?'

'Ah, that would be nice. White, one sugar, please.'

Karen switched on the coffee machine. Nick took the lid off the top of the box and was about to start taking things out when Karen suggested that they moved across to the dining table. He went over and carefully set the items on its surface. Nick began explaining what had happened when they came to empty out Monty's desk, then he faltered for a moment. He saw that Karen wasn't fully paying attention.

'I'm sorry, this must be very difficult.'

'You have launched into the subject matter rather quickly,' she said. The coffee machine gave out a timely grinding noise. 'Let me make those coffees first.'

'Yes, yes, of course. I'm sorry.'

Karen went back to the kitchen and continued the conversation across the open plan space as she prepared the drinks.

'So, how have things been at Cartmel House?'

'Oh, gradually getting back to rights. You know how it is. Life goes on.' It was typical Nick, clunky and mildly insensitive. 'And how have you been?'

Sam entered before she could respond, on the prowl for biscuits. He noticed Nick sitting at the dining table and said hello. Karen turned to see him checking the cupboards.

'You remember Nick, don't you? Your dad's business partner.'

'Yes', he replied, then turned to Nick. 'You were at the funeral.'

'Hello Sam. Yes, that's right.'

Sam left with a fistful of chocolate digestives. Karen took the coffees across and stood them down on two table mats.

'Would you like a biscuit?' she asked, noticing how Nick had eyed the ones in Sam's hand.

'Ooh, that would be nice. I've not really eaten since lunchtime, and I expect it will have to be a takeaway again this evening.'

'I imagine you do a lot of cooking?' Karen asked as she returned with six chocolate biscuits on a tea plate.

'No. Never mastered it. I keep looking out for someone to take care of me instead.'

He suddenly felt embarrassed. Perhaps Karen might misinterpret that as some sort of leading line. He shuffled uneasily on the chair, took a biscuit and a sip of coffee. He returned to talking about the Monty memorial box.

The visit lasted about thirty minutes, by which time he'd hoovered up every crumb on the tea plate. Karen thanked him for being so kind and bringing the box around, there were some sentimental pieces that she was pleased to see. Some of his very old drawing instruments and an expensive pen that she had bought for him one Christmas. As Nick stood up to go he mentioned that Monty's laptop was missing from the office and asked Karen if she had found it around the house.

'Yes. Pat phoned about a month ago and then she called in the following Saturday to collect it. She said that someone at Hanson Scott had asked her to do it because they knew that she and I were quite friendly.'

Nick was taken aback and had to hide his double dismay. Not only had he embarrassingly asked about a missing laptop that wasn't actually missing, he had the anxiety of figuring out who had sent Pat off on that errand and what had been done with the potentially offending item.

'Oh yes,' he bluffed, 'how silly of me to forget.'

He apologised as she showed him to the door. He stepped over the threshold and turned back to face her.

'Forgive me for asking, have you made much progress with the life assurance policies?'

'Yes. It's very slow, but my solicitor tells me that it should come through in another four or five week's time.'

'Hmm,' he rubbed his chin. 'They do take an eternity. Monty was a great partner and a great friend. If there's anything I can do to help, all you have to do is call.'

He delved into his inside pocket and pulled out a business card and a pen.

'Here's my contact number at work and my mobile. And ...' He wrote on the back of the card. 'That's my home number, just in case.'

He handed it to Karen and gave her a friendly, but awkward, peck on the cheek.

'Yes. Erm, thank you.'

Nick walked off down the drive just as Gemma was returning from Explorer Scouts. He nodded to her as they passed. He got to his car and sank into the driver's seat. As he set off along Conway Road he couldn't help thinking how he'd like to see a lot more of Karen.

'What a creep!'

'Gemma, that's not nice. Nick was your dad's business partner and used to be his close friend.'

'I know that. But he's still a bit of a creep. And what was he doing kissing you on the doorstep?'

'It was only his way of being kind. I think he can be a little bit odd when he's talking to women, but he doesn't mean it. He just gets embarrassed, that's all.'

21

Ged waited until he saw Nick's car exit the car park at Cartmel House. He figured it was now safe to go and find Clare. He knew she was around in the office today because someone had mentioned being in a design review meeting with her in the morning. He found her at her desk and asked if she would join him for a cup of coffee as he wanted her advice about a steel and glass structure. She looked up at him, recognising the coded request. She accompanied him downstairs and into the kitchen. It was empty, so they were able to talk in hushed tones as the kettle was filled and gradually came to the boil.

'What news from the front?'

'Nick had a word with me before lunch, called me into his office. Said he'd called in at Monty's house last night to drop off a box of his belongings and had enquired if Monty's wife had seen his laptop. She told him that Pat had collected it. So he's checked with Pat this morning and she's told him that I'd asked her to do it.'

'And ... what did you say to Nick?'

'Just like we agreed. I told him that I'd used my initiative to recover the firm's property. Given that he wanted the PC clearing down so fast, I was being proactive and making absolutely sure that the same happened to the laptop.'

'How did he take it?'

'He was pretty cross that I hadn't told him, so I politely sought his forgiveness and he didn't really have any answer to that. He asked a few questions about whether I'd looked at any of the contents.'

'And you said ... ?'

'No. I might have copied the files over for you, but I hadn't opened them and looked.' Ged could have been practicing for a court hearing. 'You can accuse me of being economical with the truth' he continued with a glint in his eye.

'Well done. Thanks for helping. We should keep this hush-hush, don't tell him where the files are on that main computer. Mind you, he's not that good with the technology anyway, but let's not tempt providence.'

'Have you found anything of any interest?'

The kettle had boiled and Clare was pouring the water into two mugs, where it instantly turned a dark brown. She scrunched her face up and turned her head back towards Ged.

'I found a couple of word documents and another spreadsheet, although I'm not sure how important they are.'

'Clare, I really think it's better if I don't know any details. I'm happy helping you with the technical stuff, but ...'

'OK. You're probably right. The less you know, the safer it is.'

'Thanks. I don't think I would have felt comfortable facing Nick's probing this morning if I actually knew anything of any substance.'

'It's the same for Pat. She's innocent by virtue of her ignorance.'

'What are you going to do?'

That was the tough one. Clare didn't really know what to do with the little snippets of information that she had managed to piece together. Their privacy was interrupted. The door pushed open and in came one of the other girls.

'Ooh, hello. Someone been making coffees and not thought to make a full round?'

Clare engaged in conversation with her and Ged stepped past to make his way back upstairs with his mug half full and his conscience acceptably clear.

22

Monty had found his feet back at home, even managing to forget all about George and Betty Franklin. He'd got used to working his way around the computer system and had even experimented to a degree with some of his personal parameters. Mr Sowerby turned out to be a real gem of a man. Full of interesting conversation and a crafty old sense of humour. At first Monty thought that he was sharp for a person of 70r/7h, but he soon grew accustomed to everyone in Hinteraevum having their wits about them. All down to that transition process. It really did a good job of resetting people.

During the summer he decided to do a grand tour of the UK. With a little help from his mother he soon worked out what he needed to do when it came to finding somewhere to stay. Some of the hotels were like drop-in centres and didn't even need to be booked ahead. He researched for a few days then plotted out a route that would take in all the places of interest that he'd always wanted to see, mixed in with a fair number that he decided he wanted to revisit. Along the way he pitched up at some beautiful country hotels and thoroughly enjoyed his travels.

It was just edging towards September and he was ready to have some time at home again, but not before dropping in for another visit to Darlington. He was round at Jacko's house enjoying a peaceful Sunday afternoon.

'Crikey. It's ages since I last played backgammon. Might even have been sixth form days.'

'It was a lunchtime ritual, matey.'

'That Common Room used to get very smoky, there were days when you needed fog lights to get round the place.'

'Nah, just needed a fume cupboard for Steve Watson to sit in. He loved himself, thought he was so cool. Smoked like a chimney and reckoned he could go out with any girl in the year.'

'Mmm. How about you? Any girlfriends along the way?'

'There's been a few. Not many women of my age here, though, as you can imagine. However, when you have the mature mind of a forty-two year old coupled with the physique and virility of an eighteen year old... That is an attractive proposition for some older women.' He winked and smiled.

'Go on ...'

'I've had a couple of moderately serious relationships, but they broke up in the end. There's one woman that I still see, off and on, which turns out to be a nice arrangement. Sometimes go on holiday with her. She's 36r/7h.'

'Strange measurements.'

'Yes,' Jacko gave Monty a knowing look. 'Actually, you might remember her, she was a year above us at school. Julia Henderson?'

'Hendo's older sister?'

'The very one.'

'You lucky devil. Everyone used to go on about her. Drove Hendo mad listening to people talking about his sister all the time. Is she still as pretty?'

'Yup, sure is, matey.' Jacko couldn't take the smile off his face. 'Let's change the subject, otherwise I'll be off in dreamland for the next hour. What are you doing in the second half of October?'

'Bear with me, I'll have to consult my busy schedule.' Monty pretended to earnestly flick through a diary. 'No, nothing planned for that fortnight, you're in luck.'

'How do you fancy two weeks in the sun? Nice beach. Relaxing holiday?'

'Sounds terrific, but what about your football? You'll be in the thick of your fixtures, won't you?'

'Yes, but we all take time off. We have a squad, so it all works out. I just need to give them some notice that I shall be away. Come on, let's take a look on ViSITs.'

Monty had used ViSITs to book bits of his recent tour around the UK.

'Maybe you can help me with some questions about some of the other things on the system. I tried changing some of my parameters to see what effect they had.'

'Yes, everyone does it at some point. But you have to be careful, don't mess with the wrong ones. Remember, that's what your mum did.'

It was a sobering thought.

'Did you try altering your GRASP setting?'

'Yes, it was bizarre. I set it high so that I'd see a lot more of the Realworld objects, but it was overload. There was so much going on. Seeing peoples' clothes with no bodies inside. Very spooky.'

'I know what you mean. It's like being high on drugs.'

'I wouldn't know.' Monty paused and looked Jacko in the eye. 'Have you been trying that since you've been here?'

'No, you can't. It's blocked, not allowed. I tried it a couple of times when we were at sixth form.'

'You kept that quiet.'

'I can be very circumspect when I need to be. You may be my best friend, but I don't have to tell you everything, matey. Come on, we'll go take a look at your vital statistics.'

He lead the way to the study and booted up his machine. Monty logged on and went into his parameter setting screens.

'The key ones are GRASP and TRIP. They help to moderate how much you see changing in Realworld. Most people find that the best thing is to allow yourself to see the world develop slowly around you whilst blocking out all the ephemera.'

'Ephemera?' Monty prompted for an explanation.

'Sorry. F-M-R-A. Fast Moving Realworld Artefacts' Jacko replied. 'You cut out all the regular movement from Realworld, so you don't get polluted with all their traffic and day to day objects floating around in front of you. It's easily blocked out. You see new buildings getting constructed, I'm sure that will appeal to you. But your view of them only alters on a regular time lapse interval. I subscribe to a daily update, and that works fine.'

'So... TRIP and GRASP. I'm fairly familiar with them already.'

'Good. Yours look reasonable. You might want to knock your GRASP down a little bit, maybe to naught point two five. TRIP is good, it's going to let you go on trains, flights and cruises - they're the unobtrusive forms of transport. You've got the road traffic filtered out, which is perfect. All of that will help us when it comes to going on holiday.'

They continued and within half an hour they had dealt with the items that really mattered. The next half hour was spent investigating holiday options. It was extremely simple. Resort booked, flights booked, all set to depart for the Maldives on Saturday the 16th of October.

'Remind me how the V-U bit works' said Monty. He was thinking of how it was going to pan out with the oversubscribed business class cabin.

'You don't notice it at all. Every passenger has their own virtual view of the surroundings. You don't need do a thing, it all works itself out as if by magic. You just sit back and enjoy a relaxing flight. You'll see.'

Monty was intrigued, rather than bothered by it all. There again, he thought, it would be an extension of sharing the house with George and Betty, and that was no longer keeping him awake at night.

23

Karen and her mother found a table and flopped themselves down with all of their bags. It was the Thursday before the school half term holiday and they had decided to do an early Christmas shopping spree. It had been a regular calendar event for her and Monty when the children were young. They would do a full day and break the back of the task during Half Term whilst Pauline was looking after Sam and Gemma for them. It meant that the children's presents could be sorted out and stored away in the loft without giving the game away.

Pauline had enjoyed the morning with her daughter, but it was half past one and they were both ready for a sit down and some sustenance. They'd arrived at the shopping centre at opening time and had been on their feet for over three hours. Karen had suggested they try the Italian restaurant. The waitress showed them to a table, ran through her accompanying welcome patter routine, then left them with a pair of menus to peruse.

The two women reviewed their purchases and complemented each other on some well thought out festive gift ideas. The waitress returned to take their orders. Karen was driving, so it was a fresh orange juice for her. Pauline could have a sparkling white wine. They requested salad and bruschetta, followed by different pasta dishes. As the girl walked away, Karen picked up a feint buzzing.

'Is that your phone, mum?'

Pauline looked to her right and found her handbag amongst the shopping, unzipped it and rummaged around inside. Like a proud angler, she pulled out the sleek white source of the signal and said 'hello'. Nothing.

'You have to press that button ...'

Pauline managed to accept the call just before the other end gave up. It was Debbie. She hadn't been able to get the day off, otherwise she would have been sat there with them right now. Pauline began with a busy description of the morning's retail assault. Karen took out her Christmas list and a pen and began checking off who she had bought for. Then she noticed her mother slowing up. Debbie wasn't really engaged at the other end and Pauline's pace had faltered, having detected an uncharacteristically subdued daughter. Karen's

110

concentration level increased, something wasn't quite right with her sister, but she was only privy to one side of the conversation.

'You're very quiet. What's wrong?' Pause. 'Oh no. I'm really sorry to hear that. Are you alright? Where are you now?' Pause. 'Is this all about having children?' Pause. 'I thought something wasn't quite right.' Pause. Karen was piecing together the clues like some game of twenty questions, arriving at possible explanations. She was ninety percent sure she'd worked it out. After a good five minutes Pauline handed the phone across the table to Karen.

'Hi Debbie, what's happened?' she asked in a slow, caring voice.

'Chris has left me. We've split up. Can I come and spend a few days at yours?'

'Of course you can. Whatever I can do to help. Whereabouts are you?'

'At work. Coming up to the end of my lunch break, so I'm going to have to go in a minute. I'll tell you all about it later. Or mum can explain, I've just told her the sordid details.'

'Oh. Okay, see you this evening. We'll open up a nice bottle of wine.'

'To celebrate?'

'I'm sorry, I didn't mean it like that, Debbie.'

'I know you didn't. But I did. Got to go, see you about six.'

Karen handed the phone back. The starters had arrived in the middle of this news and they both picked away whilst Pauline filled the gaps in the story for Karen.

Chris had originally been going out to Qatar for a couple of weeks because of work. Then it turned into a couple of months. Then it had become a six month assignment. Debbie was going to go out during the summer for a couple of weeks holiday, but that plan had eroded because of how busy Chris was. Then the real facts had come out.

He was actually out there on a three year secondment with his business. He had met a younger Scottish woman in the office back home in England and been seeing her off and on for about two years. She had decided to take a company secondment to Qatar and Chris had followed suit shortly afterwards. He had paired up with her when he got out there and had been living the life of Riley for the last six months, unbeknown to Debbie. It was a sad end to their relationship, Chris hadn't had the guts to break up face to face, he'd relied on doing it by stealth from three thousand miles away.

And timing was everything. It just so happened that it was going to be Debbie and Chris's wedding anniversary on Sunday.

Naturally the topic commandeered all the air time during their lunch. They were both bitterly disappointed. Pauline had been happily married for more than forty years, so she found it hard to accept the news. She found Chris's behaviour totally unacceptable. She wasn't surprised though. She had suspected something was wrong for a long time. They were both concerned about how Debbie would respond. She had been far less bubbly than normal during the last eighteen months, bottling all of this up inside. What sort of release was on the horizon?

Interspersed in the dialogue, they both voiced the odd grumble about the man. In fact, he didn't deserve to be called a man. He was a coward. And much more. Why take marriage vows if you're not going to put the effort in to uphold them. Till death us do part.

They finished lunch, paid, then collected their array of shopping bags and vacated the table.

'I'll take these back to the car and come back and meet you' said Karen. 'Where will you be?'

'I was going to have a look in Harrison's for something for your dad.'

They continued shopping through the whole afternoon. Pauline had decided that she would come back to Karen's, rather than get dropped off at home. She was keen to see Debbie and make sure that her daughter was okay. She'd get Ron to come and pick her up later on.

Back at Conway Road, after ferrying in all the spoils of the day and making sure everything was well hidden from prying eyes, Karen and Pauline relaxed in the kitchen. The trusty coffee machine was made redundant by the uncorking of a bottle of white wine. Karen began preparing the evening meal and Sam and Gemma came in to see their grandma. The door bell chimed and Gemma went to answer it, expecting to see her aunty Debbie.

She came back into the kitchen alone and announced in a rather loud whisper 'Mum, it's that creep again, the one who worked with dad.'

'Gemma, don't say that. Have you asked him in?'

'Urgh, no. He's just stood at the door.'

Karen went to deal with Nick. He had another box of goodies. Karen invited him in as it had started to spit with rain and it was poor hospitality to leave him standing outside. He came through to the kitchen and was introduced to Pauline. This time he declined a drink as he saw that Karen was enjoying a glass of wine with company. The box contained several framed certificates, including Monty's degree and some architecture recognition awards. He apologised for the interruption and for not spotting these things ahead of his previous visit back in June. They had been missed when the desk and filing cabinets were cleaned out.

The door bell went again. Nick took it as a signal to leave and accompanied Karen through the hall as she went to answer the door. Sure enough it was her sister, who was a bit surprised to see a man in the house until Karen reminded her who Nick was. Debbie dumped her travel bag in the hall and asked 'is mum in there?' Her sister nodded. Debbie took her coat off and threw it over the bottom of the bannister. Visibly girding her loins and displaying two pairs of crossed fingers she went to face the music.

Now that the doorway was clear, Karen could show Nick out. She had positioned herself strategically so as to avoid any repetition of that peck-on-the-cheek manoeuvre, but Nick was avoiding eye contact with her for some reason. He shuffled, then spoke.

'Karen, I know this might sound a little strange, but I have some tickets for a dinner event. Black tie. Early in December. It's the local Round Table Christmas soirée. I wondered if you would like to come along. Err, with me?'

Strategic positioning hadn't prepared her for anything like this and she had begun to feel uneasy by the end of the first sentence.

'That's really very kind, Nick, but I shall say no on this occasion. Thank you. The whole run up to Christmas, from half term onwards, has always been very much a family thing. What with the Christmas shopping, the scouts bonfire night, and my birthday is at the end of November, then there are so many friends to see in December.'

She realised that she was garbling. 'I'm sorry' she said, regaining her composure.

'I shall be missing Monty so much. It wouldn't be fair on you if I came as your guest and sat glum faced all evening. I am sure you can find someone more suitable than me to enjoy it with.'

'Some other time, maybe. Perhaps in the new year?' he offered.

'Yes, perhaps.'

He nodded and stepped out of the door, warmed by the ray of hope that he might take her out to dinner in January.

Meanwhile, back in the kitchen, Pauline had already started to berate Chris for his antics in Qatar and was teetering on the edge of a lecture for Debbie. The latter was saved by an interrupt from Sam.

'Is uncle Chris still playing the guitar?'

'No, Sam. He's not playing the guitar. He's never played the guitar. In fact he's found something much more curvy to play on while he's out there'.

'What, like a harp, or something?'

'No, he's shagging some young Scottish slut.'

Sam was thrown by the answer. Gemma stood motionless, gobsmacked.

'Debbie .... There's no need for that, not in front of the children.' Pauline reprimanded her daughter.

'I'm sorry. Come here, you two, let me have a big hug.'

Gemma and Sam huddled up to Debbie. Karen came back in from seeing Nick off the premises.

'Has creepy gone now?'

'Gemma, will you please stop saying that?'

Pauline turned her attention to her elder daughter. 'And you should be on your guard with him. He seemed to be more than a little bit interested in you.'

'Oh mum, really.'

24

Clare had gone into the office on Monday morning to attend a meeting with Nick and some prospective clients at nine. It went well, she had some changes to make, but nothing major. That would have to wait until tomorrow though, as today was already fully planned out. She would be going across to the Dan Connor house to see the glass being fitted into the atrium end of the building. It was one of the key features and she was intent on being there to make sure it looked right.

After the meeting she escorted the clients to the front door of Cartmel House and showed them out. She went back upstairs and spent twenty minutes with some of her colleagues, finding out their news from the weekend and catching up on any office gossip. Clare said 'Happy Birthday' to one of her work mates and checked the arrangements for that evening. A group of them were meeting up for a few drinks and then going on to an Italian restaurant. It wouldn't be a late one, as it was work again tomorrow morning. If it had been much later in the week, perhaps things would have been different.

'Okay, see you in the Moon at six o'clock' she said, and left them to get on with their day. She went downstairs and called into the admin office. A quick discussion with Sienna about whether she was going home before going out again, and did she want picking up. Then a chaser from Pat about doing her expenses. Clare had to admit to being well behind on that score, which wasn't the norm. Things had been particularly busy for her following Monty's departure and expenses had fallen to the bottom of the pile. She assured Pat that she would get them done this week as there was finally some space in her diary. And she was owed over £450, which would be a welcome booster on the run in to Christmas.

She finished chatting to Pat and then she was off. Out to the car park and into her car. She had just enough time to get across to the site, the windows were being delivered at eleven o'clock and it would take most of the day to install them. Clare enjoyed the drive through the country roads. Her car had a very punchy engine and she made good time, arriving just on the hour.

There was a crane on site, but no lorry with windows was to be seen. She parked up, got out, and walked across to a small group of men near the house. She knew most of them and one turned to greet her. It was Jerry, the person managing the whole project.

'Stuck in traffic, they're going to be here in about twenty minutes' he said.

He went on to check that the others remembered who Clare was. The only one that she hadn't met before was Warren, the crane driver and operator.

'Hey Clare,' said one of the others, 'do you know how he got his name?'

'No. Go on, tell me.'

'His father took one look at him in his cot and said warren ugly fu ...'

'Argh sod off' said Warren. 'If you want those windows lifting out you'd better pack it in with the insults.'

'Ooh, look out' said Jerry, nodding his head slightly in the direction of the site entrance. A sporty two-seater had just driven in and parked up. A woman stepped out of the car and started to make her way across towards them. The group dispersed quickly, leaving Clare and Jerry waiting to greet the visitor. She was dressed in very classy clothes, certainly not conducive to being on a small building site in late October. As she drew closer Clare noted the paleness of the woman's face which contrasted with her long, auburn hair. She recognised her from somewhere but just couldn't put a name to the face, nor remember the circumstances where she might have met the lady before.

'It's Gillian Connor. Dan Connor's wife' Jerry whispered before the newcomer was in earshot. 'And you never know which Gillian Connor you're going to be dealing with.'

Clare gave him a sideways glance, then turned back ready to say hello to Mrs Connor. She had put two and two together. Gillian Connor had been involved in some of the earlier client meetings in the past, but that had been several months ago. Most dealings with the Connors were now being handled by Jerry as the project manager.

'Morning Gillian' he said. 'Don't know if you recall Clare, here. She is the architect from Hanson Scott.'

'Oh, yes, vaguely' Gillian replied, in a brusque tone of voice. 'Where the devil are the windows, Jerry. They were supposed to be here by now. I've taken valuable time out from work this morning and I can't say I'm very happy about being messed about!'

She seemed to gulp, as if trying to hold back a belch of wind, grimaced, and rubbed her tummy gently for a second. Jerry instantly recognised which Gillian had arrived and resigned himself to a cautious defensive strategy. Clare was quick on the uptake and also realised that she would have to be guarded in order to keep things light.

'The crane's here and everyone is ready for action. The lorry with the windows is about fifteen minutes away. It was held up in heavy traffic on the M1. There was a crash near junction 29.'

'Well they had better get a move on and stop holding up proceedings.'

'Erm, I think you'll have to move your car to let the lorry get onto the site.'

'That's nonsense, Jerry. There's plenty of room for people to get past.'

At least he'd tried. Everyone but Gillian could see that there was insufficient turning space for the lorry to get where it would need to be. Gillian paced around for a few minutes, then returned to quiz Jerry on some of the other details and schedule specifics. The lorry came into sight over the hedges of the country road leading up to the Connor house. It turned to enter the site, got part way along the driveway and stopped short. The driver beeped his horn three times.

What followed was a lot of huffing and puffing from Gillian about how incompetent the lorry driver was and how inconvenient it was that she had to move her car. The lorry driver simply leaned out of his window and calmly said that he'd be happy to turn round and go back, if that was what she would rather have happen. That quietened her down. The lorry got onto site and the men began the process of unloading the glazing units one by one and hoisting them into position via the crane, where they would then be fastened into the building framework. Once secured, they would move on to the next panel.

Gillian watched with a critical eye as the first two went into place, then she had had enough and was ready to go. She gave some terse instructions to Jerry and turned to Clare.

'That glass cost us a small fortune. It had better look good!'

And then she went to go. Two strides later she lost her footing on the uneven ground. As she tried to right herself the high heel on her left shoe buckled under the strain.

'Damn! These bloody shoes are ruined now!'

Gillian hobbled comically back to her expensive car, the offending heel in her hand. Clare and Jerry had half offered to assist, but were rebuked. They contained their amusement until they'd heard the door slam shut and the engine growl away down the road.

'Hmmm, nice. And what's the horrible Gillian like?'

'Sometimes she's alright,' Jerry replied. 'I know that might sound hard to believe on the evidence of that performance, but she can be very friendly.'

Clare did find it hard to believe. She had made her own character assessment of Gillian and she would proceed with great caution whenever this particular client was around. Intuitively, Clare sensed that Gillian could quite easily turn out to be very devious and underhand if things weren't working in her favour. And in the long run Clare's intuition would be proven right.

'Well, all that rushing about has given her a touch of indigestion' said Clare.

They watched another two units go into place then everyone was ready to break for lunch. Clare suggested to Jerry that they have a drive along to a cafe that she knew of nearby. They changed their protective boots for normal shoes and jumped into her car. At the cafe they ordered toasted sandwiches and a pot of tea.

'The last time I was in here was the day that Monty died.'

'Oh dear, you should have said. We could have gone somewhere different. You liked him a lot, didn't you?'

'Oh, not like that' she replied, though deep down she couldn't feel totally at one with that comment.

'That's not what I meant. You talk about him a lot at work.'

'Yes. He was a brilliant mentor. Very supportive and encouraging. Very inspiring. I miss chatting to him about architecture and design. I wish he was still here.'

The conversation centred on the remaining elements of the Connor house project and it was soon time to get back over there to see the rest of the glass wall erected. When they were on site again Clare decided that she would take a walk through the house to check on how the internals were progressing. Jerry remained outside to make sure that things were running smoothly. He didn't fancy the prospects of Gillian returning and finding that the job hadn't been finished on time. Plus the Autumn light would work against them as the afternoon wore on.

Clare walked through the entire house. It wasn't far off finished. It would be great to get it completed by the end of November so that the Connors could move in before Christmas. She spent about thirty minutes inside, including five minutes watching the glazing installation from inside on the second floor gallery landing. Fortunately all the stairs were now built in and the balustrades were secure so there was no possibility of another fall like Monty's. She decided it was time to go down and rejoin Jerry outside.

Clare walked across the ground floor of the atrium area towards the glass facade. There was a gap at ground floor level where separate door units were going to be fixed in the following day. She went to step out through the opening. Jerry noticed her approaching the doorway and started waving his yellow hard hat to warn her. Warren interpreted it as a signal and swung the crane to the left. The heavy glazing panel was only three feet off the ground, he'd not started raising it up to the second floor where it was meant to be going. It accelerated to follow the movement of the boom above.

Jerry saw it swinging around and shouted out. Warren realised the boom of the crane was going dangerously close to the house structure and stopped the rotation. The panel still had momentum and continued its swing. Clare stepped out through the gap. She heard the panic calls from Jerry and the others, but it was too late. The rigid vertical edge of the eight foot high panel swung into her, smashing her against the thick oak door jamb. She didn't stand a chance. She was crushed immediately.

25

Monty arrived back home on Saturday 30th October after a terrific, relaxing holiday in a five star hotel in the Maldives. The following day he had turned on his home computer and logged in to catch up on what had been happening while he was away lazing on a beach. He was stunned when he saw the notification from SoulSearch informing him that Clare was coming through on Monday November 8th. He sent a message which he felt confident she would see during her induction session, knowing that she didn't have a wide ranging family out there.

Monty travelled to see her on Tuesday, thinking that she would prefer to get some rest on her first evening in Hinteraevum. She had spent a largely sleepless night in her flat, having just come through from Realworld. Monty found her apartment and rang the bell. The door opened and he was greeted by a young woman with panda-like rings round her eyes. After a hug and a welcoming word, she showed him in and they went through to the lounge. She wiped away some tears and sat down.

'I'm sorry, I've not made much of an effort today' she said, referring to the lack of make-up and her dressing gown attire. 'I must have gigantic bags under my eyes.'

'Don't worry, everybody gets it.' Monty was the same calm and reassuring gentleman that she'd last seen six months ago.

Their conversation quickly accelerated up to speed and Monty was keen to know what had been happening back in Realworld. Clare explained that things were ticking along nicely at Hanson Scott and gave him the latest status of the main projects he had an interest in. Monty listened intently, pleased to be getting some news of what seemed like life back home. Then Clare stopped talking and looked him straight in the eye.

'Monty, there is something I need to know.'

'Oh. This sounds interesting. Fire away.'

'What was going on between you and Nick in the week leading up to your …' She managed to catch herself before breaking one of the most important Hinteraevum principles. She'd been here less than twenty four hours and almost mentioned Monty's fall. 'Before you left Realworld?'

'Why do you ask?'

Clare told him about Nick's abnormal paranoia relating to Monty's office computer, how Ged had helped her find the spreadsheet, then how she had looked at the files from his old laptop. The latter had contained a set of notes that Monty must have typed up during that week to keep a record of the events. His conversation with Sienna. His research. His confrontation with Nick.

'There's not much more to say. I think you've figured it all out from the notes I left. Did you do anything with this information? Did you say anything to Nick?'

'No. I wasn't comfortable approaching him about it.'

'Who else knows?'

'Nobody. Ged was happy helping me, but didn't want to be compromised further by knowing anything I found out.'

'That's very sensible of him.'

'There was something else. I heard ... I heard a rumour that Nick had tried it on with a girl around Christmas time last year. He'd used a date rape drug.'

'And what's that got to do with him fiddling the books to get an extra salary?'

She reminded Monty that he had been very uncharacteristically queezy on the day he died, which happened to be the day after a team night out. She went on to point out that he had sat next to Nick for the final course. Perhaps he had been off guard? Perhaps Nick had spiked his drink?

Monty looked thoughtful. But Clare couldn't go on. She couldn't tell him that she'd been back to the Dan Connor house the Monday after the accident and taken a careful look at the wooden bar that had yielded under Monty's weight. She had found some suspicious hammer marks near each end, potentially evidence of the bar being tampered with before she and Monty had arrived that fateful Friday afternoon. Tampered with to loosen the nails, make it easier for an accident to happen. Nick had a good idea what time they would be there. Nick knew that the view from the gallery landing was a feature not to be missed. And, well, it was a reasonable probability that one would naturally have to lean on the bar to admire the view.

If she got into any of that, she'd be telling Monty how he had come to his end. And that simply would not be the done thing here.

Monty was intrigued by the date rape drug theory that she had mentioned, but he didn't want to go exploring that right now. It was conjuring up too many thoughts of how foul play may have caused his end. The topic was a very dark one to dwell on and this was Clare's first full day in Hinteraevum. She would need cheering up, not depressing. He kept to the financial misdemeanour instead.

'He'd been fiddling the books for at least three years. Maybe more' said Monty, breaking the silence. 'He may have been doing more than simply putting that extra salary into his pocket. I didn't have time to seek any specialist accountant advice. Besides, the guy who actually did the books was one of Nick's friends, so it's highly likely he was pulling the wool over my eyes in lots of ways. I can't do anything about it here, though. We have no access to Realworld. That leaves me very cross because he can continue siphoning off money and Karen will be losing out.'

'I'm sorry Monty, I didn't tell her what I'd found. I was going to tell her but I was still trying to figure out more of the facts. Then this happens and I'm here in Hinteraevum. I'm really sorry. I should have told her earlier.'

'You weren't to know you were going to leave at short notice. Please don't be hard on yourself, Clare.'

He knew that she needed some distraction to help her through today.

'I have a plan. Go and take a shower, put some nice clothes on, and make yourself presentable. I'm going to take you out for lunch.'

Clare was happy to go along with his suggestion. They headed out to the countryside to an old inn and Monty began to give her the same education and familiarisation support that he had received from his parents and Jacko earlier in the year. And, just as Monty had found when he first came through, Clare was so distracted by the conversation that she didn't see how the food arrived. She unfolded her napkin and placed it across her lap. The action jogged her memory. She felt inside her handbag. Before pulling her hand out again, she thought to check whether it was safe to proceed.

'What was the last thing that you can remember from Realworld?'

'Being in that roadside café with you. We were about to go to the Dan Connor house.'

'Ah, good.' She breathed a minor sigh of relief. 'I've got something to show you.'

She pulled out the serviette bearing the amateur world map and Monty laughed.

'You kept it! Excellent. We should do this. It's easy to arrange, you know. Very easy indeed. No limitations. No need to book time off work.'

They began planning feverishly whilst eating their lunch, Clare failing to see who had brought the desserts to the table or topped up their drinks. She brightened up. No job to think about, no money worries, Monty as friendly as ever. She found him very attractive and always enjoyed his company. She liked him more than she'd ever freely admitted to. It wouldn't have been fair in Realworld where he had Karen and an eighteen year marriage to protect.

But here in Hinteraevum things were different. For starters there was no wife to consider. The probability of Karen coming through before the next twenty years were up was very low. Monty's feelings would surely have diminished in that time. And there was every opportunity for Clare to have established a strong relationship with him by then. With all of this swirling around her head, she brightened up as the afternoon ticked on.

Her spirits, however, dampened when they returned to her apartment. She confessed to Monty that she didn't have any friends nearby, no real connections. Her main friendships had been built up around work. Her family wasn't close knit and any relatives that she did have in Hinteraevum were distant, both socially and geographically. There was an old boyfriend from University, but he was living in Australia.

'I've got a large house and there's only me kicking around inside it. I've got spare rooms and I would welcome the company. Why not come and stay with me for a few weeks. At least until you settle into this place. It can take time'.

Clare didn't need much persuading. She packed some things and soon they were both back in Monty's car en route to Conway Road. During the drive he told her that he had an evening engagement that she could accompany him to, if she wasn't already too tired. It was an invitation to the EAST Society quarterly dinner for Engineering, Architecture, Science and Technology professionals in the local area. The focal point of this evening's proceedings was Tommy Morton who had reached a double up at the grand old age of 77r/77h. Monty then spent the next five minutes of the journey explaining the nomenclature he'd just used.

When they arrived he showed her to the bedroom at the front of the house. He thought it best not to mention that she was in a virtual share with George and Betty Franklin. Within a couple of hours she had sorted out her things and made herself at home. She found a dress to wear and made herself presentable for the second time that day. She went downstairs to find Monty in his dinner suit. They set off for what turned out to be a perfectly enjoyable night out.

Later Clare snuggled in under her duvet and looked back on her first full day in Hinteraevum. It had been wonderful. Very satisfying. She felt dreamy and in no time at all went out like a light.

26

Christmas, 2010 (R)

Karen managed a few nights out with her friends on the run up to Christmas, though she was becoming more and more subdued worrying about how she would make it through the festive period. It had always been such a family thing, there would be memories of Monty around every corner and it would be a sad time for them all. She'd done her best to make a fuss of Sam and Gemma, with a fair portion of assistance from her mother and sister who had tactically taken it in turns to get her out and about.

Debbie had remained at Karen's. A few days had turned into a few months and she couldn't face going back home after splitting with Chris. The house wasn't up for sale yet, she would kick that process off later on in January. However, Chris leaving had actually turned out to be just what she needed. She had lead a withdrawn and unenergetic existence for almost two years, putting on a bit of weight and allowing her appearance to drift. Her hair had always been long, wild and frizzy, reflecting her extrovert 'daft Debbie' personality. Sometimes she had left it deliberately unkempt to make a statement. But wild and frizzy had grown a little childish and silly. With the downbeat look, it had now become tired and worn.

She had decided it was time to snap out of her gloom and take on a new lease of life. She started accompanying Karen to the gym and set about churning through her wardrobe. By the end of November those excess pounds had been cast adrift and she was ready for a make-over. Karen had been baking on the first Saturday of December when she heard the front door. She looked up to see her younger sister walk into the kitchen. Her hair was shorter, thicker on top and beautifully layered into the nape of her neck. She twirled through a full three hundred and sixty degrees, showing off her new coat and high heeled shoes, then set down several fashion-shop bags on the floor. The coat came off to reveal a stunning new dress. 'Daft Debbie' had morphed into 'Dazzling Debbie'.

As it was the first Saturday of the month she offered to treat Karen, Sam and Gemma to a family meal to show her appreciation for their support since the breakdown of her marriage. She also wanted to celebrate her new image.

With her confidence restored, Debbie had a great time during December. There were plenty of parties to go to where she could enjoy her freedom and be stimulated by the attention she was now getting. Debbie had more dates in December than there were geese a-laying. There were trips to the recycling to offload clothes, and trips to the shops to replace them. It cheered Karen up to see Debbie enjoying life again, but she flatly refused her sibling's request to expand into Monty's old wardrobe space.

Pauline and Ron came over on Christmas Day and helped to keep things bright and cheerful. After everyone had opened their presents, a less frenetic activity than in previous years, Karen found time to disappear off for a long soak in a hot bath. She relaxed and thought of Monty Christmases. She recalled some of the surprises he had given her and the gifts that she had been proud of finding for him. She washed away a few tears, pulled herself around and put on a dress that she felt he would have enjoyed seeing her in. She went downstairs to find Debbie and her parents busying themselves in the kitchen preparing dinner.

When everything was almost ready, Ron went to carve the turkey.

'It's alright dad, Monty will do that.' Karen immediately realised what she had just said. Ron looked sympathetically at his daughter. Time is a great healer, he thought.

Despite the gaping hole that was the memory of Monty, it was a good day. Karen got through it. Sam and Gemma got through it. Pauline and Ron left at around nine, they were only a twenty minute drive away and Ron hadn't been drinking since having a red wine with his Christmas dinner. Sam and Gemma opted for early nights.

'Come on big sis, there's loads of turkey left, and plenty of wine still in that bottle' said Debbie. 'Let's treat ourselves to a snack and chill for a while.'

They returned from the kitchen, each laden with a turkey sandwich and fresh glass of wine, and slumped on the sofa in the lounge.

'You missed him really badly today,' said Debbie.

'Yes. It's been a nice day, but it's been a tough one as well. We both loved this time of year. It seems wrong that he's not been here sharing it with us all. I'd stopped crying myself to sleep by the end of September, but this last five or six weeks have been incredibly hard.'

'Thanks very much. Am I really such poor company?' her younger sister joked.

'No, it's been great having you stay. You've really cheered me up

126

and helped me through it, Debs. It's just that I miss him so much. There are so many reminders every day. Sometimes when I go to bed at night I lay there and I feel so empty. It's like the middle of my body has been sucked down through the mattress.' She looked along the settee at Debbie. 'I'm sorry. I'm being gloomy and depressing. And I'm not the only one alone. This is your first Christmas without Chris.'

'Yes. But that's very different. I've not missed him one jot. He was bad news for me. It took the separation to make me realise just how much he had stifled me and suppressed my natural spark. I'm far better off without him.'

'You do appear to have enjoyed yourself the last few weeks. And you really do look fantastic. I love the new you.'

'Thank you' she said, softly and slowly. 'I've had a great time. Lots of nights out, lots of fun, lots of compliments, lots of nice attention, and one or two …'

She pressed her top teeth on her lower lip and flashed her eyes furtively. She looked Karen straight in the eye, smiled knowingly, and gave a suggestive roll of her eyes before taking a long sip from her glass of sparkling white wine. Karen faked a look of disapproval then noticed that her sister's expression had changed slightly, becoming a little more serious. She coaxed for more with a simple 'And..?'

'There was a guy that I really liked the look of. One of the big bosses from work, he was eyeing me up at the Christmas party. He kept glancing over in my direction. The trouble is I'm sure he's married. And I don't harbour any ambitions about doing unto others what has been done unto me by the Scottish Tart.'

Karen could tell there was something else on Debbie's mind. She prompted with another 'And..?'

Her younger sister said that she had been assigned to a new project at the pharmaceutical factory where she worked. It would be kicking off in the next few weeks and she had been asked to get involved because of her specialist knowledge, but no further details had been forthcoming. It was commonplace that developing new medicines required some confidentiality, but this one was shrouded in more secrecy than any other project she had worked on there.

'I'm sure it will all become clear in January,' said Karen. 'And I'm sure there's someone nice out there waiting for you.' She looked at her watch. 'It's midnight. That's Christmas Day over, thank goodness.'

'I'm sure they will get better' Debbie offered up. 'And who

knows, there may be someone nice out there waiting for you too. But not that creepy Nick! You really ought to put him out of his misery before too long.'

'Yes, you're right. I'll do that in the New Year. Now, it's time to tidy these things away and get to bed.'

27

Christmas, 2010 (H)

Monty had enjoyed December. There were lots of events to take his mind off what Karen might be doing in Realworld. Not that he hadn't spent many an hour thinking about her. What would she be doing? How she was getting on? How were the children? It was nice having a lot of distractions to help minimise the time spent reflecting.

Clare had remained at Monty's. A few days had turned into a few months and she simply couldn't stand the idea of going back to that lonely apartment. She'd gradually moved all her clothes down to her new temporary home, generating a request to Monty for more hanging space and drawers. He wasn't prepared to allow her to use Karen's share of the main bedroom's walk-in wardrobe, but he did give her permission to expand into Gemma's bedroom for storage.

As Christmas drew closer he explained to Clare that he was going to spend a few weeks with his parents. She didn't say anything straight away, but she moped around for a few days and Monty soon picked up the vibes. After a conversation with his mother he broached the subject with Clare at breakfast one morning, asking if she would like to join his family for Christmas in Darlington. She was delighted and gave him a big hug.

Roger and Marianne made a fuss of her and she couldn't have felt more welcome. Marianne found the right opportunity to have a quiet word with her son to make sure that there was clarity over where the boundaries were between him and his friend. Monty reassured his mother that this was purely platonic and it would take a long time for him to get over not having Karen by his side. As things stood right now, he couldn't foresee ever getting to that point, so there was little chance of him falling into a new romance in Hinteraevum. Not yet, anyway.

Christmas Day duly arrived. Clare had been awake early and had gone downstairs to find herself some breakfast. Marianne was in the kitchen checking the turkey's progress in the oven. They spent some time chatting then Clare offered to take a cup of tea and some toast up for Monty. She knocked at his door and went in to the bedroom. He was still fast asleep, lying on his back with his face tilted to the left. She walked across the room, placed the plate and cup on the bedside table and sat down on the edge of the bed. She leaned over and gently kissed his cheek, adding a 'Merry Christmas Monty'.

Eyes remaining shut, he turned his head towards the wake-up call and brought his left arm up around her shoulders. They came together in a deep kiss, she felt his tongue probe into her mouth. It made her tingle. An intense burst of pleasure contending with the nervousness of being found in this rather compromising position. With a mild touch of guilt she eased back from him and he slowly drew open his eyelids.

'Merry Christmas Ka-lare! Oh, no, I'm sorry. I'm really sorry, Clare. That was very inappropriate of me. I thought...'

'It's not your fault Monty. It was wrong of me to do that. I caught you completely off guard. I didn't mean to. I'm sorry. That probably wasn't the best way for you to start Christmas Day.' She drew breath. 'I've brought you some tea and toast for breakfast.'

Monty looked up at her. She was still leaning over him, wearing a light blue silk nightdress with matching dressing gown. He had to accept that it could have been a lot worse. After all, he had enjoyed that short and swift encounter. But he also felt the little shockwave tremors as his thoughts flashed to Karen and Sam and Gemma waking up to their first Christmas without him.

'Thank you very much, that was really nice of you.' His remark caused her to let out a giggle. 'For the toast. And the tea. Thank you for ... for bringing me breakfast. Sorry. That must have been a particularly unpleasant experience for you.'

Clare eased herself up off the bed and took two steps towards the door. She glanced round at him.

'No. Far from it, actually.'

The house was busy through the day. Some of Monty's relatives came round for dinner, so the conversation rarely dried up. In the quieter moments his mind turned to what might be happening in Realworld, but he was soon snapped out of it by someone drawing him into another conversation, or asking him for some help with the vegetables, or to set the table. He began to wonder if his parents had set out tactical manoeuvres to prevent any possibility of him going all maudlin on them.

When dinner was almost ready, Roger took up the carving knife and was just about to start slicing the turkey.

'It's alright Roger, Monty will do that' Marianne interrupted. Roger looked around at her.

'It's his first Christmas in Hinteraevum,' she continued. 'The least we can do is let him carve the turkey.'

That evening Marianne and Roger decided to go to bed at 10 o'clock. Clare offered to replenish drinks and make a late supper for her and Monty. She went through to the kitchen leaving him listening to a Christmas CD. He sat staring across the lounge at the Christmas tree, thinking of how much he was missing Karen. It was his first peaceful moment of real relaxation that day and his head quickly swirled with memories of Karen Christmases. The lights on the tree had become unfocused and spangly, he sensed his eyes were on the brink of shedding tears. It was a reversal from when he'd found himself in a similar reflective state in his own home in Realworld, thinking about how much he missed his parents.

Clare returned with a tray bearing turkey sandwiches, a glass of red wine for her, and a whisky for Monty.

'Are you alright?'

'Yes, thanks.' He swept the moisture from his eyes and sniffed. 'Just got absorbed in my own little world thinking about Karen and the children. Couldn't help wondering how their day has been.'

'You've missed them today, haven't you?' To which he nodded. 'I'm sorry about this morning. It must have been awkward having me here today.'

'No, it's been nice. I've enjoyed your company. You and Jacko, it's like having a twin brother and a younger sister around.'

Clare didn't know how to react to that comment so she switched conversation to neutral subjects, like the film they had watched on television, and the relatives who had spent the day with them. Monty might take a long time forgetting about Karen, so she would have to choose her moments carefully.

On New Year's Eve they attended a party at a local hotel with Jacko, who was accompanied by Julia Henderson. She remembered Monty as one of her younger brother's friends and both she and Jacko were able to reintroduce him to several other acquaintances from his distant youth. They had a lively evening and the time soon approached midnight. They were all up on the dance floor when the final countdown came and the bells chimed in 2011.

Clare cuddled in to Monty and he held her waist. Her high heels reduced their natural height difference by such a degree that he could feel her soft cheek against his. The smell of her hair and her perfume was mildly intoxicating for him. Her lips gently pressed a kiss on his cheek and her head moved slowly. Her hair brushing lightly, slowly, across the tip of his nose, his mouth and chin. He felt another soft kiss on the right hand corner of his mouth. And another, and another, slowly edging ever more central until she was lined up perfectly in front of him. He was drawn in. Tilting his head to his left, he responded and their mouths came together.

Jacko and Julia had been locked in a long and impassioned embrace. They finally unhinged and looked round to see their friends up close and personal. They interrupted and greetings were exchanged amidst the usual frenzy that is the first few minutes of any new year. Jacko shook Monty firmly by the hand and slapped him on the shoulder.

'Happy New Year matey. This may be a bit selfish of me, but I'm glad you're here.'

'Happy New Year. I'm still not sure I'm glad to be here, but it's gradually getting better.'

'Just take things easy, Monty' he said, glancing towards Clare. 'Don't rush into something that you might regret. You've still got ninety-nine years to enjoy.'

Later in the evening Jacko asked Julia to occupy Monty on the dance floor. Clare had gone for a comfort break and as she returned he intercepted her to request help bringing some drinks from the bar.

'Clare, I know that you're very fond of Monty and you both seem to be very good friends. I hope you don't mind me offering you a little piece of advice. If you want this to work, just take things slowly. I've seen this happen several times here in Hinteraevum, and it can turn out to be a bit of a car crash when one person is getting ahead of the other. Monty is still hurting about Karen. And Sam and Gemma for that matter. But particularly Karen. He could so easily respond negatively towards you if he feels that those memories are being threatened in any way.'

Clare looked at him. It sounded like a sensible steer. He wasn't telling her to back off completely. He wasn't telling her it would never work. She gave an appreciative nod.

'I like you, Clare. You're a lovely person. If you weren't, I wouldn't have bothered giving you any advice at all.'

He smiled at her then leaned forward and kissed her on the cheek. He caught the smell of her hair and perfume. He lingered for the tiniest fraction of a second before stepping back and handing two glasses of white wine to her from off the bar.

28

Nick took his seat at the table. He was an unaccompanied guest, which wasn't quite how he'd wanted it to be. Still, he'd make the best of what the night had to offer. There were plenty of local dignitaries, including current and potential clients, so he would turn on his charm as and when he felt it would advance business matters. The event had become more popular with women over the years. As he looked around he could see that the majority were already spoken for, so his charms would probably not be required in that department.

Three weeks earlier he had made the phone call. Gemma had answered it and turned to her mum mouthing 'creep' and pointing at the handset. As Karen took hold of the phone, Gemma gestured putting her fingers in her mouth as if making herself sick. Karen began with a polite 'hello' and a Happy New Year greeting. After his own introductory pleasantries Nick asked if she would like to accompany him to a Burns Night supper on Tuesday the 25th of January.

'It's very nice of you to think of me, Nick. I'm not ready to accompany people to public functions like that and I really wouldn't feel comfortable going along as your guest. After all, it's less than a year since I lost Monty … my husband and your business partner. It wouldn't be right. I've hardly been going out with my girl friends, let alone even thinking about male company.'

'I thought that when we talked a few months ago you said that I should give you a call after Christmas.'

'That's not quite right, Nick. I said that November and December were full of family memories, so I was going to spend that time very quietly at home.' Karen remained calm and affable. 'I am truly sorry if there was a misunderstanding but you should not have misinterpreted that as an open invitation to call me in the first week of January.'

'I thought we could at least be good friends.'

'We can remain good acquaintances. That makes a lot of sense considering that we are joint owners of the Hanson Scott practice.'

Ouch. Nick didn't like being reminded of that, but he caught himself before he uttered a whiplash comment that any reasonable person might regret later.

'True. And I sincerely hope that you trust me to continue growing its good fortune.'

Karen wound the call to an amicable close and stood for a few moments staring at the telephone in her right hand, wondering if she had been clear enough.

Nick relaxed back in his leather armchair and tapped his mobile against his lips, subconsciously kissing Karen a remote goodnight. She had apologised for the misunderstanding and was keen to remain good friends, but needed a bit more time to acclimatise to being single. She wanted him to keep her informed about the business and avoid asking her to any more events until later in the year. 'But how much later should he leave it?' he thought to himself.

The following day he had gone along to the club after work and practiced with one of the rifles. The previous evening's phone call had been replaying in his mind and he was beginning to question whether he'd got it wrong. She had accepted her part in the misunderstanding but had also accused him of misinterpreting. Had he? How? And was he misinterpreting again? And what was that throwaway line about her having girlfriends? Was she ...?

'Thsssst.'

He was unable to concentrate on his shooting. It was one of the rare occasions when he just couldn't settle. He gradually grew irate, stomped back to the store room, selected the emergency exit door by mistake and set off the alarm again.

Now he was at a round table with nine others. Four couples and Liz, sitting alternately man-woman. He was between two of the wives and he found it terribly hard to maintain conversation with either of them. He attempted to join the discussions to his right and left, but the others at his table were very good friends and kept gravitating back together. Nick was the odd man out. He slowly followed the proceedings and partook of a lonely meal. Directly opposite him Liz was having a fantastic evening, effortlessly breezing in and out of conversations with everybody.

After the meal he jumped up at the earliest opportunity and made his way across to the bar where he sunk a couple of stiff Whiskies in quick succession. Liz caught up with him as he was being served a third.

'Enjoying the evening?'

'Yes, very nice. Excellent meal. Very ...very good. Yes.'

'Really?' She pressed him for a more honest response.

'No. I rather hoped that I would have had some company.' She looked at him. 'Somebody let me down at the last minute,' he lied.

'Come with me, there are some people I want you to meet.'

She introduced him to four contacts that she had been talking to earlier in the evening. Three were businessmen who had potential projects that would be of interest to Hanson Scott. The fourth was a local sports personality who was looking for someone to design a futuristic house on a piece of land that he had his eyes on. She was turning out to be one of his best sales reps by proxy.

With the drink and the assistance from Liz he began to enjoy the latter part of the evening. Whilst chaperoning him around the room after the meal she had brushed against him, subtly and slightly suggestively, on three occasions. Nick had thought her a tad clumsy and put it down to the drink. Nevertheless, she invited him home for a nightcap and they shared a taxi back to her house.

He made himself comfortable on her sofa and sipped at the smokey malt, savouring the warmth as it coated his palate. Liz sat down close beside him and drew her legs up onto the seat. She was wearing a dark green dress highlighted with a tartan sash. It wasn't the longest in her wardrobe and as she made herself comfortable she deliberately drew the bottom hem up her thigh, exposing a glimpse of her stocking top.

She began by asking if he had managed to enjoy the function, despite having been something of an outsider at the dining table. She anticipated they would ease into a mellow exchange of small talk about how nice the evening had been. She was sadly mistaken. Nick bemoaned the way he had been rejected and began asking Liz for her advice on how best to woo the absentee third party. She realised there was no point fighting it so she sat back, rearranged her dress, and humoured him with some coaching.

Is the woman married? Err, she was no longer living with her husband.

Was that recent? It happened just under a year ago.

Does she have feelings for you? I believe she does, but she needs time.

It didn't take Liz much effort to work out who was the subject of Nick's desires. She told him to back off gracefully for a while, give this woman a lot of space to adjust, finish his Whisky and go sleep in the spare room.

29

It was a dull and unpleasant day. Clare was skulking around the house having been out to the shops in the village. She had hoped they could have gone for a longer walk in the countryside but the weather was far from favourable. She went upstairs to get a novel from her room. It was on the dressing table. She picked it up and turned to go back downstairs but something caught her eye. She looked back. It was that serviette.

She went downstairs into the kitchen and found Monty sitting at the island doing the crossword from the weekend's newspaper. She set the serviette down on top of the paper, derailing his attempts at 35 across - 'I carry a flower backwards in the Middle East'.

'Come on, it's about time we planned this grand tour and got it off the ground. Napkin-world 2011! That's what we're going to call it. We can even get tour tee-shirts made if you'd like.' She switched the coffee machine on.

'Napkin-world, eh? Yes. Let's set out a schedule, we've been meaning to do this ever since you came through.' He left the room and returned with an atlas.

They began working out their list, putting the flesh on the bones that had been laid out in the roadside cafe nine months before. He wanted to do the route in phases of three weeks, allowing for time back at home between each spell. Clare was keen to have more extended periods abroad, figuring that the longer Monty was away with her the more frayed his ties to Karen might become. She would also have the opportunity to slip in a few twin room hotel stays. Or even the occasional double room if she was lucky.

The cities were plotted, taking climate variations into consideration. There was nothing preventing them from departing straight away but pragmatism prevailed and they gave themselves a couple of days to straighten things around the house and pack. They would begin on Saturday. Monty asked to be reminded where they had agreed to start. She confirmed it was Dubai.

'That's it! Dubai!'

Clare was surprised by Monty's sudden burst of rampant enthusiasm. Monty looked at her. He reached for the pen and the newspaper.

'Dubai. 35 across. I carry a flower backwards. I, a, bud, backwards. Dubai.'

Clare took it as a positive omen.

30

Debbie was just about finished, she had been working on the project late into the afternoon. The senior boss walked in and started chatting to her. He was the one that she had often noticed looking across at her during project meetings. She felt an electricity between them. She was sure he was attracted to her, but he was keeping it under control. She was definitely attracted to him but had major reservations about getting caught up with a man who was wearing a wedding ring.

He was a little anxious about the project and was keeping a close watch on it because the client was very important. He suggested going for a drink at the local pub where many of the employees tended to go on a Friday after close of business. When they arrived there were very few work colleagues around, chiefly because it was already past six thirty. Most of them would either have gone home by that time, or moved on to spend the evening in the town centre venues. He insisted on buying the drinks and they spent a long time chatting with a couple of other people from the factory, a production guy and a female marketing manager. Debbie didn't know either of them but found it interesting mixing with some totally different people for a change.

The woman asked him about his wife. He became a little guarded and just offered that she was OK and had gone away to Brussels with some of her friends for the weekend. Debbie got the impression that there may be something not quite right there, possibly a skeleton in the cupboard. He took another mouthful of his lemonade and immediately perked up. He asked if anyone would like to join him for something to eat, he was in need of some more company this evening. It had been a busy week at work and he couldn't really face going home to cook, nor did he fancy a take away. Debbie was up for it, but the other two declined. This made her feel a bit awkward and she gave him a get-out clause, suggesting that he may want that take away after all rather than having to put up with her for another hour.

'Of course not' he replied, brushing her self deprecating comment aside. 'I hope you won't feel odd, it just being the two of us. We're simply work colleagues.'

She considered it for a moment then replied.

'Sure, a meal with a friend from work is okay. And as there's two of us that would make it even, not odd.'

Their conversation began with life in Ronnoc Pharmaceuticals, he was interested to hear what she thought of the company. He wouldn't be drawn into any further discussion about the project, particularly where it meandered too close to the specifics of the client. The time flew by. Debbie had a few glasses of wine, not enough to lose any of her controls, but enough to relax and be her old bubbly self. He kept to soft drinks as he was driving. Debbie found that he was very personable and had a caring attitude for the staff at work. He never strayed anywhere near being inappropriate and she felt as though he had treated her like a peer, there was no sign of this being a top level manager talking down to the proletariat.

He offered her a lift home and on the way she recounted her situation with Chris and how she had moved in to stay with her older sister for a while. They arrived on Conway Road and she showed him where to pull over near Karen's driveway. He turned to her.

'Thank you for being great company this evening, I've really enjoyed it. I found it refreshing being out with someone from work who has personality and a backbone. You speak your mind. I see so many of our employees fawning and gushing around me because I run the place. Or, worse still, going completely overawed and clamming up.'

'You treated me with a lot of respect and made me feel comfortable. That can't be said of all bosses.'

'I'd also like to say thank you for the way you are dedicating yourself to the project. I can see the value that you are bringing and it is appreciated. Please keep up the good work.'

The recognition made her feel warm inside.

He got out of the car and walked around to open the passenger door. Holding out his hand he helped her out of the car. She almost stepped into him as she rose out of the seat and stood up. For a second or two it felt awkward. As Debbie composed herself he said goodnight. Impulsively she said 'thank you' and pecked him on the cheek. He gave a chuckle.

'You would raise a sexual harassment case if I'd done that to you.'

She looked up at his dark eyes.

'Hmmm, I don't think I'd be lodging any complaints.'

He stared at her and realised that he was still holding her hand. He released it but remained standing between her and the entrance to

Karen's drive, accidentally blocking her path. She swayed her body a couple of times to signal that she wanted to get past him and he stepped aside with an apology written right across his face.

'Is it a take away tomorrow evening?' Debbie asked.

'I'll have you know that I am capable of cooking for myself. But …' he paused, 'I will probably end up in Marco's again.'

'If you find yourself short of company …' she joked.

And that's how it started.

31

Karen had been preparing for Sam going off to university, sorting out bedding, clothes, cutlery, crockery. They had all been away for a break in France during the Summer holidays and had arrived back in time for him to pick up his exam results, which had satisfied his entrance requirements with ease. Now that the day had finally arrived Karen was beginning to find the reality of him leaving home more painful than she had anticipated, even though it was a temporary term time arrangement.

Sam was feeling the butterflies. He was gathering things together and taking them out of the front door to load them into the car. Every trip back and forth onto the driveway made him wonder just how much his father would have been proud of him today. It was also fair to say that Sam had some self inflicted suffering. He had been out with his friends on Friday evening celebrating their imminent departures by having a late night down at The Blue Lion in the village.

Debbie and Gemma were helping. It would be more accurate to say that Gemma was interspersing helping with annoying. It was her way of coping with the realisation that the house would be emptier without her brother at home. Pauline and Ron called round to give Sam their love and best wishes, the latter taking the form of £50 and a twelve pack of lagers.

The postman walked up the drive just as Sam was completing another loading operation. There were four letters, two for Karen and two for Sam. He opened his as he ambled back into the house. They were both 'good luck' cards. The first from his uncle, Monty's brother. He was puzzling over the second as he walked into the kitchen. Karen took a look, it might be from one of their distant relations. She was upset by what she saw.

The card was from Nick. There was £50 inside with a message saying 'enjoy Freshers week'. She took the card and told Sam that he couldn't possibly accept this. It was inappropriate and Karen would return it next week via Cartmel House. Sam was disappointed. Maybe Nick wasn't so bad after all, and that cash would have bought a few beers in the bar.

Debbie wasn't going with them today, she had another engagement. Karen could tell something was going on because her younger sister was in high spirits. Debbie had been enjoying life without Chris. There had been a string of boyfriends, but there had been something more permanent and more interesting afoot for the last two months. At the same time Karen had seen her sister intensely absorbed about her work, to the point of being strained. She was very secretive about who the new man was. She wouldn't give much away at all. Debbie had never conducted a relationship like this and it worried Karen that her sister was getting into something dangerous.

It was true that Debbie was finding work exciting and stressful. The research and development of a new drug was highly fulfilling and was giving her a lot more to think about than her normal role. She was still unable to get any real insight into who the beneficiary was. She was handed a case file that had been desensitised. From what she read it looked as though there was only one person, a female, lined up to test the results of her endeavours. That seemed really odd. Without breaking any confidentiality she had talked to other colleagues and got the general opinion that any new medicine would be tested by a broader group of people. It crossed her mind that this could even be someone on a personal, and perhaps private, mission.

Outside work Debbie had slipped and stumbled headlong into an affair with the boss. It happened so quickly that she hadn't given fair consideration to the potential consequences. He had a wife. There was definitely some instability about his home relationship, but it wasn't obvious what that was. It didn't seem to be the usual 'my wife doesn't understand me' routine. He wasn't that trite. He seemed to be strained and upset by something, rather than cross and angry. With Debbie it wasn't so much a case of being hoisted by her own petard, it was more like 'gamekeeper turned poacher'.

Karen and Gemma returned home late in the evening. The house was very quiet. Gemma remarked that she liked it that way, without Sam's music and guitar blaring from his room. Karen disagreed. Monty had gone. Now Sam was absent too. At least she'd still be able to see her son. She and Gemma both opted for an early night.

32

Thursday November 24th, 2011 (H)

Clare woke first. She was facing the edge of the bed and could hear his soft breathing behind her. She turned carefully so as to avoid disturbing him and lay on her left flank, her head in the soft pillows, just eyeing him casually. It was the start of another glorious Spring day in Sydney and they would be setting off on the return journey to England this afternoon, marking the end of their Napkinworld 2011 grand tour. They had seen a lot, but there were still plenty of sights to see, buildings to look up to, and bridges to admire.

'Would there be a Napkinworld 2012?' she pondered.

She reflected on her strategy. Taking her time and playing her cards sensitively had been the right thing to do. She had Jacko to thank for his tip on New Year's Eve. Yes, she had managed to persuade Monty that they could stay away a little longer than he had wanted. She had reminded him that if the worst were to happen to Karen back in Realworld he would get two week's notice of her arrival in Hinteraevum. That would be ample time for him to make his return from anywhere on the planet. That said, she did find herself coming out in sympathy. This trip to the Far East was now in its fifth week and even Clare herself had to admit to being ready for home.

She had introduced twin bed rooms during the summer when they were in the USA, claiming that she felt less secure in separate rooms in the large cities. This had become more the norm during this trip, particularly in Kuala Lumpur, Singapore and Shanghai. She found herself 'accidentally' naked on occasions when Monty stepped back into the main room after his morning shower. He gradually found himself increasingly comfortable with the arrangements and they both became more laissez faire about living in close quarters. The odd double room was thrown into the schedule, leading to a lot of playful exchanges about invisible boundary lines down the middle of the bed. But Clare would make illegal border crossings during the night in search of a reassuring arm that could be cast around her.

Monty was still very stoical about it all. He was coming to terms with this new life and was certainly enjoying being with Clare, but he still seemed to be thinking of her as that younger sister he had mentioned. He didn't seem happy to commit to anything more than close friendship. Clare was hoping he might get to the breaking point where he would indulge in a bit of incest with that younger sister, but so far that had remained a pipe dream.

There had been some close moments. He had shown romance and a hint of passion a number of times. Like the evening in Chicago. After spending the earlier part of the day going up the Sears and John Hancock Towers they ate at a fantastic steak house then went to a bar on Rush Street to take in some live music. The drinks went down very easily, the atmosphere was truly relaxing, the blues music was velvet smooth. Clare thought it might be the night. The regular replenishment of gin and tonic rendered Monty very affectionate but incapable of anything other than a sound night's sleep with an irregular snore.

When they arrived in Australia Clare was beginning to wonder if anything would ever happen with Monty, her Plan A. The slow game was wearing a little heavy on her and she could sense an inner frustration. During the last few weeks she had been thinking about Plan B. She had looked up her old University friend Sean on SoulSearch only to find that he was happily paired up with a very attractive local woman. She hid her disappointment well and concluded that Plan A was worth a more concerted effort. She would turn up her powers of persuasion with Monty during their last few days in Sydney. After all, it was a year since she had first arrived in Hinteraevum and moved in with him.

One of the highlights on the original serviette was Sydney harbour. They spent a lot of time on Wednesday exploring the details of the Opera House, then found somewhere to sit and look up at its majestic sail-like roof structure. It was a true icon, they'd both seen it in so many books, it was so familiar. Yet there was nothing to compare with sitting nearby simply gazing at it. For almost an hour they talked about its beauty, its architectural qualities. This was when Clare felt closest to him, the pair engrossed in their shared passion. She saw her ability to engage with Monty on this topic so fluently, so naturally, as her big advantage over Karen. It was a good strategy to end the trip on this high.

Clare's friend Sean had recommended a restaurant in the city, not far from their hotel. They enjoyed dinner, stepping through a critique of what they had seen during the recent weeks. Which had been their favourite buildings? And why? What had caught them by surprise? What was the biggest disappointment? Clare had made it a regular feature of all their tour legs, rounding off each phase on her strong bonding topic.

Monty felt chilled. He had been a little uncertain of Clare's motivations for seeing her old friend. He'd not let on to her, but he was quite nervous that she had intentions of staying here with her old flame. And he realized he would miss her. They'd lived together for the last twelve months and he'd had a truly marvelous time doing Napkinworld 2011 with her. He was relieved when things turned out as they did. He would have felt very lonely going back to Conway Road and living in solitude.

They returned to the hotel with Monty's arm around her waist and her head resting into his shoulder. Upon arrival in their room he was first to use the bathroom. He reappeared and walked across towards her. He pulled her in towards him, put his arms around her and kissed her. It was long and slow. Clare sensed passion bubbling to the surface.

'It's been another fantastic trip' he said.

She nodded in agreement and eased herself away to go to the bathroom.

Monty stripped off and slumped into bed. He was tired. He often felt this woozy sensation when he knew he was about to return home after a foreign visit. It had always been the same in Realworld. It was as though the adrenaline had run out, like he'd been switched into hibernate mode for the flight back.

Clare finished her preparations in the en-suite. Teeth brushed. Squirt of perfume on. Stripped down to her nothings. She looked herself up and down in the mirror, then opened the door. She walked over to the bed and rolled in next to Monty who was facing away from her. To her surprise he was completely naked too. She drew in close to him, her right nipple touched his bare back as she wrapped her arm around him, her hand sensing the hair on his chest. But there was no reaction at all. Monty was sound asleep and could not be roused.

And there she was, the following morning, looking at him from her side of the bed. Every opportunity had deflated to nothing. It was almost comical, she thought. He was a fantastic friend, so she didn't want to break that bond. But she longed for that bond to be just that little bit closer and more permanent.

Clare was feeling mellow. She inched herself across no man's land in the middle of the bed and felt across for the hairs on his chest again. She stroked her fingers through them and down to his stomach. Then onwards to below his waist line. She detected an early morning erection and began to fumble with it. Monty tensed and inhaled in reaction to her playful fingers. He opened his eyes and turned his body so that he could see her.

'Do you like your wake-up call?'

'I do. It's very nice indeed.'

But she knew from his apologetic look and tone of voice that something wasn't quite as enjoyable as it ought to be.

'What's wrong?'

'Clare, I've so enjoyed these trips and we've become such very, very close friends.'

'But … ?'

'I'm still not sure this is right for us. For me. You are fantastic. Excellent to be with, you're lively and fun. I find you attractive and very sexy. The 'but' is that I have loved Karen for twenty years. I love her with all of my heart. And I can't simply erase that from my mind. I realise that it may be many years before she comes through. I long for that day, yet I really don't know how I will deal with it. What she might look like. How the age difference will work out. I know that these feelings will gradually diminish. What I don't know is how long that will take.'

The erection had certainly diminished and Clare retracted her hand. She rolled onto her back, gazing up blankly at the white ceiling.

'I'm sorry if my repetitive rejections are hurting you' he continued. 'The last thing I want to do is put our friendship at risk and I really believe that could happen if we embark on something now. Particularly today.'

Clare turned her head towards him, her face projecting the question 'why?'

'Today is Karen's birthday,' he said.

Clare let out a slow sigh and rolled her way out of the bed. She stood up and he was presented with a full frontal. She had a gorgeous body, he couldn't deny it.

'So, we stay good friends?' she asked. He nodded. 'Is it alright if I continue to live with you?'

'Yes, I'd like that. I'd like that a lot.'

She slinked across to the bathroom. As she showered, Clare tried to rationalise the situation. Monty had said that this would probably work out some time, though Karen was etched into him so deep and so indelibly that Clare translated 'some time' into 'an exceptionally long time'. In all practical terms Plan A was also out of the window.

Her mind wandered to the vision of her loosely formed plan C. She liked the idea of another option that might bear fruit in the shorter term. She definitely fancied him. He was good fun. Very interesting. Enigmatic. And, importantly, there was no matrimonial baggage attached. And she had a strong suspicion that he fancied her too. The more she considered it, the more she warmed to the idea.

By the time she was towelling herself dry Monty had been relegated to Plan B, and Plan C had been promoted to become the new Plan A.

33

Debbie read the set of notes. The test subject, the lady, had been taking the medication for four months and there were encouraging signs that her condition might be stabilising. However, this was not without some side effects. The patient was demonstrating an increase in blood pressure and occasional, though more frequent, headaches. Debbie carefully assessed this input and spent most of the day working out how to modify the medication. She eventually sat back and took a look at the time. It was already twenty past one. She hadn't taken a break since coming in at eight so she left her desk and walked round to the cafeteria. She paid the cashier and joined her team leader at a table. He asked how her morning had been and listened carefully as she explained her next steps.

'I'm still very puzzled by this assignment though,' she said. 'There's a lot of mystery about it. A rare condition, only one person as a test case. No hint of a large pharmaceutical taking this on as a longer term product. There are some rumours circulating about who the subject .. sorry … the woman is. I think there's something fishy going on.'

'There are some other rumours, Debbie.'

She looked up from her lunch tray. He cast his eye around, then leaned forward and spoke quietly.

'Is there something fishy going on between you and somebody at the top table?'

She looked back down at her lunch and pushed pieces of her salad with the fork, a reaction that signposted a 'yes' answer.

'You know he's married. You're into some complicated circumstances here, Debbie. Try not to make it more knotty.'

'I know he's married. I've known all along. Believe me, I never thought I would do this, especially with someone at work. So I accept that there are some compromises. I can't see him as often, or as freely, as I would like. Actually, despite us both working here, I rarely see him in the office and that means that I can keep my relationship distinctly separate from my work.'

Her final comment seemed to resonate with him. He knew that her work was more closely linked to her relationship than she was giving credit for. He had finished his fish and chips and was due in a two o'clock meeting. He stood up and lifted his tray.

'Try not to get too close Debbie. Nobody wants to see you get hurt by this.'

She continued pushing the salad around the plate, more puzzled now than she was when she sat down to eat. Tonight would help. A night out with her friends, time to let her hair down. He was going to a function where it would be too risky to be seen in public with Debbie. He was taking his wife. It was a compromise evening.

Karen was also going out this evening. After much persuasion and cajoling by friends she had finally agreed to stop moping around at home and make it along to the Millingtons' party. They had a large house on the other side of the village and always held a Christmas event early in December. Karen and Monty had known the Millingtons a long time and were sadly missed last year, Karen being in no great mood for such a social occasion.

Julie and her husband called round to give Karen a lift and to make sure that she didn't have to walk into the party alone. She soon got into the spirit of fun, slowly but surely becoming relaxed about being there with no Monty at her side. She was enjoying meeting up with neighbours and acquaintances from the various village societies she supported. She went into the kitchen to refill her glass and came across a familiar face. It was Liz, who she had met a few times before at this very same house party.

'Hello, how are you? I didn't see you here last year, everybody missed you.'

'No, I was hibernating. I lost Monty in the April and I declared myself unfit for social duties.'

'Yes, I heard. It must have been terrible for you. I'm really pleased that you've come this evening, it's lovely to see you again.'

They stepped away from the drinks table and continued their conversation. Then Karen felt a tap on her shoulder and turned around. It was Nick. He had come along with Liz. He welcomed her effusively, catching her off guard with his peck on the cheek greeting. It was a bit too effusive for Karen who found it made her cringe. It wasn't unlike many of the greetings that she had had from the males this evening but because it was Nick she squirmed almost visibly. Liz noticed and took Nick by the arm.

'Would you excuse us Karen, I'm beginning to feel peckish. Nick, come and help me get some of that delicious buffet.' As she ushered him out of the kitchen and in the direction of the dining room, she gave Karen a little wink.

Karen left it a few minutes before she ventured through to get something to eat. There was a considerable buffet spread out on the dining table in the middle of the room, the food looked sumptuous as usual. She picked up a plate and worked her way around, starting near the salmon. She noticed a couple on the opposite side of the table. He was tall and muscular, with dark hair and swarthy features. The woman was a little taller than Karen, her hair was brown and flared with a copper hue under the light. It was Dan and Gillian Connor, though Karen wasn't to know that. She found him very handsome.

Dan happened to glance across at Karen then looked down at his plate again. He immediately did a double take, thinking he recognised her. He froze for a moment. She reminded him of someone else but, thankfully, it wasn't who he thought it was. Karen and Dan found themselves staring across the table at each other. Gillian also looked up, noticing that Dan had stopped putting food on his plate.

Karen gave a friendly 'hello' across the table. Dan responded with an equally pleasant 'hi'. Then all three returned to the job in hand.

'Who is that?' asked Gillian

'I don't actually know' her husband replied. 'I thought it was someone from the office, but I was mistaken.'

Gillian had also taken a close look. She had grown increasingly suspicious of Dan over the last two months and had followed him at least three times in the past fortnight. The person her husband had just spoken to bore some similarity to the other woman, but Gillian knew this wasn't the one that was intruding in her marriage with Dan.

Nick engineered four further opportunities to encounter Karen during the evening. She was rescued twice by Liz running interference, once by the fictitious demands of her own bladder, and finally by her friend Julie pulling her away to meet another neighbour. Karen was attempting to escape Nick's company by telling him that it was time for her to leave the party, a move which backfired because he took it as an invitation to walk her home. Julie appeared just as Karen was trying to make it clear that she was happy to get a taxi alone. Julie and her husband gave Karen safe passage and Liz was once again left to listen to Nick's lament.

Dan and Gillian Connor left shortly afterwards. Dan had been in full swing at the party, but Gillian was hit with another bout of indigestion and had become irritable and tetchy. They had come close to having an argument, so Dan felt that an earlier and more dignified exit was for the better.

34

February-March, 2012 (R)

Pauline and Ron looked up as Karen entered the room. Debbie was still a little groggy but she smiled, pleased to see her sister. It was the first time they'd all been together in a hospital since Karen had had Gemma eighteen years ago. Debbie was resting, she looked as white as the sheets that enveloped her. Thankfully she wasn't very far into the pregnancy when the miscarriage had occurred.

It had been a horrible three months for her. Back in December she had recommended an amendment to the formulation of the trial medication. It had been reviewed carefully by her superiors and several other specialists at the lab and her conclusions had been supported by them all. A new batch had been prepared and the recipient had begun taking them early in January. The results were positive at first, then in February there was some shocking news. The trial was brought to a standstill because the test patient had lapsed into a coma. Debbie was distraught when she heard.

Debbie got great support at work. Everybody stood by her, recognising that she had taken all the correct steps. It also became clear that the patient's condition was far more complex than had first been diagnosed. The consultant treating her had reported that there was a possibility that Debbie's medication had triggered the event, but in his learned opinion he considered it a very low probability.

Interactions became difficult with the boss at work. He was very close to the family who were involved and it affected him very badly. He told Debbie he strongly suspected that his wife had found out about their affair and he really needed to be with her right now. He was, however, blissfully unaware that she had been following them since Christmas and knew far more than he could have guessed. She had made a point of tailing Debbie and had found out where she lived. And that she worked at the same place as her husband.

A fortnight after the project had hit this dramatic brick wall he found Debbie alone, working late again. He had been watching out for the opportunity to catch a quiet moment to speak to her. He asked if she would accept a lift home, he wanted to talk in private with her. She could sense what was coming, so she went to the door of the lab room and looked out. There was nobody around. She turned back to him and said that this was private enough. It put him on the back foot. He composed himself and calmly broke off the relationship. It was very simple. Too much discomfort at home. The intense distraction of dealing with the fallout from the drug test.

Debbie asked about her professional future. Should she be concerned about it? Had this caused serious damage to her career? What about her job here?

He reassured her that she had behaved correctly and that she was supported by professional opinion. But the project had had to be stopped. An independent review was being done and the patient was now receiving all the necessary medical care and attention in the hospital. He would avoid any contact with Debbie at work for fear of causing her embarrassment or difficulty. He asked if she was okay. She nodded. He nodded. He shuffled across, unlocked the door and left the room.

Stress can be a strange condition, creeping up on people when they least realise it. Debbie had enjoyed the project. She felt that she had gained energy from it. She had enjoyed the relationship. It had boosted her self confidence and made her feel good again. As the two crumbled away her adrenalin levels dropped and she felt the weight of the woman in the coma on her shoulders. The miscarriage was a natural reaction at such a vulnerable time.

'I'm OK' she said, looking across at Karen who had taken a seat next to the bed. 'Really, I'm OK. I didn't even know I was pregnant. I had a suspicion, but I didn't feel particularly different.'

'The doctor said she was only seven weeks' Pauline added from her seat at the other side of the hospital bed. 'It could have been a lot worse.'

'Thanks mum, that doesn't actually make me feel any better.'

'I'm sorry dear. I tell you what, now that Karen's here, your father and I will go and get a cup of tea. Then you two can have a good natter. We'll be back in half an hour.'

After they'd left the room, Karen checked again to make sure that her younger sister was all right and not just putting on a brave face in front of their parents.

'Yes, I'm fine, thanks.' As she spoke, she cast her eyes towards the ceiling. 'It was someone up there punishing me for doing a dirty trick. I should have known better, especially after the experience of my own husband leaving me for the Scottish Tart. I shouldn't have meddled with a married man. And certainly not a married man at work.'

'Does anyone at work know?'

'No. Well, maybe. Not really. One or two were asking questions. There were some suspicions.'

'Who was he?'

Debbie just looked at Karen. By pretending to pull a zip across her lips she confirmed that secrecy remained the order of the day. Karen nodded. If her sister didn't want to disclose the detail then she was happy to respect that wish and remain ignorant of the man's identity.

'Do you know anything more about your drug trial patient?'

'No. She's stable, but unresponsive. I have no idea who she is, nor do I want to find out.'

'And do you know anything about your ..' Karen was grasping for a sensitive way of phrasing her next question. 'Do you know anything about your man's wife?'

'No. He never spoke about her. Never said anything about his home life. They probably had a rocky patch and pure serendipity brought us together' she said with a mild artistic flourish.

Karen drew in closer to the bed and spoke quietly, even though they were alone in a private room.

'Gemma and I have spotted someone on Conway Road. We've seen her a few times recently.' Debbie turned her head towards Karen, inquisitive and attentive. 'A woman in a sporty looking car, parked up across the road. We were walking back from the village last Saturday and she was there again. She seemed to be watching our house but as we walked closer she buried her head in the property guide. I suspect she was trying to make out that she was interested in Sandra and Dave's place on the other side of the road, as that's up for sale.'

'It could have been her. He said that he thought she suspected something was going on.'

'Are you worried that she might do something stupid? Confront you on the doorstep and make a scene?'

'I don't know. I doubt it, now that it's all over. Anyway, I've made a decision. You've been great letting me stay so long at your house and I am very grateful. But it's time I reinvested the proceeds from my broken marriage. I'm going to look for a new place to live.'

'You know that you're welcome. There's no issue at all if you want to stay. I've loved having you around the house.'

'I know, but this is a sign for me. I'm upset about what's happened. I need to jump back up again and carry on with my life.

Not let it get me down. I'm going to go to mum and dad's for the next few months. Dad can help me with all the fuss and nonsense that comes with buying a new place.'

'Okay, I understand. I'll miss you though. I've got used to you being around.'

Ron and Pauline returned from the café bearing refreshments for their daughters. They all got talking about Debbie's house hunting.

It would be an even more dramatic set of circumstances that would lead to them all being in the hospital together again. And the consequences would run a lot deeper.

35

Nick had turned up on Karen's doorstep again one Sunday morning in May. She hadn't seen him since that party before Christmas, a gap that had reassured her he had finally got the message that she wasn't interested. Perhaps not.

'Morning Karen. I'm sorry for disturbing you at the weekend. The Hanson Scott accounts have just been completed and I've brought you a cheque for the annual dividend.' He pulled out an envelope from the inside pocket of his blazer and handed it to her. 'It's broadly similar to the last few years.'

'Thank you. I have to admit that I never really used to look at the accounts. Monty would give them a read, but even he found them uninteresting. His heart was in the designs, not the numbers.'

This was music to Nick's ears. He could continue keeping the accounts to himself, which gave him carte blanche to exploit them further. He made a mental note.

'I'd also like to say sorry for being a tad overbearing at the Millingtons' party.'

Karen thought it a little odd that he was apologising for something that happened five months ago, but she accepted gracefully.

'I wonder, have you given any thought to selling your share? I'd be happy to make a reasonable offer.'

'I haven't. It's not the top thing on my mind at the moment.'

There was an uneasy pause which made Karen feel as though she had to fill the silence with some sort of explanation.

'Gemma has some serious exams coming up which will have a bearing on which universities she will shortlist. It's her big A Level exams next year. Sam will be coming to the end of his first year soon and I'll have to bring him home for the summer. Worst of all, I haven't done anything about arranging a holiday. Bless them, I've denied them a holiday for the last two years – we've not been away since Monty died.'

She paused again.

'Sorry. I'm rambling.'

'I have an apartment in Turkey and nobody is renting it during

155

the last few weeks July. You could use it … for free. Just think of it as my little thank you to Monty. No strings attached. You could take your children and you'd have complete run of the place for a fortnight. It's in a small village near the sea. Lovely restaurants, great beach, great weather. It's idyllic.'

'I couldn't possibly do that, Nick, though it is very generous of you. Why wouldn't you take advantage of those two weeks yourself?'

He explained that he had some other commitments that would keep him in England. He was very persuasive and as he walked off down the drive Karen was beginning to give the idea some very serious thought. She talked it over with her close friend Julie, whose children were the same ages as Sam and Gemma. They had all been on camping excursions before and the children were very good friends. They were going to Turkey during the same period, spending two weeks around the south west coast followed by a week in Istanbul to enjoy the culture and explore all of its history. In that first spell they wouldn't be far away from where Nick's property was.

Karen came to the conclusion that it seemed a good idea to take him up on his offer. After all, he had cooled off and this was a no strings attached offer.

He telephoned a few days later, guaranteeing that she would have private use for the two weeks and extending his marketing pitch by explaining that a brochure was available along with some notes about how to get there, which airports to use, which flights to book. He also paid a local family to look after it for him and they would do the transport runs to and from the airport. He could arrange for Pat from the office to bring copies of all the information around. It was enough to get Karen to say yes.

The apartment was everything that Nick had made it out to be. It was on the outskirts of a small fishing village and the beach was only a few minutes' walk away. The village had several restaurants and the atmosphere was relaxed and friendly. Gemma was able to learn a few Turkish phrases with help from the flirting waiters. The couple that looked after the apartment were wonderful, helping with any questions that Karen raised and even going so far as to invite the visitors for a meal on the first Sunday evening of the holiday.

At the end of the first week Karen, Sam and Gemma took themselves off to the beach on the Saturday afternoon, after having a stroll around the village in the morning. They returned to the apartment at around five o'clock so that they could shower and prepare to go out for an evening meal. As Karen entered she almost tripped over some luggage just inside the door.

'Brilliant!' she said. 'He's gone and double booked it.' Then thought to herself 'What possessed me to trust him?'

Sam and Gemma followed her in and began asking what was happening. Karen walked through to the lounge and immediately saw that the doors out onto the verandah were open. And there was Nick. Sitting on one of the chairs, kitted out in his shorts and a pair of sunglasses. He turned his head as he heard them come through from the hallway.

'Hi everybody. Isn't this fantastic?'

'Hello Nick. Well, it's a surprise. I thought you said that you wouldn't be using the apartment.'

'I know. I had a lot of meetings cancelled, people on holiday. Just happened to find that I was able to take this week off so I thought I would come and join you, have some fun in the sun. I've got a hire car too. I can take you to see some of the other sights along the coast.'

The enjoyment drained out of her holiday in an instant. It suddenly felt soiled. He had broken his word and now she found herself in a very compromised position. She remained calm, as ever. She could sense that Gemma was seething just behind her. She would have to usher the children off to the bedroom to avoid the possibility of a caustic remark from her daughter.

'We've been down on the beach all afternoon. We'll just go put our things away and get tidied up.'

'It's OK. Don't mind me. I'll sort my luggage out later. I'll sleep on the sofa.'

Karen, Sam and Gemma withdrew to the main bedroom. They sat on the bed and talked in hushed tones. They needed an escape plan, but it wouldn't be straightforward.

'Why has he come, mum?' Gemma was exasperated.

'I really do not know. It is his apartment, so he is at liberty to use it as and when he wants. But I am cross, I can't deny it. He gave me his cast iron guarantee that we would be here by ourselves.'

'Mum,' said Sam, 'what about the Wilsons?'

They had met Julie Wilson and her family on Wednesday last week, as planned.

'Yes. Julie told me that they were going to Istanbul this week.'

'Can we go there instead?' Sam pulled his phone from his pocket. 'We may be two thousand miles from home, but that's nothing when you've got one of these.'

Gemma and Karen sat in anticipation while Sam searched for an evacuation route. He found a Turkish Airlines flight leaving for Istanbul the next morning and there were plenty of hotel options available in the famous city. With Karen's credit card details he was able to get everything booked and a sense of calm returned. All Karen had to do now was to inform Nick. She considered her best tactic would be to have Sam and Gemma by her side. She briefed them on the communication plan which hinged around having heard from the Wilsons that Istanbul was fantastic and they were being urged to join their friends there for the rest of the holiday.

They returned to the lounge. Nick had come back in and was trying to watch something on the television, despite the broadcast being in Turkish. Karen explained the situation and apologised for the fact that they would be making an early departure the following day. She argued that it would be a far better break for him if they were out from under his feet. Nick insisted that there was plenty of room and he was looking forward to exploring some of the coast with them. Sam and Gemma jumped in at all the right times with pleas to see their friends again. Finally Nick had to accept their wishes. He offered them a lift to the airport which Karen accepted in order to avoid imposing further rejection.

On Sunday morning they waved goodbye to Nick as he dropped them off with their luggage. They checked in and made their way through to departures. It was a slightly anxious wait. Gemma kept looking around, suspicious that Nick would have parked the car and bought himself a ticket for the same flight. Finally, with no Nick in sight, they boarded the plane and settled down in their three seats on the left of the aisle for the short hop north.

36

The plane flew over Istanbul and tracked north east, out over the Baltic Sea. From the left side they got a great view of the northern reaches of the Bosphorus before the plane banked to the left and did a hundred and eighty degree turn to line up its approach to the runway. On their final descent they looked out of the porthole windows to see Istanbul stretched out below. It was a bright, clear day which gave Monty and Clare the perfect opportunity to distinguish some of the major landmarks.

They were reunited on another architectural tour, their first joint visit since that trip to Australia at the end of 2011. Christmas had been spent at Monty's parents again, though Clare had departed on Boxing Day to spend New Year with some other friends down in the Cotswolds. They'd had a few nights out with Jacko, but he was also planning to have New Year away from home. He told Monty that he was going to Bristol to visit some distant relations. He had offered to give Clare a lift and they'd both set off with a spring in their step.

Monty saw in 2012 very quietly, a long way from the fun of the previous year. He remembered Karen. He remembered Sam and Gemma. He also looked back on the Napkinworld tour and just how much he'd enjoyed it. How much he'd enjoyed the time with Clare. Then he remembered that kiss with Clare at the New Year party. He missed her when she was in the Cotswolds.

She arrived back at Monty's house in the first week of January. She was very upbeat. Monty was convinced that she had met a man during the week away. 'And good luck to her' he thought, 'she deserves somebody nice'.

Clare was unable to accompany Monty on his next two trips. She already had other engagements. Then she cancelled from the next two as well. He ended up travelling alone, just like he had done before Clare came through. Occasionally he went with one or two of the engineer and architect members of EAST, but he missed having Clare by his side.

In July there was a slight change again. Clare booked her place on the trip to Istanbul with him. Monty detected there may have been some cooling off between her and the boyfriend that she had been spending a lot of time with.

She opened up a little during their time in Istanbul. What had begun as a minor disagreement with the boyfriend had grown disproportionately, so she was glad to get away for a break and enjoy some different company. Clare was convinced that things would right themselves easily enough once she returned from Turkey. The boyfriend wasn't so sure. He wasn't totally enamoured that Clare was falling back on her old friend Monty, whom he saw as a possible threat. From his viewpoint, this would put extra strain on the relationship.

She never mentioned his name to Monty. He understood it to be somebody from near Gloucester, in which case it wouldn't make any difference what the man was called as Monty wouldn't know him from Adam anyway.

Having got some of this off her chest Clare was able to unwind and get back to immersing herself in the architectural wonders of this fantastic city. They both agreed that Wednesday was the best. They visited the Hagia Sofia and the Blue Mosque, which sat close together in the old town. It was hot, the sun was blazing down. They found cool air beneath each of the huge domes. Monty stood looking up, quietly absorbing the majestic beauty of the Blue Mosque.

Less than five metres way, at precisely that same moment in Realworld, Karen and Sam and Gemma stood with their necks craning upwards. Karen pondered what her husband would have said had he been able to see this structural feat when he was alive.

37

It was the Millingtons' house party and Karen had grown comfortable with going out socialising again. What with the Book Group, theatre evenings, and general girls' nights out to celebrate whatever could be celebrated, she was back to her normal self. It had taken two and a half years from Monty's departure, but she had eventually learned to live without yearning for him every hour of every day. She had been looking forward to this evening with slight trepidation though, remembering Nick shadowing her movements at last year's party.

Whilst talking with some friends from the Book Group, she was distracted by a very handsome man that she could see over Julie's shoulder. She probed the depths of her memory to recall where she had seen him before. Then it struck her. It had been a year ago at this very house. She had seen him across the dining table when picking up food from the buffet. He was well built. He looked rugged and swarthy, yet his face was kind and smiling.

He took a drink, emptying his glass, and broke from his conversation to glance around the room. She didn't divert her gaze quickly enough and he caught sight of her looking at him. She felt embarrassed and turned away quickly, tuning back into the conversation with her circle of friends. She noticed him move away, presumably to get a refill. Quarter of an hour later she decided it was time to replenish her glass. She turned towards the kitchen and bumped into Liz. Karen scanned the horizon for Nick but the coast was clear. It meant that she could relax and enjoy Liz's company.

'Hello Liz, are you going to introduce us?' The mellow voice came from over Karen's left shoulder. She swung to see who it was as Liz responded.

'Hello Dan. Of course. Karen, this is Dan Connor. Dan, this is Karen Scott.'

It was him. Karen felt a youthful tingling sensation. She hoped that Dan hadn't noticed her go red earlier. Liz gave each a pen picture by way of introduction, explaining that Karen was an interior designer and Dan owned the Ronnoc Pharmaceutical business.

'Hello, it's nice to meet you. My sister works there. She seems to like it.'

'Good. We try to look after all of our staff.'

'Did I see you here last year? With your wife?'

'Mmm, yes.' He looked uncomfortable with the question.

'I'm sorry, have I said the wrong thing?'

'No. It's just that, erm, we're not, err ... I lost her early this year.'

'Oh I am sorry. Forgive me.'

'There's nothing to forgive, you weren't to know. Are you by yourself too?'

'Yes. I lost my husband two and a half years ago.'

At that point Nick appeared between Dan and Liz. Karen took a deep breath.

'Ah, I see you've met' said Nick. 'Dan, this is Karen Scott. Her husband, Monty, was the one who died at your place during the building work.'

It was a conversation killer. Nick at his worst, as subtle as a brick. Karen bowed her head and looked down at the carpet, softly biting her lip. Five seconds of silence seemed more like an hour. Liz spoke first, to check if Karen was alright. Then Dan tried to smooth things back to normality.

'I really had no idea he was your husband. I don't know what to say.'

'It's okay, you weren't to know' replied Karen. 'Would you excuse me? I need to get some fresh air.'

She left them and went out onto the patio via the large glass doors at the end of the room. Liz followed. Karen wiped a few tears from the corner of her eyes. Liz offered some warm consoling words and waited until Karen felt composed enough to return to the party. Despite there being two large patio heaters out there they soon felt the cold of the December evening. Back inside the dining room Karen told her friend Julie of the encounter as they sampled the buffet. Nick found Karen alone near the drinks in the kitchen. He homed in on her.

'I was really sad that you had to leave the apartment in Turkey in the summer, I was hoping we could spend some time together there. How about I take you out for dinner next Saturday night to make up for that lost opportunity?'

Karen was aghast. She leaned towards him and whispered 'Nick, can we just step outside and talk in private for a few minutes please?'

'Finally,' he thought, 'the time is right.' He followed her out to the patio.

'Nick, I want you to keep away from me.' She spoke with a directness that was terse and peremptory. 'I really do not have any feelings for you at all. I have no idea where you would ever get such an idea from. To be perfectly honest, you make my flesh creep. Stop following me around. Stop asking me out to dinner. Stop asking me out anywhere. Stop bothering me!'

He was lost for words. Karen wasn't. She merely needed to draw breath.

'The only reason that I have any connection with you is through the architecture practice. And I would like all further communication on that topic to be delivered to me through Pat in the office. Now, please keep out of my way for the rest of this evening and don't bother me again. Ever. Do I make myself clear?'

Nick was still lost for words. He was cold. He couldn't bring himself to make eye contact with the woman he'd not been able to take his eyes off.

'Do I make myself clear?' Karen repeated forcefully.

Nick gave a muffled 'Yes' and continued looking down at his boots.

'Good!' She left him and went back inside, feeling much warmer than she had done when coming in from the patio an hour ago. She updated Julie straight away. Her sense of relief was palpable. Her friend immediately went off to bring Karen a glass of champagne to celebrate. As she stood alone, Dan Connor walked over.

'Do you mind if I say hello again? Our first conversation didn't really get very far and I sincerely hope the house connection hasn't ruined your evening.'

He spoke warmly and she found his expression very caring and empathetic.

'Hello again. I'm pleased to say that you haven't ruined my evening at all. Somebody else managed to do that.' She smiled up at him.

'Well, you do look happier than you did earlier. That must have been a bit of a shock for you. It was for me too, by the way.'

'I am happier, thank you. I've just got something off my chest. It's something that I should have done some time ago.'

'Nick Hanson?'

She nodded.

'He can be a bit irritating at times,' agreed Dan.

Julie returned and handed Karen some bubbly. Karen introduced her to Dan and they eased into some small talk about plans and preparations for Christmas. Julie saw that Karen was very much at ease with Dan and took her leave of them to go and seek out her other friends. Karen and Dan continued chatting for almost forty minutes, taking themselves through to the kitchen to top up their glasses at one point in the conversation.

'Did my husband's death cause you a lot of disruption at the building site?' she asked.

'A little. Though nowhere near as much upset as it caused you, I'm sure. Actually, the second one had much more of an impact. The girl …'

'Clare,' Karen reminded him

'Yes, Clare. The site was shut down for three months. To have one accident was bad enough. To have two … I thought we'd never get the house finished.' He took another sip of wine. 'You must miss him very badly?'

'I do, but I have grown to accept it over the last year or so. It is true what they say, time is a great healer. Now and then I am hit by the thought that I'll never see him again. Ever. And that's the bit that really hurts most. I expect you feel the same about your wife?'

'Oh, err, yes.' He appeared to stumble over the topic. 'Sorry. It's a complicated story and I have a hard time trying to put it to the back of my mind.'

Julie tapped Karen on the shoulder. It was time to be thinking of going home. The interruption distracted Karen enough for her not to read too much into Dan's reply. Julie went off to get their coats.

'Forgive me for being forward,' Dan said, seeking a final few moments of Karen's attention. 'Could I see you again before Christmas? Take you to dinner?'

'That's the second invitation I've had this evening. And the first person was sent away with a proper flea in his ear.'

'Oh. In that case I'd better retract my last comment. I have enjoyed meeting you and it would be sad to end this lovely evening with a bitter rejection.'

Karen ruffled her hand around in her handbag for a few seconds then looked back at Dan.

'I must have only brought one flea with me this evening. You're lucky, I don't appear to have another one for your ear.'

Dan was warmed by her engaging expression and tapped Karen's contact number into his mobile phone.

Nick had been watching from a safe distance, gritting his teeth. He extended his night with a visit to the Black Jack Casino then spent most of Sunday afternoon at the rifle club venting his anger by propelling bolts from his favourite crossbow. Every other one was accompanied with a mutter of 'that bastard Connor'.

When he'd had enough he went to leave the store room via the fire exit door and triggered the alarm yet again. A mistake that had become second nature to him.

38

Since the trip to Istanbul Clare's love life had troughed again. Her boyfriend had taken umbrage about her going on a jaunt with Monty and the slightest of things frequently deteriorated into petty disagreements. Clare couldn't seem to subdue these jealousies and their relationship faltered. She settled back into life at Conway Road and accompanied Monty on another architecture viewing trip in October.

On Saturday the 8th of December Monty and Clare were going to attend the EAST Society Christmas Ball. Monty had tried to contact Jacko to see if he wanted to join them, but had got no reply whatsoever. His best friend had been a bit moody during the year and Monty felt at times as though he was deliberately being blanked by his old pal. He pondered this cause for concern whilst he sat in his dinner suit and black tie, waiting for Clare to get ready.

Monty heard her coming down the stairs. Sitting on a bar stool at the island, he was methodically retracing some of the clues in the jumbo cryptic crossword that he had started earlier in the day. He'd successfully worked out almost half of the answers but there was a large array of white squares staring back at him from the top right quarter of the grid. Nothing at all to work with, no letters to give him a head start in that section of the puzzle.

6 Across, 'Excited, pant endlessly in short advertisement (7)'. He stared but no inspiration was forthcoming.

Clare came into the kitchen, her stilettos on the tile floor marking out her entry like a sonar signal. He lifted his head from 6 Across and found himself totally distracted from the newspaper. She was wearing a stunning red dress that came to just above her knee. A five centimetre wide black belt ran round her middle, a little higher than her waist. A stylish, modern black necklace hung perfectly around her neck. She had tied her hair up at the back of her head and the front flopped down on her eyes. Black tights and patent black, high heeled shoes completed the outfit. Clare looked amazing and Monty was struck dumb. Not that he'd ever doubted her looks. It was simply that he'd grown so accustomed to her being around all the time that he'd taken for granted just how pretty she was.

'Very smart, Mister Scott' she said, looking him up and down. 'That yellow shirt would have been another Monty mishap fashion statement.'

'Yes, you were right to encourage me to put on this white one.' He paused to collect himself. 'You look fantastic, that dress suits you perfectly.'

'Thank you. Is it Christmassy enough?'

'Absolutely! You'll be the star of the show. Shall we go?'

They gathered their coats and made their way through the hallway and out.

The organisers had done a great job. It was held at a countryside hotel which was well known for its food. Clare and Monty recognised a lot of the people there through their regular social events with the society, so they found it easy to mix and enjoy the ambience.

After the meal Monty stood talking to Ralph, a combo-centenary at the ripe old age of 73r/27h. Monty was absorbed with Ralph's tales from his days in the steel industry. Clare approached across the busy room, swinging her body playfully as she walked towards them. She was pleasantly merry.

'Hi, you boys look engrossed in something. Would you like me to fetch you a drink Monty?'

'That would be great. I'd like a whisky please.'

'One whisky coming up. And what about you Ralph? Can I tempt you with a glass of port?'

'Yes please. You know me too well young lady' he laughed

She pecked Monty on his right cheek, turned and tottered off slowly towards the bar, slinking her hips gently and balancing a wine glass in her left hand. After a few steps she stopped to rub the cheek of her bottom with her right hand. In doing so, she deliberately managed to inch her dress up just enough to give Monty and Ralph a clear sight of the top of her stocking. Then she flicked it down nonchalantly and continued off through the crowd towards the bar.

'Goodness me. That was a sight for sore eyes' said Monty.

'That was a sight for your eyes, Monty. I'd say that was a dashed clear mating call.'

'Come on Ralph, you know me. I'm not sure I'm ready for that.'

'Look Monty, you've been here over two years. You're a fine fellow of a man and I know that you still long for that dear wife of yours. However, you have to rationalise this situation. Balance your emotions against the simple facts. Yes, you'll see your wife again. Unless, of course, you do something drastically stupid before that day arrives. But take note, you can continue with this course of abstinence until you're 42r/42h and she still might not have come through. And when she does … how do you know that you will still have all those same feelings for her?'

'I simply can't imagine feeling any different about her.'

'See Joyce over there?' Ralph gestured with a shrug of his right hand at a lady who was 72r/58h, the wife of one of the other older members.

'Yes.'

'Do you fancy her? How would you like to see yourself having sex with Joyce?'

'No, I'd rather not, thank you very much. What's your point?'

'Well, Monty, when your wife comes through, thirty-five years from now, and looks rather wizened like that … you're not going to be quite so hasty about doing all of that French kissing stuff when there's more than a fifty fifty chance of her false teeth falling out on the end of your tongue. What do you say?'

Monty couldn't help but laugh at Ralph's logic. Clare reappeared from the bar carrying her wine, a port and a whisky. Ralph sagely offered Monty a last word of genial advice before she reached them.

'Now … her hips look splendid in that sexy dress. But I'm far too old to do it any justice, so you're going to have to undertake the task on my behalf. And I'll wager she's not got false teeth.'

There was a glint in Ralph's eye.

Monty and Clare arrived back at Conway Road shortly after one in the morning. Monty felt mellow. He wasn't ready for bed so he went into the kitchen in search of a cup of coffee. Clare took off her coat and drooped it over the banister in the hallway before joining him. She took over the coffee making duty and Monty found himself back on the bar stool at the kitchen island, the crossword in front of him. It was a relaxed way to wind down after a memorable night out.

Clare minced around the kitchen in a very teasing fashion, her high heels clicking on the tiled floor again. He tried to concentrate on 6 Across, 'Excited, pants endlessly in short advertisement (7)'. He kept getting distracted. Clare was tidying up slowly, regularly bending over the open dishwasher to load some of the items that they had left near the sink when heading off to the party. She knew he was having trouble with 6 Across.

'Pants, trousers' he thought. 'Pant .. singular .. trouser. Trouser, with the ends chopped off .. becomes rouse.'

With her back to him, she hitched her dress up a little more than before so that she could bend over to put two saucers in the dishwasher. Monty got a private viewing of her stockings, red knickers, and the fleshy tops of her legs.

'With the ends chopped off .. becomes rouse. In small ad.' He carried on decoding in his head, mesmerised by the glimpse of her underwear.

'Aroused!' he blurted out. Clare stood up and turned towards him, her dress returning to hang down normally as she did so.

'Sorry. 6 Across is Aroused' he explained.

She stood smiling for a few seconds then walked round him to go to the downstairs toilet. As she passed by, she leaned in to his side and gave him a long and lingering kiss on the cheek. Her left hand found its way to his lap and rubbed his groin firmly.

'I hope it's not just 6 Across that's aroused.'

Ralph's encouraging guidance echoed through his ears.

8 Down, 'Voting swings left to right for building (8)'. He looked at the grid. Because of Aroused, the first letter must be an 'E'.

Clare returned from the downstairs toilet and picked up where she had left off.

'Voting .. X .. polling station .. election.' The word connections jumped around in Monty's head. Clare had picked up some cutlery and repeated her dishwasher loading procedure. Monty glanced over again. He couldn't help but look. This time he saw the stockings and the full fleshiness of her sexy bottom. She had discarded her underwear when she went to the bathroom. He was breathing heavily.

'Voting, election. Swap out L, replace with R. Erection'. He printed the letters in the boxes and put his pen down. He slid off the bar stool and stepped up to Clare. He stroked her bottom softly with his left hand and his fingers eased in between her legs. He hurriedly unzipped his trousers with his right hand and swiftly entered her from behind. He made love to her in the kitchen with a sense of urgency. His passionate release a pent-up reaction to her seductive behaviour throughout the evening.

39

2013 (H)

Over the first three months of 2013 Clare felt the excitement and heat between her and Monty diminish slowly. After all the fun around Christmas, things returned to the mundane. It was a long winter. The poor weather wouldn't go away so they made a long haul trip out to South America to see Buenos Aires and Rio. But it wasn't the same. It felt rather flat for both of them.

At Easter they sat and had a heart to heart discussion over a Sunday lunch out at the Old Swan in one of the nearby villages. Things had been far more relaxed and natural when they were just straightforward, best friends. By mutual agreement they returned to a platonic relationship. It had been right to try it, if only to find out that it wasn't going to work in the long run.

Clare decided to go for a break by herself. In fact, not that Monty knew, she arranged to spend some time with her boyfriend from last year. Perhaps this would work now that she had got the Monty experience out of her system. It turned out that she was correct. Her boyfriend could see that Monty was no longer a distraction for Clare. He was disappointed that she had spent the last few months finding out, but he had been in Hinteraevum long enough to understand that these things happened and there would be sufficient time to try again.

Monty simply went about his life as he had been doing before. Enjoying his trips, exploring the world, happy that his friendship with Clare was back on an even keel. Happy also that Clare seemed to be at one with how things were. He decided it was time to go and see what had been bugging Jacko. He would drive up to Darlington the next time that Clare went off with her boyfriend. However, this plan fell at the first hurdle because Jacko happened to be off at some training camp with the cricket club. After some diary juggling, he managed to find a suitable date when Jacko would be around. Clare didn't want to get in the way of their men's talk, so she made a reason for not accompanying him.

Monty and Jacko sat at the cricket pavilion where they had met shortly after Monty came through.

'What's the matter? You've been a real arse this last year. No fun at all. I can't think what the devil I've done to upset you.'

'Arrr, it's not your fault matey. Suffered a bit of woman trouble. Just woman trouble, that's all it was. Got myself wound up about it because I really like this girl.'

'Julia Henderson?'

'No, no. Not her. Mind you, I've always had a soft spot for her. Gorgeous breasts. But no. Someone else.'

'Well, if they're not Julia Henderson's breasts, whose breasts are they? Who is this damsel that has thrown my best friend into such a spin?'

'Oh, I doubt you'd know her.'

Monty was curious, Jacko was being more guarded than he had expected.

'So, help me understand this situation a little more. You were really off with me. If I don't know her, why was it that I got the rough end of the stick?'

'You know what they say, matey, you always hurt the ones you love.' He looked to his left to gauge Monty's reaction. But Monty was bemused rather than amused. 'I'm sorry. I didn't mean to mess things up with my oldest pal.'

'Okay, I believe you. But…'

'But what?'

'If this woman trouble happens again …'

'It won't.'

'Okay. One condition …'

'Name it.'

'If this develops into something important, I want to be the first person to know. Okay?'

'Okay matey.'

40

Throughout the year Nick smouldered. He became steadily more attached to that crossbow but couldn't kick the habit of opening the fire exit door instead of the one that lead to the main hallway of the club. Ken quizzed him about it.

'You seem to have a problem with that door, as it were.'

'I know, I know. Damned stupid thing. I just forget every time I come in here.'

'Well, no harm done, but it does irritate a few members, Nick. Trouble is, people will get a bit 'cry wolf' about it. We'll not notice when a real alarm is happening, as it were.'

'Yes, I understand. Sorry, Ken. I'll do my very best to remember in future.' Nick took the opportunity to ask Ken about the crossbow. 'How would I get hold of one of those? Where can you buy them?'

Ken looked at him oddly.

'I really like it, but it's a touch on the heavy side for me. And being left handed ... I was wondering if I could get one for myself and keep it here in the club house.'

'Oh, I see. Yes. Your left hand. I don't know whether there are any special differences, but you could look it up. The internet is the best place to go searching, but don't ask me about that, I haven't got a clue how to use it. Ask one of the younger lads.'

So Nick went off to the bar, got himself a beer and sat down with one of the younger members to get some education on the web.

Karen's friendship with Dan gathered pace. She liked him a lot. He was very considerate, interesting, and full of good ideas about things to do and places to see. What she liked most about him was his caring nature. He would call in to see his mother almost every day at an Old Peoples' home not far away. Karen kept the maturing liaison to herself, she didn't even tell Gemma. She didn't want her daughter to worry about the remote possibility of dealing with a new father figure, certainly not when she already had her A Levels on her mind.

Debbie had managed to buy her new house and move in, with a lot of help from their father. Karen was pleased to see that her sister was settled, but was reluctant to let on that she had been seeing the person whose company name appeared at the top of Debbie's monthly salary slips. Debbie instinctively knew something had changed in Karen's life, but couldn't prize the information out of her sibling. Mind you, she had precious little right to know given that she had kept her boyfriend's identity highly secretive. When Debbie had raised the subject with her parents, Ron had expressed his view that it was good for his elder daughter to be getting over her loss at last and she should be given some room to do so in privacy.

In May Karen received her annual dividend cheque from Hanson Scott, complete with a short typed letter from Nick. He simply commented that the company was starting to find the going hard and the dividend this year was ten per cent down on last year's figure. He painted a picture of challenging times and recommended that she consider selling her share to avoid losing out in the longer term. He would, of course, be prepared to make her a kind offer. She responded with a polite rejection, though Nick's letter did leave a modicum of concern at the back of her mind.

Dan took her out for dinner shortly before she was about to venture off with Sam and Gemma for a two week summer holiday in the Vendee. She felt very happy when she was with Dan. She had been out to his house on a handful of occasions. The first time set her heart racing, coming to terms with the place where Monty spent his final painful moments. It had become easier, but she wouldn't go near the top gallery landing from which he had fallen. At Dan's request she began to give the house extra flourish with some of her design ideas.

'It all sounds a little suspicious to me. Would you like my accountant to look over the books for you?'

'No thank you. It's a kind offer, but I don't have the last two sets of accounts anyway.'

'You really should get hold of them. After all, it's your business as much as it is his.'

Dan didn't press the matter any further than that. She valued the support he was prepared to give her. Equally, she respected him for leaving her to deal with her own issues. In fact he hadn't been overly pushy about anything. He had been romantic, he had been amorous, but he hadn't pressed anything more sexual or intimate. She was very comfortable with the pace of developments. When she sat back and assessed the situation, she concluded that she was actually falling in love with him.

'I have a suggestion' he said. 'And you can say 'no'. Let me check something first. Have you got any of those fleas in your handbag?'

'Not today. You're safe to proceed.'

'When you've got Gemma off to university, would you like to take a holiday with me?'

He didn't have any children of his own. He and his wife had always put their careers first. He also hadn't met Sam or Gemma, as Karen wanted to keep that piece of her life set to one side for the time being.

'That sounds like a nice idea. Somewhere in the sun. Tell me, are you thinking of a twin room or a double?'

'A double would be perfect. But I would be fine with a twin if that would make you more comfortable.'

'I think it might be an appropriate time to consider a double.'

He dropped her off near home later that evening. Probably because of where he stopped the car, it occurred to Karen that she hadn't seen that woman in the sporty Mercedes again. She put that down to the fact that Debbie's affair had been broken off some time ago and was no longer living in Conway Road.

41

With Sam and Gemma both at university Karen found the house big and empty. She was looking forward to getting them home for Christmas. On the other hand, there were things that Karen liked about not having them around. Things were easier - weekly food shopping, the washing and ironing. And she had more freedom to do what she wanted to, including inviting Dan over for dinner.

They had had a wonderful fortnight in the Caribbean, in a double room. If they were being honest with each other, both had found it strange sharing a bed with someone else for the first time in a long while. On their fourth evening away they opted for the Dutch courage approach. A pre-prandial drink, several glasses of wine with the meal, followed by a post-prandial cocktail. That was sufficient to remove any inhibitions whilst not immobilising them for the night. During the remainder of the holiday they had been very romantic and grown close.

They reflected on the holiday during the starter that Karen had prepared. Dan cleared the plates away as Karen attended to the final steps with the main course. She looked over at him as he bent down to load the crockery into the dishwasher. She couldn't help thinking he had a very nice backside. They sat down again at the dining table and began to eat. The conversation turned to 'what happens next?' It had to be discussed. Especially now that they had actually slept with each other.

It was tricky. Karen didn't want to think about leaving Conway Road. That would be a tough decision and it would take some time to come round to the idea, should it arise. She also didn't want Dan to move in. Not yet. And he didn't want to give up the terrific house that he'd had built, with all of its mod cons and low heating bills. In fact there were emotional memories in both houses for Karen. Happy in one and devastating in the other.

It was early days, so there was no sign of any tension in the discussion. Both respected the other's point of view. There were strong ties that demanded sensitivity in both camps.

Then there was a noise from the front door. Karen pricked up her ears and looked across at Dan with a puzzled expression on her face. It was the sound of a key turning. She was frozen to her seat. They heard the door open.

'Hi, it's only me.'

'It's my sister.' Karen jumped up from her seat. Mildly panicked by the interruption.

'Well, I suppose this had to happen at some point,' she whispered to Dan across the table. 'I was hoping I could have effected a more controlled introduction.'

'Never mind, I'm sure it will be fine.'

Debbie was a little worse for wear, having been out for most of the afternoon at her office Christmas lunch. The weather was horrible. There had been a lot of snow through the day which had triggered an impulsive urge for her to drop in at her sister's for coffee, a warm through, and to catch up on the gossip. She knew that Karen would be alone and in need of some company. She threw her coat over the banister. It slipped and fell onto the hall carpet. She bent down, picked it up, stood upright, felt a bit woozy, and slung it over the banister again. It slipped and fell to the hall carpet. She looked at it and shrugged her shoulders. It could stay on the floor after all.

Debbie could see signs of life in the kitchen so she stepped through from the hallway to say hello. She looked over to the left where she saw Karen standing up at the dining table. And she had a guest! Wow! Debbie was finally going to get to meet whoever it was that had been clandestinely courting her big sister.

Dan stood up and turned to be introduced.

'You!' Debbie let out a shriek. 'What the hell are you doing here? Karen! What are you doing with him? Is this who you've been seeing? No! Tell me it's not true.'

'Debbie,' Dan spoke calmly. 'Debbie, please don't make a scene.'

'You clearly know each other,' said Karen. 'Is there some issue at work that I ought to know about?'

'At work? At work? There's a lot of issues you ought to know about. Like he's a married man, for starters! And, for seconds, he was the cause of my flaming miscarriage!'

The room fell silent. Karen was trying to assimilate the two allegations. Dan was absolutely floored by the news of the miscarriage. He had never heard a word about it.

'This was who I was seeing. Who I had the affair with. He's married. She was the subject of my trial drug project. She is the one who is laying flat out in a coma in the General Hospital.' Debbie turned her attention on Dan. 'What the bloody hell have you told her? You've not said anything about any of this, have you?'

Dan couldn't get his mouth to work. It was totally dry. There was nothing coming out. In any case, he couldn't find words that would make sense.

Debbie turned to Karen again.

'I can't believe this. What a nightmare. You've got yourself tied up with this … this …' Debbie was unable to pluck the right word out of a memory bank slowed down by a fair dose of alcohol. 'Tell him to go. Get lost. Leave you alone. You don't need his sort.'

Debbie spun round, hurried into the hall and picked up her coat. Karen raced after her.

'Debbie … wait … please.'

'Karen, tell him to have the guts to tell you the truth. Then tell him to get out.'

That was her final word on the matter. She stormed out, slamming the front door behind her. There was no point Karen following after. She composed herself, ready to go back and challenge Dan in the dining room. Thankfully Karen could do 'composed'. She could do 'composed' very well.

'I had no idea Debbie was your sister. Look, I'm sorry about this. I can explain …'

'Dan, sit down, please.'

She walked round and sat at the dining table. Dinner had long since gone cold, but that was the least of their worries. She calmly reminded him of her position.

'Dan, I like you. I've enjoyed being friends with you. I've trusted you. I loved our holiday. You've been very caring. I've told you the truth. Monty was my husband. When I say I lost him, I mean that he died. I buried him. That was over three years ago. I'll never see him again. He's dead. I'm single. Whichever way up you look at it, I'm single. Now, tell me your truth, Dan.'

He waited a few seconds.

'I am married. My wife, Gillian, was suffering from a very rare blood disorder and she put a huge amount of pressure on me to find a way to make things better for her. She thought it would be easy for me to get some research done, develop a cure within my own pharmaceutical company. She was a workaholic. This illness was affecting her work, and in turn that was affecting our home life. Debbie was involved in the project. Things were difficult at home. I fell for Debbie and did the wrong thing.'

He looked up at Karen.

'Go on,' she invited him to continue.

'The drugs knocked Gillian into a coma. That was when I realised I had to break it off with your sister. I didn't know about the miscarriage. Honestly. Nobody made me aware of that. I'm so sorry she had to endure that experience because of me.'

He paused. Karen could see he was ashen.

'Debbie's perfectly correct. Gillian remains in hospital to this day. That's who I go to see most days. Not my mother. When I say I lost her, I mean that I lost any real contact with her. She is ... and I hate to use this expression ... she is nothing more than a cabbage. I go and see her as often as I can, but there is no real connection. There hasn't been for the last twenty two months.'

'I want you to take me to see her.'

'But...' Dan was totally thrown, surprised at Karen's request.

'I want you to take me to see her. Tomorrow, please. Pick me up here at five o'clock.'

Dan nodded his head dutifully.

'And now, I think you should go. I would like some time to myself.'

He left with a sombre goodnight. It was a far cry from the Caribbean goodnight.

The house returned to being big and empty. Emptier than she had ever known it. The phone rang several times during the remainder of the evening, but Karen left it to trip over onto the answering machine. She could hear her mother's exasperated voice recording repeated pleas for Karen to get in touch. Karen couldn't face talking to anybody right now. She could only throw herself into bed and churn the whole story around until she dropped off to sleep.

42

Karen got up and went straight out to work. As luck would have it, she had a full day ahead of her which would serve as a distraction from the hammer blow news she had received the night before. The appointments schedule included allowances for travel between clients but the snow would slow down her planned timetable. She remained stoic about it all.

Pauline tried to contact her repeatedly during the day, but Karen's mobile was auto forwarding every call to voice mail. Karen had done it by mistake, it was another example of her low familiarity with technology. Consequently, she didn't even think to look for messages between meetings. Besides, she was also somewhat preoccupied with negotiating the state of the road surfaces. Pauline grew increasingly worried about her daughter as the day went by. Debbie had told her all about what had played out the night before and she was extremely concerned that Karen would not be in a good frame of mind to be out on the treacherous roads. The radio silence increased her anxiety.

Pauline eventually made contact with Debbie to see if she knew any more about where Karen was, or what she was planning to do. Debbie was able to contact one of Karen's work colleagues and found out that there had been mention of going over to the hospital this evening. Debbie put two and two together and called to update her mum. It was already quite late in the afternoon and Pauline, her emotions running high, jumped in her car and set off to get across to Karen's house as fast as possible. She was intent on reasoning with her daughter, persuading her not to have any further contact with this man.

Dan called to collect Karen bang on time. His four by four was at ease dealing with the snow and they made it to the hospital safely. He took her to the intensive care ward where his wife had spent the best part of the last two years, wired up to all manner of contraptions and intravenous drips. It wasn't a pretty sight. Karen recognised the woman as the person she had seen with Dan at the Millingtons' party last year. She also identified her as the lady who had been sat in her Mercedes on Conway Road ducking behind the Property Guide.

It all clicked into place and made sense now. Karen could

179

understand why Gillian had been there. She had been stalking Debbie. And there had been no more sightings on Conway Road because she was detained by this coma.

Karen and Dan sat quietly, watching the trace on the display counting out Gillian's life systems like a metronome. Life systems. Life. This was Gillian's life. A peaceful orchestra of medical instrumentation.

Dan finally spoke.

'They can't do anything for her. It is simply a matter of time.'

'I'm sorry.'

He looked at Karen.

'I'm sorry. I'm very, very sorry to have disappointed you like this. I don't make any excuses. I just hope that you can begin to understand why …'

Karen tried to get her head around all of the facts that had become known to her in the last twenty hours. She looked sadly upon Dan's wife. Gillian's hair still burned with a bright copper brown glow, contrasting vividly with her pallid face. Deep under that motionless facade, undetectable by all the advanced machines and monitors, Gillian was somehow sensing that her husband was making his daily visit. With a stranger. Another woman.

Pauline arrived at Conway Road. The car had lost traction in a few places along the way, but nothing that had put her in any serious danger. The lights were on but it was apparent that Karen had already left. Pauline was overcome with a raging desire to protect her daughter from any more pain. She got back into her car and set off out of the village. Her head was full of inner noise, she wasn't giving her driving the full concentration it demanded.

The road out of the village ran true for a hundred yards leading to Oak Dip Bend, a shallow drop into a left hand turn. Lured by the straight, she accelerated too fast. The car was already losing its grip as it sped into the downward slope and by the time the bend arrived she had lost control. The slippery layer of snow prevented the wheels from gaining any hold and the car was unable to take the corner. It skidded at great speed straight across the road and smashed headlong into the huge oak tree that gave the location its name.

It took time for the emergency services to arrive at the scene and complete the operation, the weather conditions made everything more taxing. Eventually they were able to take Pauline's badly impacted body to the hospital mortuary. The police traced the vehicle and went to inform Ron.

Having worked out where Karen was heading, Debbie had been making her way cautiously to the hospital when the crash happened. Her phone went shortly before she arrived but she couldn't answer it whilst driving. She walked into the hospital foyer and was met by two police officers who gave her the bad news. She knew which ward Gillian was in and raced off to find Karen. She burst in and disturbed the tranquility of the room. Karen and Dan looked round at her.

'It's all right Debbie, I've just come to see everything for my own eyes,' said Karen.

'It's not all right. It's mum…'

'What?' Karen could see that Debbie was in a very distressed state. This interruption wasn't directly related to the coma victim. For a brief moment, under this most bizarre set of circumstances, Dan found himself surrounded by his trio of lovers.

'It's mum. She's had a crash. It's horrible.'

The rest of the evening was dreadful. Ron arrived. Accompanied by his two daughters he went to identify the body. They were lost for what to do next. The police constable suggested that they go home and get whatever rest they could. There was nothing more for them to do here at the hospital. Karen went back to see Dan while the constable set about arranging a car for them.

'I can't continue this, Dan. Debbie's my sister and … mum's accident … it's just unthinkable under these conditions. And it is very disappointing because … because I'm very fond of you.'

Ron and Debbie stayed at Karen's that night. They couldn't face being at their respective homes and each felt that they needed to tap into the strength that came from being together. Ron went off to bed early, distraught and hollow. Karen and Debbie broke out a bottle of red wine and ruminated over the events.

'I feel awful for bringing everything out into the open last night' said Debbie. 'If I hadn't come round none of this would ever have happened.'

'You mustn't say that. It would have come out at some point. You can't blame yourself. I just think it's so strange that we both had a fling with the same married man.'

'Typical. Married men, they're all the same. What will you do about him?'

'I've told him it's over. It has to be over. I recognise that the position with his wife is extraordinary, but she is still his wife. And I'm sad that all of this has stirred up some bad memories for you. We could have fallen out over the whole business.'

'We wouldn't have fallen out.' Debbie smiled at Karen. 'Do you know what?'

'What?'

'You and Dan would have made a good pair. Far better than me and him.'

Karen received a Christmas card from Dan a week later. It contained a beautifully written letter, offering his condolences for the sad loss of her mother and giving a sincere apology for letting her down so badly. She wondered whether the future might yet hold something for her and Dan.

43

It was a surprise for Monty, seeing the alert message that Pauline was coming through. After all, she wasn't that old and she always seemed to be in decent health. That must have been an awfully bitter blow for Karen, he thought. Indeed it must have been a double blow, being so close to Christmas and knowing just how much his wife enjoyed that time of year. Pauline would come through the day after Boxing Day in the lull before New Year. He expected that she would want to make contact with all of her other family first, older relatives that hadn't been seen for many years. He had already made plans to spend the time with his parents in Darlington, so he posted a message to say he would come over to visit his mother-in-law on Monday the sixth of January.

When the day arrived, he duly drove around to her house. He was genuinely keen to make sure that she was all right, but he was also aching for news of Karen and his children. He got a shock when she opened the door to him. Aside from the bags under eyes she was as white as a sheet and quivering. He went in and followed her through to the living room. He had heard of people having this sort of rough landing in Hinteraevum, failing to sleep, struggling to acclimatise with the new world around them, and lacking the companionship in their own home. She began to chatter to him.

'Oh Monty, I don't know where to start. This feels so horrible. I've been to see my parents, and grandparents. I've been to see Frank, and Vince, and Merv.'

For a moment he thought she said Frankincense and Myrrh, but realised that she was talking of her brothers, Karen's uncles. She continued a long ramble about the family, what they were up to, how it had been so emotional to see them all again, and news, and more news, and more news. He let her go on. It was the best way, really. Let her get as much of it out of the system. He sat very patiently whilst she got it all off her chest, offering up the occasional words of comfort and sympathy at the right moments.

He interrupted to suggest a cup of tea. She shook her head as if to declare what a poor hostess she was being and they got up and went to the kitchen. Monty knew his way round parts of Pauline and

Ron's kitchen, though they had had a bit of a reorganisation of the cupboards in the last three years and he had to use trial and error to find the tea bags. Pauline sat down and continued at a pace, though a lot of it was washing over Monty. Far too much talk of Karen's long gone relatives that he had very little knowledge of. He put the tea pot, milk, sugar, and cups on the kitchen table and took a seat.

She had finally slowed down and come to a rest, allowing for the tea to be poured in a moment of peace and quiet. Monty thought a good cup of tea would calm her nerves and they would be able to talk more steadily. Pauline was clearly feeling the stress of her first few weeks, so Monty spoke for a few minutes about his experiences, aiming to make her feel better about this new place.

She listened in that 'not fully absorbing' way, then stepped in again at a suitable gap in his flow.

'Monty, things have been terrible. Karen has a new man, and I don't like the sound of it. Turns out he is married. And his wife is in a coma. All because of Debbie giving her some bad drugs. And she had a miscarriage because of him and was in hospital. And Gillian is in hospital in a coma. Debbie shouldn't have been seeing him. Especially after all that carry on with Chris. And I couldn't get hold of Karen to stop her going to see the woman. I wanted her to see sense. Stop seeing him...'

Monty gripped the handle of the mug. He was lost. Who had had a miscarriage? Was it Karen or Debbie seeing this man? Who was Gillian? Drugs?

'Excuse me ... Pauline ... just take things slowly please. I have to say I'm a little bit lost. You're rushing and jumping between parts of the story. It's all getting a little bit confusing for me. Just try to start at the beginning and go one step at a time. And don't forget, I have been here in Hinteraevum for almost four years now.'

He managed to moderate Pauline's speed by asking her to explain everything one step at a time. At the back of his mind there was something burning. He was sure he had heard her say something about Karen having a new man in her life. And it stung. Perhaps it was one of the confused bits. He hoped it would be.

But he was disappointed to find that it was the case. Pauline explained the tale of woe that had evolved around her younger daughter. Firstly the new drug then how she had got mixed up with this man, Dan, who owned his own pharmaceutical company.

'Dan Connor?'

Pauline confirmed the name then explained how it had turned out the drug trial patient had sadly ended up in Intensive Care at the local hospital. She went on to tell Monty that Karen had become involved with this same man a year later, only to find that he was married, culminating in the revelation that it was his wife Gillian in the coma. There was no more to the story. Pauline's recall only went as far as trying to reach her daughters on that December morning. The rest had been removed in the transition process on the way through.

'Dan Connor?' he asked, seeking confirmation that this was his wife's new partner. A married man. With a wife in such a dreadful condition.

'Yes.'

'How could she do that, Pauline? How could she embark on a relationship with a married man? It certainly isn't what I would have expected of her.'

'Well, Monty, I was very cross to find out. But I would say, in Karen's defence, she only got to know this the day before I .. before I ..'

'I understand' he said, saving her the unpalatable job of referring to her own death.

There was a natural break again, a quietness descended over them. Monty took it all in. He was disturbed by the events and deeply saddened to hear that Karen was now building a new life with one of Hanson Scott's clients. At the mention of Hanson Scott, Pauline's body language flashed like a lighthouse beacon. He challenged her about it. Was it something to do with the company? He thought back to Nick's devious manipulation of the money. Was there some financial trouble that had impacted Karen?

No. Pauline explained Nick's over zealous attentions towards her daughter. Towards Monty's wife. Monty was finding the conversation tough. Upsetting. He'd arrived full of hope that he would hear wonderful things about his wife. It was a case of being careful what you wish for.

Now it was Pauline's turn to pour the tea and serve up some empathy. Her shaking had settled down and she had got a little bit of colour back in her cheeks. Only a little, but she did look in a healthier state than when she'd first opened the door to him an hour ago.

'You would be so proud of Sam and Gemma,' she announced in a more upbeat voice. 'They have both got into good universities and they're doing so well.'

Monty felt the tears ease out and trickle their way down the edges of his cheeks. He couldn't hold them in. He took out his handkerchief and wiped them clear. They spent another hour chatting, concentrating on the positives. As he was getting ready to leave Pauline offered a sympathetic comment.

'I'm sorry to have to tell you about Karen and Dan Connor. I'm sorry I blurted it out. This place has got me all at sixes and sevens.'

'I know. I hope you're feeling better soon. More settled.'

'I wasn't very settled the other week. I was very cross about Karen doing this. I didn't like the idea of her seeing someone, let alone it being a married man. I'm a big believer in the sanctity of marriage, you know. And in my eyes she is still married to you, Monty.'

'There is a difference Pauline ... you and I know that we will see her again. But she doesn't know that. She has to live her life to the full in Realworld. I wouldn't want her to live the rest of her life as a reclusive nun.'

Pauline absorbed Monty's statement.

'I left her quite a few messages on the phone. I must have sounded cross with her. I couldn't help it. Now all I can do is sit and wait until she comes through. I'll be able to explain to her when we're reunited again.'

He was relieved that he hadn't made mention that Clare was living with him. It was all innocent and above board, save the three months when he had given in to her charms. However, he thought it likely that his mother-in-law would misconstrue the situation and be unhappy that he wasn't waiting for Karen in absolute domestic celibacy. He invited Pauline to pay him a visit at Conway Road. He advised her to arrange a time so that she could be sure that he would be in and not gallivanting around the globe on another architectural trip. The real reason behind the advance scheduling request was that he would have due notice to ask Clare to make her presence scarce.

He waved goodbye and returned to Conway Road.

He joined Clare in the lounge and recounted what he had learned from Pauline. Clare felt for him. More than anybody else, she knew how he missed Karen. How much she meant to him, how long he was prepared to wait for her. Clare had to stop herself mentioning Monty's accident at the sound of Dan Connor's name. On the other hand, the comments about Gillian Connor didn't register. Clare's meeting with Dan's wife at the building site had been scrubbed during transition and she couldn't picture the woman from those earlier project design meetings back in 2009. Monty stood up and left the room to open up a bottle of wine in the kitchen.

He was in the middle of pouring the second glass when he heard Clare give out a yell of surprise. He splashed wine on the kitchen work surface, put the bottle down and raced through to see what had happened. Clare was slightly shaken, but otherwise okay. There was no sign of any sort of accident.

'What's the matter? What happened?'

'There was somebody at the window. Just appeared like a ghost. I was sitting here reading this book, I looked up and there she was. Very pale face and golden brown hair. A white blanket wrapped around her. She was looking straight at me through that middle window in the bay. Then she vanished.'

'Which way did she go?'

'That's the point, Monty. She didn't go either way. She just vanished. Disappeared. It was really weird.'

Monty stepped outside and had a walk up to the front gate. He surveyed the road, but there was no trace of anyone fitting Clare's description.

A similar appearance and disappearance happened some ten days later. This time Monty saw it with his own eyes. She was only at the window for moments. Five seconds at the most. He decided to take a walk around to the Church Hall to seek some advice and enlightenment.

'It sounds like a Nordy.'

'A what?'

'A Nordy. Not Ready Yet. It is a rare phenomenon. It happens when someone is at death's door in Realworld and they aren't quite ready to come through' Pete told him. 'Did you say this has happened twice?'

'Yes. This morning. And the previous time was just over a week ago.'

'Hmmm. Sounds like somebody who is in very grave health, slipping between life and death. In such a condition a person can lose real life for a few moments and they find themselves here momentarily. Their functions kick in again, possibly because they have been revived in Realworld, then they shoot straight back out of Hinteraevum. We only see the odd few cases every year.'

'Should we expect more sightings? Do we need to take any protective measures?'

'It could happen again. It just depends on how close this lady is to the point of finally coming through. But don't worry. She can't do you any harm. Do you know who she is?'

'No. I have a funny feeling I have seen her before, but I can't place her. It's definitely not someone that we knew closely.'

'We?'

'Yes. I have a friend staying with me.'

When he got back to Conway Road he and Clare weighed up the situation.

44

Dan went to sit by Gillian's bedside as regularly as he had done ever since she lapsed into her coma. It was an uneventful, sad and quite depressing duty. He arrived one day to be greeted by one of the consultants. It was unusual for this to happen, he normally had a monthly review to receive the update that her condition remained exactly the same. The consultant told Dan that Gillian had almost passed away earlier in the day. Her heart had stopped, the monitors had alarmed, and the medical staff had dealt with the emergency. She had revived within minutes. The monitor traces showed nothing unorthodox in the period immediately prior to the incident but there were some strange flutters during the recovery, so further analysis was ongoing.

Normality returned for the next nine days. On the tenth day the consultant was there again. There had been a repeat occurrence and the monitor traces were very similar. The doctor thought that this behaviour demonstrated Gillian was very close to the end. They discussed turning off the life support but Dan was not prepared to do that. He had sat there at her bedside for this long, why not let it run on to a natural conclusion. Who knows, he thought, this turn of events might even signify some miraculous reversal. His hopes of that were realistically low, but the positive spin might make the act of turning up each day a little bit more bearable.

The only other thing that helped distract him was thoughts of Karen. Sitting next to his inert wife and thinking about another woman didn't feel totally right, but he couldn't stop his mind drifting.

By February the process of Gillian flitting out of life and back in again was happening more frequently. At one hospital visit Dan spoke with two of the other medical staff. When analysing her monitor traces one had come up with a bit of 'outside the box' thinking. The strange and repeating pattern that was showing up on Gillian's restart had thrown up no leads at all, so any fresh hypothesis was better than none at all.

'I was looking at the recordings during my lunch break last Friday and some of the patterns seemed to connect,' said one of the young doctors. I've done a bit of Morse Code in the past and I just thought

I'd have a stab at mapping the fluctuations.'

'Morse Code? Gillian knew Morse Code' said Dan.

It was one of those things that she had done in her youth and it always stuck with her. She had been involved in her local scouting movement and the Morse Code gave her something with which she could compete against her two brothers. It was an opening worth pursuing, as crazy as it might have seemed. The doctor took out some note paper and showed his scribbles. He had got

'm-o-k-y-c-l-a-l'

'Always seems to be that sequence. I'm a bit rusty, that's the best I can do.'

'May I take this please?' asked Dan.

'By all means. Do you know Morse Code too?'

'No, I don't. But I'm sure I can take a look on the internet and find some information about it. As outlandish as it sounds, maybe I can make some sense of this.'

The concept of Gillian communicating with them all from the inner depths of her coma was completely barmy. But it was an interesting distraction from the boredom of these hospital visits. Later that evening Dan did some research. He set out the dots and dashes to spell out 'mokyclal' and began exploring whether there might be a slightly different translation that would make some sort of connection.

He found a possibility. Dash-dot-dash was K. But he found that dash-dot gave him an N and a single dash gave him a T. So dash-dot-dash could be intended as NT instead of K.

That would morph 'mokyclal' into 'montyclal'.

He continued to work on the remaining letters and saw that the final L, dot-dash-dot-dot, could also have suffered some misinterpretation. Dot-dash-dot could be an R, which would make the final dot an E. He looked down at the sheet on the desk in his study.

'm-o-n-t-y-c-l-a-r-e'

Dan was very spooked by the revelation. The names of the two people who had died in accidents at the site of their new house. It was a bit too close for comfort for it to be a quirky coincidence. And it had shown up seven times now. Why on earth would Gillian be transmitting that? What was her message? What was he supposed to do with it? Or about it?

Then his mind strayed to whether she was trying to communicate something from beyond? At that thought he decided it was high time to go and get a stiff brandy. He'd need something to help him get off to sleep after all that.

Nick, meanwhile, had been told that Karen had broken off from seeing Dan Connor. The horrible story had been making its way around the grapevine, fortunately some of the details had been kept away from the airwaves. Liz had picked up on the news and had informed Nick. She had long given up the idea of finding any fun with him after recognising that his singular, unhealthy fixation on Karen was not going to budge.

As was his wont, Nick decided to go and see Karen. He figured that she might actually come round, now that she had seen that the grass wasn't so green on the Dan side of the fence. He called at her house on his way home from work late one afternoon. She was completely speechless when she opened her front door to see him standing there yet again.

'Hello Karen. I heard that your friendship with Dan Connor was over. That must have been very difficult for you. I couldn't help thinking that you would be feeling rather down and lonely, so I came to offer some alternative company.'

Karen didn't invite him inside. She was alone in the house and felt very nervous of the situation so it was best to keep him on the doorstep. She found his persistence totally incredulous. Having collected herself she gave him both barrels, blasting at him that this was none of his business and asking why he thought it made any difference to what she had told him before – to keep away from her. She told him in no uncertain terms to clear off and then she slammed the door in his face. She quickly paced through to the kitchen and stood shaking near the telephone, hoping that he would go away. She began to cry.

Having got short shrift from her, Nick turned and briskly walked down the drive, got in his car and sped off.

'Thsssssst.'

The following day he was back at the rifle club, perfecting his ability with that crossbow. He liked the fact that it was silent. Unlike the explosive crack that accompanied the use of a rifle, the crossbow wouldn't attract attention.

45

The day's post was scattered on the doormat below the letterbox. Karen picked up four letters and two advertising flyers and walked into the kitchen. She recognised one from Hanson Scott. It would simply be the annual dividend cheque, but she still felt a shiver run down her spine at the thought of anything connected with Nick Hanson. It was unfortunate timing, getting the pay out from her husband's legacy shortly after the anniversary of his death.

She opened it as she had her breakfast. Sure enough, there was a cheque there for her and an accompanying letter. She had become used to the format over the last few years and was inquisitive to see what angle Nick would come from this time. The amount on the cheque was noticeably small. Even Karen could see that. It was just less than a quarter of the 2013 payment.

She read the note from Nick. He had very bluntly set out that the Hanson Scott architecture partnership was facing a severely competitive market and, without the strong design leadership that the company had previously enjoyed when Monty and Clare were on hand, they were losing out on far too many tenders. He added that some difficult decisions had been forced upon him and he had let several people go. The future of the practice was in jeopardy. He was prepared to make one last generous offer to buy out her stake. He urged her to accept that offer now and avoid losing everything. The final sentence was a thinly veiled threat – her home and possessions could be at risk if she failed to sell now and the company went into major debt.

It was worrying. Karen thought back to last year and could see that things were getting much worse. Perhaps it was time to cut and run. She would give some very serious thought to the matter, but she felt much in need of some trusted advice. She could ask her father, but his experience in these matters was extremely limited. At this point she was reminded that she hadn't received the copy of last year's accounts. She was sure she had requested them, but none had been made available. She would make a note to call Pat in the admin office, if indeed she was one of the members of staff that had been lucky enough to keep her job.

Her diary appointments were busy over the next week and she didn't find a suitable time to call the office of Hanson Scott. On the Saturday she made up her mind that she would go and get some retail therapy. She wouldn't be able to do so the following weekend as she had already made plans to go up to Durham to see Gemma at university. She went to Barker's Court, the shopping centre that Monty had designed five years ago. It had now been open for three years and was flourishing. Karen had a list of luxuries that she was keen to find, including a nice outfit for her trip to see Gemma in a week's time. She was meandering through the women's section in one of the major department stores when she bumped into Pat.

'Hello, how nice to see you Karen. You look great.'

'Hello Pat. Thank you. You're looking really well. I've been meaning to call you for the last week or so. Is everything alright with your job? Are you still working at Cartmel House?'

'Yes, I've not quite decided to take retirement yet.'

'Oh, sorry, I didn't mean it that way Pat. It must be horrible there, with people losing their jobs and no work coming in.'

Pat gave Karen a very puzzled look.

'I don't know what you mean. It is hard at the moment, but that's because everyone is working like Trojans. There are so many new designs on the go people are doing a lot of overtime. We've actually taken on two more people since Christmas. What gave you the idea that people were being sacked?'

Karen thought of that letter. It was a tissue of lies. He was trying to con her into selling so that he could have complete autonomy over all of the profits. And how had he worked her profit share out to be so low this year? There was some Nick skullduggery at the heart of this. She was angry but managed to hide that from Pat.

'I've just received my annual dividend cheque and a letter from Nick. That was why I was going to call you. It occurred to me that I have never seen copies of the accounts. Not since Monty passed away. Nick never sends them to me.'

'I can get you copies. I'll print some off for you on Monday and send them in the post. Better still, I'll call in after work to drop them off for you. If that's okay, of course. That way you will get them quicker.'

'That would be great, Pat. Thank you so much. What are you planning to do right now? It's almost one o'clock and I'm feeling peckish. Would you like to join me for a bite to eat?'

They took a break from clothes shopping and went off to catch up on each other's news over a light meal and coffee.

After lunch Karen set about her shopping again. She returned to the department store to find her outfit. Her route towards the store's exit took her past the jewellery section. She saw someone that she recognised. As she drew close she juggled whether to meet and speak or to detour and avoid. She decided on the former.

'Hello. How are you?'

Dan turned to see her standing next to him. His eyes lit up and his whole face filled with a warm smile.

'Hi. How lovely to see you.'

Karen looked down at the counter. There were three expensive ear-ring and necklace sets laid out for his perusal.

'A special occasion for a special wife?' she asked.

'Err, no. I'm afraid I lost her.'

Karen looked at him, not sure whether he was being economical with the truth again, or if she had completely put her foot in it. The odds were tipping towards her having put her foot in it and she would have no claim to the moral high ground.

'Yes, Gillian finally gave up the fight at the end of February. She had been going through cycles where her heart would stop momentarily then recover. In the end she just lapsed and didn't come back.'

'I'm very sorry. And that was extremely heartless of me. I'm sorry to have instantly doubted you.'

'You had every reason, given my past performance.'

'Why didn't you call to tell me?'

'Should I have called to tell you? I think that would have seemed very predatory, wouldn't it? Look … erm … is there a chance that we might be friends again?'

'Do you need some help choosing this present?'

He nodded.

'And who is it for?'

'My big sister. She's going to be fifty at the beginning of June.'

Karen guided him, based upon the pen picture he painted. He made the purchase and they left the store together.

'You're my saviour. I could have been stood there another hour if you hadn't come along. Can I buy you a coffee in return for your expert feminine advice and guidance?'

They found a café and chatted about what had happened in the last two months since that fateful Friday in December. Karen got round to talking about the Hanson Scott situation. She was sat having coffee with somebody who knew business, somebody with access to an accountant who could possibly rake over the financials for her. Dan was immediately keen to help. He had found Nick a painful person to deal with when he was selecting a team to help him with his factory developments. And he could also see it as a step towards rejuvenating his ties with Karen.

'The man's trying to con you. He's making you a generous offer whilst claiming that the company is on the rocks. If the company was about to go bust he'd be stupid to shell out a lot of money to another stakeholder to buy their share. Why would he do that?'

Karen hadn't looked at it that way, but it seemed so blindingly obvious when she heard him say it. Dan made two proposals. Firstly, he would come over on Monday evening with his accountant and they would begin work on unraveling what Nick had been up to.

'Secondly,' he said, 'there is the small matter of what I am going to do for dinner this evening.'

'And you want some expert feminine advice and guidance on that too?'

'Better still, I would like some expert feminine company. Do you know of anyone that might consider joining me?'

'Well, I can't think of anyone off the top of my head. Although, I don't have any plans of my own… and I've just spent a lot of money on a new dress …'

46

Gillian came through in February. Because of the house design there was a connection to Monty and Clare and they each received a posting about the new arrival. Clare checked the full entry for Gillian on SoulSearch and, sure enough, the photograph confirmed that it was the same person that had been appearing randomly at the bay window during the last seven weeks. But why? That was the question that neither she nor Monty could find a sensible answer to.

Gillian's Hinteraevum welcome meeting was a little irregular for the hosting team. It took place in the primary school close to the Connor's modernised farmhouse. The school hall was unfamiliar territory for her, not having had children of her own to guide through the education system. Unlike most other people, Gillian most definitely wanted to know her own cause of death. And she expressed a great deal of interest in the workings of the life choice parameters and associated HappySys computer applications. More than the typical new entrant would.

Overall, the host team was surprised at how unfazed she was by Hinteraevum. They were aware that she had been a Nordy, but that didn't usually make that much difference. In fact it often worked the other way, those odd 'not ready yet' excursions tended to make people more nervous and vulnerable about what was going to happen to them.

Gillian spent her first few days absorbing everything, concentrating most of her energy upon her connections list. Above all else she wanted to know more about the events that had ultimately brought her here from Realworld. She knew that her husband's company had been developing a drug for her. She knew that Debbie was one of the scientists behind that formulation. She had been okay with all of that until she started to suspect Dan of having some other love interest. She had tracked his movements and seen him with the other woman. And she had identified that other woman as Debbie Robinson, the person who was integral to the development of Gillian's potential cure. She had followed Debbie, found out where she lived.

And then she had been thrown off the scent when watching the premises, parked up on Conway Road in her sleek Mercedes. A different woman appeared to live there with Debbie. And there was a child, a teenage girl. Fortunately Gillian had had a newspaper with her and was able to shield herself from any suspicion. However, she couldn't quite piece together those last few facts before she plummeted into a coma.

During the next two years she had spent most of the time in a deep sleep. In the periods when she felt awake she couldn't seem to move or make herself heard. Gillian had no control of her bodily functions. Nor did she really know where she was, her best guess was hospital. She could vaguely perceive what was happening around her on those semi lucid occasions. Something was registering very deep in her subconscious. She could tell that her husband was often there by her bedside. At one time she sensed he was there with another woman, but not one that she knew. It wasn't a relative. Then there was a trauma in the room, and that affected her.

Soon after that she had found herself waking up in a peculiar mix of places. Most often it was at the front of that house on Conway Road. But the people inside weren't who she expected to see. It wasn't Debbie, or that other woman and her daughter that she had watched from her car. It was a man and a woman. She had recognised them as the architects who were instrumental in building her and Dan's new home. She had seen that young woman on the day of the awful accident that had taken her life. And the man, she remembered him from the earlier discussions and site visits to the old farmhouse.

The injustice from her husband and his liaisons with Debbie were anchored firmly in the deepest canyons of her brain. They made her arrive at that bay window each time. The surprise at seeing Monty and Clare was strong in her veins. Would Dan have spotted her attempted communication? He knew she was fluent in Morse Code.

As Gillian ran through her list of Hinteraevum connections she came across Pauline Wilson. It wasn't a name she was familiar with so she clicked on the entry out of curiosity and opened up the details. It revealed the nature of the link between Pauline and Gillian.

Mother of Karen Scott (nee Wilson, married Monty Scott, two children). Mother of Debbie Robinson (nee Wilson, married Chris Robinson, divorced, no children). Debbie Robinson conducted affair with Dan Connor (husband to Gillian Connor), 2011-2012. Karen Scott conducted affair with Dan Connor (husband to Gillian Connor), 2013.

Gillian was a tough character but she found this was a hard set of facts to have spelt out in front of her. Upset, she decided to curtail her research and relax in a lovely warm bath.

She set about SoulSearch again the following day, exploring Pauline's connections and finding Monty Scott. Working through his entry she saw that he was living on Conway Road. And there was Clare Jenkins, work colleague and friend, also living at the same house.

So it was the Scotts who lived there. Debbie, divorced, must have been staying at her sister's house. Gillian pieced it all together, along with the new information her host had provided – that her death came about following a two year coma which was triggered by a small trace of a toxic impurity in the medication she had been taking.

As in Realworld, Gillian began hatching her plan to seek some revenge in Hinteraevum. She decided her first step would be to go and introduce herself to Pauline.

She had located her prey and by the end of May had been following Pauline's whereabouts for two months. She felt that the time was right. She tailed Pauline to Barker's Court Shopping Centre one day and approached her as she sat at a table in one of the cafes.

'I'm sorry to disturb you … aren't you Debbie's mum? I'm sure we've met before.'

Pauline looked up from her Cappuccino at the complete stranger.

'I worked with Debbie. At Ronnoc Pharmaceuticals. She probably hasn't mentioned my name to you. I'm Gill Patterson, pleased to meet you.'

Gillian spoke quickly and with a familiarity that gave Pauline no latitude to deny all knowledge of this acquaintance. Using her maiden name would throw the scent. She held out her hand to a bewildered Pauline who shook it, more as an instinctive reaction than a conscious welcome greeting.

'May I join you?'

She sat down without waiting for an answer and began chatting about the factory. She told Pauline that she had been involved in the drug trial project with Debbie and how awful it must have been to find that her daughter was caught up in the middle of that horrible episode. She oozed sympathy for Debbie and claimed to have been one of her biggest supporters in the aftermath of the poor drug trial lady taking ill. Pauline was caught off guard but she began warming to this new friend, touched by the protection the stranger had offered her daughter in those difficult days at work. She hadn't known all the detail of what had upset Debbie at work, so Gillian's chatter absorbed her and she didn't think to ask when or how Gill Patterson had come through.

Gillian spent a good half hour working her way into Pauline's confidence. As they were about to leave she made an arrangement to see her target again. She was very clever, very manipulative.

'You must come and have lunch with me tomorrow at my house' she said. 'Are you free?'

'That's very nice of you. I don't think I have anything planned.'

'Oh, no, wait a minute. I have a lot of redecorating going on. What about yours? I'll bring a bottle of wine around and some nice nibbles.'

She was too fast for Pauline.

'That's settled then, I'll come around at eleven. It's been lovely meeting you. Debbie was such a great friend of mine. She was a real life saver.'

With that ironic twist she picked up her handbag and hurried off. Pauline was a little taken aback by the experience, especially by Gillian's forceful nature. That aside, she thought that any friend of Debbie's was worth connecting with.

The next morning Gillian arrived ten minutes before eleven in a deliberate attempt to put Pauline on the back foot at the start of their encounter. She had a few stories lined up about Ronnoc Pharmaceuticals and coerced Pauline to be more talkative about her daughter. She weaved in a question about Debbie's sister, who she claimed to have met on a few occasions when they'd all been on a girls' night out. This drew Pauline on to talk about Karen. At the right moment she laid down the next piece of bait.

'And didn't her husband die in a nasty accident at some building site?'

'Yes. He was called Monty. He's here, living in the village at their house on Conway Road.'

'Monty? Conway Road, you say? Yes, I've come across him here in Hinteraevum. It must be the same one. He's living with Clare now... yes?'

She stopped momentarily, just like an irritating stand-up comedian who makes out to move onto the next joke straight after the previous punch line then deliberately waits for the laugh from the audience. Glancing across at Pauline, she saw that the throwaway comment had had exactly the desired effect.

'Oh! You didn't know? What have I said?'

'He's with Clare? Clare from the architect's office?'

'Err … yes … I'm sorry,' she said sheepishly. 'I thought you would have known all about it, especially as they'd had a history of seeing each other in Realworld.'

'What?'

'You didn't know that either? Oh, me and my big mouth! I've really put my foot in it this time.'

'I don't believe it. I've been around to see him several times and he's there by himself.'

'Are you sure? Do you call in to see him regularly? Do you just drop in?'

'Well, no, not really. He often calls around here. And if I'm going to his house he usually asks me to tell him in advance. He's often travelling, you see, and he has a lot of interests … it saves me from a wasted journey if he's not going to be there.'

'How very convenient.'

Gillian decided that that was enough for now. She apologised for dropping such a bombshell, gathered her things and left. She made sure that Pauline knew how to call her if she was in need of any help.

For now, Gillian could let Pauline develop the next stage of the plan on her own from here. All she had to do was sit back and wait for the right moments to drop more poison in Pauline's ear.

47

Dan's accountant was a shrewd individual. He reviewed the sets of accounts that Pat had sent across to Karen and found many discrepancies. He asked Karen if there was anything that she could remember that might help with the case. Anything suspicious. Odd. Anything that Monty had mentioned?

'There was one visit from Nick … but I don't think it would have any bearing on this.'

'Anything at all. Just tell me, then let me work out whether it is of any importance or not.'

'He came one evening asking for Monty's laptop computer. Pat, the lady from the office, had been around to collect it a week or so earlier.'

'Well, I can understand Nick wanting a work laptop back in the office. What did you think was strange about the request?'

'Not the request, it was his reaction. He was clearly angry about it. Not just angry, he seemed on edge about it. I couldn't imagine why.'

'Perhaps he knew Monty had something on there that was revealing. Perhaps Monty had picked up the scent.'

'This sounds very sinister.'

'The accounts have got a lot of anomalies. Anomalies that all work in Nick's favour. And they go back to when Monty was still alive. I would like to get access to their computer systems … but without Nick knowing.'

'I'm sure that Pat can help.'

Karen contacted Pat the following day and asked if they could meet for coffee. She explained that it was a sensitive matter, not to be discussed with anyone else in Cartmel House. Pat agreed to drop in to Conway Road later that day. She was surprised to find that Karen was not alone. Karen introduced Pat to Dan and the accountant before asking if she was willing to be sworn to confidentiality.

'Oooh, this sounds very intriguing. Yes. My lips will remain sealed.'

Karen reminded Pat of the day they had met at Barker's Court and the revelation that Nick had been feeding Karen some deliberately false information about the state of Hanson Scott's financial stability. She explained that Dan's accountant had been analysing the annual figures and there was some strange arithmetic going on. Dan's accountant took up the reins.

'I would like to talk to someone at work who has knowledge of the computer system. Someone who might have dealt with Monty's laptop when it was returned.'

'Oh, that's easy. That would be Ged. He's awfully good with technology. He looks after all the computers.'

Pat agreed to act as the go between, arranging for Ged to accompany her to Karen's house the following afternoon. Ged felt rather nervous about the whole situation but was reassured by both Karen and the accountant that this was the right thing to do. He recounted how Nick had been cross with him in the office, how he had been instructed to scrub the laptop, and how Clare had carried out a successful investigation. He couldn't offer anything more as he and Clare had decided that it was best for him to know no more.

'You completely scrubbed the laptop. All of that data is lost. We've hit a brick wall,' said the accountant.

'I scrubbed the laptop … but only after I had copied all of Monty's files to a secure area on the main server computer. Those files are still in Cartmel House. And I'm the only person who can get sight of them.'

Ged could remember the particular file that Clare had worked on. The one that enabled her to crack the mystery. It was a spreadsheet. He could get it tomorrow and email it over to Dan's accountant.

Ged felt excited the next day. He was alone at lunchtime and most importantly he knew that Nick was out wining and dining a potential customer. He found the spreadsheet. He'd never gone back to look at it. Never opened it. But now … he'd better take a look to make sure it wasn't empty. He remembered that Clare had worked out it also had a separate password. After all of that conversation the day before it would be embarrassing if he couldn't even open the file. Thankfully he'd noted the password down at the time.

K-4-R-E-N-5-C-O-T-T. Enter.

He was relieved to see that the spreadsheet was intact. There were several work sheets and he saw that one was titled 'Notes'. He selected it. Brilliant! Clare had made detailed commentary about how Monty had entered the data, including the key to identifying each individual in the salary list. Dan's accountant would be very happy indeed.

48

Pauline had stewed on the information supplied by Gill Patterson and in her heart of hearts just couldn't believe what the woman had said. But she was a friend of Debbie's and why on earth would she come out with something like that if it wasn't true? And had Monty really been carrying on with that girl from work before he came through to Hinteraevum? Surely not? But what if it was true? It was churning Pauline's insides. She felt sick at the thought of him cheating on her daughter.

Monty had been away touring central Asia again. This time his trip was six weeks long and he was taking in some of the world's ancient civilisation ruins. He had left just before Gill Patterson had infiltrated Pauline's peaceful routine, so his mother-in-law had not had any possibility of a face to face meeting with him. Pauline was becoming increasingly anxious to see him.

She called round at Conway Road the day after she understood he was due to return. He was a little surprised to see her, but welcomed her in and began catching up on her news. Fortunately Clare was away with her boyfriend. Pauline couldn't hold back any longer. The question was simply bursting to get out of her mouth.

'Monty,' she began nervously, 'I met someone when you were away.'

He wasn't sure where this was going. His immediate reaction was that she was about to tell him that she had a new man, which he considered would be a totally astonishing revelation, knowing her views on marriage.

'One of Debbie's friends. She told me some very upsetting news.'

Monty was becoming more puzzled as she proceeded.

'Tell me … have you got someone living here that you haven't told me about?'

He gathered his thoughts and decided that the best thing was to get everything out in the open. After all, it was simply an old friend from work who was sharing the house, affording each other some comradeship in this strange existence. There was nothing more to it than that. It was innocent.

And that is exactly how he explained the position.

'And why didn't you tell me this when I came through six months ago?'

'You're right, Pauline, I should have done. I thought you might be cross to find that I was sharing the house with a female friend. This is mine and Karen's house. I didn't know quite how you would take that news. Particularly when you had just come through, yourself. That's when most people are on edge. Highly emotional, very sensitive about things.'

'Who is she?'

'It's Clare, an architect who worked at Hanson Scott. She came through about six months after me. She didn't have many connections nearby. Not much family. Hardly any friends here in Hinteraevum, mainly because she's quite young.'

'And are you two … ?'

'No. Not at all. We're very good friends. House mates. That's all.' Monty took a long deep breath. 'Hold on a minute … are you suggesting something? What has this friend of Debbie's been saying to you?'

'Is she here now?'

'No. She's away with some of her friends.'

'That's very convenient. I thought you said she didn't have many friends.'

'Pauline, I have to say that I don't like the undertone of accusation here. Clare is actually away with her boyfriend now.'

That's exactly what Gill Patterson had predicted Monty would say. Pauline's suspicious mind had been fuelled too dangerously by Gillian.

'Does she go with you on your trips?'

'She has done. We're both architects. We share a joint passion for buildings, ancient and modern.'

'And you've been staying in hotels together?'

'I'm not going to continue this line of conversation, Pauline. The simple fact of the matter is that Clare and I are former work colleagues and she is living here. We have a platonic relationship, nothing more. End of story. Now, can we change the subject please?'

'Did you share a lot of passion in Realworld … ?'

'Pauline … really … I don't know what to say. I truly cannot believe that you have just asked me that question. I don't know what has been said to you, but somebody is polluting your mind.'

'You seem very defensive about it. If you have cheated on my daughter, Monty, I will never forgive you.'

'Well, you have no reason to worry in that department, I can assure you.'

Somehow Monty kept his cool. But Pauline was not totally convinced. Gillian had planted a cancerous cell in her mind and it wasn't going to be removed as simply as that. In fact Gillian had been continuing her research and had found out about Monty and Clare having a three month period which strayed beyond the platonic. She would soon set to work dropping some of that into her little chats with Pauline.

49

Dan's accountant had put together a complete picture of what had happened to twist the Hanson Scott books in Nick's favour. It wasn't limited to siphoning off a second salary. He had been putting a large amount of his own personal entertainment and luxuries through as business expenses, including the upkeep of that apartment in Turkey. This practice had been minor when Monty was around, but had blossomed after his partner's death. In short, he had been unscrupulously fiddling Monty, and more recently Karen, out of a considerable amount of money.

He briefed Karen and Dan of his findings. Karen made arrangements via Pat to go into Cartmel House to meet Nick. She used the premise that she wanted to talk to him about the future of their partnership and she would bring her accountant along to help explore options. She made it sound as though she might be ready to accept his offer, making it appealing to him to agree the meeting. The date of the meeting was set as Tuesday the 23rd of September. Karen had managed to take Sam and Gemma off to their respective university cities over the weekend and could now concentrate on the issue of the accounts.

'Thsssst.'

Nick was zoning in on the target. He was trying to picture himself on the top of Lose Hill. It was nine in the morning and he was using some spare time before going into the office to meet with Karen at eleven o'clock. This was the best way for him to prepare. It was his therapy. His way of releasing some of the tension. He rarely used the rifle these days, it was always that crossbow. And he was very good with it. This practice session was much like the many that had preceded it. Worthy of a gold medal, he thought.

An hour was ample. He walked through to the arms room and returned the crossbow, locking it away carefully. Then he pushed at the door. The alarm blared immediately, causing him to jump. Despite it happening every time, despite him making the same mistake, it always caught him by surprise.

'Shit! I wish I could get that bloody door right!'

He stepped back so that he could look up at the closed circuit camera in the top corner above the main doorway. He waved an apology. He knew that one of the members of staff was on the reception desk and would be checking to see what had happened. He walked through via the desk and gave a verbal apology, then stepped outside and got in his car to go to the office.

As he drove, he thought about the meeting that was less than an hour away. This could be a good day. Karen might only want a small settlement for her fifty per cent. He might get away fobbing her off with a ridiculously small cheque. He arrived at Cartmel House, settled into his office and waited with a slightly smug grin on his face.

He heard them coming up the stairs then there was the knock on his door. Pat entered, followed closely by Karen then Dan's accountant.

'Good morning, Nick. This is Ian, my accountant. And I think you already know Dan Connor.'

Dan followed the accountant into Nick's office. It threw the host.

'Err .. what … I don't understand. Why is he here?'

'Dan has been advising me on this matter. After all, he runs a successful business. I remember that you took a keen interest so I'm sure you'll be pleased to hear that Dan and I have got back together … we're seeing each other again.'

Karen's introductory words were all aimed at ruffling Nick's feathers, and the plan worked. The smug grin had been wiped clean within seconds. He tried to regain his calm. It wasn't often that he thought of Lose Hill as a tactic to moderate his temper at work, but this was an exception to prove the rule. He sat back in his chair behind his oversized antique desk.

'Well, good morning, let's get this over and done with quickly, I have a busy afternoon lined up. Please take a seat. I understand you've come to consider an offer for your fifty per cent share in the business. So… I'm prepared to buy for ten thousand pounds, Karen. Are you prepared to accept?'

'I'm not prepared to accept that, Nick. It seems far too low. Ian has been looking at the recent figures and has a very different view.'

'What do you mean, looking at the figures?'

Ian stepped in to explain.

'Karen asked me to do a thorough review of the annual accounts in response to your suggestion that she sells to you before the business fails and she risks losing everything. I have been back over the last five years. My first observation is that the business is far from failing. Indeed, it is enjoying a growth spurt. My second observation.

I have taken a look at some very interesting spreadsheets that Monty had constructed shortly before he died. They show that you were receiving a second salary, Mister Hanson. I have found a great many other suspicious things tucked away, some very curious practices.'

'What the hell is this?'

'Nick,' said Dan, 'you've been doing some very underhand things and now you've been found out. You're a crook and you have swindled this woman out of a large amount of money.'

Nick couldn't hold it all together. His blood began to boil.

'You lot can't come in here and start making wild accusations like this.' His voice was raised. 'I'm going to have my solicitor sort you out.'

'They're not wild accusations' said Karen, her tone mild and controlled. 'And you know they're not. You know you've been caught red handed, don't you?'

Nick had finally had enough. He jumped up to his feet in a rage. He shouted at the accountant, then turned his sights on Karen as he made his way to the door.

'And you … I've had enough of trying to be mister nice guy to you. I only bothered because you were his wife. I felt sorry for you being left like that. All of that time, oblivious. Oblivious to the fact that your sacred Monty was having an affair with Clare here in the office.'

Karen was shaken to the core.

'Yes. No point in me keeping it from you any longer. I was there when she pushed him off that balcony at your house' he said, turning a glance at Dan.

'I knew they were going over there,' he continued his rant. 'They'd made their sordid little plan the evening before at the team night out. I decided to go and see what they were up to. No doubt they'd stopped off somewhere so that he could shag her in the back seat of that new car of his. Then I heard them arguing, he said he wasn't prepared to leave you because of the kids. Next thing she'd pushed him over the edge and was running down the back stairs to make it look like she'd not been up there.'

Karen was in tears. She couldn't believe what she was hearing. Dan had risen from his chair, but Nick was already disappearing from the room.

'And get your bloody arses out of my office before I get back from my lunch!'

The door slammed. Karen held onto Dan's arm.

'Don't,' she sobbed. 'Don't waste your time going after him. He isn't worth it. We'll see him in court.'

50

For the last three weeks Gillian had been drip feeding bile into Pauline's mind. Stories about Monty and Clare's deeply intimate friendship. All exaggerated from what she had managed to find out about the three month period when they had in fact been close. But she made it sound much worse than that and Pauline was in a receptive mood. Gillian had constructed a negative perspective from each and every account that Pauline had given of her interactions with Monty. She put her spin on each situation, weaving uncertainty and doubt until Pauline couldn't conceive of any other truth.

Monty had been away again. He'd always wanted to see the works of Frank Lloyd Wright so he and a fellow member of the Engineering, Architecture, Science and Technology society had created a summer holiday to fit the bill. It had helped take the bitter taste out of his mouth that had been left by Pauline's unpleasant assertions about his rapport with Clare. He arrived back home at the weekend and was now readjusting to the local time zone. He hadn't had a great night's sleep, but he was determined not to go back to bed and let the jet-lag get the better of him. He put his dressing gown on and went down to get some breakfast. Clare was already up and about in the kitchen, dressed in her silk nightie.

The door bell rang. Monty set off to answer it as Clare was already in the middle of her cereal. He opened the door to see Pauline and he felt a sudden deflation. He thought about conducting all conversation on the doorstep, but that would look wrong. She would merely construe it as him having something to hide. So he invited her in. She could see the facts for themselves. Him and Clare living like house-mates would if they were sharing rooms at university.

'Come on through, I was just making a coffee.'

She followed him into the kitchen and the sight of Clare in a not so modest silk night dress was enough to convince her that she had been quite right to listen to her good friend Gill Patterson.

'Pauline, this is Clare. Clare, this is my mother-in-law, Pauline.'

'Hi Pauline,' Clare spoke in a bright voice.

'I've heard all about you,' said Pauline in a tone that was

210

bordering on derogatory.

'I'm going to pop upstairs and get dressed, Monty. I'll leave you two to talk in private. Excuse me.'

'Pauline … I don't think that was entirely necessary.'

'What?'

'I think a more civil greeting wouldn't have gone amiss.'

'A more civil greeting? I walk into my daughter's kitchen and find that girl sitting half naked having breakfast. What a cheek! What do you expect me to say? How lovely to see you stealing my daughter's husband, why don't you make yourself at home?'

Monty resisted rising to the bait. He moved away from her to select his cereal and pulled a bowl out of a cupboard. He slowly emptied some bran into the bowl and poured the milk. His strategy was to defuse Pauline's angst.

'How have you been Pauline?'

'How have I been? Monty, I have been beside myself with grief about this terrible situation.'

'Tell me, Pauline, what situation are you referring to and what is so terrible about it?'

'You know damned fine what I am talking about. You having an affair with that young woman upstairs. And the thing that upsets me most is that you were carrying on in Realworld behind your wife's back.'

'Now steady on Pauline, you've got that wrong. I never did anything behind Karen's back. And that young woman upstairs has a name.'

'I beg your pardon?'

'She's called Clare. That young woman. That's her name.'

'Yes, I know that all too well.'

'Good. So that's one fact that we both agree on.' Monty was remaining unflappable, which he knew would take some of the steam out of Pauline's attack. 'Now, why don't you tell me who has been putting these ideas into your head and what proof have they given you?'

'I have it on very good authority from one of Debbie's friends and every time I raise the subject you avoid talking about it. And for goodness sake, I've just seen the proof in front of my very eyes. She hardly had anything on.'

'Pauline, let me explain everything to you. The facts. And then I don't want to hear any more about this.'

'It's high time you told the truth.'

'Clare and I were work colleagues at Hanson Scott. We were very good friends and we had a healthy mutual respect for each other's abilities. And that was it. That was all there was to it. Nothing more. Whether you want to believe it or not, I can stand here and categorically deny any wrong doing in Realworld. I never cheated on your daughter. It simply didn't happen.'

'I don't know how you can have the face to continue this tissue of lies.'

'When Clare arrived here, I'd been in Hinteraevum for six months and I had found my way about. She had no close friends, so she came here to stay. We've been touring the world, enjoying our love of buildings. As friends.'

'I've been told that people have seen you together … here … together…'

'Two years ago, just before Christmas, Clare and I did have a short relationship. It lasted less than three months. It wasn't right, we were always meant to be friends not lovers. I know that my heart is still waiting for Karen, and I don't know whether that feeling will ever go away.'

'So you admit to having an affair!'

'Pauline, have you not listened to what I've just said? I'm not going to continue defending myself. I don't have to. I don't have anything to feel guilty about, other than perhaps a short liaison with Clare here in Hinteraevum. And I do not call that going behind Karen's back.'

He walked across to put his cereal bowl in the sink then turned back to look at his adversary. He heard footsteps on the stairs and Clare reappeared, fully clothed. Monty continued.

'Did you give Karen an impossible time like this when she said she was seeing Dan Connor? A married man with his wife sick in a coma? What did you say to her about that? How much grief did you give her, Pauline?'

'That's none of your business' she retorted.

'Equally the way that Monty decides to live his life in Hinteraevum isn't really any of your business,' Clare piped up.

'You stay out of this, young madam!'

'You throw wild, unfounded slurs around about Monty and me, then you say that I have to stay out of it. You're incredible. Whoever has got to you has done a very good brainwashing job. You need to get it into that head of yours that this son-in-law here behaved impeccably towards your daughter, unlike your other son-in-law.'

'How dare you talk to me like that?'

'Look, you may be a relation of Monty's but I have to say I think your behavior is nothing short of disgraceful. I don't want to see you anywhere near me again. I'm going to get some fresh air, it's too foul in here for me.'

Clare walked out, picking up her coat on the way through the hall.

Pauline was becoming increasingly enraged. She didn't know whether to chase after Clare or reconvene her fight with Monty. But he had picked up a sign from her reaction to his last comments.

'You had a fall out with Karen … about that Dan Connor situation … that's eating away at you, isn't it? You left under a cloud, you need to make it up with her.'

'I'll make my peace when she eventually comes through, I have nothing to worry about there. Unlike you, cavorting with that slut!'

Pauline had really lost it. The red mist had descended in front of her eyes. Monty kept his cool.

'That's enough, Pauline. That is absolutely out of order. I'd like you to leave now, please. And if you ever come to accept the truth, maybe we will talk again. Otherwise, I'm afraid to say that I don't want to see you again.'

'I'm going. But I will be back to get to the bottom of this, even if it kills me!'

Her feet thumped on the floor as she made her way to the front door, then there was an almighty slam that signalled her exit. Monty let out a huge sigh. He remembered Clare. He went upstairs and got some clothes on so that he could go out and track down where she had got to.

Meanwhile, Pauline had jumped in her car and erratically jerked the keys in an attempt to get the thing started. On the fourth go the engine kicked in. Monty heard the car reverse off the drive and roar along the road in response to a very clumsy right foot on the pedals. She turned onto Beverley Road and forced the pedal to the floor again, accelerating along the straight towards Oak Dip Bend. Then she caught sight of Clare up ahead, walking on the right hand side of the road where it curved in front of the tree.

A sudden impulse gripped her. There was no ice today but she didn't know that this was where she had met her end in Realworld. She felt an unstoppable urge to punish Clare for her part in luring Monty to unfaithfulness. She was now hurtling down the slope leading to the bend. Like a world war fighter pilot, she had Clare directly in her sights. She hadn't thought the step beyond … how would she keep the car in control once she'd run Clare down.

Clare heard the noise of the car approaching. At first it just sounded like another stupid driver treating the country road like a race track. But there was something different about this one. The car's engine didn't seem to be preparing for the bend as she would have expected. She turned her head to satisfy her curiosity. She could see a car coming straight towards her at an alarming speed. It was forty yards away. She froze to the spot, not knowing which way to jump to get out of the way.

Time slowed. Clare could see Pauline behind the wheel. She could see her madly intense face staring through the windscreen, getting closer by the millisecond. But Clare's life didn't flash before her eyes. She watched the car draw closer, disorientated by the snail's pace progression of each second. Was this how her transition to the Afterworld would be? Was this deceleration how it worked? Deceleration to a standstill?

The car was five yards away from her. It was becoming fuzzy around the edges, less focused, less defined. Four yards away. It began to pixelate. Three yards away. It was disappearing in front of her very eyes. Two yards away. It was almost gone, Pauline undistinguishable in the driver's seat. One yard away. It was gone.

Clare stared at the open road. It was silent, save the sounds of nature around her. Time had snapped back into its steady rhythm. There was no sign of the car.

Pauline had deliquesced.

Clare began walking back along the road in a daze. As she made her way up the slope she saw Monty's head come into view. She gathered pace, breaking into a jog, then ran towards him and threw herself into his arms. Monty hugged her as she sobbed out a description of the terrifying incident.

51

Nick had been keeping a close eye on that bastard Connor since that unpleasant meeting just over a week ago. He'd found a neat place in Boothby Hill Woods where he could spy on the bastard's movements. He figured that the morning was the best option. When the bastard took his dogs out for a walk.

'Thssssst.'

He controlled his body for one last shot with the crossbow. The bolt hurtled out with its usual lethal velocity. It was a perfect aim, yet again. Smack in the centre of the bull. He returned to the arms room. He went through the usual motions and turned for the door. He paused, readying himself, car keys in his hand.

Go!

He pushed open the emergency door and depressed the button on the key to remotely open the boot of his car. He had parked it right outside this very exit. Deliberately. It was perfectly positioned. He'd left sufficient space to get the door open and it was close enough that he could throw the crossbow in quickly, get the boot lid closed and step back into the room in time to wave at the CCTV camera.

'What is it with you and that bleeding door?' said the guy in the office as he went past.

'I'm sorry, it won't happen again. I promise.'

He walked round to his car, feeling a little smug, a little nervy. He drove home and put the car in the garage. He usually parked it out on the road, but this evening was an exception. He didn't want anyone prying. He went inside and threw back a stiff whisky whilst he heated up a take-away curry from the local supermarket. He had a few more before he went to bed, but the drink didn't stop him from remembering to set his alarm clock. He was all set for a walk in Boothby Hill Woods.

Tomorrow was D-Day.

Tomorrow was Dan-Day.

52

Thursday October 2nd, 2014 (R)

He had parked up on the other side of the hill in the same place he'd left the car on the day of Monty's accident. He inspected the surroundings to make sure nobody was about, before getting out and going round to the rear. He surveyed around him again then opened the boot and took out the crossbow, a spade and a fold up camping stool. He closed the lid, quickly and quietly, then turned and made good pace into the bushes. He was soon well hidden. It was drizzling. Perhaps that had put some of the dog walkers off. Perhaps it was just a little bit too early for them, especially on these darker Autumn mornings.

He set the stool down and made himself comfortable. The position he had finally chosen got him within fifty yards of Dan Connor's house. It was just up the start of the hill and offered him a clear sight of the gates and the drive leading up to the garage. That's where he had watched the target park up and step round to let the dogs out of the back. He checked his watch. The minute hand was ratcheting round towards six. The small hand was just ahead of it, between seven and eight. That bastard Connor was normally back on the drive by about seven thirty-five. Not long to wait. Time to get everything under control.

'Thssssst.'

He didn't really feel any sense of humanity. He just felt an intense hatred. He knew that they'd got him trapped in a corner with all that accounting business so this would be his pay back. It hadn't helped when he blurted out about being there when Monty fell. They were now accusing him of perverting the course of justice.

He took a swig of brandy from his hip flask.

'Thssssst.'

He brought the weapon up to begin getting his range adjusted. The rain had become heavier, but that didn't put him off. He could still hit what he needed to hit from this distance, rain or no rain.

Seven thirty-five was gone. He stayed focused. The rain would slow the bastard down getting those dogs back in the vehicle. He'll be here soon.

'Thssssst.'

The faint noise of a vehicle could be heard just above the constant patter of the raindrops on the trees and bushes around him. Yes. He could see the car approaching. The engine noise rising as the car drew closer and closer. It slowed as it got to the entrance gates and smoothly pulled round off the road to make its way up the modest driveway. It came to a stop in the normal spot, facing away from the woods. He concentrated all of his attention on the rear door.

'Thssssst.'

Take aim. Get focused, wait for him to step round to the back. There he is, now, walking down the right hand side. Typical. Green wellington boots. A long, dark green wax coat. That ridiculous brown, wide-brimmed hat pulled down over his eyes. He was opening the rear door. Just a moment now, he'll stand back and wait to let the dogs out. That's the time to do it. It's only a matter of seconds now.

He was ready. Don't rush it, make sure it's accurate. Rear door's open. He's taken a step back. OK, now....

Thwang!

No going back. He felt a huge buzz as the bolt flew away from him. Silently.

Now all he had to do was watch the deadly act complete. And it did. Quickly and quietly. A thumping blow in the back and the body lurched forward into the boot space of the car, then fell backwards onto the block paving. The dogs both jumped out with sheer surprise and scampered around the freedom of the drive a few times. They went back to the slumped heap of a body and began to inspect. They could sense the blood that was spilling from the point of impact of the bolt.

Nick didn't wait to see any more. That bastard Connor seemed to be as dead as a doornail. Result! Now all he had to do was dig a hole and bury the crossbow in the bushes, then he could make his way back round to the opening to gather his car and depart the scene of the crime. Just like that day back in April, 2010. He had to wait for a few minutes as a woman set off on the track into the woods with her dog. As soon as he was sure she was well out of the way and there was no sign of any other movement, he threw the spade and camping stool into the boot, jumped in and calmly drove off.

Job done.

53

The alarm broke Dan's sleep. He rolled to his right and swung his hand across to tap the button on top of the bedside clock. Another forty winks. Today was going to be a long day for him and he needed to be up early. That hadn't stopped him from purposefully setting the buzzer to give himself the psychological bonus of an extra ten minutes in bed before he must get in the shower. He rolled a full hundred and eighty degrees and cuddled round Karen who lay beside him.

The buzzer triggered again and Dan sprang into action, hitting the snooze button to give Karen a further ten minutes under the warm duvet. Dan went into the en-suite to shave and take his shower. When the buzzer sounded for a third time Karen made sure she switched off the alarm and pulled herself out of bed. She walked into the en-suite just as Dan was finishing off drying himself. He gave her a gentle hug and kissed her cheek, then went back into the bedroom to get dressed.

They had been out for a meal at their favourite country pub the previous evening and she had planned to stay over so that she could help him this morning. It had been a mild autumnal evening but the weather had changed during the night and it was now drizzling persistently outside.

Since that confrontational meeting in Cartmel House she had found it hard reflecting on those horrid comments from Nick. The accusations about Monty having an illicit relationship with Clare had been heart wrenching. Dan had done his best to encourage her to see it rationally. This was just a case of Nick acting like a cornered rat, lashing out with any rubbish he could dream up on the spur of the moment. The more she went over things in her own mind, the more Karen began to settle herself about it. She concluded that there were no signs of her former husband being anything other than totally faithful to her.

Dan had been very careful to select the most appropriate time to tell Karen about the strange signals that had emanated from the life support monitors during Gillian's final weeks. He explained it all as an incredibly strange coincidence that couldn't possibly mean

218

anything, but if it was some sort of subconscious message it was probably a reflection that both individuals had met their end at the Connors' new house. He was keen to tell her everything he knew, however small, however far-fetched, because he didn't want a repeat of the damage that had resulted from him withholding the facts before. Karen agreed that the entire Morse code signal bit was too outlandish to have any real significance. However, it did manage to lodge itself at the back of her mind.

Within three quarters of an hour of getting up Karen was standing in the large utility room, she was almost ready to go out of the house with Dan.

'What's the matter?' he asked.

'It's raining and I didn't bring a coat or umbrella with me.'

'Ah. That won't do. Here.' He opened a cupboard and pointed at a pair of Wellington boots. 'I'm afraid they were Gillian's, but they're your size and they will keep your feet dry.'

'Dead woman's shoes, eh?' She looked at him with a twinkle in her eye.

'And you'd better wear these too. They will drown you in terms of size, but they'll prevent you from coming to any harm in this weather.'

He handed her his long waxed coat and his hat. She put them on. Whilst they were on the large side they would certainly keep the rain off. Dan stood back and looked her up and down. There was another advantage, he thought. She definitely looked cute in that hat.

They made their way out into the darkness of the morning, the two dogs excitedly bounding around them on the driveway. Dan opened up the rear door and ushered Kansas and Lincoln, the English Setters, into the spacious luggage area. Karen climbed into the passenger seat. Dan clambered into the driver's side, reversed the car and drove off down to the gates.

After a short twenty minute journey they pulled into the drop off zone at the railway station. The monotonous cyclic beat of the windscreen wipers had provided a constant accompaniment to the sound of the news topics on Radio five. Dan leaned over and gave Karen a long and warm kiss goodbye.

'I'll see you at about ten thirty this evening,' and he opened the car door to get out. Karen braved herself out of the passenger seat into the rain and hurried around to the other side of the vehicle. She managed another kiss from Dan under his umbrella before watching him walk off for his train to London. She got back in the car, closed the driver side door to shut out the weather, then started up the engine as he disappeared from view inside the station building.

She set off back towards the village, taking a detour when she reached the half way mark as she knew a good place nearby to exercise the dogs. After a short trudge along the country path she turned and lead them back to the car. It was already quarter past seven and she had appointments to fulfil, starting with one at nine. She hadn't bothered with a shower earlier, thinking that she would be better off doing all of that once she returned from walking the Setters. She dried them off as best she could using the old towels in the boot compartment, then she was able to warm up in the front seat for a few minutes before moving off again.

It didn't take long to get back. In the grey morning light she turned off the lane and into the grounds of Dan's house and followed his normal parking procedure, drawing the car to a halt on the drive. She switched off the engine and braced herself for another short spell in the rain. Karen opened the door and stepped out. She walked along the side of the car and around the back, where she could let the dogs out. She opened the boot compartment and stood back to make way for Kansas and Lincoln to jump down.

The next thing she felt was an immensely powerful and excruciatingly painful thud in the middle of her back, right between her shoulder blades. The impact was not spread out like a punch would have been, it was intensely localised in a focal point. The impulse knocked her forwards, her feet stumbled, she had no control at all, it was all too quick, and she was blacking out as she fell. Her body folded over and her chest collided with the lowered sill of the boot, recoiling her backwards. Her limp and now lifeless body dropped to the ground and became still. The dogs yelped with surprise and scrambled out of the car. They each loped around nervously for almost a minute then approached Karen's dead body to explore and make whatever sense they could of the situation.

The rain kept beating down. Dan continued his breakfast in the first class carriage on his way to London. Nick had distanced himself from the scene of his miscalculated crime.

Two hours passed by. Karen's mobile began ringing. It was the nine o'clock client checking why she was late. Then it was her work colleagues ringing to find out where she was.

The postman made his way up from the road. He was surprised to see the dogs come bounding up to him. He knew them well, so it didn't alarm him. It seemed unusual though, it wasn't normal for them to be out in the garden on a week day, and certainly not in this sort of inclement weather. He went to give them a friendly pat and a stroke, but decided against it as they were soaking wet from the constant drizzle.

'Hello boys. Come on Kansas, Lincoln, let's get you inside out of this rotten weather. Where's your dad today?'

Then another thing caught his attention. There appeared to be somebody lying on the paving near the car. He quickened his step. Had somebody fainted? Or had a bit of a turn? Had there been a robbery?

He got to within five yards of the curious body and came to a complete standstill. The person was face down with a dark bloody roundel shape seeped into their coat. At the centre of which stood what looked like a very short and thick arrow. He couldn't move his feet. He looked around. For a split second he wondered if he was on some sort of television spoof show. Finally he took another step closer. And another. He bent down and inspected without touching. He was mesmerised by what he saw. With wobbly legs he rose up and sat himself down in the boot hatch of the car. It would keep him out of the rain while he made some calls. Police first. Then he called into work to explain why his round would take longer than expected today. The man in the sorting office thankfully realised that his colleague would be in a state of shock and sent out another two postmen in a van to help.

The police isolated the crime scene and got onto the rifle club straightaway. It was the obvious place to start enquiries whilst the guys down at the station rummaged through what information they had about local arms license holders. It didn't take long to identify the bolt and make a connection to the crossbow. The arms room was inspected and no crossbow could be found. There was only one person who had used it in the last week. In fact Nick was more than a casual user of this piece of equipment. A rerun of the rifle club's CCTV from the day before also gave strong supporting evidence that he was the culprit.

In preparation, Nick had sold all of his assets, including the apartment in Turkey, and put all of his money into an offshore account. He had worked out a route across Europe involving a mixture of modes of transport, thinking that he would have time to exit England before they found the murder weapon. That would surely take them a while, in amongst all the trees. He would travel light and include steps that would make him harder to track down, like hiring a car and abandoning it to throw the scent. He had called in to Cartmel House to pick up some important items from his desk drawers and was waiting for the taxi that Pat had organised to take him to Manchester Airport.

But the police arrived at Cartmel House far sooner than he had thought. His arrogance had given him much more of a time window to get away. He'd not allowed for them tracing the bolt in the absence of the crossbow itself. It was a lot easier than removing and tracing a bullet. It may have been a quieter option, but he'd been hoisted by his own petard.

The police visit aroused suspicion in much the same way as it had done when they came to inform Nick about Monty's fall four years ago. This time they left with Nick in the back seat of the police car. There was little point in putting up any form of alibi, he went quietly. No parting rant. The Hanson Scott team gathered at the windows of Cartmel House to watch the unorthodox activities unfold and there were some perplexed faces when the police took great care lifting the spade out of the boot of Nick's car.

At the police station he was interrogated by two detectives who had been assigned to the case. In the interview he was informed of the victim's identity, at which point he found he had to accept that he'd be paying a large price for a revenge that he hadn't even managed to pull off correctly. During questioning he would finally admit to pushing Monty off the gallery landing four years ago, in the mistaken belief that being open might encourage a bit of leniency when it came to the sentence.

Dan was in the middle of a presentation to a group of senior executives at a London company he was targeting to do business with when the meeting was interrupted by Sally, one of their personal assistants.

'I'm extremely sorry Mister Lawrence, the police are here and they want to talk to Mister Connor immediately. They said it is both serious and urgent.'

James Lawrence, one of the directors, turned to Dan.

'I hope this is nothing irregular. We'll take a break for five minutes. I could do with a top up of coffee. Sally, the police can see Dan in my office.'

'Thank you James. I assure you I don't make it a regular habit to be questioned by the police,' Dan replied.

He was stunned by the news that the police conveyed. Instinctively he knew who the perpetrator was. The officers assisted by explaining to Sally that Dan was in no fit state to continue with work today. In turn, she explained to James Lawrence who came back from the meeting room immediately.

'We're all very sorry to hear what has happened. I am astounded. How could anybody do such an awful thing? I've asked Sally to arrange some transport for you. It's the least we can do. I've arranged for one of our drivers to take you over to King's Cross, it will be quicker than waiting for a taxi. I think you will have far more important things on your mind than flagging down a cab out on the street.'

'Thank you. Thank you very much.'

'I hope it works out for the best.'

54

Thursday and Friday had been busy days for Monty. There had been a conference at the EAST society with visiting speakers from the USA, including architects and engineers who had played a part in the construction of some of the country's major landmarks. Monty and Clare had heard first hand accounts about the trials and tribulations of constructing the Empire State Building, and the elation felt by the team upon its completion. The event closed with a formal dinner on the Friday evening.

On Saturday morning Monty fought with a bit of a headache that had persuaded him to remain in his bed for longer than usual. He got up at around ten and went downstairs to find some paracetamol and a large glass of water. He ate a light breakfast and went back upstairs. He called into Clare's room and said 'Good morning', presenting her with a fresh orange juice and some Muesli. They talked about the conference for a while. When Clare had finished her breakfast Monty vacated the room to let her get up and get dressed. He walked across the landing and into the study to catch up on the news. He logged on to the computer and began browsing his Hinternet emails and communications.

It was the third one in his inbox. He froze. He stared at the screen. He wasn't sure if he had read it correctly, so he read it again. Five times. But it still said the same thing each time. He wasn't sure if he wanted to believe it. Yes, of course he wanted to believe it. But he didn't really want Realworld to have terminated for Karen. Not yet. Not at her age. Finally he eased back in the chair. His eyes were moist as the intense feelings took hold. He sat forward again, his elbows on the desk, fingers interlocked, thumbs under his chin, and his eyes scanning all of the letters on the screen just in case they might have altered in the last thirty seconds. They hadn't.

Karen Scott, died Thursday 2nd October, will enter Hinteraevum on Thursday 16th October.

He heard the sound of footsteps on the landing and Clare appeared in the doorway of the study. Monty turned slowly on the chair to face her and she knew immediately that something was wrong.

'It's Karen,' he said in a vacant voice.

'Karen? When?'

'Thursday. Two days ago. She's coming through on the sixteenth.'

'Oh Monty, I'm so sorry. That's awful news. I'm so sorry that she's come through from Realworld at such a young age.'

Clare paused, knowing that he would be so happy to be reunited with his wife. Knowing how precious she was to him. Knowing how restrained he had been about falling in love with somebody new. Knowing that his attachment to Karen had prevented anything of real significance materialising between herself and Monty.

'Are you alright?' she asked him.

'Mmm. A little bit shaken. I just hope it wasn't anything dreadful. I hope she didn't suffer. Oh, good grief, I don't know what to think.'

'It will be okay,' said Clare, recognising he was in a daze. 'Don't fill yourself with pain, Monty. Think about the silver lining. You get to see Karen again. You get to touch her, hold her in your arms. You get what you have really been yearning for since you first arrived here.'

'I know that, but it seems so selfish of me to think about my gain at the time of her loss of life.'

'I am sure she wouldn't look at it that way. You're allowed to be happy. You're going to get a hundred years together now.'

'I must tell her about you living here. And what happened to Pauline. That will be difficult for her. I still can't rationalise what that was all about. I would love to know who was getting to her with all of those lies. But I must come straight with Karen on day one. I can't run the risk of the saboteur turning Karen against me. That would be even more painful than being apart for the last four years.'

'I'll get out of your way, let you have the house to yourselves.'

'You really don't need to do that.'

'Yes I do. And you know that I do. It's unthinkable for you to have a lodger here when you welcome Karen back to this house.'

Monty knew she was right. And Clare was already making plans for where she would go.

Another person who had been hatching plans was Gillian. She had seen the notification about Karen when it was first posted on Thursday.

'Well, well, well. I can't believe my luck' she thought to herself. 'First the mother manages to drive herself into oblivion. Now the daughter is coming to join us. But this isn't the one who had the miscarriage. No. This is the one who was sniffing around my husband's affections when I was in a coma. I'm going to have some fun and games with you, you bitch.'

Gillian linked to Karen's nascent SoulSearch page and read everything very carefully, making sure that she absorbed as many facts as possible.

'She's coming through on the sixteenth of October and her birthday is on November the twenty-fourth. Now that is an interesting target. If I can create enough havoc in five weeks she won't want to spend her birthday with Mister Monty Scott.'

55

Karen felt her senses begin communicating with her brain. Her eyelids wouldn't move. They seemed to be glued tight in the closed position and it needed a real effort to tease them open. The shock infusion of light forced them to shut immediately, her reaction an instant protection mechanism. She eased them open again, gently, narrowly, so that a more diffuse light could fall into her retina and gradually warm them up for more. The fuzzy shapes were unrecognisable at first, but clarity came as the aperture widened with every additional millimetre. There came a tipping point where she could make out that she was in the entrance of the Village Hall. She was sitting on the same seat where Monty had woken over four years ago. But she wasn't to know that. Nor was she to know that he'd be sat there again very soon.

She was groggy. Angela greeted her and took her through into the main hall to begin her induction process. Karen's back was restored to perfect condition, of course. No sign of the damage that had been caused by that horrific crossbow bolt. She could feel no pain, but she was full of nervous anxiety. She was starting to remember the mottled patterns, the snapshots of her life fading in and out of focus as she was lying prostrate and incapable of movement. The experience had had a certain beauty. And a calmness. A calmness beyond anything else she had known before. But now she was bewildered by it all and a little emotional.

Angela set about her task, just like she had done for the past two thousand years. Perfectly eloquent and sympathetic. It was a preference that a host would welcome members of the same family, thus Angela was chosen to hold the meeting with Karen. It was especially helpful in situations where a new entrant would ask about relatives. Angela had to be on her toes with this one following Pauline's recent exit from Hinteraevum after what had been a very short stay.

Monty hadn't slept much. He was so looking forward to seeing the person he loved so completely. What would he say to her? Would she look much different? He hoped she hadn't changed her hairstyle as he always liked it the way it was. Would she still be as slim and elegant? Surely she must be. How would she describe the last four years? How would she describe her recent relationship with Dan Connor? Would she miss Dan Connor? What if she had found herself more in love with Dan than she had remembered being with Monty?

What if he detected a slight disappointment in her eyes when he got to see her at the Village Hall? How would he cope with his own broken heart if that were to happen?

The hours had crept past very sluggishly because of the airtime these thoughts received overnight. He knew what time to get up. He knew when he had to be around at the Village Hall. He'd been round to check everything three times in the last twelve days since seeing the notification. It threw him back to that day in 1990 when he had waited for Karen to join him at the head of the aisle in Saint John's in front of their proud and supportive families. His bride would be arriving in the Village Hall shortly after seven thirty in the morning. Her induction would take some two hours. So it would be advisable for Monty to arrive no later than nine thirty if he was intent on being there to greet her.

He entered the Village Hall and spoke to the lady in the reception lobby to check that everything was in order. That Karen had arrived. Nothing had gone wrong. Suitably reassured, he parked himself on the chair that Karen had occupied two hours before and waited. He'd brought a book to keep himself amused, or distracted, until Angela delivered his wife into his company again.

In the rear room Angela was coming to the end of her procedure. Karen hadn't been able to take everything in, especially the range of parameters and their various uses, advantages and disadvantages. This was no surprise, considering her capability level with gadgets and technology. Her host gave her some simple and direct advice – 'don't meddle with anything and I'm sure it will be fine'.

SoulSearch was the biggest talking point. Karen smiled when she saw Monty in her connection list, but she was puzzled by her mother's absence.

'It was a very unfortunate set of circumstances that brought about your mother moving on from Hinteraevum. She was only with us for a short time. Less than a year, in fact. I would prefer to leave it for you to discuss the finer details with your relatives. It is the way that we work here. We had so much negative feedback in the past about delivering this sort of information that we chose to alter our policy. We find that relatives are much happier to inform their own family members of such matters. If that doesn't work for you, for whatever reason, please do come and see us and we will be happy to fill in any blanks. But please try with your family first.'

It was time for Karen to leave the hall.

'I think there might be somebody waiting to take you home,' the host said as she guided Karen back towards the foyer. Karen saw the motto on the wall and stopped for a moment to ponder its message.

'Hinteraevum – A Satisfying And Wonderful Afterlife'

'It doesn't sound as though my mother had a totally satisfying and wonderful experience here,' she said, casting a glance at Angela.

'I really am sorry that it didn't work out for your mother.'

She gestured to the doorway near the corner of the hall. It was an invitation for Karen to step through to the foyer and meet a close friend. Karen felt her stomach flutter. Her feet were attached to the floor with the same glue force that had held her eyelids down earlier in the morning. She loved Monty. She had missed him so much. She had battled so hard to quell the sheer pain of being apart from him. She had put on a brave face so that Sam and Gemma would gather strength from their mother. She knew that her best friend, the man she always felt so happy with, was sitting just through that doorway. A tear droplet made its way out from her right eye and slowly traced a smooth path down her cheek.

He heard the heels clicking on the wooden floor. Instinctively he knew it was her approaching the doorway. The reversal of when those heels had stepped away from him and out of the kitchen on a distant April Friday. He stood up. His heartbeat accelerated. The adrenalin seized hold of his veins. He hoped that this moment would be as magical as he had forecast it to be. No disappointments. Please, no disappointments.

She appeared through the doorway and stopped after taking two steps inside the foyer. She looked straight at him and her tired face warmed at the sight of her husband. They walked towards each other, met and embraced. They stood together for a few minutes and nothing was said until they were interrupted by the woman on the reception desk sliding her chair backwards as she stood up. Monty looked around at her.

'I'm sorry … erm … we …'

'No need to apologise. I've seen it so many times before and I'm sure I'll see it again. It is nice to see you finding each other again. I hope you'll both be happy here.'

Monty turned to Karen again.

'Come on, let's walk home.'

They left the Village Hall and traced the familiar route back to Conway Road. Karen was still very unsteady and Monty could see that it would take some time for her to begin feeling settled. But he was fine with that. He would be there to support and comfort her through the next few weeks, or months, as she stabilised into Hinteraevum life.

'Monty,' she said as they walked, 'what happened to my mother?'

He knew that question would be one of her first, but it still caused him to falter ever so slightly. Monty felt her pull at his arm as their strides fell out of step momentarily. He looked sideways at her and saw she was looking up at him.

'Let's get home and we can catch up on each other's lives. I'll explain everything over a nice coffee. And you can tell me everything that has happened in Realworld since I left so abruptly.'

They continued walking and their conversation reverted to smaller and less controversial subject matter.

56

Monty switched on the coffee machine and Karen ambled around the openness of the dining room and kitchen. It felt wonderfully normal for both of them to be sharing that space again. Karen stood looking out of the glass sliding doors onto the garden. Her head was like porridge, she didn't know what to make of everything. She felt Monty put his arms around her and she relaxed her weight backwards into his body.

'I love you,' he whispered into her ear. 'I've missed you terribly. There hasn't been a day go by when I haven't thought about you.'

The coffee machine signalled that it had finished preparing the second cup. They eased apart, gathered their drinks and went through the hallway to the lounge. They parked themselves on the sofa, ready for a long conversation. Monty knew he had to start. Monty knew that Pauline was the most important topic to be covered and Karen would not be receptive to anything else until she had a full understanding of what her mother had done to deserve an untimely removal from this easy going place.

Monty took a breath and composed himself. Then he began to explain. He'd rehearsed it several times, but he still felt anxious about it. Why? He hadn't done anything wrong. Other than the short romantic liaison with Clare. Pauline had made him anxious about this moment. No, that was unfair. Someone had twisted Pauline to behave in such a way that it had made him feel anxious about the innocuous. A voice of reason in his head was reminding him that there was nothing for him to feel guilty about.

'Your mother deliquesced in a car accident at Oak Dip Bend.'

A look of shock instantly appeared on Karen's face.

'Oak Dip Bend? A car accident … I don't believe it.'

Monty was surprised by her reaction, he could tell immediately there was something deeper to this story. Something that he hadn't been aware of. His expression beckoned more background from Karen.

'That's where mum died last December … in a car accident … in the snow. She was driving too fast and lost control at the corner.'

The revelation just made things a little harder for Monty, but he

231

had to tell his side of the story.

'I'm sorry Karen. We didn't know. None of us knew how Pauline had passed on from Realworld. And your mother certainly didn't know. Look, this is a long story and there is a missing piece of the jigsaw that I just can't figure out.'

'That sounds intriguing.'

'I am absolutely sure that someone was filling your mother's head with a whole lot of lies.'

'That sounds even more intriguing. Lies about what?'

'Lies about me having a relationship with a woman.'

'Why would anyone want to do that? What would be the point?'

'That's what I can't fathom out. I don't know why anyone would want to set your mother against me like that. Who could possibly have a motive?'

'And who are you supposed to have had a relationship with?'

'Clare, from work. She came through six months after me.'

'I think you'd better start from the beginning and tell me everything.'

At the sound of Clare's name Karen felt an impulsive chill down her spine. She recalled Nick's outburst at the end of that meeting in his office, his lurid remarks about Monty and Clare. And there were Dan's comments about Gillian's Morse code messages. There was something not quite right here. Her ears were wide open and tuned in. She took a sip of her coffee.

'When Clare first arrived she felt very alone and isolated. She had no close friends so she came to stay here with me. I let her have the front bedroom. In effect, she became a lodger. I liked the arrangement because it meant I had regular company. It prevented me from going a bit stir crazy.'

'Go on.'

'Well, we're both architects and we set off on several legs of a world tour, visiting all the buildings we've admired. Buildings we could only have dreamed of seeing in Realworld. We've been and seen them all here in Hinteraevum. It's so easy to travel.'

'And when you were away …?'

'We stayed in hotels. We started off in separate rooms then switched to twin rooms, chiefly for the company. And the increased sense of safety for Clare. It was all purely platonic. Just good friends sharing a common interest in architecture.'

'And did you progress to a double bed?'

Monty dried up. He didn't like the question. Or, more to the point, he didn't like the answer he would have to give to the person he loved more than anything else in the world. He felt partly embarrassed and partly as though he had let Karen down. He spoke slowly.

'Yes, we did. But only on odd occasions. And ... I know you're going to find this hard to believe ... but it remained platonic.'

'She was very pretty.'

'She is,' he conceded. 'But not a match for you. I couldn't stop thinking about you. I knew I would see you again, but I didn't know when. I didn't know how long I would have to wait. I held out for two years. Then, just before Christmas in 2012...'

Karen looked at him. She thought back to that time. The Millingtons' party when she first met Dan. Monty looked disappointed with himself, but he was determined to tell the full story. He continued.

'I had an encounter with Clare. We began a closer relationship. But it wasn't right. I couldn't stop feeling guilty. You were on my mind all of the time. It was unfair on Clare to be false with her, so the whole thing fizzled out in the space of a couple of months and we went back to being good friends. It's been that way ever since.'

'I was worried that I'd be getting worse news than that.'

'No. There's nothing worse about it.'

'So ... how does all this relate to my mum's plight?'

'Well, everything seemed okay when she first came through. Then she started to ask lots and lots of questions about my friendship with Clare. Then it became much more pointed. She started to make some very hurtful insinuations that I had been doing something wrong in Realworld.'

'Something wrong?'

'She said that a trusted source had told her that I had been seeing Clare for a lot longer. In Realworld. Before I died. She accused me of having an affair with Clare behind your back. I would never have done anything like that, Karen. Never. Absolutely never.'

'Who was the so called trusted source?'

'That's the big mystery. I don't know anyone here who would want to subject me to that sort of vindictiveness. But they really got to your mother. She got very heated about the situation. And it came to a head at the end of September. She came around here early on the Tuesday morning when we, Clare and I, were having breakfast. She was very rude to Clare. She all but called her a slut, which I thought was out of order. Clare left the house in an attempt to calm things down. Your mother jumped in her car and raced off. She must have caught sight of Clare walking along the lane and decided to… she just drove straight at Clare. The car got to within five yards of running her over and deliquesced.'

'Deliquesced?' Karen had heard the term in her induction, but couldn't quite remember what it was. There was so much to take in.

'She dissolved. She was carrying out a very aggressive act, which is not permitted here. She disappeared in front of Clare. Your mother. The car. Everything. Gone in a few seconds.'

Karen felt another tear dribble down her cheek. She had had a very emotional and tiring morning. The process of coming through invariably hits people hard on their first day, very similar to the after effects of a general anaesthetic.

'Monty,' she began, 'tell me truthfully … did anything happen before you died?'

'No. Absolutely not. I swear to you. Nothing.'

She looked very weary. Contented by his answer, but weary all the same. He was keen to find out about the last four years of her life, but he could see that she needed some rest. He helped her upstairs and watched as she curled up in their bed to sleep off the transition. It would be equally upsetting to hear of her time with Dan Connor, but he could understand how and why it came about.

That could wait. He looked at her, asleep. For now, he was happy that she was here with him.

57

Gillian locked the door and walked over to her Mercedes. She had set herself the arbitrary target of five weeks, so she had to get moving quickly. She drove off to the village feeling very chirpy. And why not? She had nothing to lose. And she had more to work with having followed Clare earlier in the week.

Gillian had decided to make use of a house on Conway Road, almost opposite Monty's. With the help of some VU privacy settings she was able to go there when she wanted without raising any suspicion amongst the other families who were already living on the road. It gave her the ideal eyrie from which to carry out surveillance on Monty and Clare. She figured that Clare would leave to allow Monty the space to welcome his wife and she wanted to be ready to gather more intelligence.

There were a few false alarms, Gillian tailing Clare to the local gym and over to Barker's Court shopping centre. Then on Wednesday morning she saw Clare stepping out to put a lot of bags and a case in her car. Gillian made her way out to her own car and waited for Clare's white car to make its way off Monty's driveway. She followed, keeping her distance, along the minor road out of the village then on the main road towards the motorway. Northbound on the A1. All the way to Darlington. All the way to Durham Road.

Clare parked up outside Monty's parents' home. She got out of the car and unloaded some gift-wrapped items from the boot, carrying them up to the house. Gillian watched Roger and Marianne warmly welcome Clare with hugs. She had seen enough. Once they had all gone inside she was able to drive on past and find her way back out to the A1. She returned home to the Connor farmhouse, knowing that she could pop back to Conway Road to resume her watch once Karen had come through.

Now it was Saturday and she was driving over from the converted farmhouse to her hide. As she turned into Conway Road her concentration was broken when she spotted her prey walking along the pavement towards the centre of the village. She quickly parked her car outside the temporary address and began walking back towards the village. She found Karen in the fruit and veg store on the

High Street. Karen didn't actually need anything, she was just taking a walk around the shops to gain a feeling of normality.

But when she turned to leave the shop she saw Gillian standing between her and the doorway. The last time Karen had seen her, Gillian looked like a ghost, lying in the depths of a coma on the hospital bed. Now the woman in front of her was strikingly attractive. Healthy. Full of colour. Karen knew who she was and she didn't think to disguise the fact. She could also understand why Dan had picked her for his wife.

Gillian clocked the look of recognition on Karen's face. It was as though a referee's whistle had blown her a signal that she could begin her game. She returned Karen's stare, scrunching her eyes up as she pretended to explore her memory banks to put a name to this woman in front of her.

'Good morning. Forgive me for being rude, but I feel I know you from somewhere. Have we met before?'

'No, I don't think so,' Karen lied. 'I've just arrived. This is all new to me. I came here two days ago.'

'Oh no ... are you ... are you Karen?'

'Yes,' said Karen. Inquisitively, guarded, not wanting to give anything away.

'Pauline's daughter? Debbie's sister? You are. Aren't you?'

'Yes ... but ...'

'I'm very good friends with your mother. Sorry. I was very good friends with your mother. You've just missed her.'

Karen was confused. She looked around the store.

'No, not here in this shop. She was in Hinteraevum until a couple of weeks ago. It must be so sad for you that she has gone through. Oh dear, it was an awful set of events. But this isn't the place to talk. Come with me, let's go to the café across the road. I'm Gillian, by the way.'

'Yes, I ...' she stopped herself short of saying 'I know', managing to twist it into 'I'm Karen.'

'Yes. I'd worked that out. Come along. We can get to know each other. I'd like that.'

Karen wasn't convinced. How could she keep up the premise that she knew nothing about Gillian? But, at the same time, she was curious to know more about Dan's wife. And Dan's wife was very keen to know more about her.

As they crossed the High Street Gillian was already feeling very positive about her chances. She had caught Karen very early, at a time when she would be feeling the strain of coming through. A vulnerable time for most people. A very vulnerable time for Karen.

They found a corner table and coffees appeared in true Hinteraevum style without Karen noticing. Gillian gave some preamble about how much she enjoyed her new home and how she had to push the thought of the two site accidents to the back of her mind.

'So, how did you know my mum?'

'It was through knowing your sister, Debbie. You probably weren't aware, your sister worked on some new medication for me. My husband, Dan, owned Ronnoc Pharmaceuticals.' She made sure she was looking Karen direct in the eye when she made the reference to Dan. 'Debbie was an amazing girl. We chatted on many occasions and she was so caring.'

'I know that she had worked on a confidential project, but I thought the patient wasn't known to her at the time,' said Karen.

'Not quite true. I spent a lot of time with your sister, but she wouldn't have told a soul because it was all confidential. She had to do all sorts of tests with me. Anyway, when your mother came through I met with her and made sure that she knew just how much I appreciated the efforts that Debbie went to in order to save my life.'

Gillian could see Karen squirming in the knowledge that reality hadn't quite worked out that way.

'What I hadn't realised was the connection to Monty and Clare. I was surprised when I found out that Pauline was Monty's mother-in-law. I was more surprised when she said that she didn't know anything about …'

Gillian stopped talking. She looked down at the tablecloth and took a slow drink of coffee.

'About … Monty and Clare?' Karen asked.

'Yes. It was very … erm … difficult.'

'Monty explained everything to me as soon as I got home from the Village Hall on Thursday, after my induction.'

'Oh, I see. Everything?'

'Well, that depends on what you mean by everything. It certainly seemed like a full description of the facts to me.'

'Tell me, was Clare there when he explained it all to you?'

'No. She's gone away to spend some time with her friends in the Cotswolds. She wanted to give us the house to ourselves for my first few weeks here. I expect she will move out in due course.'

'The Cotswolds? She seems to spend a lot of time in the

Cotswolds. At some very convenient moments, too.'

'What do you mean?'

'I don't wish to sound patronising, Karen, but … do you know where the Cotswolds are?'

'Of course I do. We've had some holiday breaks there with our children.'

Gillian waited a moment, before dealing her next card.

'I've been very suspicious about those two, especially since your mother disappeared. I'm a lawyer by profession, not a private detective, but I couldn't help wanting to know the truth behind it all. I followed Clare when she left the house on Wednesday.'

She noted Karen's reactions all the time.

'Yes, Wednesday. She got out of the way at the very last minute before your arrival. I'm surprised she didn't cut it even finer and leave on Thursday morning instead. Anyway, as I was saying, I followed her out to the A1. She went north, not south. I kept on her tail, though at a suitable distance so that she wouldn't spot me. Can you guess where she has gone to hide out?'

'No,' Karen said, her heart pounding, waiting for Gillian's next revelation.

'She is at Monty's parents' house. They are giving her safe refuge in Darlington.'

Karen was in a muddle. Forty-eight hours ago she had heard Monty expound his truth. That truth was now being undermined with apparent ease.

'I think I had best go home. I'm still feeling very unsettled after the transition ordeal.'

'I understand. It takes a few weeks to feel right again. I'm very sorry for being the one to bring all of this to your attention, but you really ought to know the facts. I don't have any axe to grind, I'm here to help you. If you need anything at all, just call me. Or come around. I assume you know the farmhouse. After all, it was where …'

'Yes, I know where it is. And thank you for your offer of help. I'm just feeling very confused at the moment.'

'Your husband seems to have been awfully impatient to tell you his side of the story. And Clare was quick to get out of the way before you arrived. Speaking as a lawyer, it all smacks of a guilty man.'

'Monty thought someone had poisoned my mother against him.'

'Well, he would say that, wouldn't he? To put you off the scent. And if you tell him that we have been talking this morning I am sure he will leap to point the finger of blame at me. Even though he doesn't know me from Adam. Or Eve, for that matter'

'I didn't think Monty would be so deceitful.'

'Well, all you can do is challenge him about the truth. Ask him again where Clare is. I bet he denies that she is hiding out with his parents. He'll probably come out with some cock and bull story about her having to drop off some presents there. On the way to the Cotswolds? Really? That seems like a very long scenic detour to me, Karen. Isn't it a bit odd that he hasn't offered to take you to see his parents this weekend?'

That was enough for the first day. Gillian was happy with her work.

58

Karen walked back to Conway Road in something of a daze. Her limbs ached and her head was completely fuzzy. It was similar to how she had remembered feeling when suffering from having a heavy bout of flu the winter after Monty had died. Auto pilot steered her back to the house. She went inside and found Monty working his way through the cryptic crossword at the kitchen island. He heard her come in through the front door.

'How was your walk?' he called out. There was a muffled reply and he turned to see her come into the kitchen.

'Crikey, are you alright? You don't look well. Here, come and sit down. I'll get you a nice coffee.'

She had removed her coat and scarf in the hallway. She sat down at the island and sighed.

'Where have you been to? Is it cold out?'

'I went along the High Street and called in at some of the shops. Then I bumped into somebody.'

'Oh. Who?'

'Gillian Connor. Dan Connor's wife.'

Monty was preparing the coffees. The response interrupted his routine actions and he turned to look at Karen.

'That must have been strange for you, after everything that happened back in Realworld.'

After a long rest on Thursday afternoon Karen had explained all of the events that had taken place in Realworld since he had come through to Hinteraevum. Some of the story he had learned from Pauline, but the part about Karen breaking off then returning to a relationship with Dan was all new news.

'It was strange. I had to pretend I didn't know her. She said that she knew my mum, Monty. She said lots of things. We spent some time talking.'

'I've seen her around, but not spoken to her. She appeared at the lounge window a few times before she came through. It was a bit alarming, to be honest. What did she have to say?'

'She … she …'

Monty looked at his wife. She was clearly disturbed about

something.

'She told me a very different story to the one that you told me. About my mum. And her disappearance.'

Monty was very puzzled. This was going the same way that his conversations with Pauline had gone. He was overcome by a worrying sense of déjà vu.

'What has been going on, Monty? Between you and Clare? And for how long?'

'I told you everything on Thursday.'

'And where is Clare now?'

'She has gone to see some friends in the Cotswolds.'

'She's not staying with your parents?'

'No. Why on earth would she want to stay with my parents? Karen, darling, what's this all about?'

'Gillian has been very suspicious since she found out that my mum was having some disagreement with you about this situation. She followed Clare on Wednesday, Monty. She followed Clare. Not south to the Cotswolds, but north to your parents.'

'Yes, I know she was going to call in to drop some presents off.'

'Darlington has never been on the direct route from here to the Bristol. And that's exactly what Gillian said you would say.'

'What? I'm very confused by this, Karen. I'm beginning to think that Gillian Connor may have been the person polluting your mother's mind.'

'That's strange Monty. She said that you would probably try to turn me against her. A woman that, by your own admission, you hardly know. You've never spoken to. She has no axe to grind, Monty. No motivation to do any harm to you. Yet she seems to know where the truth is.'

'She certainly does not know the truth. Or if she does, she's deliberately pushing this story to make my life difficult.'

'But why would she want to do that, Monty. It doesn't make sense.'

'I don't know. I don't understand what that woman's problem is. Where do you think she's getting these lies from?'

Karen looked disheveled. She began to sob. She didn't have the strength to continue the discussion. She didn't have the rational mind to make a decision on who to believe. She desperately wanted to believe Monty but the evidence from the independent witness had thrown so much doubt upon the case.

'Monty, this is very upsetting for me and I'm struggling to think straight. I'm going to find somewhere else to stay for a few weeks. I need some time and space to work things out for myself.'

'Don't leave, Karen. Please. Please don't do this. Where would you go?'

'I'm going to stay with my grandparents. They're not far away. I'll keep in touch.'

It was a bitter blow for Monty. One which he couldn't reconcile, no matter which way he looked at it. And if it was Gillian Connor at the root of it … why? What on earth had he done to set her against him?

59

Nick was in custody awaiting his trial and the Hanson Scott practice was left rudderless. Two of the older members of the team had stepped up to act as a temporary management team but neither wanted a permanent leadership role. Liz had taken an interest, primarily because she had already lined up a lot of clients for the firm through her own contact network and didn't want to see it all fall in a heap. That would be highly embarrassing. She called Dan Connor. He had a business head on his shoulders and might be willing to help.

Dan had jumped at the suggestion. After all, the success of Hanson Scott would have some bearing on the livelihoods of Karen's son and daughter, Sam and Gemma. He felt that he owed it to the girlfriend he had lost recently.

Dan and Liz had met and conceived a plan. Nick's half of the business was up for grabs. He couldn't continue in any capacity, certainly not where he was going to be spending the next twenty five years. His parents were the only other option, but they were disgraced by his outrageous actions and wanted nothing more to do with him. So Dan and Liz were able to purchase Nick's fifty percent share in confidentiality through an intermediary. There was paperwork to be completed, but a deal was struck relatively quickly.

Dan and Liz met mid-morning. They had an appointment at eleven o'clock at the solicitor's office to propose a strategy for the future of Hanson Scott. Sam and Gemma would be there, accompanied by their aunty and grandfather, Debbie and Ron. The solicitor had already prepared the adults and part brokered the agreement in principle. It helped that Dan had made his peace with both of them during the last year, whilst going out with Karen.

They all congregated in a meeting room at the offices of Knight & Donnelly. The proposal was read out. Liz and Dan would own half the company, Sam and Gemma would inherit the other half from their mother's estate. Liz would run the firm with Dan as a business advisor. In this way they could steer the practice with the intention of protecting and growing the legacy for the son and daughter of Monty and Karen. The company name would change to become 'Monty Scott and Partners'.

Everyone nodded acknowledgement. They had read through the particulars in advance. But before pen was put to paper, Liz interjected.

'We would like to add one more clause, if we may.'

'This is a little extraordinary,' said Donnelly, who had conducted affairs.

'Hold on,' Debbie said, 'you can't twist things when we're about to sign on the dotted line. We've read and understood all the papers. You can't change it now at the eleventh hour. That's unfair.'

'Please,' Liz continued, 'just hear us out. It might be to your advantage.'

Donnelly nodded for Liz to proceed.

'With this agreement, four of us have twenty-five percent each. Nobody has a majority. Specifically, Sam and Gemma hold no majority over Dan and me. We would both like to sell a one percent share to each of you. Dan sells to Gemma. I sell to Sam. That would mean that you would hold a fifty-two to forty-eight majority.'

'But we don't have that sort of money' said Ron.

'We have our offer prices here, in these envelopes.'

Liz passed her envelope to Sam and Dan handed one to Gemma.

'Go ahead, please open them. Let us know whether you accept or not.'

Debbie and Ron looked on, not knowing what to think. Sam and Gemma looked at each other.

'Let's open them together' said Sam.

They tore their way into the envelopes and each took out a piece of note paper which was folded in half. They looked at each other before turning the paper up. Both sheets bore the same figure.

£1

Ron began to laugh. He dug into his pocket to bring out some loose change.

'No. Not you Ron,' Dan said. 'The money has to come from them. They will think more of this moment if they use their own money to pay for the extra shares in Monty Scott and Partners.'

60

The weeks with her grandparents had been therapeutic for Karen. Monty aside, they were her nearest relatives in Hinteraevum and she had spent lots of time visiting them during her childhood. They had provided her with a calm and neutral bolt-hole and her grandmother, seeing her as a Godsend after the surprise disappearance of Pauline, had nursed her through the acclimatisation period. She had hardly been out of the house, apart from two journeys around the Dales with her grandparents.

Karen had dropped a note to Monty to say 'don't give up on me' and to explain that she really wanted to be alone for a while, to gather her thoughts and make sense of everything. She had been back to Angela for some counselling and now understood that she was suffering from post-traumatic stress after the transition. It was not uncommon. It was a phenomenon found in thirty-seven percent of people and the average time to recover was five weeks. Recovery depended upon the softness of the landing in Hinteraevum. Karen hadn't really had the smoothest first few days, what with the counter arguments being presented by Monty and Gillian.

Monty respected Karen's wishes and decided to play a waiting game, despite how much it hurt. He'd seen what things were like in Hinteraevum and he was convinced that ultimately the truth would out itself. He had ninety five years left to go, so he could afford to be patient. He could afford to give Karen that much needed time to come round.

Gillian, on the other hand, was keen to maintain the momentum. She had attempted to contact Karen but to no avail. She had followed her on the two excursions through the Dales, but there had been no point where neither grandmother or grandfather was at her side. Three weeks. Three weeks out of her target of five weeks. Okay, it was only an arbitrary target. But Gillian was a competitive animal and the target was a target, no matter how soft. She was becoming more irritable about it. There had to be a breakthrough moment some time soon. Surely.

Saturday the eighth was to offer that opportunity.

Karen decided it was time for her to go out by herself. She felt much better after the rest and was so grateful for the safe haven, but she was getting a little too house-bound. It was time to take the next step. She would have a drive over to the village and then call in to see Monty. Perhaps they would be able to talk things over and life could get back to normal.

She parked up on the side of the High Street and began browsing the shop windows. Unbeknown to her, Gillian was watching her every move from fifty yards away. Karen reached Maxine's, the most expensive shop in the village. Offering outfits for that 'special occasion', it was owned by a French woman who had married a local businessman and settled in the area. Instinct made her go inside. Something was drawing her towards the idea of an outfit for a wedding. Nobody had mentioned one. She didn't have an invitation to one. But she felt compelled to go in and find herself one.

Gillian gave it a few minutes before crossing over the road and entering the same shop. It wasn't large inside but she was able to make her way into a spot where she could skulk behind a rail of dresses and watch. Karen was chatting happily to another lady about a selection on the other side of the room. Gillian worked her way around the displays. She wanted Karen to bump into her, not vice versa. It would seem a little less forced that way. Moments later Karen turned to look at a different rail and found herself next to Gillian.

'Hello Gillian. Fancy meeting you here.'

'Oh, hello Karen,' she replied with a false air of surprise. 'You're looking so much better. I'm really pleased to see you. Are you shopping for a wedding?'

'No, not really. I was just seeking some retail therapy and my instincts brought me in here. And you?'

'My cousin is getting married. He wasn't happy in his Realworld marriage, so it's no surprise that he's found someone new here.'

Gillian had her tactics lined up for today. She would woo Karen with kindness and pleasantry, whilst giving the Monty-Clare subject a wide berth. If Karen mentioned it, she had some snippets ready to wield. But otherwise, she would avoid talking about it. Today was all about winning Karen's trust and friendship. She picked a dark blue dress from the rail in front of them and held it up against Karen.

'Oooh, that looks so good next to you. It really highlights your hair. Try it on. Please. I bet you'd look fantastic in it.'

'Thank you. This is one of my colours.'

Gillian was already flicking her way along the rest of the rail. She couldn't believe her good fortune, Karen had walked into the perfect shop for her charm offensive. She continued to pick out dresses and she certainly had an eye for which would suit and which would not.

Within five minutes Karen had half a dozen hung up to try on. She was enjoying it. After all, it was a harmless distraction. And Gillian did seem to have a genuine desire to help her get back to rights. She went into the changing cubicles at the back of the shop and began working her way through the six items. She came out dressed in the first one, the dark blue number.

'Ooh yes. That is you. That is so you. The colour, the style, the length. It looks great!'

Karen took a look at herself in the mirror. She had to smile, it was an ideal outfit for her. She went back in to try another one. As she was getting changed Gillian brought her two more wisely chosen dresses. There was a similar reaction when Karen stepped out in the next dress. And the next. On the fourth showing, Karen came out to see that Gillian was holding up a pair of shoes, a matching handbag, and the most gorgeous hat. All to go with the dark blue dress that she had tried on first.

'I think you need to go back to dress number one. You look fantastic in the others, don't get me wrong. But that first one … it was just perfect. Here … take these in with you and put the blue one back on. I think the contrast will work really well.'

It had been a long time since Karen had had such informed fashion support during a shopping trip and she was basking in the fun of it. She appeared again, this time in the full array from head to foot. She looked truly elegant.

'You simply can't walk out of here and leave those in the shop. If you don't take those home with you, then I will have to gift wrap them in a box and give it to you for Christmas.'

'Well, it is my birthday in just over two weeks' time. No. You're right. I'll just take everything right now. Why not? There's no need for me to wait.'

'Brilliant. Even better. Then you can always get some different gifts for your birthday.'

They were getting on famously. Karen was being sucked into a trap.

'I've got an idea.'

'Go on …'

'Let's go over to my house and we can have lunch there. I can show you around the place. You've never been, have you?'

'Yes.'

'Oh,' Gillian gently seized on the response, 'you have been there?'

'No … I meant .. yes, I have never been there.'

'Ah. Okay. Come on. Let's go. Have you got your car, or do I need to give you a lift?'

'I've got my car parked just along the High Street.'

'Okay, you can follow me. I'm in a sporty red Merc.'

Karen remembered a Mercedes parked along Conway Road back in Realworld. She didn't know that following Gillian would constitute an interesting role reversal. They soon arrived at the Connor farmhouse building. Karen parked up near Gillian and they walked into the house via the main front door. Gillian lead the way into the kitchen and began arranging a light lunch with some soup and bread rolls. They chatted about outfits and events, both recalling special times spent with loved ones. Weddings. Milestone birthdays. Christmas balls.

'Come on, I'll show you around.'

She began giving Karen the guided tour, making her way through the ground floor to the lounge.

'I love this room,' said Gillian. 'It is so spacious and full of features from the original building.'

'Yes,' agreed Karen, looking around as if she'd never seen it before. 'I much prefer it in greens and yellows.'

Gillian turned to look inquisitively at Karen. The room was decorated in grey and silver toned wallpapers. Or at least it was when she had last seen it in Realworld and that was how her VU had preserved it.

'Greens and yellows?'

Karen had been caught out. She looked around the room again, just enough to give herself time to construct her next sentence. She remembered that the room had had grey and silver wallpaper when she first saw it, before she had helped Dan to give it a refreshing facelift. Her VU settings were picking up that more recent colour palette.

'Yes, sorry, the room … it would look good if it were decorated in greens and yellows. I was an interior designer,' she said, by way of explanation. 'I think the greys make it look a little darker. More gloomy.'

'I see. Perhaps Dan and I should have hired you to do all of that for us.'

'I'm sorry if I've offended.'

'No, don't worry about it. The whole thing was done by a company from Harrogate.' She turned to face Karen and continued. 'One of Dan's friends handled it. You'd have loved Dan. He's a wonderful man. So kind and generous. Come on, let's look upstairs.'

She walked out of the lounge and they made their way up to the top floor. Gillian showed off the bedroom suites and the main bathroom before turning into the master bedroom. Karen followed in her footsteps, knowing that this one was going to be quite jarring for her. In a manner of speaking she had already followed in Gillian's footsteps in this bedroom.

'This has to be my favourite room,' Gillian said, and threw herself onto the bed in a theatrical fashion. 'Oh, Dan and I used to have such a lot of fun on this bed. And it is so luxurious.'

'Yes, I know.' Karen slipped up again. 'It certainly looks comfortable.'

She turned to the window to cover her embarrassment and recover composure.

'I'm sorry, Karen. I've embarrassed you with all of my musings. It's just that I get the impression that we have so much in common. I seem to be able to talk to you about anything … and you seem to know exactly what I'm talking about.'

She raised herself up from the bed and showed Karen the dressing room and the en-suite. Karen shuddered as she caught a vivid memory of Dan drying himself off early one morning. It was the last thing that she could remember from Realworld, so it must have been getting close to the time of her exit. Gillian, ever observant, noticed.

'Are you alright?'

'Yes. Just felt a little draught as we walked in here.'

'The window is open, I'll close it. Then we can go back out to see the piece de la resistance! The gallery landing. Oh … no … err … would you be okay with that? It was where … Monty …'

'Yes, I'll be fine. It's a fantastic view.'

'It is. But … I can't believe this, it's … it's as though you know this house like the back of your hand. Are you sure you've not been here before?'

'Yes, sure. I meant that you get a fantastic view from up the hill here, looking out over the vale and the village. Monty and I often went walking up Boothby Hill Woods, just behind here. I'm probably familiar with the layout because Monty used to talk so much about the designs he had done.'

'Ah, I see.'

They stepped through to the gallery landing and it was a tremendous sight. Gillian had achieved her objective again. She had made Karen feel her friendliness and hidden any suspicion that she knew anything of what might have happened between her new friend and her old husband. And she had managed to lure Karen into some give away comments for good measure. They went back down to the kitchen.

'When did you say your birthday was? In a few weeks?'

'Yes. The twenty-fourth. Two weeks on Monday.'

'And have you got any plans?'

'Err, no. No, I haven't, actually. I hadn't given it much thought.'

'In that case, I suggest that you come here and I will lay on an evening meal. We can drink lots of wine and get giddy. There are plenty of spare rooms so you wouldn't have to worry about driving home. You could just crash here. And I would love the company. If I'm perfectly honest it can get a bit lonely out here.'

On her way back to her grandparents Karen called in to see Monty. Clare was still on her travels, so the pair had some time to chatter. She told him that she had bumped into Gillian Connor again and had just been over to see her house. Monty remained sanguine at the sound of her name.

'I thought you said that you had been to Dan's house several times?'

'Yes. And I let it slip on a couple of occasions, but I don't think she suspected.'

'Look, Karen, I don't know what she has said to you today. And, frankly, I'm not interested. At some point you will find the truth, I am sure of that. And when you do, I will be waiting for you. Even if that takes years. I'll wait. I've waited for four years already, I can wait some more. It hurts, though. This is like having a stake driven through my heart. It really hurts. Twenty years together, but you still find it hard to take my word over someone that you have known for three weeks.'

'Monty, let's not go through that just now. I'm starting to feel better, but I'm still not quite right. I'm going to spend a few more weeks with grandma and grandpa. Let me work things out in my own head.'

'OK. I'll be waiting for you. I love you. That will never change.'

'Thank you.'

'I have some trips planned, with members of the EAST Society.

Conferences. Skyscraper visits. Boring stuff.'

'It's not boring stuff. I know you get a lot of enjoyment from it.'

'Just so that you know, I'll be out and about a bit. Just call me if you need me and I'll get myself here. What are you doing for your birthday?'

'I'm afraid I've already got something planned.'

'Ah, okay. I'm disappointed, but I did commit to give you some space. I hope you enjoy whatever it is that you've decided to do.'

61

Her grandparents had spoilt her with some lovely presents on the morning of her birthday and she had been out for lunch to celebrate with them before driving off to Gillian's house at around six o'clock. She took two bottles of her favourite wine as a contribution to the evening's entertainment.

Gillian welcomed her in and showed her to one of the spare bedrooms. Karen dropped off her overnight bag and saw a present on the bed. She opened the wrapping to find a dress from Maxine's. This one was a deep wine coloured red, another first rate choice from Gillian. Karen held it up against herself in front of the long mirror on the wardrobe. 'Ideal for Christmas parties,' she thought. Gillian was very clever

Karen could smell the divine cooking aromas from her guest bedroom as they drifted up through the high atrium and along the top floor via the gallery landing. She changed into the new dress and went back downstairs to join her hostess in the kitchen.

'Thank you for the dress, it's lovely.'

'You're welcome. I'm pleased you like it. What did Monty get you for your birthday?'

Karen's answer was sheepish.

'Oh ... err ... nothing. Yet. He's away on another trip looking at world architecture. I'm sure he'll bring me something back from his travels.'

Gillian gave a nonchalant 'oh' and returned her attention to the vegetables she was peeling and slicing. She was a very accomplished cook. She had applied some careful thought to the menu choices and each course played on their taste buds. They also got through a considerable volume of wine between them, both white and red. After dinner they retired to the lounge to relax. Karen had to be very careful to remember that the room was grey and silver, not green and yellow as she had seen it in Realworld.

'I took your advice,' said Gillian. 'I had the room redecorated in yellows and greens and it has turned out much brighter. You were absolutely right about that.'

'So, I have a gift with interior design, you have a gift choosing

252

dresses.'

'I'll drink to that. Happy Birthday!'

Gillian raised her glass again. Then she began the serious business.

'Have you done anything with your settings on HappySys? Your parameters.'

'No. I was told to leave them exactly as they are. Don't tamper with them and everything will be alright. So I haven't even considered looking at them.'

'Oh, you should. It's worth it. I've known people find that their settings have not worked to their best advantage. Come on, let's go and have a look. I'll show you what I mean.'

They walked across the hallway to the study. Gillian made sure that she took the half full, or half empty, bottle of wine with her. She logged in to the computer and brought up her own settings to illustrate some of the nuances she had learned in her research over the past months. She picked out a few lesser points to begin with, gently luring Karen in. Then she went for the big one.

'This is the one you have to be very careful with. LE. The Life Expectancy parameter. Lots of people get this wrong. They worry far too much about working out the number of years they have left in Hinteraevum.'

'Oh?'

'Yes. You have to reset it each year so that it drops down from ninety-nine to ninety-eight, to ninety-seven, and so on. What a fag. And if you get it wrong ... it can have some devastating consequences.'

'Really?'

'Really! That's why I went in and changed mine to the maximum setting. You see here ... I've got it set to 01 M. That means the default maximum. One, maximum. Once you've put that in there, HappySys works it out automatically for you, year on year. You don't have to worry about going in and trying to remember how many years you've been here and subtracting that from a hundred. So much simpler, in my humble opinion.'

'I didn't realise I'd have to go in and change this every year. I'm hopeless with technology and computers. I couldn't even make full use of all the gadgets we had in the kitchen, so this is way beyond me.'

Gillian had to stifle her delight at hearing this admission of incompetence. This would be easier than she had bargained for. The investment of five minutes earlier in the day to alter her LE for this very purpose had been time well spent. All she had to do was remember to reset it back to 99 Y tomorrow.

'Let's see what you've got set up. I'll log off and you can take over at the keyboard.'

Karen did as directed and was soon bringing up her parameters. They checked the others that Gillian had spoken of and they were all correct. This built up a greater sense of security and confidence for Karen in her adviser. Then she selected the LE parameter. 99 Y stared back at them both.

'Ah, I see I've got that one wrong, haven't I?'

'Yes. It's a good job we found it.'

'What do I need to do?' Karen took another sip of wine.

'So … you need to change the 99 to 01 first.'

'Okay.'

It was done in a jiffy.

'Now … you can change the Y to an M. Simple as that.'

Karen altered the letter.

'Now click on 'save' and you're all sorted.'

Karen followed her friend's instructions and the screen refreshed. A warning message was posted in the middle of the panel.

'What's this? Has it gone wrong?'

'No, that's normal. Just click on OK.'

The one month warning message was cleared and Karen hadn't bothered to read it. She had relied on the guidance from Gillian.

They tinkered around for a few more minutes before Gillian gave Karen the 'all clear'. Everything was now in good order and Karen need not worry. She was set up for life. Though not a very long one.

It was almost eleven o'clock and time for bed. Gillian had managed to hit her five week target and was very pleased with her competitive self.

62

Karen had been out for an evening meal with Gillian on Friday. They had arranged to meet in the Blue Lion in the village at seven o'clock, but Gillian had texted to say she was running fifteen minutes late. Karen used the free time to text Monty.

'Hi. Where are you?'

'In US. Philly. Arch tour of Liberty Place'

Karen had vague recollections of Monty talking about a Liberty Place before, but she couldn't remember much about it. For Monty, it was one of his favourite buildings. Or one could say it was two of his favourite buildings, as it comprised a pair of towers reaching up towards a thousand feet in height. He had seen it before but this was an in-depth internal tour and he was especially keen to see the art deco glass spires.

'Clare with you?'

'No, she's away with a friend'

'When's she back?'

'Sunday'

'When are you back?'

'Sunday'

'Should I pop over?'

'No, best not'

'What about Monday?'

'No, don't come Monday. Tuesday evening OK. Wednesday OK too'

'OK. Safe trip home. See you next week'

'Thx. Love you from afar'

Gillian arrived and sat down at the table with Karen, who was just putting her phone away. She couldn't help noticing that Karen looked a bit unhappy about something. It must have been the phone call.

'Are you alright? Who were you speaking to?'

'Monty. I was texting.'

'Oh. Something wrong?'

'I don't think so. Well … no, I'm probably adding two and two and making five.'

'Tell me … what was the message?'

255

'I was asking him where he is and when he is back. He's in America and is coming back on Sunday. And Clare is also away. Not with him, she must be somewhere else. And she's also getting back on Sunday.'

'So … there doesn't seem to be anything wrong in that, so far.'

'Hmmm, I know. But I asked if I should call round on Sunday and he said no. Same for Monday. The earliest he would be happy for me to call round would be Tuesday evening. Or Wednesday. I don't understand why.'

'I can offer an explanation, but I don't think it will be one that you will thank me for.'

'I suppose I ought to hear it.'

'Well, it seems to me that he wants to spend some quality time with that tramp, Clare. He's been away. She's been away. They're both eager to see each other again on Sunday. And it sounds like a mammoth session.'

'Why?'

'If they're going to be at it all the way through to Tuesday. I hope they both have the dignity to get up and shower before you call round on Tuesday evening.'

Karen didn't like what Gillian had said. And she found it hard to think of Clare as a tramp. But she was more than curious about the situation and Gillian had fuelled her fire on that front. Karen thought of calling on Sunday, but she couldn't bring herself to do so. She thought of Monty's travel and satisfied herself with the argument that he would have jet lag after an overnight flight back from the States. She would, however, muster up the courage and go round on Monday, despite Monty's replies to the contrary.

By the time she had got herself organised it was mid morning. She got in her car and left her grandparents' house at half past ten. She pulled onto the drive at Conway Road and parked up behind Monty's car.

'So he's here,' she thought. 'They must be up, it's nearly eleven o'clock.'

She walked up to the door, opened it gingerly and walked inside. She could see that there was nobody in the lounge so she walked through to the kitchen. It was quiet and unoccupied. A few breakfast pots littered the sink and the nearby work surface. The dining area was pristine. Nothing out of place, all quiet. She could hear a pin drop. In fact she could hear something upstairs. She stood rigid on the spot and strained her ears to listen carefully. Nothing. She must have imagined it. No. There it was again.

She made her way out into the hallway again, taking care with every footstep on the tiled floor. Once out of the kitchen she would be muffled by the carpet. She stopped once more, motionless. Heart thumping. If only it would calm down, it was distracting her and she might not hear the sounds upstairs over her own heavy internalised beat.

And again. Playful giggling. It was true, she hadn't imagined it.

She took her shoes off and put her right foot on the bottom step. She didn't go any further. Could she face what she was going to find in that bedroom? Could she confront the pair of them this way? Or should she just walk out of the door and leave it all behind her? If she did that, would she ever get another opportunity to expose the truth, once and for all?

Her left foot eased down on the carpet on the second step. Then she was on her way. No looking back now. Only one way, and that was forwards. Courage.

It was Clare's voice she could hear. She was sure of that. The female was saying the odd phrase. The groans coming from the man were less distinguishable.

Karen continued. She carefully stretched to miss out the ninth tread, it always made a squeak. She got to the top step. She now knew that the noise was emanating from the spare bedroom at the front of the house. That's the one Monty had said Clare could use.

'Thank the Lord they're not using our bed' she thought.

She was now standing outside the bedroom door. It was slightly ajar, but not enough for her to see in. Or for the occupants to see out. Not that that was their current priority, given the sounds of panting and frolicking coming from within. Karen had to draw herself together. For a moment she rehearsed what she was going to say. Then she burst in and blurted out in pain.

'Right, you two. There's no more hiding. No more lying. It's all over!'

She looked straight ahead. The bed was directly in front of the door, the headboard against the opposite wall. Karen saw Clare's naked back. She was sitting astride her man. She let out a scream of shock and fell forward onto the bed, pulling the duvet up to hide her from whoever the assailant was behind her. Her action exposed the naked body of a virile man, flat on his back and clearly excited.

Karen slowly took on board the details of the scene. The man, much younger than her Monty, craned his head up off the pillow so that he could see her.

'Hi. You must be Karen. I'm Jacko. I rather hoped I might have been fully dressed when I met my best friend's wife for the first time.'

Karen lurched back out of the room.

'I'm sorry … I'm sorry … I've got everything wrong … '

She hurried her way downstairs, a far cry from her stealthy ascent. Jacko jumped out of bed and ran out on to the landing.

'Karen,' he shouted after her, 'please don't go anywhere. Wait there. We'll be down in two ticks. Just wait, please.'

Jacko and Clare came downstairs having quickly thrown some clothes on. They found Karen sitting in the lounge. She was in a bit of a state with herself. Jacko sat down on the other sofa and Clare went to the kitchen to make teas and coffees.

'Are you alright?'

'Yes,' said Karen in a shaky voice.

'If you don't mind me asking … what was that outburst about?'

'I thought you were Monty.'

'Monty! What on earth would give you that idea? Monty's in London today and tomorrow. He's visiting an old university friend down there. And why on earth do you think Monty would be in bed with Clare?'

Karen began explaining the background, covering the last few weeks and including the information that she had received from Gillian. Jacko listened carefully before asking Karen to expand on some of the events from Realworld that she had briefly touched on. Clare joined them with a tray of drinks just as Karen was finishing her story.

'Let me tell you what I know,' Jacko began. 'Monty lied to me once. It was over a girl when we were in sixth form, about a year before I lost my life and came here. He never admitted to telling a porky, but I knew. I knew from the look on his face, his actions, how he kept looking away. He couldn't maintain eye contact. He's never lied to me since. What I'd like to know, Karen, is … how was he when he was telling you his side of the story? Could you see the falsehood written all across his face?'

'No,' Karen replied, a little sheepishly.

'Hmmm. Let me tell you about me and Clare. Monty brought her up to Darlington for their first Christmas in Hinteraevum and I fell for her the first time I saw her. She was off doing this Napkinworld tour with Monty for most of 2011, so it took a while for me to make progress. But we started going out in 2012. I put my foot it at one stage and the relationship cooled off. Monty and Clare had a brief thing going around Christmas that year. But it fizzled out as quickly as it started. She was back with me by the February. She says she's going to the Cotswolds to put Monty off the scent.'

'Monty doesn't know about you two?'

'No. Monty doesn't know about us two. I'm surprised he hasn't guessed, but it remains our secret. Until today, when you burst in.'

'I'm really sorry.'

'There's no need to apologise to me. But ... I do think you owe my two best friends an apology. We were planning to tell Monty tomorrow when he gets back. Clare took him to the railway station this morning then collected me. I arrived on the train from Darlington just after he had left on the train to London. We came back here and ... well ... you know what happened next because you caught us in the middle of the act.'

'I'm sorry.'

'We're going to inform Monty that we are getting married on the Monday before Christmas.'

'That is weird!'

'Oh, thanks. I think congratulations is the more traditional response.'

'No, I didn't mean that ... err ... congratulations. A few weeks ago I suddenly had a strange urge to go and look at wedding outfits for no apparent reason.'

'Well, we would dearly love you to iron out all this nonsense with Monty because we want you both to be our chief witnesses on the big day. Oh, and give us a lift to the airport the next day. We're flying out to the Caribbean for our honeymoon.'

'But ... what about all of Gillian's evidence? I can't ignore that?'

'Yes ... Gillian's ... evidence.'

Jacko put great emphasis on the final word.

'Monty has a very weak connection to Gillian. Her house was designed by Clare, who worked with Monty. That's all. But her connection to you...?'

'Well, that's through her knowing my sister, then my mother.'

'But you told me that you didn't realise she knew your sister. Did ... sorry, was it Debbie, the name of your sister..?'

'Yes, Debbie.'

'Did Debbie ever mention her? Ever say that she knew the patient in the medication project?'

'No, but it was confidential.'

'Did Debbie seem to be hiding that when she told you? Or did she seem genuinely perplexed about it?'

'She seemed genuine, actually.'

'She's your sister. She could have been lying to you all the time.'

'No. Not Debbie.'

'Okay. You said Gillian knew about her husband having an affair with Debbie. That she followed them, like a private detective. Yes?'

'Yes.'

'And does she know about your affair with her husband.'

'Absolutely not. I've not said a word about it, and I don't think my mother would have done. Besides, Gillian is clueless about it.'

'Excuse me a moment,' Clare interrupted. She had been tapping away at her laptop. 'Look at this. It's the SoulSearch entry for Pauline, showing that she was named in Gillian's connections list when she came through. And the entry is very revealing.'

Clare handed the laptop over to Jacko who read it and turned to Karen. He gave her a knowing look and showed the entry. Karen read it. She was speechless.

'She knew, alright' Jacko said. 'She knew from the very first day she arrived here. She already knew about Debbie from stalking her in Realworld. How did you meet her?'

'I just bumped into her in the village, a couple of days after I arrived.'

'Sounds like more than a coincidence to me. I bet she was alerted to you arriving and she was watching out for you. Have you just bumped into her again since then?'

'Yes. She happened to be in Maxine's when I was shopping there a few weeks ago.'

'Did you notice her in the shop as you walked in?'

'No. There was another lady, I got talking to her. But there was nobody else.'

'So Gillian mysteriously happened to come into the same shop a few minutes after you.'

'She was looking for an outfit for her cousin's wedding.'

'What cousin?' said Clare. 'She hasn't got any cousins here in Hinteraevum. Nothing showing up on SoulSearch. Jacko … she was a Nerdy. Would that have any bearing on the situation?'

'You mean a Nordy.'

'What's a Nordy?' said Karen.

'Somebody who is teetering on the edge in Realworld. Terminally ill, for example. It's short for 'Not Ready Yet'. It's very common for

Nordy folk to roam in and out of Hinteraevum again before they finally pass away and come through. They can pick up some signs here. There have been reports of some finding elaborate ways of getting messages back to people in Realworld.'

'The Morse code messages,' Karen uttered. They both looked at her. 'Gillian was in a coma for a long time. Dan thought that she was transmitting Monty and Clare's names using Morse code. It seemed laughable at the time.'

'She saw Monty and me in this very room' Clare explained. 'She appeared at that bay window.'

'In that state they can often sense more about what is going on around them than the people in Realworld could ever believe. Did you ever see her in that coma condition?'

'Yes. Once. The night my mum had her car crash. The night after everything had erupted about Dan being married, Debbie's affair, the miscarriage. Everything.'

'I wouldn't be surprised if she picked up the vibes. But the fact remains that she knew from that connection entry. I wouldn't put it past her to think that Debbie had deliberately tampered with the medication to send her off into a coma. She doesn't have any motive against Monty. But she does have a motive to take out her revenge on you and Debbie. She's already done that once by pushing your mother beyond the limit. Now she's hounding you. She may even be out there now, spying on you at this very minute.'

'She followed Clare,' Karen said. Jacko's comment sparked her recognition of a conversation with Gillian.

'When?' Clare asked.

'The day before I arrived. She knew you had been north to Darlington. Not south to the Cotswolds.'

'I did go north. I dropped off some Christmas presents for Monty's mum and dad, then I went to pick Jacko up and we went to Scotland. Gillian seems to have a habit of snooping around behind people and twisting what she has seen.'

'What should I do next?'

'Where did you wake up when you came through?' asked Jacko.

'In the Village Hall.'

'OK. So, firstly you and I are going to go around there and ask them for help. They have access to every bit of history and they can confirm the undisputed facts. Then I think that you must confront Gillian with the truth and see how she reacts.'

63

Karen had a date at Gillian's again for an evening meal. Jacko had accompanied her to the Village Hall where they had asked to see all of the facts relating to Monty and Clare's friendship. As expected, the computer system confirmed Monty's story and blew a gaping hole in Gillian's. Karen set off from the house on Conway Road after working out tactics with Clare and Jacko. The latter agreed to go with her, he would hide outside and be on hand if anything went badly wrong. She dropped him off near the gateway to the property and then continued up the drive. Jacko walked up under the cover of darkness.

Gillian opened the door and welcomed her friend into the farmhouse. They went into the kitchen where she had already begun preparing the vegetables. The hearty smell of a casserole drifted through the air from the oven. Karen sat on a high stool on one side of the island. Gillian poured her a red wine then went round to the opposite side and resumed her vegetable duties.

'How often did you meet with Debbie during the project?'

'Oh, several times. I can't remember, precisely. It was about once a month.'

As she spoke she kept her eyes on the carrots that she was peeling.

'Did you ever go out socially?'

'Oh, a couple of times, yes. She and her friends were really good fun.'

'Yes, they were a great gang. You must have met Sandra Beckett and Linda Ward. She never went anywhere without those two being around.'

'Err, yes, now that you mention it, yes. They were very nice girls.' Her attention remained focused on the vegetables.

'Did she ever tell you about how her husband had done the dirty on her and left to go to the Middle East?'

'No. She never mentioned that.'

'That's when she came to live with me. It's funny, we've shared a lot in our lives. I remember when I was in upper sixth at school and Debbie was in the fifth form, she tried her hardest to steal a boyfriend away from me. He turned out to be a bit of a jerk, so I let her have him in the end. She soon found out.'

Gillian was listening intently. Where was this going? She began slicing the red cabbage.

'It was hardly surprising when we found out we'd done it again as grown-ups.'

She paused for a moment, just like Gillian had done when slowly twisting open the lid of her bottle of poison. She could see that her quarry was taking it all in. Not giving any eye contact at all, much as Jacko had predicted.

'I'm sorry. I'm bordering on a thorny subject. Oh, but I'm sure you must know already. About Debbie having an affair with Dan? And about me having a relationship with him too?'

She had lit the blue touch paper. Now, what sort of fireworks were in store?

'I don't understand. Where's all of this nonsense coming from, Karen? You and Dan? Debbie and Dan? What are you talking about?'

Gillian was trying to make light of it, almost laughing off the suggestions.

'You know. You know perfectly well. You were following Dan when he was having the affair with my sister. I saw you sitting in your car on Conway Road, disguising yourself with a newspaper. You were spying on my house, watching for Debbie. What were you going to do? Did you have a nasty accident planned for her?'

'Don't be so silly, Karen. I was out house hunting.'

'Really? And why were you out house-hunting when you were in the middle of having this amazing redevelopment done? I don't think so. But the accident with the medicine got in the way and thwarted whatever devious plans you were concocting, didn't it. You couldn't carry out anything in that coma? Or could you? How much were you aware of underneath that cloak?'

'This really is a very strange turn that you're having. I befriend you and give you support because I know that your husband has been lying to you all along. Carrying on where he left off in Realworld. I think you're still feeling the transition trauma, aren't you?'

'No. Not at all. I feel fine. And I now know who's been telling the truth. And it's not you.'

'Come on, Karen. I know it isn't very nice, but you do have to face up to the facts about Monty.'

'You knew about Dan's affair with Debbie before you went into your coma. And you found out about me and Dan whilst you've been here in Hinteraevum.'

'No, that's not true. Who has been putting you up to this?'

'Look me in the eye and tell me.'

'Please, Karen, stop drinking the wine. I don't think it's good for you in this condition.'

'Look me in the eye and tell me.'

Gillian squirmed. The vegetable preparations had just about come to a halt. She'd put the knife down on the chopping board.

'You simply can't do it, can you? You knew all about Debbie and me, it was on the connection notification when my mum came through. So you homed in on her to play your game. And Debbie's friends … I made those names up. You never went out socially with her. You never had any meetings with my sister during that project. And what happened when my mum came through? How did you latch on to her?'

'What do you mean, latch on? I simply became friends with her through knowing Debbie.'

'And you simply bumped into her, did you? By chance? After tailing her for how many days? Or was it weeks? Like you've been tailing me?'

'I don't go around tailing people.'

'You told me that you followed Clare all the way up to Darlington …'

Karen could see that Gillian was cornered and beginning to get irritable.

'I went to the Village Hall this afternoon.'

'Well, congratulations. I am very pleased for you. So what!'

'So … I was able to check on the occupants of Conway Road. I found something very strange. Gillian Connor was listed as taking up residence at number seven. That's just across from number eight. Very odd, don't you think, when you have this beautiful house with its spacious rooms. Moved in on Thursday the ninth of October. One week before my arrival. And we all know who lives at number eight, don't we. Monty and Karen Scott. Now, wasn't that coincidental. Or … what's the word you use for it … convenient?'

Gillian was now glowering across the island at Karen. She chose to say nothing.

'You were already spying before I came through. No wonder you were able to … bump into me … at the shops on the High Street. Since then you've just been stirring up fear, uncertainty and doubt in my head. No wonder I've suffered from transition trauma.'

'I really do think you're still suffering. You should get some proper counselling.'

'And when I was there I asked them to pull up the records about Monty. Specifically the details of his friendship with Clare. Both here in Hinteraevum and spanning back through the whole of Realworld. There's no truth in your accusations, Gillian. It's all over for you.'

'What on earth do you mean by that? Don't you go threatening me!'

Gillian had enjoyed Hinteraevum up until now. She was not in a good position. She had no fresh spin to deflect Karen with, and for the first time since Realworld her feisty side was rising to the surface. Karen stepped down from the stool and picked up her handbag.

'What do you think you're doing? Where are you going?'

'I'm not staying for dinner this evening. I'm going to go back to the Village Hall and explain everything to them so that they can deal with you. I hope it will gain my poor mum a reprieve as well, once they understand that you drove her to do what she did.'

'Wait! No. Don't do that. We can sort this out. Don't you go running off telling tales. Just sit back on that stool while we figure out how we can fix this. You and your sister had a fine time with my husband. That cow Debbie even tried to bump me off, disguising that contamination as an accident. And you … I bet you thought you were on to a winner with my Dan. Fantastic house. Nice bank balance. No snotty kids to get in the way. I bet you were thinking your pockets were very nicely lined. And all at my expense.'

'When they find out about all of this they'll have no option but to remove you.'

Karen began to step across the kitchen, but Gillian sprang around the island, making sure that she cut off Karen's escape route to the hallway. Unconsciously she had picked up the chef's knife as she reacted to Karen's movement. She confronted Karen, menacingly pointing the knife at her. She didn't intend using it. She was only wanting to stop Karen from going and stirring up the truth with Pete at the Village Hall. But her actions were enough to trigger the Hinteraevum protection procedure.

Karen kept her eyes on Gillian. She wanted to step backwards to get out of the way but her body just wouldn't respond quickly enough. No matter how urgent the signals were from her brain, her legs felt as though they were forcing their way through a pond of treacle. She was edging away at an infinitesimal speed. Gillian's right hand was stretched out towards her, the knife only an arm's length away from her chest. One slip and it would connect.

But … but the tip of the knife … the knife didn't finish at a point. Karen was convinced it hadn't been broken when Gillian was cutting the carrots. And Gillian … Karen couldn't pick out the details of her face … even at this close range. She thought she was about to faint, but she could see the rest of the kitchen clearly. It was just Gillian that was out of focus. And three feet in front of her eyes the knife was disappearing. Karen's heartbeat was a dull and deadened thump, its frequency lowered by the retarded rotation of time. Gillian was evaporating to nothing.

Then she was gone. No knife. No clothes. No sign of her at all.

Jacko had seen the events unfold inside and could tell that things had taken a turn for the worse. Karen must have panicked, she hadn't followed the plan which was to head straight to the glass doors onto the patio at any sign of danger. He hurried from his hiding place, across the patio, up to the door. He tried the handle just as Gillian dissolved from view. The doors were locked. He banged on the window, giving Karen another fright. Then she heard an almighty crash as a terracotta plant pot came through the window next to her and time resumed its regular pulse. Jacko stepped in carefully through the broken glass panel. She fell into his arms and they stood, not knowing what to say. Eventually he eased his head back a little from her and spoke.

'Are you okay?'

'Yes … yes! I'm okay. That was terrifying. Did she …?'

'Deliquesce?'

'Yes.'

'Yes, she did. It had to happen, once she began waving that knife around in front of you like that. I guess you were safe all along, but it's easy to get caught up in the moment. Are you ready to go home?'

'Just give me a minute, I need to calm down.'

He held her a little longer.

'Jacko?'

'Yes.'

'I know this may be wrong of me, but I'm going to say it anyway.'

'Go on.'

'This is where … this is where Clare had her accident. Right here. This very doorway.'

'I'm pleased you told me.'

'And the landing … up there,' she pointed, 'that's where Monty had his fall.'

'I will bring Clare here some day. Not now. Maybe when she is 50h. That would seem to be a good time.'

'And I will do the same with Monty.'

'We should go now … back to the comfort of eight Conway Road.'

64

Karen slept in until lunchtime. The shock of the previous evening had worn off and she took a long relaxing bath. It was a cold morning but an ideal one for a walk around the village. It cleared her head. She was back at Conway Road before three o'clock, in time to see Clare and run through the plan one last time. Then Clare left for the railway station. Karen and Jacko had three quarters of an hour to kill, then they took up their positions.

Clare and Monty entered the house. He took off his coat and hung it in the hall.

'I've got a surprise for you,' she said. 'I've brought my boyfriend. I'd like to introduce him to you.'

'Oh, that's fantastic. Where is he?'

She pointed to the kitchen entrance. He signalled for her to go first. Jacko was sitting at the kitchen island, deliberately facing away from the door. He had also disguised himself with a ridiculous party wig of long blond hair. Monty's first impressions were not strongly positive.

'Hello, I'm Monty. It's nice to meet you at last.'

'Hello matey,' Jacko said without turning to see his host.

Monty pricked his head up at the response. There was only one person he knew who used that word. He looked at Clare who couldn't stop grinning. Jacko stepped off the stool and turned round, casting off the blond locks as he did so. Monty looked backwards and forwards at the pair of them. Then he opened his arms wide and they all came together in a scrum hug.

A short summary of the courtship finally helped Monty understand all of the Cotswolds trips and why his friendship with Jacko had gone through a fractious phase.

'I have something to tell you, matey.'

'I'm all ears.'

'Remember I made you a promise … if anything important happened in this respect … you'd be the first to know. Well … Clare and I are going to get married in three weeks' time. Just before Christmas.'

'That's brilliant. My two best friends. Congratulations. I'm so happy for the pair of you.'

'We want you to be one of the witnesses.'

'I would be honoured. Thank you.'

'We had hoped that Karen would be the other.'

The comment knocked the wind out of Monty's sails for a moment.

'Well, I guess you're going to have to ask her yourselves. She's been a little bit distant with me. I think she might be coming around this evening. I'll have to get in touch with her to confirm.'

'I'll be here,' came a voice from behind him.

Jacko and Clare had kept Monty facing away from the hall, which gave Karen time to come down the stairs and softly step towards the doorway. He whipped round in surprise.

'In fact I'll be a permanent fixture here now … if that's alright with you.'

Monty couldn't restrain the tears. She walked into his arms.

She explained the events of the last two days and how they had got her to see that she had made a monumental error of judgment believing anything Gillian said. That was all over now. She knew that she should have trusted her husband all along. She offered her apology. He didn't really need it. He was just delighted that she was there with him for good now.

65

There was a warm buzz at 8 Conway Road on the morning of the wedding. Jacko and Monty steadily went about getting ready for the event, donning charcoal morning suits, off-white waistcoats and blue cravats. Monty had been given a dilemma. Jacko wanted him as his best man whilst Clare had also asked him to give her away. Then Ralph from the EAST Society had stepped in to be Clare's surrogate father for the day. Clare had also been invited to stay at Ralph's house overnight to prevent Jacko seeing his bride on the morning before the ceremony.

Karen had decided to return to Maxine's to choose a different outfit. She simply couldn't face wearing the clothes that she had bought when shopping with Gillian. Instead, with help from Clare, she had selected a purple and black dress with a matching hat.

Karen had spent most of the morning round at Ralph's helping Clare to get ready. She set off ahead of the bride and found Monty waiting for her at the entrance to the church.

'Do we need to renew our vows whilst we're here?' he asked.

'No, I don't think that will be necessary. However, I do feel the need to make a new one.'

'Oh?'

'Yes. I promise to trust you, like I always did in Realworld. I won't doubt you again. Ever.'

'I love you. I've felt that way since 3 months after I first met you and it's never changed.'

'Walk me into the church, Monty. Escort me down the aisle.'

'I'd be delighted to, Mrs Scott.'

It was quite a small gathering, but special. Monty's parents were there to support Jacko, along with his grandfather and all of the bowls club, and his close friends from football and cricket. Clare had no family to invite, but that didn't bother her. She was pleased to see a large number of members from the EAST Society had come along to mark the day. The service was short and simple, Monty held Karen's hand throughout.

The reception dinner was equally relaxed. There was little formality, except for a short toast from Monty to the new couple and a few words in response from Jacko. As things died down Monty caught Jacko at the bar. They each ordered a fine whisky and looked back on recent events.

'I have you to thank again,' Monty said.

'How do you mean?'

'You saved my mum from an early exit and then you opened Karen's eyes, made her see sense.'

'I think she saw a little bit more than sense that morning, matey. She got a real eyeful of my middle stump.'

'You know perfectly well what I mean.'

'I know. I'm just pleased it's worked out right for you two in the end.'

'And I'm really pleased it's worked out for you and Clare.'

Clare, meanwhile, was having a quiet word with Karen.

'I think it's official.'

'What is?'

'Monty is totally besotted with you.'

Karen smiled.

'Clare, I'm so happy for you and Jacko. I feel dreadful. I didn't just doubt Monty, I doubted you as well. That was awful of me. I hope you can forgive me.'

'Karen, it's fine. It's all behind us now. We can both look forward to many years of wedded bliss here in Hinteraevum.'

'Here's to long and healthy marriages!'

They chinked their glasses.

The following day Monty and Karen took the newly-weds to the airport and saw them off on their honeymoon. Now they could relax into Christmas.

66

It was just after ten o'clock in the evening on Christmas Eve. They had spent the day doing final preparations for Christmas. Tomorrow they would take a trip up to Darlington to see his parents, Roger and Marianne, who had travelled back home after Jacko and Clare's wedding on Monday. There was time for a quiet chill before bed.

Monty angled the bottle and listened to the familiar glug as he poured two equal glasses of wine. The kitchen, Karen's kitchen, was dimly lit and a Christmas tree glowed in the far corner of the open plan dining area. An artistic mix of pretty red baubles dangled amongst the crystals from the long steel light fitting that hung above the island. He put the bottle back down and paused for a moment to admire the tiny twinkling reflections bouncing back off the shiny surfaces around him. It was his favourite time of the year. It was a perfect time for reminiscing.

To say that this had been a difficult period in their relationship would be an understatement in anyone's books. One hears of couples going through trial separations but this separation had been totally different. They had been worlds apart. He loved her deeply, he'd never given up hoping and waiting. She hadn't stopped loving him but, as far as she knew at the time, she'd never see him again. And now they were back together. It wasn't quite the way he'd have wanted things to work out. His mind was a confusing cocktail during their time apart. Desperate to be reunited with her. Desperately not wishing that transition journey on her so soon in her Realworld life.

He picked up the two glasses of red wine and carried them through to the lounge where she was sitting on the sofa with her legs tucked up. He walked across and handed her one of the glasses, kissed her cheek, then sat down beside her. Karen shuffled her legs around so that she could lean in to his side. He raised his right arm and wrapped it around her as she drew in close. They chinked their glasses together, implicitly declaring a mutual love, before each taking a sip.

They began to chat. Across the room was another Christmas tree, one that was ritually laden with memorabilia decorations from all their time together as a family. Mind you, they both recognised that it would be a long time before they might share another festive season as a complete family with their children, Sam and Gemma. In the background a CD was playing a selection of the "best ever" Christmas songs at low volume. Monty loved Karen more with every day that went by. It had been such a heart aching time waiting for her since he came through after his fall at the building site.

They fell silent. Simply enjoying each other's warm company. Monty felt drowsy, the lights on the tree were becoming spangled and diffuse. Suddenly he felt Karen's glass drop onto his knee and his lap became soaked with red wine. His arm dropped under its own weight, there was no longer anything there to support it. He sat up with a start. Where was Karen? She must have got up while he was nodding off. Why had she left her wine glass balanced on his knee?

He got to his feet and inspected the sofa. Thankfully his trousers had taken the hit from the glass of wine, none of it had stained the upholstery.

He walked through to the kitchen but she wasn't there. He called her name, but there was no response. He checked the downstairs toilet, but the door was unlocked and the room empty. He made his way upstairs and checked their bedroom. Again he drew a blank. He began to feel more anxious. Where had she gone? He explored every room upstairs, calling her name repeatedly, before going back to the ground floor and doing another run through the dining room and kitchen. Nothing. The house was silent and still. He went back into the lounge and stared at the sofa where they had been sitting. Only a delve in the seat and the placement of the cushions were left to show where she had been. She had gone. But how? And why? Was she unhappy with him? Surely not. He couldn't think straight.

He had a spark, an idea. He put his shoes and coat on, grabbed a scarf and set off towards the Village Hall. He walked fast, sometimes breaking into a jog. He was beside himself with anguish. He passed several sets of people on the way, all wishing him a Merry Christmas. He could see the crowds in The Blue Lion and the steady drift of people walking across to the church to join the midnight mass service.

He got to the Village Hall and banged on the door. He turned the handle. It was open. He hurried inside and found Peter. On the way he had racked his brain, thinking of a rational explanation for her sudden disappearance. In mild panic he garbled out all he knew to a very compassionate listener.

'Let me take a look at some things on the system.'

Monty followed him to a desk and sat nervously as Peter worked his way through some of the HappySys screens. He had access to everything and everybody. He opened up Karen's record and went to her settings. He looked sad. Upset.

'Monty, you need to prepare yourself. This will come as a bit of a shock for you …'

'Go ahead. I just need to know what the hell's happened.'

'Karen has gone.'

'Gone where?'

'She had her Life Expectancy parameter set to one month. It was altered at 10:37pm on the twenty-fourth of November. I'm very sorry to bring you this bad news.'

'Twenty-fourth of November … that was her birthday.'

'Why would she have done that?'

'I haven't got a clue. I know she was a little bit depressed after the transition, but she had overcome that. Wait a minute. She spent the evening of her birthday with that witch, Gillian.'

'I can't condone calling anyone a witch. However, if you tell me the lady's full name I might be able to find some more information.'

'Gillian Connor.'

'Ah, yes. Gillian Connor. Deliquesced on Monday the first of December. I remember it well. Not a pleasant story. Let me see.'

He tapped away at the computer and then scoured the screen, tutting.

'What is it? What have you found?'

'Well, our friend Gillian Connor altered her LE parameter earlier that same day. She changed it to 01 M at 3:15pm. And I can also see that she reverted it back to 99 Y at 1:37 the following afternoon.'

'Can you tell where Karen was when she altered her LE setting that day?'

'Hold on, I'll just go to her activity log. It should show which computer she made the change from. Bear in mind, Monty, only Karen could have changed this. Gillian couldn't possibly have done it for her. Ah … here we are. Yes. She changed it on the computer at Gillian Connor's house.'

The facts whirred their way around Monty's brain.

'She had invited Karen for a meal to celebrate her birthday. I remember Karen telling me. That bitch has tricked Karen into changing her LE, then she's reset hers afterwards. Peter … bring her back … please … this is all wrong. You can't allow this. Please, bring Karen back to me.'

'I'm afraid I can't do that, Monty. As much as I would like to, it is beyond my power to do so.'

'Who can do it?'

'Nobody. I'm very sorry.'

'Where has she gone? I need to know.'

'She has gone through to the Afterworld. It's a one-way process. There's no option of a return ticket.'

Monty was heartbroken. He and Karen had just begun settling in to their Hinteraevum life together. Now she was gone. They were split apart again by someone else's devilry.

He left the Village Hall with Peter advising him not to do anything rash or hasty. Awash with turmoil, he wandered home. He didn't absorb anything, his head was like fog. He was seething about how that woman had misled his darling Karen. How could she have been so heartless. So intentionally cynical?

He arrived at Conway Road and clambered upstairs to his study. His stomach was churning in an uncharacteristic fury. He logged on to HappySys, brought up the Life Expectancy screen and stared at his LE parameter. He weighed up a precarious choice.

Should he set his own LE to 00 so that he could follow Karen into Afterworld immediately?

For a moment he pondered what was left for him if he remained in Hinteraeveum?

His fingers hovered over the keyboard, they were pulsing with nervous energy. Should he stay? Or should he go?

BRIAN LANCASTER

Brian was born in 1961 and lived in Redcar on the North East coast. He read Engineering at Cambridge University, influenced by being raised in the shadows of Teesside's heavy industry. After a brief stint in a building engineering firm Brian turned to the world of IT and has worked for two large corporates. He has spent the majority of his adult life in Sheffield with his wife, Andrea, and two sons, Joe and Tom.

Hinteraevum is Brian's first novel, arising from a wave of inspiration that came to him when relaxing on a beach in sunny climes. Perhaps it was turning 50 that did it.

13978470R00155

Printed in Great Britain
by Amazon.co.uk, Ltd.,
Marston Gate.